ESTHER'S DIARY

THE HEART OF THE MATTER

A Novel
by
James V Genovese

Esther's Diary
The Heart of the Matter

Copyright © 2008 by James V Genovese

This is a work of fiction. All of the characters, names, incidents, organizations, and dialogue in this novel are either the products of the author's imagination or are used fictitiously.

iUniverse books may be ordered through booksellers or by contacting:

iUniverse
1663 Liberty Drive
Bloomington, IN 47403
www.iuniverse.com
1-800-Authors (1-800-288-4677)

ISBN: 978-0-595-51867-8 (pbk)
ISBN: 978-0-595-62068-5 (ebk)

Printed in the United States of America

DEDICATION

This story is dedicated to my sweet and wonderful wife, Audrey. We have been married, as of this writing, for over fifty one years, and boyfriend and girlfriend for fifty five years. She has been inspiring and encouraging to me for all of that time.

On January 9th 2005, after over three and one half years of fighting breast cancer, Audrey passed on. She still however encourages and inspires me and will always. I will love her forever,

TABLE OF CONTENTS

FORWARD

March 30th, 2004

In the telling of this fictional story, I have incorporated many elements of events that happened to me and my family. Things that I saw and heard, and about people that I knew while growing up in Brownsville Brooklyn, N. Y., in the early forties and fifties. The characters are either fictitious or are composites of people that I knew way back then. It is my hope that the reader will not find this story to be a sad story based on any single event within the story. I did not intend in writing this, for it to be sad but on the contrary, to be a story of beautiful, everlasting love between two people and several families. I also wished to show how these people who came from different cultural and religious backgrounds can and did get along as one big happy family.

A person's life should not be judged or measured by one or two aspects in their life, but by the entire story of that life. My hope is that the reader will view this story in the same manner, by reading the entire story before judging it. As I've noted before, it was written as a story of unending love and also to impart to the reader some positive food for thought about enjoying life and all that it has to offer. I hope the reader will find that to be true. I hope too, that when Esther speaks to her diary through her pen, the reader will hear her voice.

ACKNOWLEDGMENTS

I cannot possibly name all the people who have helped me with this story, either by direct input or simply by their encouragement. Of course I'd be remiss if I didn't mention by name, my wife Audrey, my son Jimmy and his wife Cheryl, my daughter Lori and her husband John and my two wonderful grandsons, David and Matthew. They have always supported me from the get go. I have to also extend my gratitude to all my nieces and nephews who have always been there for me too, especially my nieces Kathy and Adrienne Giannone, who helped me review and edit this book. I have to mention as a group, all of the friends, the ones that I grew up with so many years ago and with whom I'm still in regular contact, and the many friends I have made in my adult life. They too, have always supported me. I guess until you sit down and count your blessings, you never really know how many you have. I now realize that I have so many more than I thought. I thank them all from the bottom of my heart.

PROLOGUE

"A MOST BEAUTIFUL THING

There is nothing more beautiful is this world
Than to see a guy and his girl
Laughing and having fun
With two hearts beating as one
With their souls entwined
In an ever loving embrace
Each one shining
With a beautiful smiling face
Walking forever side by side
Sharing a joy they cannot hide
Always together, hand in hand
Sharing a life
That was Heavenly planned
Their hearts so happy
They always want to sing
This is truly a most beautiful thing

CHAPTER 1

The big, white, stretch limo pulled up in front of the brand new, glimmering in the morning sunshine, "Sackman" building, in New York City. Four very big bodyguards immediately jumped out of the limo. They each looked around, carefully, before opening the rear passenger door. A lot of people walking by stopped to look to see who this celebrity might be. Finally, after about a minute or two, out stepped a man of about seventy, well dressed, who no one seemed to recognize. However one person did know who he was and yelled out to him, "Hello Mr. Sackman, lots of luck in the big race on Saturday." "Thank you very much. That's very nice of you", Mr. Sackman replied. The man who yelled out turned to a guy standing next to him, and said, "That's Harry Sackman. He built and owns this big skyscraper. It's the newest and biggest one on Park Avenue. It's his headquarters. He is one of the richest men in the world."

"No kidding", said the other fellow. "What does he have to do with the big race on Saturday, The Belmont Stakes?" The first guy replied, "He owns the favorite to win the Belmont, "Big Bucks Baby." The horse has already won the "Derby" and the "Preakness." You know I've seen him here many times, on my way to work, and many times I've called out to him, but this is the first time ever, that he answered me. He usually just ignores me. In fact he always seems to ignore everybody." The second guy said, "Well maybe he is very happy about his horse's chances in the big race on Saturday. I bet there's a lot of money in it for him if the horse wins." "You're probably right about him being happy about the horse, but he doesn't need the money. He has so much now, he couldn't spend it all if he tried."

As Mr. Sackman walked into the building, he headed toward his own private elevator, that was sided by two uniformed security guards.

One of the guards said, "Good morning Mr. Sackman, lots of luck in the big race on Saturday." "Well thank you very much John. I really appreciate it", Mr. Sackman responded. The elevator doors closed and John, the security guard turned to his partner and said, "That's the first time he ever answered me. Will the wonders never cease?"

As Mr. Sackman got off the elevator, he immediately looked at his secretary, Anna, and asked if Mr. Christopher, one of his main partners, was in yet. When she answered to the affirmative, he said, "Would you please ask him to come into my office as soon as he is able to. Oh, and one more thing, I'm expecting a small package. It could be here anytime today and I would like to see it as soon as it arrives, and by the way, good morning Anna." Anna, looked a little bit taken aback, because Mr. Sackman never said please to her before or even "good morning" in such a nice tone. "Right away, Mr. Sackman and I'll be on the lookout for that package.", she said. Mr. Sackman looked at her with a half smile on his face and said, "No hurry, Anna."

After settling down in his office, Anna came in with his usual cup of hot coffee, fixed the way he liked it, and said, "Mr. Christopher will be here in a few minutes, Sir."

"That's very good Anna, and by the way I don't wish to be disturbed so hold all my calls until I tell you otherwise. Of course if you need any help with anything, feel free to come in or call me anytime you want to. Oh, and thanks for the coffee Anna. I've been meaning to tell you for a while now, how I look forward every morning, to this nice cup of coffee. You fix it just right." "Wow! What in the world has gotten into him today," Anna said to herself. "I always thought that deep down inside he was a good guy, but I never thought I'd see the day when nice things would come out of him. Well no matter, thank God it happened, even if might be just for today."

"Good morning Harry", Sid Christopher said, in his usual somber tone, when greeting his partner. "Ah, yes, sit down a minute Sid, there's something I want to talk to you about", Harry said, in a semi jovial way. "Oh before you start, let me just tell you that your ex wife called before you got in this morning", Sid quickly said. "She said something about a possible reconciliation. Is that true Harry?" "Sidney, in the first place, Sarah is not my ex-wife because we're not divorced yet and in the second place, it's not a, "possible" getting together again, it's going to happen", Harry said with conviction. Sid, with disbelief in

2

his voice, exclaimed, "What the hell is going on here? Just yesterday morning you were saying the nastiest things about Sarah! What in Heaven's name changed your mind about her?" "Nothing changed my mind about how I feel about Sarah. I've always loved her it's just that I didn't know it for a time, that's all Sid. I know, with all my heart that we'll be getting back together again. As a matter of fact, she was probably calling me this morning to set the time I have to pick her up on Saturday", Harry explained. "You mean you're taking Sarah to the Belmont Stakes on Saturday? Sid asked. "No", Harry answered, "I'm going with Sarah to Brown University, along with our daughter Rachel and her family to watch her son, my grandson Matthew pitch in his first start for the University. He has been a relief pitcher for them all year, but now that they are in the tournament for the collage world series, he's going to start a game."

Sid in complete disbelief, grabbed his head with his hands, started to walk rapidly in a circle and in almost a shout, excitedly said, "Harry, Harry, Harry what the hell is wrong with you?" Before Harry could respond, Sid continued, "The Belmont Stakes on Saturday could mean millions for you! If Big Bucks Baby wins the race, you get a five million dollar bonus, plus the purse is worth over a million and last but definitely not the least, the horse's value in stud will be worth twenty to thirty million more! So tell me Heshy, oh I'm sorry, I mean Harry, I know for the last forty years or so you didn't want anyone to call you by the Yiddish name of your youth, I am sorry Harry, it's just that you're getting me so crazy this morning." Harry smiled at Sid and said, "It's okay Sid, you can call me Heshy anytime you want to. I like it now. As for the money, let me ask you something Sid, how much money are we worth right now? I know you don't know and neither do I, but I do know it's in the billions, am I right?" Before Sid could say a word Harry went on, "So what difference does it make to me, twenty or thirty million, one way or another? Do you see what I mean, Sid? There are things in this life that are more important than money."

"Wait a minute, oh just a minute here", Sid said, with exasperation clearly in his voice, "Am I the one who is going a little nuts here or is it you? I mean aren't you the same Heshy Abromovitz that I have known since I was 16 years old? Are you or are you not, the same guy who always and I mean always, had to win in every game we played when we were kids? And when we grew up and entered the business world, you

3

had to come out on top in each and every deal we ever did, no matter what it was?" All the while he was near ranting to Harry Sid was pacing around in a circle with a wild eyed look on his face. Harry said, "You are so right Sid that has always been me. I had to win in every thing that I got involved in. But that was then and this is now."

Sid almost lost control after hearing Harry's reply. He was almost shrieking when he said, "Whadda ya mean that was then and this is now? We're talking about yesterday Harry, yesterday when you were saying all kinds of negative things about Sarah. You left the office early to go to Belmont Park to check up on Big Bucks Baby and now, now you're not even going to see the race. And worse yet, you don't even care if he wins or not! No Harry then was yesterday! Not twenty or thirty years ago! I wanna know what happened between yesterday afternoon and now to make you talk so crazy!" Harry started to laugh and said, "Alright Sid, I suppose I owe you an explanation."

Harry took a deep breath, leaned back in his chair and started to explain, "You're right Sid I did leave here early yesterday to go to the stable area of the track. As I walked through the shed row area, going to where Big Bucks Baby is stalled, I heard a voice call out, "Hi Heshy, how're you doing? Are you still mad at me?" I stopped dead in my tracks. I looked over to where I thought the voice came from, and said, "Who is it? Who are you? Come out in the light where I can see you". With that, an old looking guy steps out of one of the stalls. He looked like a groom, I thought. He was slightly bent over and his face, while still revealing a good looking man, was a bit weather beaten. I didn't recognize him at all, so I asked him, "Who the hell are you? Am I supposed to know you? And besides, who the hell are you to call me Heshy? I haven't been called Heshy in almost fifty years. Today I am called Harry, but only by my friends. Everybody else calls me Mr. Sackman." So the old guy looks at me and with little bit of a laugh in his voice says to me, "Ok Mr. Sackman, I am sorry. You are right. I haven't seen you in about fifty years or so, in person that is. I have seen you many times on TV and in the newspapers over the years, so to me it seems like I've always been close to you." "Who the hell are you?" I demanded of him. Again, he sort of laughed and said, "Well, when we were kids I knew you as Heshy Abromovitz. We were such good friends back then, I always felt like we were brothers. We played basketball and softball together, do you remember now?" "Keep talking", I said

4

as his voice and demeanor were becoming a little ore clear to me. So he continued, "We went through Jr. High and High school together. I know that you were mad at me for some reason but I had to leave the area at that time, before my senior year in high school, so I never really found out why. Does that ring a bell, or do I have to tell you who I am?"

Sid, my jaw must have dropped, I must have looked startled, because I was startled. "Joey Balducci!" I exclaimed. I couldn't believe it. After all these years, I thought Joey was dead. I used to hear things about him from my parents and Joey's parents but since they have all been gone I haven't heard anything. You do remember Joey Balducci, don't you Sid?" Sid, scratching his head and looking like he was trying hard to remember, said, "I think so, Harry. If I remember correctly, he was your sister Esther's boyfriend when she died. Is that right Harry?" Harry shook his head in agreement and then went on with his meeting up with Joey Balducci. "You know Hesh eh, I"m sorry I mean Harry or do I have to call you Mr. Sackman? Joey asked me. I told him he can call me Harry. He then said, "I had heard from my sister Mary I think, that you were mad at me. I think she said that she was talking to one of our freinds and they told her that you were mad at me for something or other, but I still don't know why you were mad at me. Are you still mad at me after all this time?" I told him, mad at you, mad at you, hell I hated you all these years and I probably still do.

Sid, he was incredulous. He blurted out, "Hated me! Harry you hated me! Why? I knew you were mad at me, but hate me! I can't believe that. I can't figure out why you were mad at me, let alone why you would hate me. How could you hate me when we were so close, we felt like we were brothers, no I can't beleive that you hated me." I said to him, "Believe it Joey, but to tell you the truth, it has been so long I'm not sure now, why. I know it had something to do with my sister, Esther. About when she passed away, I think." You know Sid, right about then, thinking about those days, with Esther being sick and my mother and father trying to cope and of course seeing Joey Balducci, I got a little emotional and angry at the same time. I could feel tears welling up in my eyes. Joey looked at me with the most beautiful deep look of his soft blue eyes and said in a very soft, caring voice, "You know Harry your sister was a very special person. You and your parents were

5

not the only ones who loved her. Your family was not the only one who was impacted by her passing. My family and I grieved for her too."

At this point Sid, I'm not ashamed to tell you, I started crying like a baby, uncontrollably. Joey opened his arms wide and came to me and held me in his arms while I cried. The next thing I know I'm hugging him back and he says to me, "It's okay Harry. It's alright. As strong as I thought I was, I went through the same thing. Anger, guilt, it's all part of the healing process. For some of us, it takes a little longer than for others, that's all. But we all have to go through it." His words sunk in. I was too busy crying to respond, but he continued, "Remember this Harry, the greater the love, the greater the pain." Finally, I was able to speak and I said to him, "Boy did I hate you. I mean I hated you and missed you terribly at the same time." "But why did you hate me?", he asked. "I don't know exactly why Joey but I think it was because I was very close to my sister, after all we were twins. You do remember that we were very close, don't you?" "Oh of course I do Hesh, I mean Harry." Sid I heard myself saying, "Oh you can call me Heshy any time you like. To tell you the truth I kinda like it now. You know, Joey, Esther used to confide in me her innermost secrets. Before she ever told you that she would like you to be her boyfriend, she told me first."

At this point Sid, I thought it best that we stop hugging, in case someone came by and saw us and got the wrong idea about one of the worlds richest men. In the meantime I'm still teary eyed you know talking about that hurtful period of time. Still on the verge of tears, I heard myself telling Joey that when he came into my sister's life, as a boyfriend I mean, because of course we all knew each other for a lotta years, I felt that he kinda stole some of the love that my sister had for me and that's one of the things, I think, that made me mad at him. Even my parents were crazy about him, even though he wasn't Jewish. Sid, I don't know why I said that to him, I don't even know where that came from.

Anyway, Joey looks me right in the eyes and says, in the sweetest way, "Harry, what are you talking about? Esther loved you very much, About a month or so before she passed away, while she was still able to talk, she told me that she was very worried about you and how you would handle her passing, You do know that she knew for a long time that she was not going to live, don't you? It wasn't that she didn't want to, but she just faced up to the facts and because of the way she was feeling. I mean, and I'm sure you also know it, she put up one hell of a fight. Oh she loved you Harry, boy did she ever. I never realized that you had doubts about that. I'm truly sorry about that Heshy." Brushing away some more tears I told him that I was so glad to hear what he just told me. You know Sid I just came to realize that what I felt about Joey all these years was not hate but I think it was jealousy. Sid, it's amazing, when all the tears stopped flowing, I felt so much better about myself and everything and everyone else in my life.

Now do you understand about me and Sarah getting back together again?" Sid, now slouched in a chair, trying to clear his head of all this news, said, "Not really Harr, er, I mean Heshy, but I'm trying to. Go on Heshy, finish your story." Heshy said, "By the way Sid, Joey remembers you." "Really, he does"? Sid asked in disbelief. "Yes he does Sid. In the course of our conversation, he asked about you. What he said was, "I see that, probably for business purposes, you changed your name. Because you lived on Sackman Street, you changed it from Abromovitz to Sackman. Your partner, what's his name, oh yeah, Sid Christopher, is that the same Sidney, what was his last name, Bernstein or something like that?" I said Bernbaum. "Oh yeah, that's right and he lived on Christopher Street, so he changed his name to Christopher!" I told him he was right and he continued. "I guess because I lived on Powell St. I should have changed my name to C.R. Powell.", Joey said with a big grin on his face. I asked what the C.R. was for and he said laughing, "Corner Riverdale Ave.!" I told him he still tells lousy jokes. Since we were kids he always told corny jokes. He laughed louder and said, "Heshy, there is no crime or shame in trying to make someone smile or laugh." Sid I had to laugh with him even though I had heard that joke many years ago but about someone living on the lower east side."

Sid, having regained his composure some what, asked, "Do you still hate him Heshy? 'Cause it doesn't sound as if you do." Heshy said, "Are you kidding me Sid? Hate the guy. Hell no! I realize that I still love the guy. How could anybody hate a guy like that? You know Sid, since we were in grammar school together, I mean me and Joey of course, not you Sid, Joey and I were the best of friends. By the time we got to Jr. High School, I felt like we were brothers. Even our families grew very close, even way before Esther got sick, that's how close Joey and I were at that time." Sid asked, "So what's the rest of the story?" "Well, when he told me about Esther still loving me, like she always did, even as she lay there dying, I asked him why he never told me about those talks he had with my sister. He told me that he had written to me a few times but the letters kept coming back. He told me that he even tried to send me Esther's diary that she kept and that came back too. Now he knows why. We changed our names.

He said that Esther had given him her dairy, for safe keeping, after she wrote her last entry, about two or three weeks before she died. Now he would like me to have it. He said that because he moved around so much, he gave the diary to his sister Mary to hold for him. His sister has since passed away, but he will call up his brother-in-law and ask him to send the diary directly to me at my office. He told me to read it in private because it might make me get emotional. In reading it, he said, I will see how much Esther really loved me. He told me that when Esther passed away, and he was there with her and of course all of our family, he had a hard time coping with the situation, so he quickly and quietly quit high school and joined the Army, for twenty years, I think he said. He said he got his high school GED while in the Army. He told me Sid, that he did a lot of things in a lot of far places, like working on a ranch out west, picking crops on farms and sailing with the Merchant Marines. Sid, when I asked about other women in his life and if he ever got married, he told the most incredible story.

He told me the following, and I'm gonna quote him now, "Heshy, I don't care about the age, but at any age, now I'm not talking about six year olds, but the age that your sister and I were when we first fell in love with each other, when you find that certain someone, like I found in Esther and she found in me, it's a love that is pure and unending. It's a love that comes only from the heart and that is all you need in this life to really sustain yourself. You see Heshy, the time that we had together on this Earth is not what is important, but the quality of the time is what matters. I loved Esther, and I still love her. I will forever, with all my heart, soul and being, love her. You do know Heshy she loved me the same way? Don't get me wrong now, she still loved you and your family very much, it's just that this is a different kind of love. I think you understand. At least I hope so.

Sometimes it's hard for me to explain to people what it is that I'm feeling about Esther, but maybe this will help. When I fell in love with your sister and she returned that heart full of love for me, well we had two hearts beating as one. When she died, her heart was and is still

8

beating in my heart, right along with mine. They still beat as one and it will always be so. You know Heshy, I still talk to Esther. I'm not ashamed of that. I tell everyone, who happens to hear me talking aloud sometimes, exactly what I'm doing. If they think I'm crazy, so what, I don't care. The point is Heshy, that I have lived my life, and will continue to do so, to honor Esther. If you remember, and you should, Esther loved helping people and making people smile and spending time enjoying all of Nature's beautiful work that surrounds us all, and that's what I've been trying to do for the last fifty years or so. In answer to your question Heshy, no there has never been another girl in my life and there never will be for I will always have Esther. I have all the love that I need for I still have Esther and her love. What more do I need? Does that answer your questions Heshy?" Joey asked.

Sid, I was not able to speak for a while for I was too choked up. When I was able to speak, I asked him what his plans were and he told me that he was going to be moving on with the small stable that he had been with for a number of years. He thought they may be going to Canada, but he was not sure. I asked him if he needed any money and he laughed and said that he thought that was very nice of me to offer like that but he had all the money that he needed. He said though, that if I wanted to part with some of my money to please make a nice donation to a food bank to feed the poor. If I wanted to, he said, I could maybe set up a trust fund for the food bank, this way they would have a steady source of income. Here's the clincher Sid, he says make it in the name of Esther Abromovitz. He says that would be a nice touch. He says that Esther would like that.

"Sid," Heshy said while laughing, "that son of a bitch knew all the right buttons on me to push. I called the lawyers late yesterday afternoon to set up the trust fund for a food bank and not only that, but if Big Bucks Baby wins on Saturday, a big part of his winnings will go to the trust fund too. I then asked Joey what he was doing to help the poor and he said, "Heshy, while you will be putting food in their tummies and a little color back into their cheeks, I will try to put hope in their hearts, a little twinkle in their eyes and hopefully, a smile on their faces."

"You know Sid, Joey Balducci, since we were kids, always seemed to come up with the right words for any situation." Sid, looking dumbfounded, said, "I dunno what's goin on right now. I think I got a headache. You know Harry, er Heshy, what ever the hell your name is, I don't remember too much about Joey Balducci because I was only on the scene for a short time when your sister died, so do you think you could talk about it now? I know that before this incident yesterday, you would never want to talk about it. It's not important, but I'm just very curious about how that romance not only got started, but how it got the okay from your mom and dad. So wadda ya say, can you tell me about it?" "Okay Sid. I'll tell you their story as best as I can remember it."

"I'm not sure of exactly when it was that we all met, but I would guess that it was when we were all about nine or ten years old or maybe even younger, in grammar school, like I said before. Well anyway, Joey was a quiet kid then, the kind of kid who listened while everyone else did the talking. He never even offered an opinion about anything. I don't remember when it was when he came out of his shell, but when he did, it was with a bang. He was funny and witty and soon became one of the most popular kids in the school. The girls, for the most part, loved him and my sister was no exception. Of course, at that time in our lives we guys had no interest in girls. After all we were only about eleven or twelve at the time and sports was our thing, especially baseball.

As the years went by we started to develop our personalities a little more. I remember, before I met you Sid, I entered an essay writing contest about Wall Street, the free enterprise system, stocks and bonds and things of that nature, if you know what I mean. Well anyway I won! I mean it was a national contest and I won. I was so proud, as you can imagine, Sid. The prize was a day at the New York Stock Exchange and a mini portfolio of stocks. It consisted of one share of stock in ten of the most solid companies in America, at that time. Sid I felt like I was on top of the world, not only because I won the contest, but Sarah and I were also boyfriend and girlfriend. Esther and Joey became boyfriend and girlfriend I think, the week before on a boat ride to Bear Mountain State Park. But as luck would have it Sid, on that very day that I went to the New York Stock Exchange, when I was not in school, Esther got sick.

We didn't know it at the time of course, but that was the beginning of her battle for life. At that particular time there were a lot of health scares going around so when Esther started to get sick, throwing up, dizzy and feeling week, nobody would come near her for fear of catching something. Nobody that is, except Joey Balducci.

My sister didn't want to go to see the school nurse for fear of having to go to the hospital, maybe in an ambulance. Up steps Joey. I was told, by my sister and others, that there was not even a little bit of hesitation on Joey's part. He went right to her side, helped her up out of her chair and without even getting the okay from the teacher, took Esther home. My sister later told me that he practically had to carry her home. Can you imagine Sid, on the biggest day in my life, up to that time, 15 years old and win a national contest like that. Winning those shares of stocks are what got me started on my business career but of course, after what happened to Esther, it really didn't matter to me, about the prize, I mean. I only cared about Esther and if she would get well.

I remember the next day, when Esther wasn't in class, Joey was asking me about her and at that time I really didn't know anything was seriously wrong with Esther. The family doctor was coming over that day to check her out. Remember those days Sid, when doctors still made house calls?" Sid nodded in agreement. "That afternoon", Harry went on, "after school, Joey came by the house, to see how Esther was feeling and he brought her a single, beautiful rose, in a pretty vase. My mother was standing in the doorway to Esther's room when Joey handed my sister the flower and he said the difference between that rose and Esther, is that the beauty of the flower will soon fade, but the beauty of Esther, will last forever. Of course Esther had tears in her eyes when Joey told her that, but when I looked over at my mom in the doorway, she was wiping away what I know was a tear, but she said she had something in her eye.

We didn't know yet the seriousness of Esther's illness. After a few days, when the results of all the tests were in, the doctor's worst fears were confirmed. Leukemia! That dreaded disease! To this day, I hate the sound of it. My parents and I of course were devastated, as was Esther. But I never thought that Joey would be affected like he was. He came over as soon as Esther felt well enough, physically and emotionally. He always came over upbeat, with a smile on his face. After a few days of visiting, one afternoon, after school, Joey came over with a bunch of Esther's school mates and friends. Joey organized it all by himself. He even brought Esther some make up school work, to keep her mind occupied during the day. Esther loved every minute of it. She brightened up so much that the next day she said that she felt like going out for a walk. So as soon as Joey came over, after school, he took her out for a walk. It was a nice, warm day for it too, as I remember.

Esther was having good days and bad days but everyday Joey came over to visit and that seemed to make a bad day into a good day and a good day even better for Esther. They would sit and talk for hours, helping each other with home work, laughing and sometimes Joey even had Esther singing. The prognosis, you know Sid was terrible! The experts, the specialists, only gave her six months to one year to live, but after about 7 months, Esther was feeling pretty good, for a short while. We all thought that maybe the doctors were wrong. We were wrong. The doctors explained to us that sometimes a patient will be in remission for a short period of time. A time when she will feel good, but they said don't be too optimistic, because the disease always comes back. Back then Sid, they only had one drug to prolong the fight against this awful disease. It was Methotre something or other, wait a minute I think it was Methotrexate, yeah that was it. Esther was taking that and when she was feeling a little better, she went back to school, always tired and a little weak, but she went back. Joey was always by her side, always walking with her, always helping her as I was too.

She told me that she loved Joey very much and that he told her that he loved her the same way. Joey was always writing stuff to her, you know, like poems and notes and things like that. He even used to make his own get well cards for her. The pictures on the front of the cards were not too good but Esther told me that the words that he wrote inside were from the heart and precious. She loved each and every one of them. On Valentine's Day, of the following year, Joey gave Esther a poem in a picture frame that he had written for her, with a beautiful pink heart on the top of the page. Esther loved it so, she showed it to my mother, and she also loved it. In fact, my Mom liked it so much she hung it in the dining room for all to see. You might have seen it Sid, It was still hanging there when you started to come around." Sid said, "You know, I think I do remember seeing it years ago. Where is it now Heshy?" Pointing to a corner file cabinet, one of the few that he kept locked, Heshy reached into his jacket pocket, pulled out a key, handed it to Sid and said, "I think it is that cabinet, in the top drawer, in a file marked, "Esther's things". There are a lot of papers in that file, but the one you're looking for should be right near the front. When you find it Sid, read it aloud, would you Sid?" Sid turned to give Heshy a look of wonder, for Heshy, even though they were friends and partners for all these years, seldom spoke to Sid in such a pleasant manner. "I found it", he said, then started to read the poem:

"A MOST BEAUTIFUL THING"

There is nothing more beautiful is this world
Than to see a guy and his girl
Laughing and having fun
With two hearts beating as one
With their souls entwined
In an ever loving embrace
Each one shining
With a beautiful smiling face
Walking forever side by side
Sharing a joy they cannot hide
Always together, hand in hand
Sharing a life
That was Heavenly planned
Their hearts so happy
They always want to sing
This is truly a most beautiful thing

When Sid finished reading the poem, neither one of them could speak. They each cleared their throats and then Heshy continued with his story. "My mother loved that little poem because, she said it reminded her of my father and her, when they were teenagers in Europe. It hung on her wall until both my parents were gone. It has always reminded me of myself and Sarah.

As Joey and my sister were getting closer and closer, spiritually and emotionally I mean Sid. Our families by this time were very close, like us going to Joey's house one year for Easter Sunday dinner and on Christmas to see their tree and sample some homemade holiday treats. And they came to our house for a Passover Seder. My parents and Joey's parents really liked and respected each other very much, so it was a very happy time for all of us. My father loved Joey as did my Mom but he became a little concerned, you know because of the different religions, so he asked Joey to come sit with him in the kitchen for a little talk.

My mother and I were there too. My mother was very mad at my father because she was crazy about Joey and saw nothing wrong with my sister and Joey being boyfriend and girlfriend. Anyway, Joey leaves Esther in her room, because Esther wasn't feeling that great at that time, and sits down with my father. My mother, to my father's surprise, sat down too. My father, with eyes almost welling with tears, because it really hurt my Dad to have this conversation with him, says to Joey that he didn't think it was a good idea for him to come around to see Esther anymore, because he thought they were becoming too serious. Joey answers by putting on a beautiful show of logic and persuasion. Joey started by saying that he understands my father's concerns and respects his strong religious beliefs. That he will abide by my father's wishes, but first he wanted to say a few things before my father made a final decision. My father, smiles and says, sure Joey, say anything you want.

Joey knows my mother is on his side just by the way she always looks at him, so he looks my father right in the eyes and says, "Mr. Abromovitz, I want you to know that what I said before, about abiding by your decision is true. But I also have to tell you, that just like you and Mrs. Abromovitz, my main concern is Esther. I only wish to make her happy, as I know the both of you do too. I only wish, as I'm sure that you do too, to fill her heart with love and joy, if that is possible. I only wish to keep her smiling if I can. You see Mr. Abromovitz, with all my heart and soul and my entire being for that matter, I love your daughter, Esther and she loves me. Now I know that you probably think that we are too young to understand and appreciate what true, real love is all about. I don't know, maybe we don't, but Esther and I really, in our hearts believe that we share a love for each other that will be forever. You see Mr. Abromovitz I share the concerns that you and your family have about Esther's medical condition. I am saddened to say that it seems that the doctor's original prognosis was correct. I cry myself to sleep some nights, wishing that the prognosis was wrong. Maybe the both of you do too. But the point is, if the doctors are right then there is nothing for you to worry about Esther and me being in love with each other. But let me reassure you that if, by some miracle, the doctors are wrong and Esther beats this terrible disease, I would do whatever it is I would have to do to satisfy you and Mrs. Abromovitz, except of course change my religious beliefs. I'm sure you can understand that. And let me say just one more thing that also comes straight from my heart.

I think that the beauty and loveliness of Esther and the niceness and brains of Heshy, are a reflection of the way you both, brought them up, in other words, a reflection of the two of you.

"Oh, just one more thing to consider is this, we all know the pain and suffering that Esther has been going through, you know that more than me, and we also know, I think, that when Esther and I are together, she seems to brighten up and smile and starts to feel a little bit better or at least a little less bad. So I think to keep us apart at this point in time would only add to her pain and I know that neither one of you would want that, am I right?" Before either one of my parents could answer, Joey said, "Well like I said before, I'll do whatever it is that you decide. Thanks for listening to me"

My father looked blank for a minute, then turned his head and looked at my mother. She had been looking intently at him since Joey finished talking. She smiled a hopeful smile, wiped away a tear, nodded her head affirmatively and said to my father, "Well?" My father looked at Joey and said, "Why couldn't you be a Jewish boy?"

He wasn't expecting an answer and he didn't get one. My father then said, "Forget about what I said before, I don't know what I was thinking about. I guess it's just all the stress and tension around here the last year or so, I don't know." His voiced tailed off as my mother softly clapped her hands as she got up from the chair and said, "So, what are the plans for today Joey?" Joey told her, as they both walked towards Esther's room, "The same as every other day, Mrs. Abromovitz, I have to try to put a smile on your daughter's beautiful face." My mother gave him a little hug as they disappeared into Esther's room.

I followed them into her room and there was Esther, a big smile on her face, arms open wide to receive a hug from my mom and from Joey. From me too, of course, when it was my turn. Boy, I tell ya Sid, she looked so beautiful and happy that day. I remember it as if it was yesterday. After that day, when the air was cleared, Joey was like part of the family. Joey spent every minute of his time over at our house. He didn't hang out with the guys any longer, he didn't play softball or basketball, he only wanted to do is be with Esther. Every day, sometimes many times a day he would make a get well card or write a poem for her. Sometimes he would just write his feelings down on paper. My mother would get to read them, but only after asking Esther if she could. When my mother would finish reading one of his writings, she would usually hold the paper to her heart heave a big sigh and say, "Wow! What a heart this boy has."

I tell ya Sid, I have to admit, he had a way with words. When I would say that to him, Joey would say, "It has to flow from the heart, Heshy it has to come from the heart. You have to mean and feel what you say otherwise it will never come out right. Whenever you're stuck for the right words to say to someone, search your heart. The right words will be there. Let it flow from the heart." You know Sid, now that I think about it, I've been trying to do that for over fifty years and I just remembered that I got it from Joey. Well anyway, the guy was good. There's one thing I'll always remember that he did that was simple, but great.

One day my mother had to go to the store to get, oh I dunno what, and Esther was still sleeping. So my mother started to write her a note explaining where she had gone, in case Esther woke up and got no response when she called out to my mother. My mother had only gotten as far as "Esther," when my sister awoke, so there was no need to finish the note. My mother just left the piece of paper on the kitchen table and went about her business. Later, when Joey came over he happened to see this piece of paper with "Esther,' written on it and asked what that was about and my mother told him what had happened. Joey looked at it for a second and said, "Let's see what I can do with this." He right away started writing and in less than a minute came up with this,

Esther, Esther,
What a beautiful name
My old, current and forever
Flame

See what I mean Sid, the guy, the kid really, he was only about 16 years old at the time, had a great way with words. You know, like I said before, even his family became close to our family. One day Joey brings over a big pan of fresh baked lasagna. Joey says his mother made it just for our family and she made it, just like she had made that Easter Sunday dinner that I told you about before, with the fact that we were a kosher house, in mind. It was vegetable lasagna, made with home made tomato sauce, with no meat in it. Not only that Sid, but she used the same special dishes and baking pans that she bought special, so that no trace of meat came into contact with it. It was out of this world Sid, just like the Easter Sunday dinner was, as I remember it. It fact Sid I think I can almost taste it right now, fifty years later." "Man that must have been some lasagna Heshy!" Sid said. "It sure was, now let me get back to the story. Anyway, Joey explains to my mother and father that his mother likes to buy her meats at the kosher butcher, because it's a better grade of beef, she thinks. "

One day, when Esther was feeling a little better and the weather was really beautiful, Joey asked his father, Giuseppe, who now owned a station wagon, if he would drive us all to Prospect Park for an outing, you know Sid, a picnic. He said he would and we all went, even me. Joey's mother was there too. She had already bonded with my Mom a long while before that day. They enjoyed each other's company very much. She understood what my mother was going through. Anyway, it was a lovely day and everybody bonded real well and got along. We had a great time too, as I remember. We even rented a row boat on the Prospect Park Lake and helped Esther get in the boat and Joey and I took turns rowing the boat and all the while keeping a close eye on Esther. In the meantime my father and Joey's father got along great, as they usually did. They were talking about how tough it was to make ends meet and how important strong family ties were to keep the family going. They talked about everything and anything. Everybody had a great time, especially Esther. That's what it was all for anyway, you know Sid, for Esther.

You know Sid, I haven't thought about that day for a long time. I should have though. There were a lot of good lessons to learn from that trip. About people getting along and the real important things in life, if you know what I mean Sid. Well anyway, that was probably the last really good feeling day I think she had. That was in the late spring or early summer and by July and August, physically she went down hill. Joey was still coming over every day, writing his usual stuff for her every day. By this time Esther was getting fevers, bleeding and bruising. But still Esther always had a smile for Joey. He was always by her bedside, holding her hand and writing his heart out to her, which she loved. Sometimes Joey would leave to go home and he would have tears in his eyes but he always came back the next day with a smile on his face for Esther. My mother once told me, long after my sister had passed away, that Joey's mother told her, that on so many nights, Joey would cry all night. That he would yell and rave and rant at God for not making his Esther well. My mother did the same thing on many nights.

Then Esther was having difficulty breathing. She was getting lethargic. Then there came a time, near the end, when she couldn't see or speak. I'll never forget the date Sid it was August 17, 1948. Joey was on one side of the bed, holding her hand, while my mother and father were on the other side of the bed, holding her other hand. I stood at the foot of the bed, gently caressing her feet. We didn't know if she could hear us but we kept talking to her anyway. Joey struggled hard to maintain his composure but was losing it a bit near the end. I'll never forget this part of it Sid, Joey started writing in his ever present pad and in a minute or two tore the page out and leaned close to Esther's ear and whispered into it, reading from the page he had just torn out of the pad, all the while still holding her hand tightly. When he finished reading I saw her smile, squeeze Joey's hand and take her last breath. When everyone in the room realized what happened, sobbing started, softly at first, but it got louder in a few seconds. Joey leaned over and kissed her face and hands and immediately started to cry loudly and quickly left the room and the house.

My mother and father followed Joey in kissing Esther and crying but a little subdued. Naturally Sid I cried too, after all, she was my twin sister. Joey, before he left, placed the paper that he had just written to Esther, in Esther's hands and I removed it when I leaned over to kiss her." "What did it say?" Sid asked. Heshy, after thinking about it for a few seconds replied, "I don't remember exactly Sid, but I'll tell you where it is now. You know Sid, you may have already seen it, because it too used to hang on the wall in my mother's house, she loved it so. I haven't looked at it since my mother passed away. Sid you'll find it in the back of the picture of Esther and Joey, and Sarah and me that was taken when we all went on that boat ride up the Hudson River to Bear Mountain. I've kept in the same cabinet that you just unlocked. Here let me get it for you. Please Sid if you wouldn't mind, read it aloud won't you. Oh, before you start reading, do me a favor Sid, see to it that you ask the girls in the office if any of them would like to go to the big race Saturday and sit in my box seats. And I think it's time we gave all the help around here a little bonus for all the good years they've given us. Don't you agree Sid? Well go ahead and read that last thing that Joey read to Esther."

With that the door opened and in stepped Anna. "I'm sorry for the interruption Mr. Sackman, here is the package you've been waiting for and I thought you'd like to know that Mrs. Sackman called and asked if you could come by the house for dinner tomorrow night. She said that if you are able to come over, then there is no need to return her call, just show up. She said that sevenish would be fine." Taking the package she handed him Heshy said, "It's okay Anna, and thank you. Oh by the way, wait in here a minute I want you to hear something. Go ahead Sid, read it loud and clear." Sid, picked up the paper, looked at Heshy and Anna, made a face and started reading:

EVERY STEP OF THE WAY

We were fifteen when we met
and yet

Our love for each other has always been in our hearts
And before our journey through forever starts,

Let me just say,
We will be together, forever,
every step of the way

Walking hand in hand,
Through Heavens never ending land

Our love makes the bad days good
And the dark days bright

Fills a sad heart with joy
And makes a heavy heart light

Night and day, forever,
We will be together

Every step of the way

As Sid choked hard, Anna, a tear welling in her eye, said, "That's very beautiful and touching. Who wrote it? What's it from?" Heshy, finding it a little hard to speak, finally said, "Oh some guy, named Joey, wrote that to my twin sister many years ago." Anna said, "Oh, I didn't know you had a twin sister Mr. Sackman. Did she marry this Joey fella?" "No. Not exactly, Anna. You see she died over fifty years ago when she just turned seventeen. I just saw Joey yesterday, for the first time since then and he feels like they've been together all these years and will continue to be together always. I don't know, but I guess in a sense, my sister Esther did marry Joey." Anna walked out of the office with tears, flowing fast down her face, as Heshy called to her, "Anna, I'm leaving the office early today, why don't you do the same thing. Turning to Sid he said why don't you leave early and have dinner with me tonight?"

Before Sid and Anna could leave the room, Heshy quickly called out to them, "Wait a minute Sid, and you too Anna, I just had an idea, Sid why don't you and your wife come to my house for dinner tomorrow night too." Before Sid could answer, Heshy turned to Anna and said, "Can you get Wayne Bartly on the phone for me?" "Wayne who?" was her quizzical response. "Bartley, You know Wayne Bartley my trainer, the one who trains Big Bucks Baby. I think his number is in my computer phone book." "Oh yes, of course. Now I know who you mean, right away Mr. Sackman." "So whatta ya say Sid? Will you come tomorrow night?" Heshy asked. "I think so Hesh but let me check with Vivian first. I'll call her right now" Sid replied as he quickly went to his office to make the call.

"Oh Anna just one more thing before you leave, as soon as I finish talking with Wayne and Sid finishes talking with his wife, please get Mrs. Sackman on the phone for me. Okay?" Heshy asked. "Of course Mr. Sackman, no problem and by the way Wayne Bartly is on line 11." "Thanks Anna. Hello Wayne, this is Harry Sackman, I wonder if you could do me a favor? There's a groom that works for a small outfit that is stabled near you, his name is Joey Balducci, could you call him to the phone for me if he's around?" "Sure, no problem Harry, hang on for a few minutes." In a few minutes Harry heard, "Hy Hesh, er I mean Harry, what's up?" "Joey how about you coming to my house for dinner tomorrow night?" Harry asked. "Well I'd love to but I don't have my car here and besides that I don't know where you live." Joey replied.

Harry laughed and said, "That's no problem Joey I'll send a car to pick you up. About six o'clock. Is that okay?" "Yeah, that'll be good and by the way Harry did you get the diary that I asked my brother-in-law to send to you this morning?" Joey asked. "I sure did and thanks again. I can't wait to read it tonight", Heshy said. "Oh I bet you can't wait", Joey said. "By the way Harry, who else will be there tomorrow night?", Joey asked. "I'm not 100% sure but I think there will be a bunch of people you might remember from the old neighborhood. That's alright with you, isn't it, Joey?" "Oh yeah, that's okay. I'll see you tomorrow night Harry." "Okay I'll see you tomorrow night Joey." Just as Heshy got off the phone, Sid walked in and said that he and Vivian would be there tomorrow night. At the same time Anna came into the office and told Heshy that his wife was on the phone, line two. Heshy thanked her and asked Anna to please send his driver into see him before she left for the day. After dinner with Sid Christopher, Heshy returned to his apartment, sat in his favorite chair and opened Esther's diary.

CHAPTER 2

Hello diary! My name is Esther Abromovitz. Today May 8, 1944, is my and my twin brother Heshy's, thirteenth Birthday. My parents made a very nice party for us and invited most of our friends and relatives. Even my aunt, uncle and cousins came all the way from the Bronx to be there. My aunt, uncle and cousins from Queens were there too. You were my birthday gift from my brother Heshy. You are just what I have wanted for a long time. I saved up all my babysitting money and bought Heshy a new baseball glove. He loved it. Even though there is this terrible war going on, and there are a lot of things that we are not able to buy, I got a lot of nice presents from everyone, even from a boy that I have a big crush on, Joey Balducci. He doesn't know it yet and I don't know when he will, if ever. I just hope he likes me too. He is very shy so I don't think he will tell me anytime soon but we shall see. Joey, for as long as I've known him, has worked part time before and after school and sometimes weekends too. He took his hard earned money and bought me some beautiful handkerchiefs, monogrammed, with my initials. It was so sweet of him. I had told Joey I was getting Heshy a new glove so Joey bought Heshy a new softball. Heshy loved that too. I have so much to tell you and I will write a little bit of what's going on with me, my family and friends every day, or whenever I can. Good night for now.

Heshy flipped through the pages until he came to an entry on the first day of school that fall.

Dear diary today was the first day of school and I was thrilled to see that Joey is in every one of my classes. In home room he even sits right in front of me and I found myself staring at the back of his head. He must have felt it because a couple of times he turned quickly to look at me. I pretended to read my notebook and then I looked up at him and smiled. I tried to look so innocent but I think that maybe he knew I was staring at him. I don't know, but Marsha Plotkin, who sat next to me, caught me and leaned over to ask me what I was doing. I thought I would die. I told her I was just daydreaming about what a great summer we just had. I think she believed me, at least I hope so.

In our History class I sit in front of Joey and to his left. I sat there the whole class trying to feel if he was looking at me. I know I must sound a little crazy, or maybe a whole lot crazy but I just have such a great big crush on him. I can't help it. I haven't even told my brother Heshy about how I feel about Joey, even though we are so close, you know being twins and all that. Well anyway, we all walk to and from school together, a big group of us, and usually I walk with most of the girls and Joey walks with most of the boys, including Heshy. Tomorrow, I think I'll walk close to Heshy and maybe I'll be closer to Joey. Nobody can say anything about that because I will look like I'm walking with my brother, right? If I talk to Heshy and he's talking to Joey then I can talk to Joey and walk close to him too. I wish he wasn't so shy. Well that's enough for tonight, good night diary.

The following day Esther wrote:

Dear diary, it worked like a charm. I walked to and from school along side Heshy. Joey at first walked on the other side of Heshy, but halfway to school, Joey suddenly came around to my other side and started talking to me. He was talking about anything and everything. It was great, for me anyway. Joey does not seem to be so shy anymore. In class he was talking up a storm. He was raising his hand to answer questions from the teachers and talking to his classmates, especially the girls. I didn't like that a bit. And he was smiling a lot too. I'm hoping that Heshy asks Joey to come over to our house some day to do homework together. Of course then I could join in and do my homework with them. That would be great. Good night for now.

Heshy flipped through some more pages and came to an entry for Halloween.

Dear diary, we had a Halloween party and a contest for the best and most original costume in school today. Just about everybody was in costume. The teacher in charge even let us join together in teams of anywhere from two to ten kids, to make "interactive", as she called it, costumes and skits. Heshy, Joey, Barry Engle, Marsha Plotkin, Sarah Gold and me, all formed a team and we tried to come up with a theme that would allow us to dress up in the same kind of costume and do a little skit. I think when we got together to plan and discuss the different ideas that everybody had, we spent more time arguing than making plans. Finally, we all agreed to put together a bunch of old clothes and dress as refugees coming to America for the first time. Being that almost all of our parents were immigrants and so happy to be in America, our parents, for the most part, were happy to help us in any way they could.

Next we had to write a little skit, which, with everybody's help, we did. Because Marsha and I are on the small side, we played young children. Sarah and Barry played our parents, while Heshy and Joey played our uncles. We only had a few days to put it all together and rehearse, which we did. Everyone, teachers and students alike, really liked our skit and costumes, but we didn't win. Gloria Rothenberg won for dressing up as Carmen, from the opera of the same name and then singing the aria from that opera. None of us thought that was fair because Gloria was studying to be an opera singer and had a trained voice. We didn't complain because as Joey said, we might look like a bunch of sore losers. It really didn't matter because we all had so much fun and besides that I got a chance to work on a project with Joey. That felt so good. That's enough for now, good night.

Once more Heshy skipped through the pages and stopped at a page dated two days before Thanksgiving Day, 1944.

Dear diary, ever since Heshy asked Joey to come over to our house to do homework together, about three or four weeks ago, it seems that Joey is over here two or three times a week and I love it. Joey was over here again tonight and as we were all helping each other out, Heshy,

Joey, and me of course, we were also talking about the upcoming holiday, Thanksgiving, and what kinds of food we were all going to be eating. Daddy, who was sitting in his favorite chair reading the newspaper, and listening to us too I think, asked Joey if his family was going to be having a turkey for Thanksgiving dinner. Joey, with a straight face, tells Daddy that they could not afford to buy a turkey this year so his mother is going to make a giant meatball and shape it to look like a turkey. Daddy, taking Joey seriously, looked at him in silence for a moment and when we all broke out in laughter, including Mom, who was listening from the kitchen, then Daddy laughed too. With a smile on his face and shaking a finger at Joey, Daddy said to him, "so you're a kibitzer, huh Joey?" Joey didn't answer, he just laughed along with the rest of us. Joey is so cute and funny. I can't wait to go to school tomorrow just so I can see him again. Good night.

About four or five pages later, Heshy came to this page.

Dear diary, well it's the first day back to school after the Thanksgiving break and I think I gained ten pounds from all the delicious food and goodies I ate. Mom says she feels guilty about us having so much to eat when most of the people in Europe are starving. For quite a while now Mom and Daddy have been telling us at meal times, to eat everything on our plates because the children in Europe are going without food, so it would be a sin if we wasted it. Mom always tells us that even though we have food rationing here in this country, because of the war, it is much better than it was in Germany back in the twenties and early thirties. Back then, she said, she and her family couldn't afford to buy much because of the runaway inflation. Daddy and Mom got married in 1929, just before the world wide depression started. Heshy and I were born in 1931 and it was a struggle for my parents to keep us fed and clothed until 1935, when we all managed to move to England.

After a year or so we were able to come to America and our lives have been so much better because of it, Mom and Daddy always say. After I hear about what's going on back in Europe now, I'm so glad that we didn't miss the boat. Well anyway, back in school everything is about the same except that Joey always seems to be smiling now and is more popular every day with all the kids in school, especially the girls. I hate it. He greets everyone with a smile so much, that many of the girls are calling him "Smiley". I don't think Joey is comfortable with that name. I still call him Joey. He really has come out of his shell this past school year. I still don't know if he likes me or thinks that I'm special or anything like that because he is so friendly with everybody, boys, girls, adults, teachers, everybody. He makes us all feel as if he likes us all. I suppose that's good in a way but I still would like it better if he made me and only me, feel special. I don't know, maybe I'm just a silly young girl living in a dream world, but that's who I am. Diary, you are the only one that I have told this to. I haven't told any of my friends because they would blabber it all over school. If I was going to tell anyone it would be my truly best friend, my brother Heshy and I haven't told him either. I don't know if maybe he suspects, the way I always get involved with Joey and Heshy on the nights that we do homework together. When it's just me and Heshy, I don't always do my homework with him. I don't know why, I just don't. Oh well, we shall see what happens. Good night diary.

Heshy next stopped at a page that indicated it was now a few days before Christmas, 1944.

Dear diary, it is now three days until Christmas and Joey invited a bunch of us up to his apartment to see his family's Christmas tree. In fact, the other night, when he was over at my house doing homework with me and Heshy, he even invited my Mom and Dad to see his tree too. I got to see it twice, am I lucky or what? I think they had just about the only window in the neighborhood that was all lit up with Christmas lights and decorations. I was told by one of the kids who lived on Joey's block that most of the people on his block and even those who lived near his block were invited and came up to Joey's apartment to see their tree. Everyone who did visit were treated to Christmas treats. We all, our friends and my parents, had a great time as well. Joey's Mom and Dad were great. They treated everyone like family, both times I was there. They offered me, Heshy and my parents some homemade cake and wine and other holiday treats, which we all ate and drank. Yes, Daddy let me and Heshy taste a little sip of wine, just like at Passover.

A wonderful thing happened when my parents visited Joey's apartment. As we were all getting ready to sip our wine, Daddy raised his glass in a toast like gesture, and said, "Merry Christmas to you all."

26

Joey's parents beamed, raised their glasses and at the same time said to my parents, "Happy Chanukah to all of your family." It almost seemed rehearsed, but I'm sure it wasn't. It was wonderful and beautiful at the same time. Everyone seemed to bond at that moment and there were smiles, hugs, kisses and handshakes all around. I thought for a moment that I might get a kiss or a hug from Joey, but all I got was a hand shake. It seemed as if he was getting ready to hug me, but at the last minute he pulled back and shook my hand. I was disappointed of course but I did get to hold his hand, however so briefly. By the way, the Christmas tree was beautiful. His family did a great job of decorating it.

Earlier in the day, when I visited Joey's house with most of our friends, it was so very nice too. His parents wouldn't give us any wine to drink without our parents being there but, the cake tasted great. Like my Mom, Joey's Mom is a very good cook. Maybe it's because they're both from Europe. I don't know for sure why, but they are good cooks. Diary, I have a little problem. I would like to get Joey a little Christmas present, with the money that I saved from my babysitting jobs, but if I did wouldn't that look a little suspicious? I couldn't afford to get all of my other friends a gift for Chanukah. Maybe I ought to forget about it. Well at the very least I think I'll sleep on it. Good night dear diary.

On December 27th, Esther wrote:

Dear diary, I'm sorry I didn't write to you for the last few days. One day the whole family went to visit my Mom's sister, my Aunt Sherry, and her family in the Bronx. We didn't get home until after midnight. The next day we went to visit Daddy's brother, my Uncle Carl, and his family, way out in Queens. Again we didn't get home until after 1am. Another night we had friends of Mom and Daddy's come over to visit and they didn't leave until after 11pm. Well anyway now I'm back and let me see, what's new. Oh yeah, I decided not to get Joey a Christmas present, not this year anyway. I didn't want to start people talking because, believe me they would be talking. Just today at the soda shop I met Sylvia Roth, who is in most of my classes. She's a nice girl but such a "yenta", in case you don't know, that means a busybody. She really loves to dish out the gossip. Today she asked me if I heard about Sandra Einhorn being crazy about Sheldon Kravitz. I told her no.

Then she asked me if I heard about Bobby Feldman and Tracy Cohen. Again I told her no. Then she really shocked me by asking me if it's true, about what she heard about my brother, Heshy wanting Sarah Gold to be his girlfriend. I told her that I didn't know anything about that, but of course I knew because Heshy had told me that a while ago. I was so nervous that she would ask me about Joey, even though I never told anyone about how I felt about Joey. I was so glad when she left.

Anyway, the war news from Europe is awful. A lot of American and British soldiers were being killed and wounded in something called "The Battle of the Bulge". I hate this war. I wish all of our troops could come home right now. Mom and Daddy get very aggravated and sad when they hear news about the war. Well like I said before I've been very busy since the holiday break started, so I haven't seen Joey around lately. I sure miss seeing him. Maybe I'll see him tomorrow. We shall see. Good night diary.

The next night Esther wrote:

Dear diary, I had another disappointment today. I was all excited, inside me of course, when I was invited to a New Year's Eve party at Sarah Gold's house and I heard that Heshy, Joey and a few of their friends were invited too. I thought that was so great, going to a party with Joey being there too. Then I found out from Heshy that Joey will not be there because he said that he always spends New Year's Eve at home with his family. He said especially this year because his brother "Buster", I don't know what his real name is, is in the Army and his parents are very worried about him. Even though he is still here in America, with all the bad news we are hearing about that big German offensive, called "The Battle of the Bulge", they are worried that he will be going overseas soon. I feel so bad for Joey's parents. I hate this crazy war. If it wasn't for this war not only would the killing stop, but I most likely would be seeing Joey at that party. Oh well there I go dreaming again.

Here is some good news. It's official! Heshy asked Sarah Gold to be his girlfriend and she said yes. Somebody please wake up Joey and tell him I'm here waiting for him. Oh well, I guess if I didn't have my dreams I wouldn't have much. Okay, it's off to beddy bye now. Good night Joey. Good night dear diary.

Heshy stopped at the next page. It was dated January 4th, 1945.

Dear diary, the days that have passed since I last wrote to you have been uneventful, except for the good news that while the war is not yet over, the Battle of the Bulge is. The Allied Armies are again on the move toward Germany, so the radio and newspapers are reporting. So I guess that is good news. Anyway that party, without Joey being there, was for me anyway, very dull. Sylvia Roth was there and she tried to fix me up with her cousin, Bobby Finklestein. He seems to be a very nice boy, and nice looking too, but I really had no interest in him. He even asked me to go the movies with him the next day, New Year's Day, but I told him a little white lie about me having to stay home and catch up on a bunch of school work that I was behind on. Heshy heard me tell that lie and just looked at me and smiled, a loving, brotherly smile, if you know what I mean. Heshy seemed to catch on right away that I didn't want to go the movies with Bobby. I don't know, are we so close because we're twins or just because we are brother and sister and also best friends?

In the meantime when Sylvia heard that I wouldn't go to the movies with her cousin, she came over to me and asked, "What school work do you have to catch up on?" I thought for a moment and realized that I couldn't lie my way out of it, so I just told her that because Bobby is her cousin, I didn't want to hurt his feelings, so I made up the story about the schoolwork. I told her that while he is very nice looking and seems to be a nice guy too, I just was not interested in going to the movies with him. Then I added the clincher and reminded her of when she did almost the same thing with Hy Glasser, a few weeks before. That seemed to do it because she just smiled at me, tapped me on my arm and said, "Yes. You are right. I know exactly what you mean." and walked away. I was so glad that she agreed with me, because the truth is, I really didn't want to hurt Bobby's feelings.

But you know dear diary, if Joey doesn't come my way soon, I might just go to the movies with Bobby that is if he ever asks me again. If for no other reason, maybe just to make Joey a little jealous. Would that be a dirty trick diary? I wouldn't want to hurt Joey's feelings either but you know I've got to get him moving. Don't I? Well, let us see what tomorrow brings. Good night dear diary.

Heshy skipped along the pages until he came to Feb. 12, 1945.

Dear diary, today in art class we all started a project for Valentine's Day. We are learning how to make our own Valentine cards. I plan on making one for Mom, one for Daddy and one for Heshy. Do you think I should still be giving my brother a card for Valentine's Day? I don't know, we'll see about that one. I'm also planning to make a card for Joey, but I'm not going to sign my name to it. I think I'll sign it, "secret admirer". I hope he won't suspect that it came from me. Ira Hirsch, I think, is going to make a card for me, because I always catch him looking at me in an admiring way and then he looks down at the cards that he is making. He is kind of cute and a pretty smart kid too, but thoughts of Joey always seem to get in the way of me thinking of anyone else. Am I being foolish or what?

Well anyway, making the cards is fairly easy, but the hard part is going to be finding the right words to put on the inside. I'm going to have to work real hard to find those words. Somebody started a rumor today that Mrs. Schultz, the art teacher is a Nazi, just because her name is German and she speaks with a slight German accent. You know diary, Heshy and I spoke German first before learning English. We don't have accents because we started speaking English at a young age. Mom and Daddy speak with mild German accents and speak German and Yiddish once in a while, but only at home. They say we're in America now so we must speak English.

Well anyway, being that more than half the kids in school are Jewish, the reaction from most of the Jewish kids, about the rumor that Mrs. Schultz is a Nazi was predictable. They didn't like her and wrote bad things about her on the walls of the stairways and halls. She was hurt by all the taunts but still taught her class as if nothing was going on. I always liked her though and even felt sorry for her when all that nonsense started. I even apologized to her for the bad behavior of the other kids. Of course I didn't name who the other kids were, although I do know most of them. I'm so glad that Heshy and Joey were not in that bunch. Oh, by the way Joey's brother, "Buster", left to go over to Europe a few weeks ago, Joey told a bunch of us today, on the way to school. I still don't know what his real name is. I keep forgetting to ask Joey. Well anyway, I hope he will be alright and I will pray for him. When I told my parents about Joey's brother going over to Europe, they too became very worried and concerned. I'm sure they will be praying for him too as we all will for all the soldiers. Well good night, dear diary.

Feb. 13, 1945

Dear diary, what a small world this is getting to be. I don't know if I told you but, Sarah Gold's uncle, who is from the Bronx, but is in the Army now, in Georgia or someplace like that down South, lives in the same barracks as the son of the man who lives upstairs from us. And now Daddy, who works for a large clothing company in Manhattan, as a bookkeeper, was transferred today to the factory in Brooklyn that makes winter coats for the Army and what they call "P" coats for the Navy. He was promoted to office manager at the factory, with more money of course, but the funny thing about it is, Joey's mom works in that same factory. She is what they call a "baster". I'm not exactly sure what that means, but I think she attaches the sleeves onto the coats, by hand, sewing a loose stitch to hold it place until it can be sewn tightly by machine. I think that's it, at least that what Joey told me.

Anyway Mom is very happy, not just because of the extra money but also because Daddy won't have to travel as far. Daddy said that Mrs. Balducci was so happy to see him that they hugged each other. Daddy says that Mrs. Balducci is such a lovely and wonderful woman. I was so happy to hear Daddy say that. Of course I already knew that to have such a nice son like Joey, his parents must both be nice and lovely people. I couldn't tell Daddy that of course. By the way, I asked Joey about his brother Buster's real name and he told me it is Aniello. I never heard of a name like that before but that's what it is.

I worked on my Valentine cards again today and they are just about finished, so now I'm concentrating on finding the right message to write on the cards. I decided to give Heshy a card this year like I've done in other years, because after all he is my twin brother and best friend. I decided that I really don't care what anybody thinks, I love Heshy, I always will and giving him a Valentine's Day card is just one little way of showing him that. I caught Ira Hirsch looking at me again today, not only in art class but in some of the other classes we share together. I think that might mean he likes me and I think he is very nice too, but thoughts of Joey are still getting in the way of me liking anyone else.

31

At least at this time, but who knows maybe tomorrow I'll be over Joey. I really don't think so but we'll see. Good night, diary.

Feb 14, 1945, Valentines Day

Dear Diary, I finished all the cards that I was making and also found the words that I think are right for each one who gets a card. On Heshy's and my parents cards I just told them how much I loved them and wanted them to be my Valentine, but in words that came from my heart. Now Joey's card was a little different, because I didn't want it to sound too mushy. I just wanted to let him know that there is a special someone who likes and cares for him, a lot. Yes diary, I still like him today. I didn't sign my name on the card of course, I want him to try and guess who his "secret admirer" is. Even if he never guesses, I'll never tell him.

A funny thing happened after I finished sticking Joey's card in one of his books, when no one was looking, I found an unsigned Valentine card addressed to me, in my home room desk, at the end of the school day. I'm going crazy trying to figure out who made a Valentine card for me. Was it Ira Hersch, or maybe Sylvia's cousin Bobby, or maybe it was Joey. Bobby goes to our school but he is not in any of my classes so I don't know how he could've put it in my desk. Of course, he could've asked Sylvia to do it for him she only sits a few desks away from me, in homeroom. I wonder. If I asked her she probably wouldn't tell me the truth anyway. She probably would tell me to go to the movies with Bobby and ask him myself. I don't think so. So that leaves either Ira or Joey, I think. Maybe it could be some other boy. I don't know diary, this is getting me a little crazy and giving me a headache too.

Well anyway, Mom, Daddy and Heshy all loved their cards and they all gave me cards that expressed the same feelings that I have for them. That alone makes me very happy but I'm still getting crazy about that other card. Oh well, maybe a good night's sleep will help me figure it out tomorrow. Good night dear Diary.

The next page is dated Feb. 28, 1945

Dear diary, I couldn't write the past couple of weeks because Mom and Daddy are trying to get everything prepared and ready for Passover.

This year it comes early, I'm not sure of the exact date but I think it is sometime either at the end of March or early in April. I was helping Mom as much as I could and I was also loaded down with homework. Sometimes when Joey comes over to do his homework with us, we tend to talk and kid around too much. Of course there are many times when he helps us out a lot and you know I just love having him around, but I had so much other stuff to do with Mom and Daddy too. Now you know why I was too tired to write. I couldn't ask Joey not to come over, could I? Beside I think my parents enjoy having Joey around too.

And last weekend I went with my parents to visit my aunt Sherry and her family, because Aunt Sherry broke her arm when she slipped on the ice in front of her apartment building. We all went to visit her to try and help her with getting ready for the Passover holiday. You know with some housecleaning, shopping and also a little cooking. I think mostly we went on that long subway ride up to the Bronx just to lift her spirits and let her know that she had family that cared about her. That's just what Mom told her sister too. I'm glad we went because it seemed to make Aunt Sherry very happy when she saw us.

Well diary I still haven't figured out who made me a Valentine card. I had all my friends ask around and they couldn't even come up with a clue. I even asked Joey directly and when he started to turn a little red in the face, I thought it was him, but he swore it was not him. I now know for sure, I think, that it was not Ira because Ira gave a Valentine card to Selma Rubin and asked her to be his girlfriend. Then, Sylvia told me, in an, I told you so kind of way, that her cousin Bobby is now Ruth Brodsky's boyfriend and that it all started because he gave Ruth a Valentine card. Now I'm really confused. Now I don't have any suspects left. I even told my Mom about my dilemma, I swore her to secrecy of course, and Mom, put her arm around me, hugged me and told me to forget about it because if a boy really wanted me to be his girlfriend, he would ask me face to face, sooner or later. I thought about it for a few minutes and realized she was right. My Mom is so smart. So I'm going to listen to Mom and forget about that card and who gave it to me, and get a good night's sleep. Good night dear diary.

The next page was dated March 5th, 1945

Dear diary, the preparations for Passover are still going on and Heshy and I are helping our parents get the apartment clean and ready for the Passover Seder. This year it is at our house. Every year it is at somebody else's house. It kind of rotates, if you know what I mean. I got up enough courage and asked Heshy to invite Joey this year because I said he is over here so often he is almost a part of the family. Heshy looked at me suspiciously, so I quickly told him to also invite Sarah Gold. He told me he already had and she is coming. Then he said that he would have to ask our parents if it was okay with them, about inviting Joey. I tried to look as if I didn't care one way or another, and said sure, that's the right thing to do. Inside of me I was dying. I hoped and prayed that they would say yes. When they did say yes, then I crossed my fingers that Joey would accept.

Heshy later told me that Joey would be coming to our Seder. I tried very hard to look blasé' about it but I'm not so sure that I did a good job because when I said, in a very matter of the fact sort of way, that was nice of Joey, Heshy gave me a very funny looking smile. He said he thought I'd be a little more enthused by his coming, seeing that it was my idea to ask him in the first place. Then he admitted that if I hadn't asked him to invite Joey, he would've anyway, because he too felt like Joey was part of the family. I wonder if Heshy suspects anything, or if I should confide in him about how I feel about Joey. I don't know, I think I'm a little bit afraid that Heshy might tell the wrong person and then it might be all over the neighborhood. I mean I wouldn't mind, if I knew for sure that Joey felt the same way about me.

Oh diary, what should I do? Maybe I should confide in Mom, because she was once my age and now she is so wise, I bet she would be able to tell me the right thing to do. I think that is exactly what I'll do tomorrow, the first chance I get to talk to Mom alone. I feel so much better now I think I'll be able to sleep very well tonight. Well, good night dear diary.

March 6th, 1945

Dear diary, well I managed to get Mom all to myself after school today, because Daddy's at work and Heshy went to the library, with Joey and some other boys, to do some research on a project for Mr. Simon's science class. As usual, Mom, by just looking at me, knew that I had a problem and needed some help in fixing it. In fact she told me that she knew for quite a while that I was worried about something, but get this, she not only guessed it was about a boy, but that the boy was Joey. I was dumbfounded! I just stared at her with my mouth wide open in disbelief. Then she put her arm around me, like she always does, and slowly walked me into the living room and sat me down on the couch, all the while soothing me with warm words of comfort.

She sat down beside me, took my hand in hers, and gently urged me to tell her exactly what my problem with Joey is. I took a deep breath, clutched her hand a little tighter and started to tell Mom of my frustration, at not being able to get Joey to even look at me, the way that Heshy for instance looks at Sarah. I also told Mom that I don't know how to let him know that I liked him, without telling him to his face. Mom just smiled and told me that thirteen, fourteen year old girls are pretty much the same the world over. She told me that she thinks that probably, Joey likes me too, but is still too shy to tell me. Now here is the best part, Mom says that she noticed the way Joey, when he would come over to do homework with me and Heshy would love to kid around with me and try to make me laugh. She thought that shows, in her opinion, that he likes me in some way, because usually, you only kid around with people if you like them. So she told me to do nothing and just be patient and be myself, always and don't worry about Joey liking me enough for me to be his girlfriend.

Then Mom really made me wake up and take notice. Mom said that she and Daddy liked Joey very much and really liked it when he came over to our house. Mom said that even though we are both still very young, I should be careful not to get too serious with Joey because he's not Jewish and Daddy would never allow us to get married or anything like that. Wow! I was devastated! I mean I have very strong feelings about Joey but I never considered it to be love or anything even close to that. I just like Joey very much, like a lot of girls in my class who have boyfriends, but I never even think about marriage. It's too far away to even think about stuff like that and besides, who knows maybe in a month, or six months or maybe a year, I won't even feel about Joey like I do now. Maybe, if Joey does like me now, he won't feel that way about me in six months or a year. I told Mom exactly that and she looked at me intently, with a slight smile on her face, and told me I was probably right, but that Daddy might still not like the idea of me having a non-Jewish boyfriend even if it is only for a few months or a year.

A thought occurred to me at that point, so I asked Mom why, if Daddy would object to Joey being my boyfriend, if he ever will be, why she didn't seem to object to him. Mom said that her only concern is for my happiness and that if we did get serious about each other and down the road wanted to marry, that would cause problems. She said that in the first place Daddy might take the very drastic step of "sitting shiver" for me as if I didn't exist anymore. "We wouldn't even, your brother and I, be allowed to mention your name again, ever, in this house. Of course even if your father were to give his blessing to the two of you, which really doesn't seem likely, the two of you would face a lot of the problems that arise in an interfaith marriage, such as which faith would any children you may have, follow. I wish for you only to be happy and I will do for you whatever I can and I hope that any problems you have will be small. In my heart my beliefs are as strong as your father's but I'm a little more flexible, that's the only difference." Mom then hugged me tightly, kissed my forehead and gave me a warm, loving smile.

Well, diary I've got a lot to think about now. I thanked Mom very much for trying to help me and asked her not to tell Daddy or Heshy about what we discussed. Mom said she wouldn't but reminded me that Daddy is a very smart, perceptive person, who may figure out by himself, all about me and Joey. So I guess now I'll have to stay in my room from now on and do my homework by myself. I hate the thought, but that'll be better than getting Daddy mad at me and Joey. I don't think I'll get much sleep tonight. Good night diary.

March 8th, 1945

Dear diary, Sunday, March 11th, is Joey's birthday and I feel so bad because I can't get him a present, after what Mom told me the other day about Daddy being so perceptive, especially since Joey got me those nice monogrammed handkerchiefs last year for my birthday. Heshy told me he bought a book all about Babe Ruth for Joey for his birthday and that made me feel even worse, but then I got this bright idea. I told Heshy I would give him half the money for the book and that it could be a present from the both of us. Heshy thought that was a good idea probably because he'll be getting half his money back. Of course he doesn't work and make money as I do so I guess he could use the money. So everything will work out okay for Joey's birthday present. Heshy even had me sign the card that he's giving him with the book. I couldn't hope for anything better than that.

For the last two days, Joey came over to do his homework and I stayed in my room. I was so depressed I could hardly do my homework. I finally got it done but it was a struggle. Imagine Joey being in the next room and I didn't dare go out to sit with him. Of course when I did go out of my room, once to go to the bathroom and another time for my nightly glass of milk, Joey said hello to me but his eyes seemed to be asking me why I wasn't doing my homework with him and Heshy. Of course I gave him a nice, warm smile, but I didn't dare linger because Daddy was sitting nearby. By the way Joey looked at me, I think maybe Mom was right, about Joey liking me, but I can't be 100% sure. I secretly made a birthday card for Joey and even wrote some nice words in it too, but I have not been able to sneak it in to his books yet. I can't try to do it here, I might get caught and in school it is usually so busy and crowded in our classes, I don't think I could do it there either. I'll have to try again tomorrow.

I guess that would be better than doing nothing. I still can't sign my name to it, so I'll let him think that it's his "secret admirer" again, which of course it is. I just got a bright idea. This coming Saturday, I'm going to be babysitting again, for the Bernstein's, who live around the corner from me on Powell St., Joey's block. I have already asked Mrs. Bernstein if I could have some of my friends over and she said I could but only after her kids were asleep and we don't do any wild things or make too much noise. Heshy and Sarah have already said they would be there. Now if only I could figure out a way to prod Heshy into asking Joey to come over too, I could wish him a happy birthday and who knows maybe I could even sneak in a little hug or kiss or both. I'd be the happiest girl in the world, but I know I'm dreaming again. I could tell them about Mr. Bernstein's bat and ball that are autographed by Babe Ruth. The way Heshy and Joey are always talking about and playing baseball, I think that would be great bait. That's it diary. That is what I'm going to do. Now I so anxious for Saturday to come, I don't think I'll be able to sleep tonight, or tomorrow night but I have to try. Good night diary.

March 9th, 1945

Dear diary, you won't believe what happened on the way to school today. Heshy and I walked down Sackman St., approaching Riverdale Ave., where we met Joey, who walked over from Powell St. to meet us, as usual. Sarah Gold, who walked from her house on Stone Ave., was there too with a small group of other friends and we all started to walk to school together. I just happened to drift to the back of the group and Joey suddenly is walking right in front of me. He turned around, looked me right in the eye, smiled a big smile at me and said, "Hello stranger. Where have you been hiding?" Before I could answer him all of his books fell right out of his hands and were lying all about the sidewalk. He turned to pick up a book that was on the sidewalk in front of him and I started to pick a book that was behind him and in front of me. The birthday card I made for Joey yesterday was in my coat pocket, so I quickly pulled it from my pocket and slipped it into the cover of his book that I picked up.

The rest of our little group was walking way ahead of us and I don't think anyone was behind us, so I believe nobody saw me do it. The best part was of course that we walked to school together, just the two of us. While we were walking I mentioned to Joey that Heshy and Sarah were going to keep me company on Saturday night, while I babysat, right on his block, and that Mr. Bernstein had a ball and bat that was autographed by Babe Ruth. I told him that Heshy couldn't wait to see it. Well I planted a seed in Joey alright because before I even had a chance to ask him to join us he asked me if he could come over too. I played a little hard to get, you know I didn't want to seem too anxious, so I said in a very slow way that I didn't know for sure but that I guessed it would be alright.

Then he wondered out loud why Heshy hadn't told him about this, so I told him that I only told Heshy about it late last night, after Joey had left my house. So now everything is looking so bright again. I think I walked on air the rest of the way to school and the rest of the day as a matter of fact. I can hardly wait until Saturday night, just two days away. When I got home from school Mom and I were alone again, Heshy, Joey and the rest of the boys on that science project went to the library again. I was so excited that I told Mom everything that happened that day and she said she was very happy for me. She also told me, again, that I shouldn't get too serious about Joey. But the smile on her face told me that I have a special friend in my Mom, who would fight for me in any way that she could.

As far back as I can remember, Mom never would let me get hurt, my feelings, my body or anything. I feel so lucky, not just because I have the Mom that I have, but also because of Daddy and Heshy. I have the best family in the world. And I also have you dear diary. Now I have to go to sleep. I can't wait until tomorrow. I really look forward to walking down Sackman St. and as we get close to Riverdale Ave., seeing Joey's smiling face waiting to greet us. It's such a wonderful feeling. Oh but wait a minute tomorrow is Saturday and there is no school. What am I thinking about? I'm getting so crazy about this I think I have to stop now. Good night dear diary.

Saturday, March 10th, 1945

Dear diary, I had a wonderful time tonight but it's 1am and I just got home so I'll tell you about it tomorrow. I'm very happy and tired. Good night dear diary.

Sunday, March 11th, 1945

Dear diary, I can't wait to tell you how wonderful Saturday night turned out to be.

First, when I went to the Bernstein's to start my babysitting job Mrs. Bernstein told me that she bought some snacks and soda for me and my friends to have that night. I thought that was so nice of her. I always thought she was a really nice person. Then she told me that even though I've only sat with her kids four or five times, her kids say that I'm their favorite sitter. Wow, isn't that great to hear. Her kids are so good they're no trouble at all. They love to be read to and I love to read to them. All the times that I've sat with them, every time I finish reading a story with them, they always give me a big hug and kiss before going to bed. And they always go to bed when I tell them to. It's such a pleasure sitting for them I really love it and them too.

Mrs. Bernstein told me that her husband, who is also very nice, was injured in a car accident a few years ago and because of his injuries, they wouldn't let him in the Army. She said he felt very bad and guilty about not being in the military service, when all of his friends were. He now works at the Brooklyn Navy Yard as an electrician, working on building and fixing up navy ships. Now, she says he feels better about himself because he is making a contribution to the war effort. They are all just a very nice family. Any way, after the kids, Sophie who is three and Joshua who is five went to bed and were fast asleep, Heshy, Sarah and Joey arrived.

Although I would've loved to play some music and maybe even dance a little, I promised Mrs. Bernstein that we would be quiet and not wake up the kids. So we sat around the whole night eating and drinking the snacks and drinks that Mrs. Bernstein bought for us. It was really nice. After the boys finished looking at the bat and ball signed by Babe Ruth, we started talking. We talked about everything, school, part time jobs that we'd all like to have this summer and after school. We all were wondering what high school was going to be like the following year and what we thought we'd like to do with the rest of our lives. Sarah thought she would like to be a fashion designer because she loves clothes so much. Heshy said he wanted to be in the business of business, because he would love to make a lot of money. Joey said he wasn't sure exactly what he wanted to do, except that he wanted to help people in one way or another. I just said what I think they already knew, I wanted to be a nurse. I want to help people too.

Of course there were a few awkward moments when Heshy and Sarah started to kiss each other, Joey and I just gave each other an uncomfortable look, smiled, shrugged our shoulders and tried to start up a conversation with the two of them. I mentioned that tomorrow, which is now today, is Joey's 14th birthday and I told Joey that just in case I don't see him tomorrow, I'll wish him a happy birthday tonight. Joey thanked me but never came close enough for me to hug or try to kiss him. Sarah then started to get into all the gossip that is going around the school and neighborhood, who is going out with who, who likes who, who doesn't like who, who has two girlfriends and who has two boyfriends and all kinds of stuff like that. I think she must have been talking to Sylvia Roth. I was so scared she was going to say something about me and Joey, but thank God she didn't.

Even though we didn't cuddle or smooch or even hold hands, I enjoyed sitting near Joey and just talking with him. At the end of the evening, when the Bernstein's got home, the four of us walked back to my house and they all bid me good night, Joey actually shook my hand as he said good night. I can't help but wonder if there was something to that or not. Well anyway, Heshy and Joey walked Sarah home, after all it was 1am, and after about fifteen or twenty minutes Heshy got home.

I just feel so good about last night I had such a good time. The weather is pretty nice today so I think I'll go down to the park across the street and maybe I'll see Joey. I think Heshy said this morning that they all might be playing softball or maybe basketball or they might just be all sitting around "shooting the breeze" as the boys call it. When I got to the park Heshy was already there and talking with Joey and the rest of their buddies and when Joey saw me coming he came straight over to me. I felt my heart start to beat rapidly because I had no idea why he was coming toward me in such a hurry. He grabbed my hand and thanked me for getting that Babe Ruth book for him for his birthday, with Heshy.

Before I could even say anything he started to put his arm around me as it to give me a hug, but then quickly pulled back. I was disappointed of course but I guess he did that because he didn't want our friends to tease him about likening me or something like that. I'll just have to do as Mom told me and that is to be patient, because everyone gets to where they want to go in their own time. Joey's so happy with the Babe Ruth Book, he was showing it off to everyone, even the girls and that made me feel so good. It really has been a great couple of days for me, I hope I have many more of them and I'm sure I will. So long for now dear diary, maybe I'll write some more tonight, we'll see.

March 14th, 1945

Dear diary, I'm still walking on air, thinking about last Saturday night. But guess what? Mrs. Bernstein came over to our house at dinner time and asked me if I could baby-sit again for her this coming Saturday. This time she wants me to watch her kids all day and then again on Saturday night. She said that her two sisters own a dress shop in Manhattan and that one of her sisters got sick, so she has to go and help her other sister. She said that Mr. Bernstein has to work at the Navy Yard that day too. That's a long day, taking care of two kids, but she is so nice to me, I couldn't say no.

I asked Mrs. Bernstein if it would be alright with her if I brought the kids to the library in the morning because I have to work on a book report for school. She said it sure was if I thought I could manage them there. I told her I was sure because they both love to have stories read to them and also they're very good at looking at books by themselves. Later I asked Heshy if he wanted to come over with Sarah again. I purposely didn't mention Joey's name and Heshy asked if I would like Joey to come over too. I hesitated for a moment, so I would look like I was thinking it over and then said, yes if he would like. Now nobody can say I asked for Joey to be there. You know Mom says that Daddy is perceptive but she is pretty good at that sort of stuff herself.

After Mrs. Bernstein left and I had that brief conversation with Heshy, about keeping me company on Saturday night, Mom looked at me, smiled a very knowing smile and said, "You did a very good job of making Heshy think that he is the one who wants Joey to be with you on Saturday night, but be careful about trying that on Heshy too often. He's no dummy you know. Sometimes he can figure out what's going on pretty good. You just be careful. But you did do a very good job of getting your brother to do what you want and made him think it was his idea, a very good job." By this time Mom was laughing and that made me feel so good, that she thought I did a good job getting Joey to come over on Saturday night without having to ask him myself. Like I said before, Mom is so smart and loving too. Now I can't wait until Saturday again. It seems that almost every week I have something to look forward to lately. I guess I don't have it so bad after all. Good night dear diary.

Sunday, March 18th, 1945

Dear diary, it was a long but wonderful day Saturday. By the time I finished my babysitting job it was midnight and I was so tired when I got home, I just fell into bed and went right to sleep. The day was so good and fun filled that I'm sure I was sleeping with a smile on my face. First, I went to the Bernstein's at 8am to start my day. I was happy to find out that Mrs. Bernstein had already fed the kids their breakfast, so that was one less thing I had to do. Then when the kids saw me they came running to me for hugs and kisses. They're such happy kids that it doesn't feel like a job to watch them.

They were all excited when I told them I was going to take them to the park to play on the swings and other things. When I told them that after we visit the park, I was going to take them to the library to read some books, they jumped up and down and clapped their hands with glee. I thought to myself, what a beautiful way to start a day, listening to and watching children being happy. Before she left, Mrs. Bernstein handed me two coloring books and some crayons and said that they might come in handy when I was trying to get some work done on my book report. She also told me that she should be home by 6pm and that Mr. Bernstein should be home about the same time. She said that after a quick supper and after she feeds the kids, she and Mr. Bernstein were going to go to the movies. If I wanted to, I could stay and have supper with them or I could go home and come back at 7pm.

I told her I'd let her know when she got home at six. Oh, then she told me to take the stroller with me for Sophie because she gets tired, walking too far. She said that Joshua would be fine walking. That's just what I did. When we got to the park it was still pretty early so the park was not crowded at all, even though the weather for this time of year is great. I took them to the swings, the see-saw and the slide. They loved it, especially the swings. They had me running from one swing to the other to give them a push. As I got one of them going, the other would be slowing down and they would yell out to me for a push, while giggling and laughing, as I ran back and forth. They sure tired me out but I loved it. Then we rested on a bench and I read to them from some of their books, that I brought with me.

While I was reading to the kids, Heshy and Joey came along and stopped to talk to me. Heshy asked me if I would like some help sitting with the kids. I told him that I had to go the library to work on my book report and Heshy told me that he and Joey were going there too, in a little while. They were working on their book reports also. So I said sure, I'd love the company and could use the help while I work on my report. After I put Sophie safely in the stroller, we all walked together to the library. It is on the corner or Stone and Dumont Avenues, about a four or five block walk from the park. At the library, Heshy and Joey left me alone with the kids for a short while and returned with hastily written book reports. I couldn't believe it. There was no way they could've read a book that fast. I had already read my book this past week and today I was just reviewing it and taking some notes so I can finish my report tomorrow. Heshy told me this morning at breakfast that they hadn't picked out the books to do their reports on yet, so how the heck could they be finished with their reports?

I questioned them about that and they laughed and said they had a secret. When I nagged them about it, they finally said they would tell me, but they would have to swear me to secrecy. When I agreed to never tell anyone about their secret, they told me. What they did was, they would look for an obscure book with an unknown author, a book they felt sure that nobody ever heard of, let alone read. Then they would read the first and last chapters and fill in the middle by making it up. Then, writing the report would be easy and fast. Heshy made me promise never to tell my parents about it. I promised, but I made him promise never to do it again. Reluctantly, he did, and Joey did too.

Well anyway, while they were away doing their dirty work, I was again reading to the kids but this time from some books that came from the library. After a short while, I gave them each a coloring book and told them to share the crayons, without fighting. We were all sitting at the same table, so I could keep an eye on them, as I tried to do some work. It was at that moment that Heshy and Joey came back from their phony work. After the kids were coloring for a short while, Joshua put his coloring book aside and picked up the library book that I had been reading to them. Now Joshua you understand couldn't really read, I mean he knew the alphabet okay and he could describe the pictures he was looking at, but he couldn't read. Because he was read to so much, he seemed to be reading a book when all he was doing was looking at the pictures and making up a story as he went along, all the while talking in a rhythm that sounded just like someone reading. I had never told Heshy or Joey about Joshua being able to do that, so you should've seen the looks on their faces as Joshua "read" on.

Not believing what they were seeing and hearing, they quietly walked behind where Joshua was sitting and moved in as close as they could without distracting him, and glanced intently over Joshua's head to see if the words he was saying matched the words on the page. It took them a few moments to figure out that he wasn't really reading, because I had just read that same story to Joshua and he remembered what part of the story went with what pictures. Actually on some of the pages he was pretty close to the right words that were written. I had seen Joshua do that at home with books that he was very familiar with. He is one

y

44

smart kid. Sophia is no dope either she's always trying to do whatever Joshua does. But the looks on the faces of Joey and Heshy made me break out in loud laughter. The librarian gave me a dirty look, put her finger to her mouth and told me to, "Shush" I thought if I didn't stop laughing she would throw us all out, so I put my hand over my mouth until I stopped laughing. It was so funny. I finished what I wanted to do on my report and the kids were getting a little tired and hungry, so we all left.

We all went back to the Bernstein's apartment, Heshy and Joey too, where I made lunch for all of us. After the kids ate, I read to them for a short while. Sophie, with Joshua's urging handed a book to Joey. He just smiled and started to read to them in a very funny, animated way. They loved it. I loved it, it was so cute. It wasn't long before they each laid down for a nap. After about an hour or so, just before they woke from their nap, Heshy and Joey left. The rest of the afternoon went fast and before I knew it Mrs. Bernstein came home followed a few minutes later by Mr., Bernstein. While I was waiting for them, I got some things started for their supper, like peeling some potatoes and getting some other vegetables ready. It was no big deal, because I had nothing to do anyway.

I told Mrs. Bernstein that I decided to go home for my dinner because I hadn't seen my parents all day and I just wanted them to see me because I was going to be out again that night. Diary, I'm getting real tired now, because I got up late this morning and spent the afternoon writing my book report. It's due tomorrow. It's getting late now so I'll write tomorrow about how the rest of my Saturday was. Good night dear diary.

March 19th, 1945

Dear diary lets go back to last Saturday night. When I went home, between my babysitting jobs, to see my parents and have supper, my parents greeted me with warm smiles and what I call, "glad to see you" looks. My Mom asked me how my day was so far and before I could tell her she said that I must be tired and I still have a night of babysitting ahead of me. Daddy was shaking his head "yes" to everything Mom said. After I assured them that I was not that tired and that I would be okay for sitting that night, I noticed Daddy smiling at me in a very funny way and maybe a tear in his eyes. I went up to him and ask him what was wrong and he put his arms around me, giving me a very tight hug and said, "Oy totala my totala." Since as far back as I can remember, Daddy has called me "totala", which means little child. "Wrong? Nothing's wrong, it's just that it seems like yesterday you were a little baby and now here you are, so grown up that you take care of other people's babies. So I guess that means that your Daddy is getting old." I quickly told him that he is not old and then Mom joined us in the middle of the kitchen and hugged daddy and me and said, "Old! Who's old? Not my Gus Abromovitz. You still have the little boy in you that you had when we first met in high school in Germany, so don't tell me you're old. You'll never grow old, my dear Gus because you are always young in your heart."

Daddy's real name is Gustav but everybody calls him Gus and Mom's name is Hannah and that's just what Daddy calls her. We all hugged each other and at that moment Heshy, having just changed his clothes, getting ready to meet Sarah and join me and Joey at the Bernstein's later that night, came out of his room. When he saw me and my parents hugging, he joined us in a four way hug. It was wonderful and delicious and felt so good. It was better than eating supper, but I did anyway.

On her way home from Manhattan, Mrs. Bernstein stopped and bought some more snacks, for me and any of my friends who may be coming over to sit with me. She is really so nice, she's more like a big sister and friend than someone I just baby-sit for. I'm so lucky to know her and her family. The kids were as glad to see me again as I was to see them, but they seemed to be a little tired from all the activities of earlier in the day. After the Bernsteins left, I read some stories to Sophie and Joshua and then they quickly went to bed and fell asleep almost as soon as their little heads hit their pillows.

A short time later, Heshy, Sarah and Joey arrived. Again, just like last week, we started eating and drinking the snacks that Mrs. Bernstein was good enough to buy for us. All the while we were talking, about anything and everything, but mostly the talk was about the progress the Allies were making on their march to Germany. We all sensed and hoped that the war would soon be over. Just like last week, when there was a slight break in the conversation, Heshy and Sarah started smooching. It was most uncomfortable for me and Joey so Joey got up, walked toward the kitchen and motioned for me to follow him. Oh diary, my heart started pounding fast. I thought that this is it, he is going to try to kiss me in the kitchen, but oh boy was I wrong.

When I got into the kitchen Joey was sitting at the table, reading a cook book. I sat across from him and he started asking me questions about cooking. Can you imagine that, cooking questions! I thought to myself that I should be mad at him but I wasn't. After a few minutes talking about cooking, I started to like it because I was finding out things about Joey and cooking that I never knew before. I found out that Joey likes to cook and that he is learning from his mother about Italian cooking. I used to wonder why, when we were doing our homework together Joey would ask my Mom questions about what she was making and how she was cooking it. Now I know why, It's just one of his interests. That made me wonder why, when we were all talking last week, about what we would like to be when we got older, Joey didn't say a cook.

Anyway, after being in the kitchen for about 10 minutes, Heshy and Sarah came tiptoeing in, looking a little disheveled. Their hair was mussed up a bit and Heshy's face had a little lipstick on it. Heshy said, "Hey why did you guys leave? We thought you two would join the party." Joey quickly changed the subject by asking Heshy if he heard about the fifteen year old kid, just a year or so older than he and Heshy, who is going to pitch in the major leagues. Joey said because most of the young ballplayers are in military service, mostly older players and a few really young ones are playing in the major leagues. That seemed to make Heshy forget all about Joey and me joining his so called "party".

Later, when Heshy and Sarah went back to their "party" in the living room and Joey and I remained in the kitchen, I told Joey that he did a very good job of changing the subject. Joey looked at me for a minute and then said, "You know Esther I really like you and your whole family, very much. I think of you all as a part of my family so that's why I get uncomfortable, sitting with you and watching Heshy and Sarah doing what they're doing now. You see, Esther, you are like a sister to me. I love to hang around you and Heshy and your parents too. All of you make me feel like I belong wherever you are at. I hope you don't mind me telling you this." I told him I didn't mind at all, and in fact I said, I feel the same way about him. I told him we all felt that way about him. Inside of me I was so mad. His sister! I don't want to be his sister! He already has a sister and I have a brother. Oh boy! What a mess.

So I thought at the time. I was mad and confused, but at least he did say that he liked me. I guess that's something to be a little happy about. I told myself I'd have to ask Mom about this. Sister huh, we'll see. On Sunday, yesterday that is, when Heshy went out to play ball, with Joey I supposed, and Daddy went to the park to sit around with some of his friends and talk politics, as he usually does on Sundays, I asked Mom if we could talk and she said yes, of course. I told her everything that happened on Saturday night and everything that was said. I also asked Mom not to tell Heshy that I told her about him and Sarah. She laughed and said that she knew about Heshy and Sarah because his clothes smelled from perfume and there were lipstick stains on his collar. Then she said that fourteen year old girls should not be wearing perfume and lipstick. I started to protest but she cut me short by saying she knows all about it being okay because we're in America.

Then mom told me that in her home town in Germany, girls that age were not allowed to wear perfume and lipstick, they were too young, she said. She asked me to please wait a while longer before I started to wear that stuff because she didn't want to get Daddy all upset, me being his "totala". Then we talked about the important part of my problem, what Joey told me that night. Mom again sat me down on the sofa, held my hands in hers, looked me in the eyes and said to me, in a most gentle way, that she thinks he has told me everything I need to know about how he feels about me. I was confused and didn't know what she was talking about, but then she continued. She said that she thinks that Joey, even though he seems to be very outgoing now, is still shy and lacking in confidence in himself. When Mom saw the look of disbelief on my face, she started to tell me a story about when she was in high school in Germany. She told me about a girl in her school, a very beautiful girl, in fact probably the most beautiful girl in the school. They used to have a party to celebrate graduation, like a prom that we have here in America.

Well anyway it seemed as if she was not going to go to this party because no boy would ask her. Every boy in the school was afraid that she would say no, so no one asked her. They were all afraid of being rejected so no one asked except one boy who no girl would go with because he wasn't very good looking, at least not at that time anyway, but he was a very nice boy and fairly smart too. He had been turned down by every girl he asked so he was used to being rejected. So he asked the very beautiful girl to go with him to the party and she said yes. They went to the party and the boy was the envy of all the boys there and even most of the girls. They had such a wonderful time dancing, laughing and having fun. It turned out, Mom said, that they were the best looking couple there. Then she shocked the life out of me by telling me that young couple got married and are still together today, with two of the most beautiful children in the world. You see, she said, that couple was Daddy and her.

Mom hugged me, called me her beautiful little girl and told me to be patient with Joey because he has told me that he likes me but he might be afraid of me rejecting him, so he covered up his feelings for me by saying he thinks of me as a sister. Of course, he may not want a girlfriend at this time, because everyone grows in their own time and in their own way. She finished by telling me again to be patient and just keep enjoying his company when I get it. It took me a minute or two to think about what Mom had just told me. Again I thought to myself how smart Mom is and then I thanked her for the advice. Then she told me that she of course, was still hoping that we both grow out of this infatuation soon, before it gets serious. I was surprised, but I understood.

As we got up from the couch I turned to Mom and asked her if Daddy really wasn't good looking when he was a young kid. She said he really was, but you had to look a little harder to see it. She said that the more she got to know him, the real him and the goodness in his heart, the better looking he became. Then she laughed and said, "but you know of course I was the most beautiful girl not only in the school but in the entire town too." As the two of us walked arm in arm into the kitchen, laughing all the way, I told Mom she still is the most beautiful girl in town. Brooklyn, that is. It was great talking with Mom, but I'm not exactly sure what the point of Mom's story is but I think it is this, a person's looks most times reflect what's in a person's heart.

For example, Howie Stein has a large protruding nose, but because he is such a nice sweet person, after a while, when you get to know him, you don't notice his nose anymore. On the other hand, Phyllis Handleman has a nose that is not quite as big as Howie's, but because she is such a trouble maker, most of the boys call her "the witch" and sometimes something that rhymes with "witch", her nose looks even bigger than it really is. Well anyway, that's what I think Mom was trying to tell me. By the way, in school today, before handing in my book report, I had to get up in front of the class, as did some other kids, and read my report to the class. When I finished, the teacher, Mrs. Levine, took my report and told me it was very good, so I guess that means I'll get a good grade on it. I hope so because I worked very hard on it, not like Heshy and Joey. Good night for now dear diary.

CHAPTER 3

Thursday, March 22nd, 1945

Dear diary, I couldn't write the last few days because Mom wasn't feeling too good one night, I think she was coming down with a cold or something, so I helped her with the cooking and the clean up afterward. The next day Mom felt better but I got a last minute request from Mrs. Bernstein to baby-sit Joshua and Sophie for a few hours. She had to go to the hospital with Mr. Bernstein to visit a close friend from Flatbush, who was in a car accident. Mom at first didn't want me to do it because it was a school night and I had homework to do and she didn't want me walking home alone at a late hour. I convinced Mom that I could do my homework after the kids were asleep and Mom asked Mrs. Bernstein if her husband could walk me home as he usually does and she said yes he would.

That was last night and by the time I got home at about 11pm I was very tired. Today I got my book report back and I got an A. I was very happy about that. Heshy and Joey each got a B for their phony book reports and I gave them both a very long, stern look. They gave me a sheepish look, turned away from me and started to laugh. Mom always says, whenever Heshy misbehaves, that boys will be boys and now I see what she means. On the way home from school I asked Heshy and Joey to walk with just me because I wanted to talk to them and I didn't want anyone else to hear what I wanted to speak to them about. Even though spring officially started a couple of days ago, the weather is still on the cool side. I actually looked forward to walking home because I hoped that I could walk very close to Heshy and Joey, to keep warm, as I usually do in cool weather. I mean, who can say anything about me being close to Joey if I'm also walking close to Heshy at the same time?

Anyway, while we were walking alone by ourselves, I told them that they ought to be ashamed of themselves. They both protested by asking why. I told them that they were both very capable of getting an A on their book reports if they would just do the kind of work that I know they could do. By cheating, I told them, they're only cheating themselves. So what if they have to miss an afternoon or two of playing ball in the park, if they were to put in the same time doing their schoolwork as they did playing ball they both would get A's in most of their subjects. That's what I told them. They looked at me, then each other and finally Heshy said that I was right and he was not going to take shortcuts anymore. Joey nodded in agreement. I felt good about myself for doing that. Well anyway, I'm glad I got to baby-sit last night because I could always use the extra money for the Holidays coming up. As a matter of fact I think we are going to be so busy for the next few weeks with Passover and a few other things, that I'm not sure when I'll be able to write again, but it will be as soon as I can. Good night dear diary, I'll write again soon.

Friday, March 23rd, 1945

Dear diary, it's late but I had to make note of what happened earlier this evening. Daddy told Heshy that he should not only invite Joey to our Seder, but his whole family also, for it's traditional to invite not just family, but good friends too. Daddy said that Passover is often referred to as the "Celebration of Freedom" and that's what all the fighting is about today, is it not? Mom was so glad that Daddy did that, because she really likes Joey and his family a lot. I'm so excited I can't wait for Wednesday, the Seder night, to get here. I just had to tell you the good news. I'll write again soon. Good night dear diary.

Wednesday, March 28th, 1945

Dear diary, oh what a day and night we had at our house. It was so wonderful and I had such a great time today. First all of my friends, including Joey, came by at about noon time and spent a few hours talking with Heshy and me and my parents. Then after a while we went down to the park and just gathered around and talked about everything and everyone. Everybody was all dressed up in their new holiday clothes, even Joey had on his new Easter outfit. He looked great in it too. It made me feel so good especially this year because the war news has been really good so far and the end of the war seems near. I hope so.

It feels good to be young and have all your friends around you, with everyone full of hope about our future. It is so good to see Mom and Daddy so cheerful and happy today too. Heshy and I went home at about 4pm, to be there when the quests for the Seder start arriving and to help Mom and Daddy if they needed us. The Balduccis, when they arrived, gave Daddy a big case of Passover wine as a holiday gift. Daddy was so happy to get it he couldn't thank Mr. Balducci enough and then I made everyone laugh at my ignorance. I heard Joey's father tell Daddy as he handed him the case of wine that it fell off a truck, so I said that it's a wonder all the bottles didn't break and everybody howled. I didn't know that "fell off a truck" meant it was stolen and I didn't realize that Mr. Balducci was only kidding when he said that. Well like Mom always tells me, you have to live and learn.

When everyone arrived and was seated, I don't know how we fit all those people, about forty, in our apartment, the Seder celebration started with the traditional passing of the plate that carried the symbols of the enslavement of the Jewish people. That was followed by the hiding of the matzah. After everyone sampled the usual Passover foods, people started to get up to make toasts with the Passover wine, not the wine that fell off the truck. Well it took everyone by surprise when Joey's dad got up and said, with a glass of wine raised in his hand,"Goot Yontif", or Good Holiday, then Mrs. Balducci, still seated said, in broken Yiddish and an Italian accent, "A Zizen Paizock". Everyone loved it. Most of them stood up and clapped their hands in approval. Inside of me I swelled up with pride. I love his parents almost as much as I do my own. At that moment I thought to myself, why can't everybody in the world get along like this without all the fighting and killing? I wish they could and would. We all had a very good time, especially me, because of Joey and his family being there. I will not forget this night for a long, long time. Well tomorrow is another day of celebrating and I'm very tired right now, so I have to say good night dear diary.

Friday, March 30th, 1945

Dear diary Sunday is April Fool's day but Joey fooled someone today. After another great day of celebrating Passover yesterday, we all headed back to school today. As we all walked through the schoolyard, toward the entrance doors of the school, Mr. DiMeola, our math teacher and guidance counselor, approached Joey and asked him if he was Jewish. When Joey told him no, he was Roman Catholic, Mr. DiMeola asked Joey why he wasn't in school the past two days. Now here comes the fun part. Joey looked the teacher right in the eye and told him that because all of his Jewish friends, out of respect for him, don't go to school on Christmas, he, Joey, out of respect for his Jewish friends, doesn't go to school on Passover. Mr. DiMeola looks at Joey for a second or two, smiled a faint smile, then turned around and went into the school building.

As soon as we all were sure that Mr. DiMeola couldn't hear us, we all burst into loud laughter and everyone patted Joey on the back in approval of what he had just done. It was great. I think a quick thinking mind like Joey's indicates a very smart brain. Maybe I'm just biased toward Joey, I don't know, but that's what I think. When word of what Joey had done got around to the whole school, most of the kids who know Joey, and even some of the teachers, told Joey that they thought it was a great and quick response. While Joey thanked everyone for the compliments, I think he was more than a little embarrassed by it all. He told me later, on the walk home from school that he didn't even think. about what he was going to say, it just came out the way it did.

At my house later, when we were all sitting at the table doing our homework and drinking coffee, Heshy, in a proud sort of way, told Mom and Daddy about what Joey told the teacher and Mom and Daddy laughed and thought it was great. Daddy said he thought Joey used great logic. Mom just nodded in agreement, and said that she thinks that Joey has a "Yiddisher Kup", that means a Jewish head. Joey asked what it meant to have a Yiddisher Kup, a Jewish Head. So Daddy told Joey that if he were to ask a hundred people that question he might get a hundred different answers. Then Daddy told Joey that he would give him an example of what it means to have a "Jewish Head" or Yiddisher Kup. In the first place Daddy said, not everybody who is

Jewish has a "Jewish head" and one doesn't have to be Jewish to have a "Jewish Head".

So then Daddy started to tell Joey and the rest of us, this story. He said, "There was once a man who could not sleep at night because he kept thinking there was a man hiding under his bed. He went to a head doctor, if you know what I mean, and after getting treatment three times a week for six months, the man was no better than when he first started seeing the doctor, so he stopped going. About a year after his last visit with that doctor, the man, by chance, met the doctor in the street and the doctor asked him how his problem, about not being able to sleep because he thought there was someone under his bed, was. The man said that he was cured. The doctor, looking surprised, said that was good news and then asked the man who cured him. The man with a smile on his face told the doctor that his wife's brother-in-law cured him. The doctor, now visibly upset, asked if the man's wife's brother-in-law was a doctor. When the man said no, the doctor was really upset and asked how his wife's brother-in-law cured him. The man said it was simple, his wife's brother-in-law told him to just cut the legs off the bed."

As all of us started to laugh, really hard, Daddy explained that the doctor, although Jewish, didn't have a "Jewish Head" but that the man's wife's brother-in-law, who wasn't Jewish or a doctor, did. Joey couldn't stop laughing and that seemed to please Daddy very much. Then Joey held up his coffee mug and said to Daddy that he guessed that was a "Yiddisher Kup" When Daddy asked Joey why that would be, Joey told him because the handle was on the outside of the cup. As everyone again started to laugh, Joey then said that if the handle was on the inside of the cup, then it couldn't be a "Yiddisher Kup". Mom laughed so hard she had to run into the bathroom. Daddy then asked Joey if he was sure he wasn't Jewish. Nobody could keep from laughing even Mom could be heard from the bathroom still laughing and that made me very happy. Mom was still wearing a big smile with tears streaming down her face when she came out of the bathroom. I was beaming too. What a great day! Good night for now, dear diary.

Tuesday, April 3rd, 1945

Dear diary, although the weather is still a little chilly, yesterday we had a little bit of snow, I can feel spring in the air. I love springtime it's my favorite time of the year. I love to see the squirrels scampering around, the flowers starting to bud and birds in the trees singing. Mom says that there is still could be some winter weather coming our way even though spring started a few weeks ago, officially that is. I have to baby-sit for the Bernsteins again Saturday but only during the day. Mrs. Bernstein's sister is still sick so she has to help out in the store again. I hope the weather warms up a bit by Saturday so I can take the kids to the park again. They really loved it last Saturday and so did I. It's just as well that I'm not babysitting Saturday night because Heshy is going to Sarah's cousin's fifteenth birthday party with her, in Flatbush, and I don't think I would've asked Joey to sit with me by himself. I don't think Mom and Daddy would like it if I did that, but It doesn't make any difference now anyway. I think I needed the break in babysitting to rest up a little and do some schoolwork. I'll probably just stay home that night, wash my hair, soak in a nice hot tub and do some homework. I'll probably do some of my homework after I get home from school on Friday, so I won't have too much left. Maybe Saturday night after taking a bath I'll read a book or something and finish my schoolwork on Sunday. We shall see. Well good night for now dear diary.

Sunday, April 8th, 1945

Dear diary, Saturday turned out to be a beautiful day, weather wise and Joey wise. Because it turned out to be a nice and warm day, I took Joshua and Sophie to the park again and they were so excited about going. We did the same things as we did last Saturday. They went on the swings and got me going crazy, pushing one then the other, all the while squealing and laughing at the same time. I was getting run down but laughing about it too. Then they went on the slide and the seesaw. When they started to get a little tired, which I thought would take forever, I read to them from their favorite books that I brought along with me. While I was reading to them, Joey suddenly appeared all by himself and offered to help me if I needed it. Heshy was playing basketball with some of his other friends. I pretended to think about

Joey's offer for a moment, and I said, sure if he wanted to. Well Sophie remembered Joey reading to her and Joshua the previous Saturday and handed Joey a book to read to her. Joey smiled at the two of them and eagerly took the book.

Then he started to read the book just like he did the week before only this time he was more animated and funny. The kids couldn't stop laughing. They laughed so hard they both wet their pants, and Joshua is toilet trained too. I not only laughed my head of, but I was thrilled knowing that Joey was so good with children. I told him, when the kids couldn't hear me, that they had both wet their pants laughing so hard, Joey wanted to know if I wet mine too, because he said I was laughing just as hard. At first I made believe I was mad that he asked me that but after a few minutes I started to laugh with him at the thought. When the kids got tired and hungry, I took them home and Joey asked if he could come too. This time I didn't hesitate and said yes, right away.

After I made lunch for the kids and read to them for a little bit, they were both ready for a nap. As soon as they fell asleep, I went into the kitchen to fix some lunch for me and Joey, but there he was fixing lunch for us. He just went into the icebox and helped himself, but when he saw me come into the kitchen, he stopped what he was doing and asked me if it was okay. I just took a quick look at what he was making for us, it was peanut butter and jelly sandwiches, and I told him it was alright. I can't find the right words to describe how wonderful I felt at that moment. We sat at the kitchen table and just talked about family, his and mine, and he told me how lucky he felt to have not only such a loving family, but also to have a second family in my family. I told him I felt the same way about his family too. At that moment I believed I knew what Joey meant when he said a week or so ago that he felt like we were brother and sister. I really did, but only for that moment.

The more I talk with Joey, the more I get to know him, the more I like about him. If only I could tell him now how I feel about him. Well maybe someday soon I hope. Anyway Joey stayed with me until Mrs. Bernstein came home, he even read to the kids again when they woke up from their nap. Of course Mrs. Bernstein knows Joey because they live on the same block. She even asked Joey how his mom is doing, because she knows about Joey's brother being in the Army in Europe. After that Joey walked me home, and I was walking on air. He had never before walked me home, just him and me. He even came in for a few minutes just to say hello to my parents. They were very happy to see him too. Finally, when he left to go home, he told me he would probably see me in the park tomorrow. I haven't been down to the park yet this morning, it's only 11am, but I'm going to go there in a minute. So long for now dear diary, maybe I'll write again tonight, maybe not.

Sunday night, April 8th, 1945

Dear diary, well I'm back again, to tell you about another great day that I had today. As I told you before, I went to the park about 11am this morning and most of the gang was there, including Joey. Somebody, I don't know who, put a tennis net up across the basketball court at the half court line and people were playing paddle ball. It looks very much like tennis, but instead of a stringed racket, they use a solid wooden paddle. I watched them play for a while and then someone asked me if I'd like to try it. I said yes and even though I had never played that before, I picked it up pretty quick and I really liked it. The girl that I was playing with, I don't know who she was, in fact I had never seen her before, said she was tired of playing and asked if anybody wanted to take her place. Well I almost fainted when Joey stepped up and said he would like to try it. He had never played it before either. Well we played for a little while, getting used to it a little bit more and then he said he wanted to play me for real. I didn't think I had a chance against Joey because he is very good at sports.

It seemed as if everybody in the park was watching us. I was playing pretty well and keeping up with Joey for a long while and then I don't know what happened, but I suddenly was beating him. Sure enough I beat him and all of the guys started teasing Joey about losing to a girl. I think he was a little embarrassed by it, but then he challenged them to try to beat me if they think it's so easy. Then he said that I was really a good player and that made me feel so good. So up stepped my brother, Heshy, to try to beat me and he yelled out, so everyone could hear him, "I can beat my sister any day of the week." That got me mad, so when we started to play I tried extra hard and it worked. I beat him easier than I beat Joey. Now Heshy took all the teasing from the other guys, but by then nobody else wanted to play me. It really wasn't that I am that good, it was more that the guys, like me, had never played paddle ball before, and they didn't play as well I did. But no matter what, it made me feel like a champ. Joey came up to me afterward and, patting me on the back, told me that I was very good and that I surprised everyone. That really made me feel good, coming from him.

When one of the boys tried to say that I just got lucky, Joey jumped to my defense and told the kid that I won because I played better, not because I got lucky. The kid just looked at Joey and shut up. Diary, I wonder if that is a sign or something, that he really likes me? I don't know, but I can only hope. All the girls gathered around me as if I was some kind of hero or something. It was a great afternoon. Right before dinner, Daddy came home from talking politics with his friends in the park and said to Mom, that Mr. Balducci is his kind of man. Mom asked Daddy what he was talking about and he said that Joey's father, who usually drives a taxi on Sundays but was off today because he worked a double shift on Saturday. After going to church, Daddy said, Mr. Balducci joined Daddy and his friends in the park to discuss politics and how things are going in the war.

It seems, Daddy said, that the American and Russian Armies would soon meet in Germany, probably near Berlin. Daddy said that Mr. Balducci thinks we should watch out for the Russians because he thinks, they can't be trusted. That is exactly how Daddy feels and he is not afraid to tell anyone about it. Many of his friends don't agree with him and many Sundays he has come home from the park very aggravated, but now Daddy has found an ally in Joey's dad. I know that Joey's parents and my parents like each other but now I think Daddy and Joey's dad have bonded even more, and that makes me feel great. Like I said before it has been a great Sunday for me. Now I'm getting tired and it is getting late so I'll have to say good night, dear diary.

Tuesday, April 10th, 1945

Dear diary, it has rained on and off for the past two days and Heshy caught a bad cold, trying to play basketball in the rain, I think. It was only drizzling at the time but still I think that's how he caught it, although Joey didn't catch cold and he was playing in the rain with Heshy, so I guess I don't really know. The good thing about it though is that when I met Joey, on the usual corner, on the way to school, Joey didn't have an umbrella so he walked all the way to school and back in the afternoon, huddled next to me under mine. I was in Heaven. It could've been a blizzard blowing out there, I wouldn't have been aware of it.

All I thought about in school all day was the walk back home afterwards. For a few moments in school I panicked, because the thought occurred to me that maybe because Heshy is not in school today, Joey might decide to walk home along Powell Street instead of Sackman Street. I quickly put an end to that thought. By this time it was raining very hard and that made me happy. I was also afraid that it might stop raining and there would be no need to huddle. So while it was still raining hard I asked Joey, in History class, If he would like the protection of my umbrella after school lets out and he said yes. I even suggested that if it's still raining as hard as it was at that moment, we could walk down Powell Street as that would be closer to his house. Again he said sure.

As you can see dear Diary, I was leaving nothing to chance. After thinking about it for a while I now realize that it's a good thing to be able to turn a dismal day into a beautiful day and if I would always try to do just that, I'll be okay in my life. The war news is getting better each day although there is still a lot of fighting going on and a lot of people getting killed and wounded. That's the terrible part and the thing I hate the most. I hope it's all over soon. Good night dear diary.

Wednesday, April 11, 1945

Dear diary, the rain has finally stopped early this evening and Heshy is feeling a little better today, so maybe by Friday he will be able to go to school. Mrs. Bernstein asked me if I could help her out on Sunday, this Sunday. It seems I was wrong about Joshua being five years old. His fifth birthday is on Monday and the Bernsteins are having a party for him on Sunday and feel that they could use my help at the party. I think also because Joshua relates to me, he probably asked his mom if I could be there. Mrs. Bernstein said that she will pay me just like for a babysitting job. I would do it for nothing, really, because I love those kids and Mr. and Mrs. Bernstein, but of course I didn't tell her that. I could use the money, with our birthday, Heshy's and mine, coming up next month.

Mrs. Bernstein even asked my parents to come over on Sunday for a piece of birthday cake and coffee. She made it a point to tell my parents that they didn't have to bring a present. Knowing my Mom as I do, Mom will not only get a present for Joshua, but also a little something for Sophie too. Mom's afraid that Sophie's little feelings would be hurt if Joshua got a whole bunch of presents and she got nothing. That's my Mom, always thinking about everyone else and their feelings. I hope that when I become a mom someday, I'll be half as good as my Mom. Oh I didn't mention that today I had the same wonderful time huddling under my umbrella with Joey as I did yesterday. Again I was able to turn another rainy, dismal day into a beautiful one and I felt great about it.

I forgot to tell you but the other day Mrs. Morgenstern, from Stone Avenue, asked me if I could baby-sit for her kids Saturday night, she has three and at the time I had to say no because I didn't know if Mrs. Bernstein needed me and she is my first choice. Now it's too late to baby-sit for Mrs. Morgenstern because she found someone else, but she did say that she would keep me in mind for the future. I guess that's good. I really could use the money because in addition to having to buy Heshy a present for his birthday, summer is not too far off and I'm going to need a new bathing suit. I have grown up a little since last year and have started to blossom, if you know what I mean. I wonder if Joey has noticed it yet. Oh well maybe soon he will, I sure hope so. I think this year many of our friends, Heshy's and mine, will be allowed to go to Coney Island and Brighten Beach by themselves. Mom and Daddy are still thinking it over about letting me and Heshy go by ourselves but I think they are going to give in to us because of all of the other kids, including Joey, being allowed to go. At least I hope so. It's getting late and I'm getting tired, so good night, dear diary.

Thursday, April 12th, 1945

Dear diary, we heard the most awful news today, President Roosevelt has died. My whole family and everybody in the entire neighborhood is in complete shock. Nobody seems to know what's going to happen with the country, and the outcome of the war. The only thing that's on the radio and in the newspapers is about FDR's death and Vice President Harry Truman being sworn in as the new President. So many people in the neighborhood were crying and distraught at the news of the President's death, it is as if a family member had died. FDR is the only

President I have ever known, he's been the President almost since I was born so it seems weird not having him as President anymore.

Later on, all kinds of reassuring statements came out of Washington that the government will continue as usual and that the war is going ahead until we win, which, they say will not be too much longer. There was a report on the radio that Hitler was so thrilled at the death of FDR that he predicted that Germany will now go on to victory. Gosh, I hope not. Nobody knows too much about Harry Truman so they are all worried about what's going to happen to the country. I don't know what's going on either, it's so crazy right now. In the park this afternoon that's all my friends and I were talking about and Daddy and his friends too. Joey was there too but his father wasn't because he was working. I wonder who feels like going for a taxi ride today.

Joey and a few others were saying that we should all stay calm and give Harry Truman a chance to show what he can and will do. Someone said, I don't remember who, that Harry Truman is the first man to be President, who is not a college graduate. That makes most people wonder all the more about the future of the country. I hope our fears are all for nothing. I'll have to try to go to sleep now although I don't know if I'll be able to. Good night dear diary.

Friday, April 13, 1945

Dear diary, Heshy was well enough to go to school today even though he still has a little bit of a cough. Mom wanted him to stay home one more day but Heshy said that he missed three days of schoolwork, although I did bring him our homework assignments, which he did and I turned in for him, he did not want to miss any more days. The whole school was talking about the events of yesterday, including the teachers. There was talk of us not having school for a few days but that was changed because they said we should not show our enemies that we are disrupted in any way. The Principal, Mr. Goodman, said that he will probably close the school on the day of FDR's funeral, which was not announced yet. We really didn't get to do much schoolwork today, mostly homework assignments, because nobody, teachers or students, could really get their minds on schoolwork.

Other than that, for me it was to and from school as usual, without any more huddles. I didn't really feel bad about it because I did what

Mom has been trying to teach me and that is be thankful for the little things you get in life. I'm just happy that I got to walk those two days huddling with Joey under that umbrella. With all the commotion about FDR dying, now we will, in school, try to catch up on some of the work we missed the past two days. We need it too, because we are only a couple of months away from the end of the school year. Just thinking about it all is making me very tired so I'll just say good night dear diary.

Sunday, April 15, 1945

Dear diary, yesterday I read in the newspaper that FDR will lie in state in Washington for a few days and his funeral will be this Thursday, so maybe we will not have to go to school that day. I guess that means we will have to somehow make up another day's schoolwork. Oh well anyway, Saturday's weather was a little warmer than it has been lately, but still a little cool and very sunny. In the afternoon, my friends and I gathered in the park as usual, at least those of us who weren't working, like Joey was.

Mrs. Bernstein came by, with Sophie in the stroller and Joshua holding her hand, heading for the playground area of the park. When the kids saw me they got very excited and begged me to go with them to the playground area. Mrs. Bernstein told the kids not to bother me, but I told her that they are no bother at all and I would be happy to go with them. When we got to the swings, I looked around and saw that a few of my girlfriends and some of the boys, including Heshy, tagged along. I was surprised and glad at the same time. Joshua and Sophie asked their mom if I could be the one to push them on the swings and she was a little reluctant at first, but then gave in. So I started the same routine as I had done the past two weeks and the kids loved it again. When some of my friends wanted to help me out with the pushing of the swings, the kids started yelling no, no, they only wanted me to do it. I think they enjoyed seeing me huffing and puffing and getting out of breath.

By this time everyone was laughing, Joshua, Sophie, all of my friends and even Mrs. Bernstein and of course me too. Mrs. Bernstein told me something very nice that I will always remember. She told me that she thinks that I'm a very special kind of person to do all that I do for her children it goes far beyond babysitting chores. That made me feel so good, because I really don't feel anything special about myself for doing whatever it is that I do. I just do it because I love to, especially for Joshua and Sophie and the whole Bernstein family. They are all very nice, special people. It's just like what Joey told me about how he feels about my family being a part of his family, that's how I feel about the Bernsteins.

After Joey came home from work, he worked at Mr. Seltzer's fruit and vegetable store   he brought over a bag full of nice, fresh fruit for my parents and told them that his parents would like our whole family to come over to his house on Easter Sunday, April 22 for a nice Easter dinner, at about 3pm. Daddy asked Mom if it would be okay with her and she happily said yes, of course.   My father asked Joey if they, his family, ever eat ham, because, my father explained, Jewish people can't, because a pig is not kosher. Diary, I'll never forget this as long as I live. Joey said to Daddy, with a straight face, and Mom was standing right there too, "Well yes, Mr. Abromovitz, we do eat ham in my house, but first we circumcise the pig!" We all started to laugh and even though Daddy was trying not to, he burst out laughing too.

I was helping the Bernsteins today for Joshua's birthday party and it was going along very well, but then some of the adults there started talking about FDR. The party was very nice, up to that point and Joshua got a lot of nice presents and so did Sophie, which made my Mom very happy. The coffee and cake was very good but none of us ate too much because we all ate a big lunch before we got to the Bernstein's and all the talk about FDR kind of took our appetites away anyway.

When we got home, to put everyone's mind on a more pleasant topic, Daddy started talking about how much he was looking forward to having Easter dinner at the Balducci's. Mom knew what he was doing and looked at him for a few seconds and then joined Daddy in saying that she too was looking forward to the Balducci's Easter dinner next Sunday. She wondered aloud what we should bring as a gift. Daddy looked at her and said that we have a whole week to think about it. They both seemed to me, to be still feeling the effects of FDR dying, as are most of the people in our neighborhood. Oh well I hope we all get over it soon. Good night dear diary.

Monday, April 16, 1945

Dear diary, everyone at school has calmed down a whole lot and things are almost back to normal. We have not been told yet whether or not we will have to come to school on Thursday, the day of FDR's funeral, but I really don't care if we don't get the day off because I'd just as soon not have to make up another day's work. I got to see Joey for a few minutes yesterday. It was Palm Sunday and I saw him just before he went to church with his family. He looked so good all dressed up in his Sunday best, as he calls it. Of course I saw him again this morning and all day in classes and that was very nice. He is so nice to me that I can't believe, or maybe I don't want to believe, that he thinks of me only as his sister. I keep walking next to Heshy, going to and coming from school and naturally Joey is always close by. I only hope that nobody catches on to what I'm doing.

A funny thing happened today. When I got home from school my Mom looked as if she didn't feel well. I don't know what it was about her but she just didn't look right. When I asked her what was wrong, she said she didn't know exactly what it was but she felt down, melancholy and a feeling of gloom. She said she started feeling that way around noontime, but she didn't know why. Later this evening, Joey came over to do homework with me and Heshy, well Heshy anyway. He said he noticed the same thing I noticed about Mom and he said that his Mom came home from her work today feeling the same way. Joey said that his Mom tried to just brush it aside by saying that it was nothing, maybe just the weather or something that is going around, like a bug or something like that. No more was said about it tonight, but it still strikes me strange. I don't know diary, but I sure hope everyone is feeling better tomorrow. Joey again mentioned Easter Sunday's dinner and said that his family is looking forward to us being there too. He also told us that his Mom's brother, his Uncle Paul might be there too and the only reason he's telling us is because his Uncle Paul speaks no English, only Italian. He was only preparing us in case we try to talk to him and he doesn't answer us, we'll know why. I'm only guessing but I think that is why. Good night for now, dear diary.

Tuesday, April 17, 1945

Dear diary, my Mom said she was feeling better this morning but not completely. She looked much better so I guess she really is. On the way to school this morning I asked Joey how his mom was feeling and he said that she went to work okay but he thinks that whatever was bothering her yesterday is still there, a little bit. For the first time Joey mentioned to me that he had gotten an unsigned birthday card and didn't know who put it in his book. I tried to look surprised but he looked at me funny anyway and then asked me if I knew anything about it. I told him no, but then I almost let the cat out of the bag. I suggested that maybe it was his secret admirer and Joey looked at me and asked how I knew about that because he never told anyone about it. I told him a big fat white lie when I told him that he had told both me and Heshy on the way home from school on Valentine's Day.

I figured that it was far enough back in time, about two months or so, that he wouldn't remember it. I was right because then he said that he didn't remember if he had told us or not so I told him to ask Heshy if he thought I was lying. Joey started to stammer a little and finally said he was sorry, that he didn't mean to suggest that I was not telling the truth. I told him to forget about it because it really wasn't all that important. Inside of me I was dying, I was praying that he would forget about it and not ask Heshy, but if he did I was hoping that Heshy wouldn't remember either. Well anyway I think I got out of it okay, because on the way home from school this afternoon and later on at my house when we were doing our homework together, Joey never said a word about it. Yes diary I know I said that I couldn't do my homework with Joey and Heshy anymore, because Daddy might get suspicious, but I figured that once is a while would be okay. Joey never said a word about it.

A funny conversation took place between Joey, Daddy and the rest of us. Daddy asked Joey how his family came to live in a Jewish neighborhood. Mom got a little upset with Daddy for asking such a question. I was a little shocked by it too. Before Daddy could explain himself, Joey told my Mom that it was okay, that he was happy to tell us all why they lived in a Jewish neighborhood. Joey said that his mother always said that she felt very comfortable being around Jewish people.

He said that was the reason and that his whole family felt that way too. Then Joey told us about a funny thing that happened to his mother.

Sometime after the war started, she went back to work, doing what she does now, basting. She hadn't worked since she was single. On the first day at work, she was seated at a big table with a group of Italian woman who were doing the same type of work that she was doing. Joey said that probably because his mother had lived in a Jewish neighborhood for so long, when she spoke English many people thought she was Jewish and so it was with this group of Italian woman. She was sitting there only a short time, Joey said when the other women at the table started talking about her, in Italian of course, and saying the nastiest things about his mother because they all thought she was Jewish. His mother naturally understood every word they said but she said nothing. Joey said she just sat there all morning working and not saying a word, not in Italian, anyway. Finally, Joey said, at lunchtime, his mother looked up from the table and asked the other women where she could go to buy lunch around there, but she asked in Italian.

Joey said the women almost all fell down in surprise and shock. They started apologizing and saying they didn't mean the things they said about her, like when they all said that she was very funny looking and other bad things. His mother, Joey said, being such a smart, clever and good person forgave all of them and they soon all became fast friends. Daddy asked Joey how his mother could befriend anti-semitic people like that and Joey said that he asked his mom the same thing. She said that they are not bad people it's just that they were brought up thinking these bad things about other people. She told Joey that if she could change the hearts of one or two of those people, then she feels she has done a good thing. My Mom looked at Joey with an approving smile and said that she thinks Joey's mom is a wonderful person. Daddy smiled too and shook his head in agreement. Wow! Every time I learn something new about Joey or his family, I like him even more. When Joey left to go home, a little later on, Daddy told Joey that he was such a "Joey boy". That was a great compliment, coming from my Daddy. Good night for now dear diary.

Thursday, April 19, 1945

Dear diary, it looks like I may not see Joey until Easter Sunday because Joey was not in school today. He said yesterday that today is Holy Thursday and tomorrow is Good Friday and he wasn't going to school on those two days. I don't remember what he did last year on these two days, but I think that maybe he did go to school then. I'm not sure but I think the reason that he's been going to church more than he usually does is because of his brother Buster being in the Army in Europe. Speaking of Europe and the war, the news keeps getting better and better. The newspapers and the radio are reporting that the Allied Armies are now in Germany, with the Americans and British troops on the west and the Russians on the east, so hopefully the war in Europe will soon be over. I will be so happy to see that day come and also the end of the war in the Pacific too. I still say a prayer for Buster every night as does my family.

Daddy came home from work tonight and told Mom that he got what he thought was the perfect present for the Balduccis for Easter Sunday. From some of the Italian ladies at the factory where he is the office manager, he found out what the Balduccis usually like to drink with their dinner, red Italian wine and nice Italian liquor for after dinner. He also asked them where the nearest Italian bakery was and went there to buy some traditional Easter breads and other goodies. Mom said that he must have spent a lot of money and Daddy said that he did, but that he didn't care because it was so nice of them to have invited us to their house on their holiday. And besides that, he said when they came to our house for our Passover Seder they gave us a very nice gift of Passover wine. I quickly added, not the wine that fell off the truck. After everybody laughed, Mom thought about it for a split second and then agreed with Daddy.

And now for the local gossip from the mouth of the official "yenta" of the school, Sylvia Roth. In school today she told me that Rose Giordano might not be coming back to school, because the word going around is that she may be pregnant. Rose lives on the other side of Pitkin Avenue, I'm not sure exactly where because, even though she seems to be a very nice person, I don't pal around with her. I believe that she's about a year or so older than me, but I still don't understand how she could let some boy do that to her before she's married. Oh I know that some girls who live right around here are messing around like that but I still don't understand why. Maybe I'm old fashioned, I don't know but that's just the way I feel. Sylvia then told me that Lillian Moskowitz, Seymour's older sister who's nineteen I think, thinks she may be pregnant too. She was overheard on the telephone, in Sussman's Drug store, on the corner of Stone and Riverdale Avenues, telling her boyfriend, that she missed her period for two months and that they will have to get married. Sylvia said whoever the guy is must have taken off for parts unknown, like maybe joined the Army or something like that because they're not married. She doesn't come out of her house lately so nobody has seen her to see if she is starting to show.

Then she told me about two girls, sisters, who are both older than we are, but not that much, from New Lots Avenue, who go every weekend night to Times Square to pick up sailors or any guy in uniform. Sylvia said they told her that that is their way of helping in the war effort, by boosting the morale of our servicemen. Diary, sometimes I think the whole world has gone nuts. I was so glad when Sylvia got done talking and went on her way to somebody else in another class, to spread that great news, I guess. I just didn't want to hear anymore. When I got home from school and Heshy wasn't around, I told Mom about all the gossip I heard and she just shook her head in disbelief and shock. She told me that back in the small city in Germany where she grew up and went to school, they had the same kind of "yentas", spreading the same kind of stories. She said that just like what I had heard today, in her hometown, sometimes the stories were true but most of the time they were not, so I shouldn't believe whatever this Sylvia ever tells me. Many times, Mom told me, these stories are not true but they hurt very innocent people, mostly the girls.

Sometimes, Mom said, when a boy and girl start to date and are like girlfriend and boyfriend for a while, a boy might try to get fresh with the girl and the girl might resist the boy and won't see him anymore, so the boy will try to get even with the girl by telling these untrue stories about what he said he did to the girl. The next thing you know everybody is repeating the story as if it were true and then the girl gets a very bad reputation. That's why Mom said, I shouldn't repeat any of these stories because they probably aren't true. What Mom says sure makes a lot of sense to me. I can't wait until Sunday when I know for sure I'll see Joey at his house for Easter dinner. Good night dear diary.

CHAPTER 4

Monday, April 23rd, 1945

Dear diary, well Sunday finally arrived yesterday and I spent a lot of time trying to look my best for our visit to Joey's house for Easter Sunday dinner. I sure hoped that Joey noticed the effort I made to look good for the occasion. Mom, Daddy and Heshy all got all spiffed up too, as they say. Finally at 2:45pm we all left for the short walk to Joey's house and up the stairs we all went to his apartment door. Joey's sister, Mary, opened the door and welcomed us and she really looked lovely. She led us into the kitchen where Mrs. Balducci was still fussing with something or other and Joey was helping her. He greeted us all as if he hadn't seen us in a year and then he led us into the living room that was converted into a dining room for the occasion. Like a lot of my friend's apartments, Joey's is called a railroad flat. That's because we have to walk through one room to get to another, if you know what I mean. Well anyway everything was fixed up so nice and the living room being right next to the kitchen made it very easy for passing the food from the stove to the table. The whole apartment and the atmosphere were very festive.

The Balducci's took the time, especially Joey's mom, to feed us nothing that would be forbidden for us to eat by our faith. Mrs. Balducci must have been up all night cooking. I found out later from Joey that she was up most of the night and his sister, Mary, was with her most of the time too. Joey said that they all pitched in and helped a little. They served one great dish after another and we were all stuffed. I don't remember the names of all the different dish's we had and if I did remember I don't think I could pronounce their names. One of the things we had was very thin flat steak that was rolled up after being

70

stuffed with some kind of vegetables, held together by toothpicks stuck through it and cooked in tomatoes sauce, homemade of course. I think they called it something that began with the letter **B.** Mrs. Balducci said that she bought all of her meat at the Kosher Butcher, even the chopped meat for the spaghetti and meatballs. It was all so delicious.

After we sat and talked around the table for a while, Daddy raised his glass of wine and toasted all of the men and women in uniform around the world who are fighting, so that we can all enjoy celebrating our holidays in peace, just like we were doing right then. Everybody joined in and then Mom said she wanted to offer a prayer that all the soldiers would come home safe and sound. All the while during her prayer, she was looking at Joey's Mom. Everyone also joined Mom in her little prayer. I thought it was very beautiful and touching. I won't forget that scene for a long time. When we had some room again in our stomachs, Mr. Balducci brought out Italian liquor, but Daddy wouldn't let me or Heshy try it, not even a taste. Daddy did let us again have a taste of their homemade wine. As I was sipping the wine I said to Daddy that it doesn't taste like it fell off a truck and again everyone laughed. Daddy looked at me, pointed in Joey's direction and asked if I was a kibitzer too, like him. More laughter. Then we had coffee and great tasting Italian pastries. We all loved it, everything was great.

What a day it was. Our families have come even closer together. It just made me feel so good and warm inside. I think we all gained a few pounds yesterday. I was so full last night that I was glad I had a little bit of homework to do because I couldn't go to sleep feeling so full anyway. By the time I finished my homework, about 11pm, I was okay. I don't know why I was so concerned about my homework when we have all of this week off for Easter week. Oh yeah, today in the park we gathered with all of our friends, as usual and Heshy and I both were still talking about how great the food was at Joey's house yesterday, and a whole bunch of our friends and even some kids who don't usually pal out with us, kept asking Joey when they can come over for an Italian dinner. Joey, after being asked that question so many times, finally said to the next kid who asked for an Italian dinner, the next time he and his family are invited to the kid's house for a Passover Seder, he'll invite not only him, but his whole family over for an Italian dinner. That stopped it right there.

I told Joey that I was sorry that Heshy and I blabbed to everyone in the park about the great food we had at his house yesterday and he told me to forget about it. He said he was really glad that we had a good time, because his family loved having us over. He said that they have nothing but nice things to say about our family. I loved hearing that, it was so sweet of Joey to tell me that. Mom and Daddy were also very pleased to hear it when I told them. Well I've got to go to sleep now so good night dear diary.

Sunday, April 29th, 1945

Dear diary, it has been a week of mixed emotions for me. I had a lot of fun hanging out in the park with my friends, playing paddle ball whenever the net was put up, sometimes handball for a little while, but mostly just gabbing with the girls and boys. Sometimes we'd walk over to the candy store for an egg cream or a ice cream soda or a frappe or whatever. It was really a lot of fun. The only thing missing was Joey all day and sometimes in the evening too. During the day, and it was a long day for him too, he worked for Mr. Seltzer at the produce store and then two or three times during this week he helped out the old Italian man who he used to work for a couple of years ago, in his hat blocking and shoe shining store on New Lots Avenue. He made a lot of money, for a kid his age anyway and Joey says he is saving it up so that he will have it for either college or a good used car or whatever.

When I did see him on those evenings when he wasn't working, he looked very tired, but he seemed glad to see his friends, all of us, even if it was for such a short time. Those times that I mentioned I was gabbing with the girls, you know that most of the gab was about the boys. They all were saying who they thought was good looking or cute or very smart and who they thought was a jerk or whatever. Of course the talk got around to who liked who and things like that and also off course Sylvia the "yenta" was in the middle of the whole conversation and taking in every bit of news she thought was worth repeating. In fact the girls decided to have a contest to see who we all thought was the best looking, the cutest and the smartest guy we know. We all, the girls that is, got to vote by a show of hands. I was scared that I would blurt out Joey's name for all three categories, but I was relieved when Marsha Plotkin nominated Joey for all three and everyone started teasing her about liking him. I was glad, relieved and jealous at the same time. Sarah Gold nominated Heshy for all three and nobody was surprised because he's her boyfriend. Sylvia did the same for Barry Engel and everyone looked surprised and then started teasing her about liking him. She started stuttering and stammering and couldn't speak, she was so embarrassed. I never have seen Sylvia speechless before. What a lovely sight. Don't get me wrong, I like Sylvia, I just don't like her being such a "yenta" all the time.

Well anyway back to the contest. Rhoda Pinsky seconded Joey's nomination and Gloria Rothenberg nominated Irv Glick, also for all three categories. What happened next was great. I had to control my emotions with the results. At the end of the first vote, Joey won all three categories and Heshy came in second. I felt bad for Heshy but I mean after all it was my Joey who came in first. It was agreed by all that Joey would be the winner of the best looking contest and that we would all vote again for the other two categories. Well to make a long story short, Heshy was voted the cutest and the smartest. I was so proud I felt my chest swell so that I thought to myself I must really be blossoming now.

Joey didn't come around to the park that night but the next night he did. When I saw him I told him that he won the contest for being the best looking guy in our group and all he said was that it was not surprising that he won, being that he is Italian. He tried to look serious when he said it, but he was trying so hard to keep from smiling that it made him laugh very hard and I joined him and also a few others who were standing nearby and heard him.

On Saturday I babysat again for the Bernsteins and Heshy and Sarah joined me again but not Joey because he had to work late for Mr. Seltzer. When he finished work he went home to eat and then he stopped by to visit us at the Bernstein's I was so happy to see him even if it was just for a short time. He told us that he would not be working for Mr. Seltzer anymore because Mr. Seltzer tried to cheat him out of his hard earned money. Joey was always paid fifty cents an hour working part time after school and on weekends but this past week he worked full time. Usually eight to ten hours a day and on Saturday he worked twelve hours. When it came time for Joey to get paid, Mr. Seltzer said that for working full time he would only be getting forty cents an hour. Joey said he was very mad but that he didn't lose his head.

He said that he told Mr. Seltzer it's okay with him but when he got home he would have to tell his father, who had a very bad temper, so Mr. Seltzer told Joey to never mind what he said about forty cents an hour and that of course he couldn't use Joey anymore. Joey said that he waited until he had his money in his hand and then told Mr. Seltzer that he couldn't and wouldn't work for anyone who tried to cheat him just because he was only a kid. Joey said that he also told Mr. Seltzer that he would've worked for the forty cents an hour this week, if only Mr. Seltzer had told him before the week started, not after. Joey said that Mr. Seltzer didn't know what to say after that so Joey just thanked him for giving him the job in the first place and left. Joey told us that he thinks the reason Mr. Seltzer never told him before hand, was that he didn't realize how much money he owed Joey, so he tried to change the hourly rate after the fact. Smart boy my Joey.

Well tomorrow we all go back to school and I'll get to see Joey again all day, I hope. Tomorrow after school, Mom and I are going to downtown Brooklyn, to the big department stores, to shop for some summer clothes and a new bathing suit for me. I think while we're there I'll look around for a birthday present for Heshy and Mom can help me pick out something nice. I would love to get a grownup bathing suit for myself this year instead of a little girl's. I've saved up almost fifty dollars from my babysitting money and I hope I don't have to spend all of it because I have to have some money to buy birthday presents for Mom and Daddy. They both come up in the fall. But then again, I suppose I'll be getting more babysitting jobs during the summer. I hope so. It can't be all fun and games for me this summer, although I wish it was. A funny thing happened today. Joey stopped by this afternoon looking for Heshy, because he hadn't seen him all week and he wanted to say hello. Mom asked him how his mother was and he said that his mother for some unknown reason was walking around with a heavy heart, and my Mom said that she is too and doesn't understand why either. Strange isn't it? Well good night dear diary.

Monday, April 30th, 1945

Dear diary, I had a really good day today. On the way to school, Heshy and I met Joey and the rest of our friends who we usually walk to school with, Joey gave us a big smile but I didn't think it looked like his normal smile. When I asked him if anything was wrong, Joey said he didn't think so but he was feeling a little bit like his Mother has been feeling. I wasn't too happy with that but there was nothing I could do about it. The rest of the day in all of our classes Joey seemed to be okay, so I felt better about that. After school I went right home and then Mom and I took the subway to downtown Brooklyn, to the big department stores. We shopped around for a good while but we did find some lovely clothes, some shoes and even a very nice grownup bathing suit for me. Yippee! No more children's clothes for me.

Mom suggested that because Heshy got a baseball book for Joey on his birthday and Heshy seemed to like it as much as Joey did, that I should look for a different baseball book for Heshy. I thought it was a great idea so that's what I looked for. With Mom's help I found a book about the history of baseball and bought it. I hope Heshy will like it. With all the stuff that I bought, I was surprised that I only spent thirty two dollars and change, so I told Mom that I wanted to buy her a nice gift of whatever she wanted, as long as it was no more than ten dollars. When Mom asked why I wanted to buy her a gift, I told her just because she's my Mom and I love her. She gave me a big hug, smiled at me and planted a big kiss on the top of my head and said she loved me too. She always makes me feel so special and so lucky to have her as my Mom.

When we were looking at the bathing suits I kiddingly pointed to a very sexy looking two piece swimsuit and told Mom I'd like to get it. Mom just gave me a look that told me there was no way that I could even bring that suit home, let alone wear it. When I started to laugh about it Mom started laughing too. I think she knew right along that I was kidding. It was so much fun shopping with Mom. We picked out a couple of nice, flowery, satiny kerchiefs and a very lovely shade of lipstick as her gift from me. I even helped her pick out the shade of lipstick that would look right for her. That's the first time Mom ever asked my opinion before she bought something. Now I really feel grownup.

On the way home we even stopped at Finklestein's bakery, on Sackman Street near Livonia Avenue, just downstairs from the El, for a nice little cheese cake to bring home. It's Daddy's and Heshy's favorite. Mom would not let me pay for it she said that I work too hard for the few dollars that I had left and that I should hang onto it for a rainy day. After dinner Joey came over to do homework with us again at the dining room table and Daddy was reading the newspaper in the living room, as usual and Mom was in the kitchen when Daddy yelled out, "Hannah, could you please bring me a banana?" Joey looked up from his books, smiled at me and Heshy and yelled out to Daddy, "Mr. Abromovitz, you write poetry now?" Heshy and I started laughing and we could even hear Mom laughing from the kitchen. Daddy rose from his chair, stuck his head in the dining room and told Joey that he is still a kibitzer. Joey left a little early because he said his Mother was still feeling a little down. He said she denies it but he can tell by the way she acts. Like I said before it was a very nice day for me, today. Good night dear diary.

Tuesday, May 1st, 1945

Dear diary today has been the worst day of my life. I'm still crying as I write this. Although the day started out nice as usual, after dinner, when Heshy and I were getting ready to do our homework and wondering if Joey was going to join us tonight, in comes Joey. He looked awful! His eyes were all red as if he had been crying and he seemed to be completely distraught. Through tears Joey told us that a short time ago his family received a telegram that his brother Buster had been killed in Germany. Like an explosion, the news hit us. Mom burst into tears and hugged Joey and Daddy started yelling and cursing about the evils of war and everything else he could think of. I never, ever heard Daddy use language like that before. Of course I started crying immediately and joined Mom in hugging Joey. Heshy got so sick about it that he rushed into the bathroom, I think to throw up. It was a horrible scene. I can only imagine how things were at Joey's house.

Joey, still crying said he had to go, but he stopped to ask me If I would tell our home room teacher about what happened and that he would not be coming to school for a few days. I was crying so that I couldn't speak but I nodded that I would. When Heshy came out of the bathroom he was very pale and uneasy on his feet. As much I care for Joey, I know that Heshy loves Joey for being his best friend. I don't think they ever had a fight or disagreement, ever. There's nothing that they wouldn't do for each other. Daddy was so visibly upset that he had to leave the house and go out for a walk. Mom, still crying and upset, kept saying about Joey's Mother, that poor woman, that poor woman what she must be going through. Then Mom asked me if Joey had said when his brother was killed and I told her I thought he said it was on April, 16th. Mom asked, of nobody in particular, what day of the week that was as she walked over to the kitchen cabinet, to open the door to look at the calendar, that hangs on the inside of the door.

After checking out the day of the week it was, Mom suddenly burst into tears again and said, that was the day that both she and Mrs. Balducci felt a feeling of melancholy and a heavy heart. She was sure of it she said. I don't know, I just don't remember right now. I couldn't do the rest of my homework and I don't even care about it. I can't describe how terrible I feel right now. I hope I'll be able to sleep tonight, I don't think my parents will be able to. Daddy came home about an hour or so after he left but he was still very upset, so he might have trouble sleeping tonight too. I have to try to go to sleep and if I can't I'll probably get up and write some more, about what I don't know. Good night dear diary, I hope.

Friday, May 4th, 1945

Dear diary, It has been an awful week that started with the bad news about Joey's brother. My heart still aches for Joey and his family. My parents are also still grieving for Joey's family too. I don't think there has been a single laugh heard or a smile given in this house since we heard the news. Going to school every day has been tough for me and Heshy, but we go through the motions of being students. I don't think either one of us has done all of our homework completely any night since Tuesday night. We have not seen or heard from Joey since then either. My parents want very badly to go to see the Balduccis to console them and offer their sympathy and any help that they can give them.

They're just waiting for the right time to go. They both agreed that they should wait a few more days until the grieving lets up a little bit. Heshy and I both told my parents that we wanted to go with them when they do go and my parents both said it was okay. Maybe, Daddy said, we will go to their house on Sunday, and Mom said, yes that would be a good time for us but maybe not for the Balduccis, so Mom suggested that either Heshy or me, or both of us, should go first to ask them if Sunday, at about 1pm, would be a good day and time for us to come.

I really didn't want to go by myself so Heshy agreed to go with me tomorrow morning.

Saturday, May 5th, 1945

Dear diary, this morning Heshy and I went to Joey's house with a little hesitation. I was a little scared at first, not knowing if we would be welcome at that time, but I should've known better. Joey and his family greeted us as if we were a part of their family and that put me and Heshy right at ease. His parents, though still with heavy hearts and sadness written all over their faces, said that yes, they would welcome our family on Sunday. I gave Joey's family, including Joey hugs and kisses when we greeted them and when we left and Heshy did the same too. Joey gave us each a big, tight hug and he gave me a little peck on my cheek. That was a first of course but it was not the way I wanted it to be. Under the circumstances, I'm not complaining. Joey did tell me that he thought he would be coming back to school on Monday. I felt good about that.

I was telling Mom that I hope all of this sadness and hurt would go away soon and she told me that for us it would, but for Joey's Mom and Dad it would never go away. When I asked Mom how she knew that, she reminded me of something that she had told me a while back. She asked me if I remembered that she once told me that before Heshy and I were born, she gave birth to a little girl who only lived fifty nine days, because she was born with a defective heart. I told her I did remember and then she told me that although that happened over fifteen years ago, she still thinks of that little baby every day. She went on to tell me that Moms don't forget these things. Of course, she added, having me and Heshy has helped her cope with life every day, but she will never forget that little life that could've been.

Daddy told us yesterday that all the ladies Mrs. Balducci works with in the factory have been in mourning with her, as is their custom. He found out from some of the women, what would be the right thing to bring with us tomorrow. I can't believe what a nice thing Daddy has done. He had one of those ladies buy a Mass card from the church, for Joey's brother, because he said they told him that would mean a lot to Joey's family, especially his Mom and Dad. Daddy said that some of his friends in the park and in the Temple might not think it was right for a Jew to do that, but he said he's doing it anyway because he thought it was the right thing to do. Daddy also bought for them what he said was, a very fine Italian liqueur, Anisette. He thinks that Mr. Balducci likes to put a little in his coffee on chilly and cold mornings.

Mom didn't seem to care, one way or the other about the liqueur but she liked the idea of the Mass card. She thought that would mean a lot to Mrs. Balducci. I had to baby-sit tonight for Joshua and Sophie and it was very hard for me to put on my usual happy face for the kids but I did. I had to. The kids are too young to understand, so I had to try to be my normal self. They are very perceptive because they seemed to know that something was not the same with me. They kept asking me if something was wrong. I could've cried when Joshua asked me if I was mad at him or if he had been a bad boy. After I reassured him that everything was okay, I told myself I had to snap out of it.

The Bernsteins, like most of the people in the neighborhood, who know the Balduccis, feel very bad for them. It's very hard not to feel for them because they are such a fine family. Heshy and Sarah came over to keep me company and I was very glad they did. I'm happy to say that there was no smooching by them tonight, at least not in front of me. We spent the whole night just talking about Joey and his family and the fact that the war in Europe looks as if it is almost over, with the Allied Armies completely surrounding Berlin. In fact Heshy said that they are already in Berlin. Heshy said that it was a shame that Buster was killed so close to the end of the war, and we all agreed. But when I thought about it, I said to myself, what's the difference when it happened, it still hurts Joey's family, no matter when the war is over.

The Bernsteins got home early, around 11pm, but they paid me for a whole night, like when they come home around 1am. That was very nice of them to do that but I was not as happy as I would've been if Joey's brother had not been killed. After seeing the Balduccis this morning, I'm looking forward to going there tomorrow but I wish it was for a happier time. Good night dear diary.

Sunday, May 6th, 1945

Dear diary, we got to the Balducci's just at 1pm and were very warmly greeted. But as soon as Mom hugged and kissed Joey's Mom, the tears started flowing. Mrs. Balducci was trying very hard to keep her composure and control but was not able to and soon she started to wail very loudly about her baby being killed and of course that made everyone else start to cry, even Joey's father and Daddy too. You know that I started to cry because I couldn't help it. So did Joey and Heshy and Joey's sister Mary too. Before I knew it, me, Heshy, Joey and Mary were all in the middle of the living room in a four way hug. It was very nice to have a shoulder to cry on.

Out of the corner of my eye I saw Daddy and Joey's father hugging and wiping tears from their eyes too. After a few moments the wailing and crying stopped to just a trickle and I heard my Mom say to Joey's Mom that it was too bad it had to be her son killed and so close to the end of the war too. Mrs. Balducci looked at Mom for a second and said that it was too bad that it has to be anybody's son. She then asked a very simple and telling question in her simple Italian way of speaking, with her little Italian accent, she asked, "Why? Why, what was it all for? Why are so many people killed, for what? There never seems to be an end to it. I wish somebody can tell me why?" Daddy tried to answer her but he only got as far as, "Mrs. Balducci" when she looked at him and said, "I know that Hitler was an evil man and that we had to go to war or they would be bombing us and killing us. I know that, but what I'm asking is why does that have to be? Why can't we just talk to each other instead of killing each other? All that I'm asking is why?"

With tears again starting to run down her face, she sat down and buried her face in her hands. Mr. B and Mom went quickly to her side. While Mr. B spoke to Mama B softly in Italian, Mom embraced her and cried a little too. No one could give her an answer. After a short while, with her composure again regained, Mrs. Balducci looked at everyone and apologized, but we all said that there was nothing for her to apologize for. Daddy by this time was very angry at all the people who brought this terrible sadness to the Balduccis. Mom calmed him down and then told him to give them the gifts he had brought. Mrs. Balducci was really taken by the Mass card and told my parents so. Both of Joey's parents not only liked the card but they also thought it was very nice of us to give them the Anisette too. While my parents and Joey's parents sat down on the couch in the living room, Joey said he had to go down to the grocery store to get a few things for his Mom. Heshy and I asked him if he minded us going with him and he said no.

When we were out of sight and hearing of his family, Joey told us that his Mother has been like the way she was this afternoon, since they got that telegram, only much worse. Somebody from the Army came by to say that his brother is buried in a U.S. Military cemetery in Holland along with thousands of other GIs, and it would be some time after the war is over in Europe and in the Pacific before his body can be brought back. I think that is awful. He also told us that he didn't sleep for the first two nights after getting the bad news, but that he is getting much better about coping with it. When we got back to Joey's apartment, everyone was sitting around calmly and talking. Mary had made some coffee and she then set out the coffee cake that Joey had just bought at the store.

Mrs. Balducci told us a very familiar story. She said before Joey was born, she had another son who only lived for about six weeks. She didn't know exactly what he died from but she thought it was a heart defect. My Mom's jaw just dropped in disbelief. My Mom then told Mrs. Balducci about the little girl she gave birth to before she had Heshy and me and the two of them had another good cry. At that point Joey then made everyone laugh when he said that Mary, who is three years older than he is, used to tease him when he was real young, that he didn't really belong to the family because they found him in a garbage can. He said he went crying to his Mom and of course she would tell that it was not true.

Then he said Mary would tell him that if that baby, whose name was David, had lived then he, Joey, wouldn't have been born, because she said their mother only wanted three kids. Again after much laughter, Mrs. Balducci denied that story too. It was really nice to hear everyone laughing, even if they are crying on the inside. Then my Mom mentioned that her little girl's name was Rachel. I had forgotten all about that. After spending what seemed like a short time, but was really about three hours, we left.

On the way home Daddy went into the park to chat with his friends and Heshy went there too to be with his friends. I could've gone too because my friends were also there, but I just wanted to go home and be with Mom. It has been an eventful day, sad at times but it was nice to see that Joey and his loving family are going to be getting along okay. It will take a while I'm sure, except for Mrs. Balducci. According to

Mom, she will never completely get over it and now I can understand it, I think.

I'm looking forward to going to school tomorrow for the first time since last Tuesday night. I only hope that when I see Joey waiting for us on the corner, on the way to school, he will have some kind of smile on his face. If he doesn't, that's okay I'll understand. Oh I forgot to tell Joey that the only reason Heshy and I didn't bring him our homework assignments was because we didn't know whether it was okay to come to his house at a time like that and also we didn't think he would be able to do the work anyway. I'll have to also tell him that Heshy and I will help him with any makeup work he needs to do. Of course by this time Joey should know that we would do anything for him. I hope so. Well good night dear diary.

Monday, May 7th, 1945

Dear diary, rumors were flying all around the radio dial that the war in Europe is on the verge of being over but nothing official was reported. I hope the rumors are true, we shall see. Well anyway, Joey was there on the corner waiting for us as usual, with a smile on his face but, it just wasn't the same. That's okay at least it was a smile. In school Joey was trying very hard to be his old self, at least it seemed that way to me but, he wasn't quite the same. I hope that after a few days around his friends and classmates, he'll come around to his old self. I'm sure that he will. Everyone in school today, classmates and teachers alike, all told Joey how sorry they were to hear about his brother.

Most of the teachers remembered his brother Buster because he had gone to that same school only a few years, maybe five, before us. On the way home from school in the afternoon, Joey was a little bit more talkative and I thought that was good to hear. I love to hear him talk because besides his kidding around talk, he always talks about and says interesting things. Even Daddy says, that is an indication of a very intelligent mind. I, of course always knew that about Joey. Ha! Ha! Joey told us that he wouldn't be coming over our house to do homework for a few days because he wanted to be home for his Mom, in case she needed him. I thought that was so sweet and caring of him and made me feel good inside just knowing what a good person he is.

I hope that if Joey and I ever become girlfriend and boyfriend and Daddy wants to object, he considers how good of a guy Joey really is. I think Daddy knows it already because he likes to kibitz, as Daddy puts it, with Joey all the time. Anyone can tell that Daddy likes Joey a lot just by the way he talks and acts with him. Mom of course makes no secret about how much she likes not only Joey but his whole family, especially his mom. I guess it's something about moms being able to relate and bond with other moms. It's a funny thing but I miss Joey being in the next room doing his homework with Heshy even if I'm not doing mine with them. That sounds crazy, doesn't it? Oh well I guess that's me just being me again. Good night dear diary.

Tuesday, May 8th, 1945

Dear diary, everyone, everywhere it seems, is rejoicing. Not because it's Heshy's and my birthday, but because the rumors turned out to be true, that the war in Europe is finally over. Hitler is reported to have killed himself, something he should have done a long time ago. My Mom went over to see Mrs. Balducci right after the news of the war's ending was announced, to try to comfort her. The news was all over the school too and we were allowed to go home early. On the way home, walking with our usual friends, I stayed close to Heshy and Joey, trying to see if Joey was having any problems dealing with the news. I had nothing to worry about because Joey accepted it as we all did. It was a relief to know that no more of our guys were going to be killed, not in Europe anyway.

Of course, he told me, he wished the war had ended a month ago so that his Mom wouldn't be hurting as she is today. On the way to school this morning Joey wished us both a very happy birthday and apologized for not getting us presents but he did give us each a birthday card and hoped that we'd understand. Of course we understood. He really didn't have to even get us the cards, which were very nice. In my card he wrote that he thinks of me as a part of his family and I didn't mind a bit. Even if he would have said like a sister, it would've been okay with me. In Heshy's he addressed it to his best friend in the whole world, forever. I could tell by Heshy's reaction to it that he was thrilled with it.

When we came home from school we met my Mom as she was coming back from her visit with Joey's Mom. She told us that Joey's Mom was taking the news of the war's end very well and in fact was glad that no more mothers with sons in Europe will have to suffer the loss of a child. Mom is very impressed with the inner strength and wisdom of Mrs. Balducci, as are most of the people who get to know her. When Daddy got home from work, Mom, as she always does, greeted him with a hug while telling him how wonderful the news is. As she went to kiss Daddy she suddenly pulled back and said, "Is that alcohol I smell on your breath Gus Abromovitz? Have you been drinking?"

Daddy opened his mouth to say something but Mom cut him right off by saying, "Gus Abromovitz, you know you are not supposed to drink. In the first place you can't handle it and in the second and most important place, it's no good for your stomach!" Daddy looked at Mom and said, "I thought the most important place came first." Mom started laughing as Heshy and I did and Daddy explained that he only had one drink at the office, along with everyone else. As the office manager he said he couldn't allow anyone to have more than that. Besides he said that we still have another victory to win, over Japan. He insisted that he was not drunk but when he tried to sit down he missed the chair and wound up sitting on the floor. He had the silliest looking grin on his face. As he was trying to get up he said he always sits down that way when he's very tired. Mom, Heshy and I laughed and said at the same time, "Sure you are tired, sure you are"

Daddy had to laugh too as Mom helped him back up to the chair and then we all sat down to eat. After dinner Mom brought out a very beautiful homemade and decorated birthday cake for me and Heshy, as she and Daddy sang Happy Birthday to us. Of course we both joined in too. Mom said that she would've liked to have a bigger party for us with some family and friends, but because of all the commotion lately she thought it best that we skip it this year. Heshy and I both agreed that she was right, as she usually is about almost everything.

Then we opened our gifts. Heshy got me a cute sun hat to go along with my new bathing suit and they look great together. I love it and can't wait to show it off on the beach. Mom and Daddy got me a beautiful beach bag that almost matches my suit and hat. I love that too. Mom and Daddy got Heshy a book of jokes, it was Daddy's idea I think, because he told Heshy now he can keep up with Joey in telling lousy and corny jokes. Heshy laughed and said that's just what he needed, and he also said he loved the book on the history of baseball that I got him. On top of everything else, my parents gave each of us ten dollars. If Joey didn't feel down today it would've been a perfect birthday for me. A funny thing, but Heshy told me the same thing without me mentioning it. I think that's probably because we're twins and think a like most of the time. Well anyway, good night dear diary.

Friday, May 11th, 1945

Dear diary there was a little bit of melancholy news today from Joey. He told us, Heshy and me, that today his brother Buster would've been nineteen. That put me in a blue kind of mood, even though I didn't know his brother, I just feel so bad for Joey and his family. Up until this morning I thought Joey was getting back to almost normal, a little bit every day. In fact yesterday he even told Heshy and me a funny story about Frances Finklestein. Her parents own the bakery on Sackman Street, near Livonia Avenue.

On the way home from school yesterday, Heshy, Joey and I broke off from the rest of the group walking home and stopped at the bakery. Joey said he wanted to get something for his Mom, like a cheese Danish or something for her sweet tooth. While we were there Frances walked in. She and her family live above the bakery. Anyway she gave Joey a big hello. I didn't like that a whole lot. Although we all knew her for a long time through school, she never really hung out with us much, I don't know why. Maybe it was because it seems like she had to help out in the bakery a lot. After Joey got what he wanted for his Mom and we left the store, Joey asked us not to repeat what he was about to tell us because he didn't want it to get around and embarrass Frances.

He told us that a few years ago when he was eleven or twelve, he used to sell newspapers on the corner of Livonia and Powell, on Friday and Saturday nights. He didn't know Francls at that time but after she saw him there one Friday night, she started to come around and sit with him while he sold his papers. For some reason, and Joey said he didn't know why, she would laugh at almost every thing that he said. She would very often laugh very hard, as he put it, at his lousy, corny jokes until she would tell him that she wet her pants. Joey said she would even laugh about that too. He said if that was him he would be too embarrassed to tell anyone. Heshy and I both said the same thing. Joey said he always thought she was a very nice girl and liked having her around for company while he was working but it was just that funny thing about her wetting her pants and telling him about it.

I told him that she probably liked him very much and felt comfortable with him for her to tell him something like that. We all laughed over the story and again Joey asked us not to embarrass her. I asked him, if he didn't want to embarrass her, why he told us about it. Without even thinking about it Joey said that because the three of are so close, almost like family and our families are also very close now, he feels like he could tell us anything. He said that he has never told anyone else that story because he has never trusted anyone like he trusts us. Wow! I didn't realize how special he thinks me and my family are.

I know that my family thinks Joey and his family are special too. Well anyway, I think he is really on his way back to his old self. Today is just a very blue day for him at least I hope it's only for today. When I got home from school today, I told Mom about today being Buster's nineteenth birthday and she gasped for a second and then said she was going over to see his mother, just to be with her. I now remember that when the notice of Buster's death was in the newspaper, it did say that May 11th was his birthday.

Speaking about that newspaper notice, Joey told us that last night an Italian couple, about the same age as The Balduccis, came to their house. They live not too far away but in an Italian neighborhood. They had seen the notice in the newspaper about Buster and their son was killed on the same day in the same area as Buster and his Army unit, his company, was only one or two away from Buster's. They came to the Balducci's house because they just wondered if maybe, because both boys were about the same age and from close neighborhoods in Brooklyn, and were in Army units that seemed to be close, that maybe they knew each other. Mr. Balducci told them that if they did meet each other, Buster never mentioned it in any of his letters. Anyway, Joey said that it was a nice visit because there was a little bit of bonding between parents of two young boys lost in the war.

When Mom came back from visiting with Mrs. Balducci, I told her the story of the couple that came over to the Balducci's last night. Mom said she knew and understood about what she called, grief bonding. I guess I'll have to wait until I grow up and become a mom myself to fully understand. I took a leap forward today. I'm going to be babysitting for the Bernsteins again on Saturday and instead of getting Heshy to ask Joey if he would like to come over that night, I asked Joey myself. I just thought it might help him forget his troubles for a little while and I told him so. He agreed with me and said he would join Heshy and Sarah and me. I don't think anyone can make something out of that, not even Sylvia Roth. Well good night dear diary.

Monday, May 14th, 1945

Dear diary, we had a sudden change of plans on Saturday. Mrs. Bernstein came over to our house with the kids in tow early Saturday morning, about 8:30 and asked if I could watch the kids for her starting right then. It seems that her sister, the one who was sick, got sick all over again and she had to go to Manhattan to help her other sister in their dress shop. While she was at our house she asked my Mom if she would like to work at their store. I say their store because I recently found out that Mrs. Bernstein became a partner. She said they needed someone for three or four days a week. Mom was so taken by surprise she told Mrs. Bernstein that she needed a little time to think about it. Mrs. Bernstein said that would be fine as long as Mom let her know sometime over the weekend and then she left, leaving the kids with me.

I don't think Mrs. Bernstein was gone five minutes when Mom, after a quick talk with Daddy, said she would love to give it a try. This was the first time that Joshua and Sophie were ever at my house and they checked out every corner of every room in our apartment. They seemed to be having a great time doing that. About 10am, after I gave them a little snack, I took them out to the park to play in the playground area. You know they had me running all over, between the swings again, squealing and laughing at me getting all out of breath. I didn't have any of their books to read to them but Heshy and Joey came to my rescue just in time, before I knocked myself out running around the play area.

Heshy and Joey both have very good imaginations so since there were no books to read, they made up stories about monsters, ghosts, wild animals and other stories and acted them out. They were very funny. Not only did the kids love it, but I did too. The kids kept asking for more and Heshy and Joey gave them more. At times I couldn't figure out who was having more fun, the kids or the boys. What a help to me they were and they made the morning go by so fast. At lunch time we all went to the Kosher Deli on the corner of Riverdale Avenue and Christopher Street, just outside the park, for hot dogs, French fries and sodas. The kids and the boys by this time, had worked up good appetites and ate well, including me.

We hung around the park for a little longer and then we all went back to the Bernstein's apartment so the kids could take their naps. When the kids woke up, about an hour or so later, they wanted to go back to my house. Heshy then suggested that maybe they would like to have dinner with us. I thought that was a good idea as long as my parents didn't mind. I left a note for the Bernsteins telling them that the kids were with me at my house and then we all went there. The kids liked Mom and Daddy when they met them in the morning and my parents liked the kids, so they said they loved for them to stay for dinner.

Just as we were starting dinner, the Bernsteins knocked on our door and they too were invited to stay and they accepted. Joey had already left to have dinner with his family and although I understood him wanting to be close to his mother, I still wished he could've stayed. Mom told Mrs. Bernstein that she hadn't worked in a while but she would love to try it again. The two of them worked out the details of the job and pay and the hours and days that she was needed. Mrs. Bernstein then turned to Heshy and asked him if he would like to work in the store on Saturdays until school let out, then he could work for a few days every week during the summer. She said it would be as a stock boy and other duties around the store. She said the store is getting very busy lately and they are thinking about expanding, that's why they are looking for good people that they can trust.

Heshy jumped at the chance and said he would do it. About an hour after we finished eating the Bernsteins left and Joey came by the house again. Since I didn't have to baby-sit that night we all decided to go to the park and hang out, which we did. Joey asked Heshy and me if we would like to come to his house on Sunday morning for breakfast and Heshy said sure but he wanted to know if he could bring Sarah. Joey said yes he could and then Joey looked at me because I hadn't answered him yet. I said yes but shouldn't he ask his mother first before inviting people over early in the morning. He said that normally he would ask his mother first, but he didn't want to give her a chance to say no. I must have looked at him as if he was crazy or something because he half smiled, looked me right in the eyes and said that he thought if his mother was kept a little busy, like with making breakfast, and having people around her, it would take her mind off her grief, even if it's only for a little while. Besides he said, he was going to help her with the cooking and probably his sister would as well. He makes so much sense it scares me.

So the next morning we met Sarah in the park and went to Joey's house for breakfast. Joey's Mom while a little surprised, welcomed us warmly. She even smiled at all of us and seemed to enjoy, if that's the right word, our company. She then asked us what we would all like for breakfast, looked at Joey and said she now knows why he bought all that food last night. We all laughed a little, even Mrs.Balducci and decided that to make things easy for her we would all have the same thing. Joey suggested, because I think he already had it planned orange juice for starters, scrambled eggs with fried salami, hot rolls and coffee, with coffee cake, just out of the oven from the Finklestein's Bakery.

Everyone's mouth was watering as we all said yes, so off to work Joey and his mom went. Joey first put the rolls in the oven to warm up then he started slicing and frying the salami while his mother started beating the eggs. At that moment Joey's sister Mary and his father came walking into the kitchen. They had been setting up the living room as a dining room, just like on Easter Sunday. Mrs. Balducci asked Mary to please put on a pot of coffee, which she started to do. The whole family seemed to work so well together and to enjoy fussing over company. Everything tasted so good that everyone wanted seconds and we got it too.

After breakfast we all just sat around and talked, well answering questions asked mostly by Joey's Mom. She seemed to want to know everything about everyone there, mostly about Sarah because she already knew a little about me and Heshy. Joey's Mother has a picture of Buster in his Army uniform and she had it blown up into a big picture in a big beautiful frame and it hangs on a living room wall. She also had the same picture printed on a large button which she wears pinned to the front of her blouse, which by the way is all black. The only color she wears now is black. Mary told me that she now makes all of her own clothes by hand. Mary told me that her mother will be in mourning for the rest of her life. How sad and yet so beautiful, I thought to myself.

Joey and his family seemed very pleased that everyone had a good time and Mrs. Balducci seemed to have really perked up since the last time I saw her and that made me feel good. I keep thinking about what Mom told me, about moms never getting over the loss of a child, so I know that even though Mrs. Balducci has perked up a bit on the outside, she's still doing a lot of crying on the inside. It must have been afternoon by the time we left. We spent a little time in the park just talking to friends. Heshy and Sarah were boasting about what a great breakfast we had that morning at Joey's house I think all of the gang we hang with are now looking to have breakfast at the Balduccis. By this time I was getting tired so I went home while Heshy stayed in the park with the gang. Daddy was also in the park talking politics as usual with his friends, so I figured Mom must be by herself. That was another reason for me wanting to go home, to keep Mom   company.

I told Mom all about the nice breakfast at the Balducci's and how well Mrs. Balducci looked. Mom was very glad to hear that. Then I asked Mom about her job and what days and hours she would have to work. She told me that they think they will need her on Thursday, Friday, Saturday and Monday. The hours are not set yet, they're still working that out. Mom told me that Mrs. Bernstein wants to know if I could, after school lets out for the summer baby-sit the kids during the day until she can work something out with a camp or something. Gee, I don't know what to do about that, I did want to spend a lot of time at the beach with my friends this summer but I would love to make some money. I wonder if I said yes I would do it, Mrs. Bernstein would trust me enough to let me take the kids to the beach once in a while. I'm sure the kids would love it, especially if Heshy and Joey were there too. Well we shall see. Good night dear diary.

CHAPTER 5

Thursday, May 17th, 1945

Dear diary, it has been a pretty good week so far for everyone. Joey, as of today, is almost his old self and his mother is talking about going back to work on Monday. Daddy told her that she could take off as long as she needed to, but she feels like she ought to go back to work on Monday. Joey and most of his family think that it would be good for her to get back to her old routine. We all feel the same way. Mom started her job today and she likes it very much. She said that not only do Mrs. Bernstein and her two sisters look a lot alike and sound alike, but they are also very nice, like her. Mom told us she did a little bit of everything in the store today from sweeping the floor to rearranging the dress racks and even selling a few dresses. Because Mom didn't get home until 6pm, I got dinner ready tonight it was easy because Mom had everything prepared last night so all I had to do was heat it up tonight. Like Mom and Daddy said, we just have to make a few adjustments in our schedules and everything will work out okay.

We found out in school today that we not only made up for the days we missed because of the death of FDR but we are even a little bit ahead of where we are supposed to be in our text books. That means that the last two weeks or so of school we will just be doing review work and have little or no homework. That will be great, having just a light schedule near the end of school. My baby sitting on Saturday for Joshua and Sophie will be during the day only but Barbara Moses, a girl who lives across the street from Joey, asked me if I could help her out and take over a baby sitting job for her. The job is in the next apartment building from hers, for a Mrs. Green, who has three kids that are four, six and seven years old. I told her I'd have to think about it and let her know tomorrow. I asked Heshy and Joey if they could help me out by being there with me and of course Heshy asked if he could bring Sarah and of course I said yes. Joey said yes too, so then all I had to do was convince Mom that I would be okay with babysitting all day and night too. I think the only reason Mom said yes was that Heshy, Sarah and Joey are coming too. Now all I have to do is find out if this Mrs. Green wouldn't mind me having friends with me. I probably should've asked her first, but we'll see what she says.

Barbara is one year ahead of me in school and is still in jr.high with me but she seems to me to be older than that. Next year she'll be in high school. I know her to talk to, but she doesn't hang out with my crowd. She runs around with a much faster crowd of older kids and has a bit of a reputation, if you know what I mean. But I always try to remember what Mom told me, about listening to and believing stories about people, so I try to make it a habit to judge people for myself. While I don't know Barbara well, what I do feel about her, from my personal contact with her, not the stories I've heard, is she's a very nice person. At least she's nice to me I mean I never heard her talking bad about anyone in school or in the neighborhood. I know that there are some people in the neighborhood who are not very nice, I could even say they are bad people, but most of the people I've come to know around here I think are very good people and Barbara is one of them. I'll know for sure tomorrow about Saturday night.

I asked Mrs. Bernstein if I take the job of babysitting her kids during the day in the summer, about me taking them to the beach with me once in a while. I told her that because the kids seem to be crazy about Heshy and Joey that I would only take them if the big boys were going to go with us too, plus there would be a whole gang of us there and I'm sure they would all keep a watchful eye on Joshua and Sophie. Mrs. Bernstein said that while she thought it would be okay once in a while, she still had to talk it over with her husband. She said she'd let me know on Saturday morning. I hope I get nothing but okay's for both babysitting jobs. We shall see, good night for now dear diary.

Sunday, May 20th, 1945

Dear diary, let me see, where shall I start? Okay, first things first. Barbara said that it was okay for me to have friends over, but just like at the Bernstein's, no wild party or loud noise to disturb the kids. Second, Mrs. Bernstein on Saturday morning told me that it was okay with her husband, about me taking the kids to the beach once in a while in the summer, as long as I promise to be very careful in watching over them. Of course I promised I would be. Mrs. Bernstein again brought the kids to my house, because she had to meet my Mom and Heshy, so they could ride the subway together to go to work. She got here a little early, so she sat and had a cup of coffee with us. When I told her about me sitting that night for Mrs. Green, she made a face and said that Mrs. Green was not well liked or respected on her block. The talk on the block is that she is either divorced, or maybe was never married and she is always dating a bunch of different guys. She told me to just be careful. When I mentioned that I was just filling in for Barbara, she again made a disapproving face and said that she's another one to watch out for. When I asked her why, all she had time to say before she and Mom and Heshy left, was that she has a very bad reputation. I already knew that about Barbara but I never heard anything about Mrs. Green, one way or another. I just brushed aside what Mrs. Bernstein said, not because I didn't respect her opinions, but because I'll just do what Mom told me about listening to rumors and stories.

Again, like last Saturday, the kids made an adventure out of inspecting every corner of every room in our apartment and seemed to have a great time doing it. Like last week, we again went to the park to play, but this time I went to their house on Friday night to get some of their books, for reading and coloring, plus crayons, in case I needed them. I even had a couple of new reading books that I had gotten out of the library for them. Because Heshy was working and I didn't know if I would see Joey in the park, I thought I better be prepared by bringing the books. It worked out well too, because I didn't see Joey until after I had read to them and had them coloring their books for a while. When the kids saw Joey they went a little wild. Sophie kept handing Joey her book to read to her and Joshua was trying to do the same with his book. Joey took charge right away, by very quietly and calmly telling them that he would read to them, one book at a time. He told Joshua, that because he should let ladies go first, he was going to read Sophie's book first. Joshua looked at Joey for a few seconds and said that Sophie is a little girl, not a lady. Joey laughed and told Joshua that he was right, that Sophie is a little girl, but she is also a little lady and they should always go first. Joshua said okay and pulled back his book and let Sophie go first. I couldn't believe it, I mean I know they are great kids and usually listen to me, but after all they are kids and once in a while in certain situations, like this one, they will act up as to who goes first. Joey was so calm, quiet and assertive, I was impressed. I almost think Joshua thought it was his idea to let Sophie go first. It reminded me of how I got Heshy to not only invite Joey to help me baby-sit that time, but I made Heshy think it was his idea. Like Mom always says, you have to live and learn.

Anyway Joey didn't disappoint the kids or me. He was his usual funny self in acting out the stories in the books. Maybe Joey should think about becoming an actor or a clown or something along those lines. That's why I think Joey is all the way back to his normal self. He was just as funny as he was a few weeks ago, only this time the kids didn't wet their pants, thank goodness. Joey told me that he didn't think he was as funny to the kids this time, because they didn't wet their pants this time. I laughed and told him to stop being so silly, so then he asked me if I wet my pants. When I made believe I was angry at the question he dropped to one knee, bowed his head and yelled out so the whole park could hear him, that he is a "has been". He yelled again that he is only fourteen years old and already a "has been" and pretended to cry hysterically. The kids laughed so hard at his antics that I thought for sure they'd wet their pants and I was right. When I told Joey about it he jumped for joy, started prancing around like a peacock and proclaimed to the world that he's back, he's back. I almost wet my pants laughing so hard but of course I couldn't tell him that. I thank God that my Joey's back.

When the kids were getting a little tired and hungry, we all, Joey too, walked back to my apartment where the kids took a nap on my bed shortly after they had peanut butter and jelly sandwiches for lunch. Joey stayed with me the entire time. When the kids were napping we decided to have the same as the kids had for lunch. While we were eating, I asked Joey if he knew anything about Barbara Moses and Mrs. Green. He looked at me a little surprised and said he thought I didn't like to get involved with rumors and gossip and stuff like that. I said I don't, but if I have to work with people, I'd like to know something about them. So Joey thought for a minute and said okay, he'll tell me what he knows about the two of them.

Barbara, he told me, he knows for a long time and she has had a tough time growing up. He said, "Before the war started back in the late thirties or maybe even 1940 or so, her father was a soldier in the Army and he was killed in a training mission or something like that. Barbara was only about nine or ten years old at the time and she was very close to him. Her mother was so devastated she had a nervous breakdown and in time she committed suicide. Barbara then went to live with her aunt Rebecca, Mrs. Roth, who is not related to Sylvia the "yenta". Mrs., Roth is widowed and lives across the street from me. Barbara had a very tough time adjusting to life without her parents, but she did it. She used to look up to my sister Mary when she was younger and hang around my house a lot. My parents felt sorry for her and made her feel welcome, like she was part of our family and treated her like she was special. I think maybe that helped her get over the rough spots. At that time she was at my house almost every day but when she became friendly with Arlene, she would come over about once a week and most times with Arlene. You know when the word about Buster being killed spread around the neighborhood, Barbara was the first one to come over to offer comfort to my family. Now she comes over to visit my mother two or three times a week, to make sure my mother is alright and to see if she needs anything. I used to think that a few years ago, she had a crush on Buster, but I don't know for sure. You and your family coming over when you did Esther, was wonderful and my family won't forget it.

"Anyway, even though I've heard the worst rumors, and that's all that they are, about her, I still like her a lot. You know that she is about two years older than we are, don't you? She got left back once at the time her mother started to have problems and she never caught up. I don't believe most of those stories and neither should you, even if some of them may be true. Mrs. Green's story is almost the same as Barbara's. The oldest kid is Alan, her seven year old son. Her husband abandoned them when the kid, Alan, was only three. The other two kids are really her niece and nephew, Adrienne, who is six and Michael who is four. Their father was killed in the Pacific with the Marines and their mother was killed in an accident in the defense plant where she was working. Mrs. Green was appointed their legal guardian. She told all of this to my mother on one of the many times she would come to my house to sit and chat with her. In order to be able to take care of all the kids, she has to work at jobs with hours that would allow her to be home as much as possible. I don't know about all those stories, about her dating a bunch of different guys, and I don't care and neither does my mother, or my family for that matter. I hope you realize that there are all kinds of really bad people living in our neighborhood and Barbara and Mrs. Green are not part of that group.

"You know Esther, one of the things that I like about you the most, is that you are just like my mother, in that you almost always see only the good in the people you meet. I hope you never lose that, because I think it's beautiful. Come to think of it, your Mom is the same way, am I right?" I didn't even have to think about it and said yes he was right. I couldn't help thinking that he almost sounds like my Mom, isn't that funny? At that moment the kids awoke from their nap asked for a snack, which I gave them, milk and cookies. Joey had a great idea. He asked me if my family's dinner was already made and I told him yes it was. Then he said how about if he went to the grocery store to buy all that he needed to make and bake an apple pie, and he thought the kids might like to help out too. That ought to keep them occupied for a good while. I agreed and we decided to all go to the grocery store, another adventure for the kids.

When we got back, with the kids helping in the mixing of the flour, kneading of the dough and the peeling of the apples etc. we finally got the pie ready for the oven and put it in. While the pie was still baking, Heshy and Mom came home so I took the kids to their house and Joey came with me. After we dropped the kids off, of course we had to promise to save some pie for them, I asked Joey if he was going home and he said there is no way he was going to leave that pie at my house with Heshy there. He always makes me laugh. By the time we got back to my house the pie was ready to come out of the oven. It smelled so good that I carried it over to where Heshy was sitting with bare feet, and bent over so he could smell the delicious pie that Joey and I had made. I was so proud. In bending over, I tipped the pie so that the juices from the apples and sugar poured out of the pie and right onto Heshy's bare foot, burning him. I felt so bad, but Joey pretended to be mad at me for wasting all the juice. Then he bent down and made believe he was going to lick all the juice off Heshy's foot. Heshy, as much as he was hurting, still managed to laugh at Joey's crazy antics. Mom was in her bedroom changing her clothes and I could hear her laughing from there too. Daddy wasn't home yet, because since he became office manager he is working longer hours and on Saturdays too. Before Joey left, he told me and Heshy that he would see us later at Mrs. Green's house. Well I'm getting tired now so I'll finish telling you about Saturday night, tomorrow. Good night dear diary.

Monday, May 21st, 1945

Dear diary, I have to finish what I was saying about Saturday night before I tell you what happened today. After I burned poor Heshy's toes with the juice from the apple pie and after we ate dinner, I had to rush over to Mrs. Green's house to baby-sit. I was supposed to be there by 7pm but I was ten minutes late. Barbara said it was okay because she didn't have to leave until 7:30 and she just wanted to have a little time to get me and the kids used to each other. She told me that they go to bed at eight. She already had fed them, so that was good. She said that she was going to her Cousin Miriam's birthday party, her Aunt Becky's daughter, who lives in Flatbush. She said that Mr. Balducci was going to take them there in his old jalopy of a car, but it still runs and that's all that counts, and then pick them up at 11pm. Barbara said that her Aunt Becky offered to pay him for the ride, but he refused to even talk about it. Barbara also told me that she's only going because that's all the immediate family she has left. She felt she had to go.

Mrs. Green left for work at 5pm and usually gets home about 1am or sometimes a little later. I asked Barbara what kind of work Mrs. Green did and she said she works at the Del Rio night club in Sheepshead Bay, a very famous and busy place. She's a hat check, cigarette girl and photographer and she says that she makes more money with tips and all, than most of the guys who are working in the defense plants and shipyards, including overtime. She only works Friday and Saturday nights except for once in a while working in the middle of the week to fill in for someone. I told Barbara that because she was here since 5pm I would give her part of the money I make, but she told me to forget about it, because even when she is not babysitting for Mrs. Green, who by the way she calls Arlene, she is always hanging out there because they are very good friends. In fact, she said that they are so close that the kids all call her Aunt Barbara.

Just then Joey came in and gave Barbara a big hello and a hug. Well I should say she gave him the hug but he didn't seem to mind. Maybe I should try that, but not in public, in front of our friends. We'll see. Joey asked Barbara how Arlene has been, because he hasn't seen her in a while. He calls her Arlene too; he really must know her. When I mentioned that, Barbara asked me if I was kidding, because he usually greets her with, "lean mean Arlene Green, the cutest chic I've ever seen, and you know what I mean jelly bean". Well we all laughed at that but Joey looked a little embarrassed. I asked Barbara what Joey called her and she laughed as she said that a couple of years ago, when she was somewhat overweight, he would call her "Bab the flab", but in such a way that she wasn't hurt by it, nor could she get mad at him for it. She looked at me for a second before she left and said that if Joey is a friend of mine, then I must be an alright person. Even though I already knew and felt that way too, it made me feel very good to hear someone else say it.

Joey did a wonderful thing, he brought the book about Babe Ruth that Heshy and I had given him for his birthday, so he could read it to Alan and the kid loved it. Of course the kids all knew Joey, because I found out from Barbara that on some nights when "lean mean Arlene Green" couldn't get a babysitter, she would sometimes bring the kids over to the Balducci's house where they would stay overnight or Mrs. Balducci would go over to her house and either Mary or Joey would stay with her to help out with the kids. I brought along some coloring books that I bought for this occasion, and three kid's books that I got from the library. While Adrienne did some coloring I read a story to Michael and after a while we switched. In the meantime Alan was really into the Babe Ruth book as was Joey. Joey is really something, I mean he can cook, he's funny, good looking, liked by everybody and great with kids. Now if only I can get him to like me in a special way, I'd be the luckiest girl in the world. You know what diary, I guess just having him for a friend, a very special friend like I do now, plus the loving family that I have, makes me the luckiest girl in the world. I guess I'm starting to sound like Mom.

Shortly after the kids went to bed and fell asleep, they're such good kids just like Joshua and Sophie, Heshy and Sarah arrived. I noticed Heshy was walking with a slight limp and mentioned it to him and he said his toes still hurt a little from the apple pie juice burn he got earlier.

I felt bad about that until he laughed and told me it was okay. Joey felt right at home there and went right into the icebox and got some soda for us and then rounded up some snacks like potato chips and cookies from the closet. At 1am Heshy took Sarah home and then came back to sit with me and Joey. Mrs. Green, I don't feel comfortable calling her Arlene, got home at 2am and apologized for being late. She said it was very busy and crowded at the club. She gave Joey a big hello and he introduced us. She really seems like a nice lady. As we were getting ready to leave, she said wait a minute and gave me twelve dollars! Twelve dollars! I couldn't believe it. I started to protest that it was too much, but she told me not to worry about it because she said she made a lot of tip money, plus commissions. Wow, twelve dollars! I still can't believe it. That's the most money I ever made for one night's sitting. Heshy and I walked home, just around the corner and Joey just walked across the street to his house.

As usual Mom stayed up waiting for us to get home. When I once asked her why she waited up, she said she wouldn't be able to sleep anyway, knowing that we were not home yet, and besides, she thought we would welcome the idea that someone was awake to greet us when we got home. Again she's so right. I was too tired to tell Mom all that happened Saturday, so I waited until yesterday afternoon when Heshy was in the park with the boys and Daddy was in the park with his "boys". I knew I'd get to talk to Mom alone then. I'm so tired right now so I'll tell you about our little talk tomorrow. Good night for now dear diary.

Tuesday, May 22nd, 1945

Dear diary, well back to Sunday. I got up late on Sunday morning, about 11:30, and sure enough Heshy and Daddy had already left to go the park to be with their friends and Mom and I were alone. Mom made breakfast for me and while I was eating, I told Mom everything that Joey told me about Barbara and Mrs. Green. Mom just shook her head and said that is just what she was talking about, people spreading rumors and false stories about other people. She said that she would, in a nice way, tell Helen, as she calls Mrs. Bernstein, the truth about Mrs. Green. She said she would have to do it in a way that will not upset Helen. She also said that it didn't surprise her that Barbara and Mrs.

Green are both friendly with Mrs. Balducci, because Mrs. Balducci is so well liked and respected in the neighborhood. Mom also said, what I already knew, that Mrs. Balducci never talks bad about anybody and seems to befriend everyone. I told Mom I still would like to ask Barbara about all that talk of Mrs. Green's many boyfriends who come around at all kinds of hours. Just to satisfy my curiosity. Mom told me to be careful and not to pry too much.

After our talk, I went to the park to join my friends. While I was talking with my friends, I saw Joey walking into the park with Barbara, who had little Michael by the hand. I went right over to meet them and again offered to give her some of the money I got for babysitting her job. She gave me a big smile and said no, it wasn't necessary. I asked Barbara how the birthday party for her cousin was and she said she had a good time because she saw a bunch of distant relatives that she hadn't seen in a long time. She said they all seemed so glad to see her and that made her feel good. To my surprise, Michael remembered me and my name too. I felt good about that. Barbara told me that the kids all told their mother that next to her, Barbara, and Mrs. Balducci, I am their favorite babysitter. That was very nice for me to hear. When I asked Barbara how many other babysitters they ever had, Joey and Barbara at the same time loudly said none, and started laughing. At the sight of the make believe look of hurt on my face, they said they were only kidding and that they had quite a few over the last few years.

I asked Barbara, in a low voice so that little Michael wouldn't hear me, about those ugly stories about all the boyfriends that Mrs. Green is supposed to have. Barbara got a little serious and said that in fact, Arlene has no boyfriends. What she has, Barbara said are some nice guys that she works with, like waiters and others who work at the club, who don't live too far from here and they pitch in and pick her up at the house to take her to work and give her rides home. Most of them are married with kids of their own and respect Arlene for trying to raise three kids by herself, and for working so hard in trying to do it too. Then Barbara added that I shouldn't always listen to all the things people say about other people. I told her I don't, that's why I asked her about Mrs. Green because I really didn't believe any of the stories, but I was just curious about why people would think these things. And now I know why. Then, to my huge surprise, Joey put his arm around me, gave me a little hug and said that he knows that I don't believe or spread rumors. It only lasted for a second but to me it will last for a long time.

When I got home and Daddy and Heshy were in the other room, I told Mom everything that happened that afternoon, including the little hug I got from Joey and the nice words too. She smiled about the Joey hug and gave a knowing shake of the head when I told her about the so called "boyfriends" of Mrs. Green. Yesterday in school, I was still walking on air about the hug I got on Sunday. I saw Barbara and she came over to me, gave me a big smile and a hug and told me that the more she gets to know me, the more she likes me. I told her that the same goes for me, and then we chatted for a few minutes and left to get to our classes. Diary, I don't know, but lately sometimes I feel like I'm blessed. Anyway we still have a lot of schoolwork to do, so we can have a few weeks of just review work before school lets out for the summer.

There is nothing new to write about today, it was the same as Monday except for one little thing. On the way to school today Joey told us that his father bought a cute little doggy for Mrs. Balducci, and she loves it. Tonight, when Joey came over to do his homework with us, Daddy told Joey that he thought he saw his mother walking a little dog on Riverdale Avenue, and asked him if that was true. Joey said yes, it was true and that his father bought it for his mother. Daddy then said that the dog looked so cute and asked what the dog's name was and what kind of dog is it. Joey putting on a much exaggerated serious face said that he was a kosher dog and his name was Porky. Daddy looked at Joey in disbelief and said how could the dog be a kosher dog if his name is Porky. Before Joey could answer him Daddy said "Wait a minute, don't tell me, I know, after you had that pig circumcised you had the dog circumcised!" I thought Joey was going to fall out of his chair, laughing so hard and everyone else was too. Then Joey asked Daddy who is the kibitzer now, and Daddy started to laugh all over again and said to Joey, that he was such a "Joey boy". That's it for now so good night dear diary.

Thursday, May 31st, 1945

Dear diary, I know it's been a little while since I wrote last, but there was really nothing new to write about except for a few little bits of news. Mom told me that she mentioned to Helen, Mrs. Bernstein, about the truth of all those ugly stories about Mrs. Green and Barbara. She said that Helen was surprised by what the truth was and expressed disgust over the way rumors get spread around like it was the truth. In school for the last week or so, Barbara has made it a point to stop and talk to me every day and I not only enjoy it, but I look forward to it now. Today I mentioned to Barbara that I noticed that she and Joey seemed very close and she told me that they are just like brother and sister. I said to myself, oh no, not another brother and sister relationship.

Then I asked her how all these nasty rumors got started about her and Mrs. Green. She told me that because she moved in with her Aunt Becky and had no parents, someone and she didn't know who, started a rumor that she was illegitimate. That was just the beginning she said, because then the stories got uglier, especially since she started to hang out at Arlene's house. Then they started telling stories about Arlene and the three kids. The rumors had the kids being all bastard children with different fathers and that Arlene was sleeping around for money. There's not a single bit of truth in any of the stories, but people still believe and tell the stories anyway. That's why Barbara and Arlene both don't care anymore. I can't believe that people can be so cruel to one another. When I told that to Mom at home later in the day, Mom said all I have to do is look at what went on in Europe with the Nazis. Nobody can figure out how or why that happened either, but it did, so people spreading vicious rumors and hurting people with them didn't surprise her and it shouldn't surprise me either, she told me. I've got so much to learn about this world, but I'm glad I've got Mom and Daddy to guide me. Well like I said before, there is not too much to write about so I'll say good night now dear diary.

Monday, June 4th, 1945

Dear diary, the past weekend has been another fine weekend for me. On Saturday I just had to baby-sit for the Bernsteins during the day. That seems to be the usual thing right now because by the time she gets home from work, Mrs. Bernstein told me, she is too tired to go out. She did ask me if I could sit for her on a Sunday night once in a while, so that she and her husband could go to the movies or something. She said that because we all have to get up early on Monday, that they wouldn't be coming home late, so I said yes I would. Oh yeah, then she told me she was sorry she said what she did, about Mrs. Green and Barbara, because my Mom had told her the truth about them. Now she has changed her opinion of them and that made me feel good.

Saturday night a bunch of us got together, Joey, Heshy and Sarah included, and went to the Premier movie theater on Pitkin Avenue. The feature film was a war movie which I didn't care for but of course the guys seemed to love it. I just don't care to see violence. However they did have a live stage show which I liked a lot, except that it was a little risqué at times. But it was very funny and the dancers were very entertaining. Afterward we all stopped at The Old Brooklyn Malt Shoppe on Saratoga Avenue, a very big and famous ice cream parlor and everybody had their favorite ice cream dish. I had a delicious hot fudge Sundae. Joey, quietly offered to pay for me, but I asked him, with a smile on my face, since when did he pay for his "sister's" ice cream and I paid for it myself. He just looked at me with a half smile, shrugged his shoulders and turned around. I thought to myself, I hope I didn't hurt his feelings or make him mad at me, but on the walk back home he was talking to me in his usual friendly way, or should I say "brotherly" way.

Yesterday was a very nice warm Sunday, so again a bunch of us, just about the same group as Saturday night, decided to go to Prospect Park, to visit the zoo, maybe go row boating on the lake and maybe have a picnic. As usual the girls all went home to make sandwiches enough for the guys too, pack some other goodies like cookies while the guys said they would bring the drinks. So off we went to Prospect Park for the afternoon. I think that was the first time we all went to Prospect Park by ourselves and not as part of a school outing. It made most of us feel a little more grown up well at least it did me. It was great fun I enjoyed it so much, especially seeing all the different and beautiful animals at the zoo. I hated to see them caged up like they were, but I guess that's the only was I'll ever get to see them.

Four of us rented a rowboat, but Joey wasn't one of my group, he went with another group of four on a different boat. That, of course was disappointing to me but he did come close to our boat with his boat and I looked at him and gave him a big smile that he returned. Then his boat came too close to my boat and we, the girls in my boat and his, started screaming because we thought that they were going to ram us. Joey, you know was steering and he did that deliberately, so when we screamed, he and the other boys on both boats, doubled over laughing. Of course after the danger passed, we, the girls started laughing too. On the walk through the park I thought I might get a chance to walk next to Joey but one or another of the guys always seemed to be on both sides of him. And what did they want to talk to him about, baseball and the Babe Ruth book he has. I can't get over it, it's the book that I paid half for and now it's coming between us.

Well anyway Prospect Park is lovely in the spring, with the flowers mostly all in bloom and the little critters scampering all about. I love Nature so much, it's so beautiful. When we left Prospect Park we all went back to our park and decided to go to the kosher deli for hot dogs, fries and sodas and eat in the park for our dinner. It was a very nice day from start to finish, but before it was finished, Joey went to Finklestein's bakery and brought back Danishes for everyone. Heshy asked him how he could afford to do that and Joey said that because it was so late in the day and they wanted to sell as much as they could before closing, he got it all for less than half price. Plus he said, Frances waited on him and he thinks she took a lot off the price too. That made me wonder if Frances still likes him as she did a while back, or if maybe he still likes her. I don't like thinking things like that, it gets me mad, jealous and a little crazy. I'll just have to push it out of my mind.

Today in school a lot of the kids, including myself, were still talking about what a nice time we spent together yesterday. I did feel a little guilty because now that Mom is working on Saturdays, I was going to try to help her on Sundays around the house with getting food prepared, not only for Sunday's dinner, but Monday's as well. And house cleaning too. I told Mom when I got home last night that I was sorry I didn't stay home to help her like I said I would. She just laughed and said it was alright, that I had nothing to be sorry for. She said I was supposed to enjoy myself at this time of my life and she was happy that I had a good time. What a Mom I have, she's the best and I love her so much. Good night dear diary.

Friday, June 8th, 1945

Dear diary, on Wednesday, Barbara asked me in school, if I would be able to baby-sit the Green kids for her on Saturday, because some guy, a junior on the high school football team, asked her to go to the movies with him that night. I told her I'd have to let her know on Thursday, after I checked with Mrs. Bernstein to see if she needed me. Well I checked and she only needs me for Saturday during the day until 6pm, so I'll be babysitting tomorrow night too. I already asked Heshy if he would come by tomorrow night with Sarah and he said he would and he'll also ask Joey to come too. Joey didn't make it to school today because, Heshy told me, he worked in his father's cousin's pizza shop in Queens last night and didn't get home until very late. I hope he's able to come to the Green's when I baby-sit. Because he knows those kids so well and they know him, it makes it easier for me. Of course there are other reasons why I would like him there, but that's a secret. Ha! Ha!

Oh, Barbara said a funny thing in school today about this date of her's. She said she thinks the reason he asked her out is maybe he heard some of those stupid rumors about her. She laughed as she said he is going to be very disappointed if he believes those stories. She said she may be a little bad, but not that bad. I told her I didn't think she was bad at all. She squeezed my hand and thanked me for that and then we went off to our classes. She may be a little fast and worldly but I don't think she's bad.

The war news in the Pacific has been good but a lot of American soldiers are still getting killed and wounded. I feel awful about that. The newspapers are full of pictures of people who were lucky enough to have survived the horrors of the Nazi concentration camps and they look like walking skeletons. It looked so terrible that I asked Mom and Daddy when they came home from work tonight, if they had seen any of this going on before we left Germany. They hadn't, but they said they knew it was coming just from the way the Nazis were acting against the Jews and other people. That's why they are not too shocked by the pictures they are seeing today. A lot of Mom's and Daddy's relatives didn't make it out alive, so I know that they both have heavy hearts about that. It's a wonder to me why they are not bitter people and mad at the world instead of the kind gentle souls that they are. I thank God for that.

Mom and Daddy have often said that they hope and pray for a better and peaceful world for Heshy and me to grow up in, I hope so too. Well the weather is getting nicer and warmer every day and I can't wait to be able to go to the beach so I can wear my new bathing suit and hat and carry my new beach bag. If I'm lucky enough to go to the beach with Joey and the rest of the gang too of course, I think because Joey likes to cook and make lunch, I'll let him make the sandwiches this year. That would be something wouldn't it. He would do it too, I'll bet. Enough for now, good night dear diary.

Monday, June 11th, 1945

Dear diary, I'm getting to be the luckiest girl in the world. I just can't believe that I'm having so many great weekends and weekdays too for that matter, lately. This weekend was another great one. Saturday morning, Mrs. Bernstein brought the kids over again and then went to work with Mom and Heshy, as usual. Again as usual now, the kids went all through our apartment as if they had never seen it before and acted as if they were discovering places for the first time. They are a couple of ham actors, but very lovable. After they had something to eat, we decided to go to the library, because the weather was a little overcast and rainy. It's a good thing that Mrs. Bernstein had brought over an extra stroller for us to keep here so we wouldn't have to carry it back and forth. Joey again worked in his cousin's pizza parlor Friday night and got home late, so I didn't think I'd see him at all during the day on Saturday.

Before going to the library, I did read to the kids a little bit and by the time I left the house it was about 11:30. Just for the heck of it, I walked through the park on the way to the library and to my pleasant surprise I met Joey, who was just walking into the park. He looked very tired and he told me that he worked over twelve hours between Friday afternoon and early, 2am, Saturday morning. I told him where I was heading and he asked if I would mind If he joined me. I decided not to play any hard to get games anymore and told him I'd love it if he joined us. Then I quickly added that the kids really enjoy it when he's around. That isn't lying because they really do.

At the library Joey did something wonderful. He actually got Joshua and Sophie to work together with him and create a story. He even got me involved. I don't know where he learned this little trick from. He said it just came to him while watching Joshua making up a story while pretending he was reading. Joey started the story and then stopped and asked the kids one at a time to think of a word that they thought would fit to finish the sentence. Most of the time they would get silly and say words that didn't really fit but made the sentence and story sound crazy. When they did that, Joey would put on these painful looks on his face and the kids would laugh their heads off. Soon they would only say silly words just to see the look on Joey's face. The funny thing is, when Joey asked me to fill in a word, I found myself saying the silliest words too and the kids laughed even harder. I guess their silliness is catching.

All the while this was going on, I was worried that the librarian would "shush" us again and maybe ask us to leave. It wasn't too long before the kids were getting tired and hungry too, so we left and went back to my house, Joey came too. When I asked Joey how come he didn't want to play ball in the park with his friends, he said there were three or four reasons why he didn't want to. First, he said it's raining on and off and he didn't like to play in those conditions. Second, he said he's tired from all the work he did on Friday. Third, he said he was very hungry and that if I would let him, he would like to make lunch for all of us. I said off course, be my guest. Fourth he said and probably the biggest reason is, at this point diary I thought he was going to say because he likes to be with me or something like that, is because he loves to be around the kids and make them laugh. Now while that is a wonderful reason and I can understand it, I was still a little disappointed.

Before we got to the house, Joey asked me if there were any eggs, milk, while bread, butter and syrup at my house. I told him that we had all of those things because Mom went shopping on Wednesday. I asked him what he was planning on making. He asked me and the kids if we liked French toast and we all said yes. The kids actually said they loved French toast. Joey's French toast was delicious and he said his secret, that he learned from his sister, who learned it in her cooking class in Girls High School, is to cut all the ends off the bread, add just the right amount of milk to the egg mixture and then let the bread soak in it for a few minutes to soak up some of the egg mixture before putting it in the pan. We all wanted seconds, no demanded it is more like it, and we got it too. Soon after lunch, even though the kids were enjoying Joey's company so much, they laid down and took their naps.

While they were napping Joey and I just sat around and talked, about a lot of different things. He told me that now he learning all about making pizza and he likes the idea. I couldn't help thinking to myself that there is no end to Joey's talents. He told me that I look taller than I used to and wanted to know if I grew. I told him that I'm sure I did grow, but I didn't know how much and besides I told him that we are all growing. I told him he looks a little taller too. Then he said something that made me laugh to myself. He said that there was something different about the way I look, but he didn't know what it was. For a split second I wanted to throw my chest out and say I not only grew taller but I got bigger too, but of course I didn't. Throw my chest out that is. Because the kids started their nap later than usual, they didn't get up until almost 4pm. I asked Joey if he could stick around for a little while longer, to keep the kids busy while I got things started for my family's dinner. He said sure and then I asked him if he would like to stay and have dinner with us, but he said no he couldn't. He said he had some things to do, but that he would see me later at "Lean Mean Arlene's" house and he'll have a surprise for us. No matter how many times I asked he wouldn't tell me what the surprise was.

By the time Mom got home at 6pm I had the dinner all prepared, I mean she prepared it all last night and all I had to do really was just to heat most of it up. I finished eating quickly so I wouldn't be late for Barbara and her big date. I got to Mrs. Green's house at 6:30 and Barbara happily greeted me. So did all the kids. I think it's great that they all seem to remember me and like me too. Barbara's date, his name is Ronnie, was coming to pick her up at 7:30, so she was able to stay with me till then. Again I offered her some of the money I'll be getting but she refused to hear of it. At 7pm Heshy and Sarah showed up and right behind them was Joey carrying a big pizza box that held a steaming hot pizza. Everyone oohed and aahed at the sight of the steaming pizza, even the kids. Joey told us that he just made it at his house with the ingredients that he brought home from his cousin's pizza shop, last night. It was a large pie and because most of us had already eaten our dinner and we weren't too hungry. There was enough to go around for everybody to have a taste and it was delicious. I've only eaten pizza a few times, but this was the best that I've ever eaten. Everyone said the same thing, it was the best pizza they ever had.

After Barbara left for her date, I read to the kids. Joey, Heshy and Sarah helped out too, as usual. At 8pm the kids all went to bed without fussing. The four of us sat around and talked the rest of the night about the war, school letting out soon, our jobs and how we all are looking forward to our last year in jr. high school. At 1am Heshy took Sarah home and then came back to sit with me and Joey. Mrs. Green got home at 1:45 and this time she gave me ten dollars which I thought was still very good for babysitting for six or seven hours.

Yesterday, Sunday, I got up late again and I asked Mom why she let me sleep so long, because I wanted to get up early so to help her around the house. Mom told me that she didn't wake me up because I got home so late and, as she put it, I need my beauty sleep. I jokingly said to Mom that she always told me I was beautiful so why do I need any beauty sleep. Mom just looked at me and smiled. Later in the afternoon I went down to the park and Heshy was already there telling everyone about the great pizza that Joey had made the night before. By the time Joey walked into the park everyone was asking when they were going to sample some of his pizza. I looked at Joey in an apologetic way and shrugged my shoulders. He gave me an understanding smile and a wave of his hand, as if to say don't worry about it. That's the way I took it anyway.

I was still a little tired from Saturday so I went home not too long after I saw Joey and tried to help Mom with some of the things that she wanted to get done. Mom saw that I was tired so she just let me help her a little bit and told me to lie down and take a nap before dinner or just sit down and rest. I can never get over what a great Mom I have. I should really say what a great family I have. Good night dear diary.

CHAPTER 6

Friday, June 15th, 1945

Dear diary, on Monday I saw Barbara in school and asked her how her date with Ronnie went on Saturday night. She said that she was right about why he asked her out. He did hear and believe those stupid stories and not only was he disappointed but a little angry as well. She shrugged her shoulders and said there was nothing she could do about it and she didn't care if he was angry. She added that she was sure he'll get over it.

Well all we have left is one more week of school and then we can enjoy the summer, I hope. Enjoy may not be a good word to use yet, with our soldiers and sailors still getting killed and hurt. On the radio and in the newspapers, all the talk is about how much tougher the fighting is getting to be the closer we get to Japan. One story in the newspaper said that the military planners expect that if we have to invade the Japanese home Islands, there will be at least one million casualties, on the Allied side alone. The Japanese losses would be double or triple that at the least, they said. How awful that would be. I hope it never comes to that.

Anyway, all of last week and all of next week in school is just review work so it has been and will be light and easy. Even though we haven't had any homework this past week, Joey, because of habit I guess, still came around to our house a couple of times after school. On Wednesday he came over about 5pm and sat around ant talked baseball with Heshy. Mom had seen an advertisement for a new home permanent hair product and bought it. Because it was new she was afraid to try it on herself and I wouldn't let her try it on me, so we both, at the same time looked at the boys. When Heshy saw what we wanted to do he ran into his room and wouldn't come out, but Joey just laughed and said sure, why not try it on him. He said if he didn't like it he would just have it cut off or shampo it away, it's only hair and it'll grow back.

So with great delight Mom and I went to work giving Joey a perm. He just sat there and didn't complain, except for the very strong and unusual odor it had. We just laughed and went about giving him the perm. Heshy, when he realized we were not after him any more, came out of his room and when he saw Joey with the big towel wrapped around his neck and this strange looking stuff all over his hair, doubled over laughing. Joey kept yelling at him to shut up because it wasn't funny and besides he said he always wanted wavy hair. When we got all finished his hair was only a little wavy but the smell was still there. The next day his hair still smelled from the stuff, but not as bad as the day before. Every time Heshy got close to him he would hold his nose and Joey would give him a slap on the back and the two of them would laugh. In a way they reminded me of Joshua and Sophie with their silly laughing and teasing of each other. Like Mom always says, boys will be boys. Tomorrow I only have to baby-sit for Mrs. Bernstein during the day and I'll have the night off to either rest up or do something with my friends. We shall see, good night dear diary.

Sunday, June 17th, 1945

Dear diary, Even though it rained most of the day today it has still been a very nice weekend for me. Joey is still helping out his cousin at the pizza parlor in Queens and working long hours and getting home late. He only works on Thursday and Friday late afternoons and nights so on Saturdays he gets up late. I guess he needs his beauty sleep too. On Fridays he has to get up early to go to school, well at least one more Friday anyway. If you remember I told you that on the Friday before last, he missed school but that was the only time he did that. This past Friday he came to school on time but did he look tired. At the beginning of every class, before the teacher would start, Joey would put his head on his desk and close his eyes for a few minutes. I felt so sorry for him that I got tired too.

With Mom, Daddy and Heshy working on Saturdays, I have no one to help me with the kids except Joey when he's awake and not tired. Yesterday was the same as last Saturday, except that the weather was much nicer so it was a little easier for me because I was able to take the kids to the park for a little while. As I was knocking myself out pushing the kids on the swings again, Joey showed up. He looked sleepy faced but smiling a big smile. I don't know if he was happy to see me or the kids or maybe it was both. As usual when Joey shows up, the kids were delighted, but they wouldn't let him help me push them on the swings. It wasn't long before he was able to talk them into letting him push them for a while. After he was pushing them for a while they didn't want me back again, because Joey would make believe that he was falling down tired from pushing them and they loved it. I don't know diary, maybe I'm blind or something, but I just can't seem to see a single fault in Joey, like I know all human beings have, so maybe he's not human. I don't know.

Anyway, after the swings we took a fast walk to the library, to get there before they closed. I let the kids pick out some books that they liked and I took them out with my library card. I told the kids that I would read the books to them after we all had lunch. Then Joey said that instead of making lunch for us, he was going to buy lunch for all of us and the kids got all excited about that. We all stopped at the kosher deli and got sandwiches to take out. Joshua wanted a baloney sandwich on white bread and you know that Sophie had to have the same. Joey and I both got corned beef sandwiches on rye, with mustard and a sour pickle. Joey even bought some big chocolate chip cookies, when the kids weren't looking, so he could surprise them when we got to my house. I forgot to mention that the reason we were able to leave my house early this morning was because the kids no longer feel that they have to explore every room in my house.

When we got back, we all ate our sandwiches and then Joey brought out the cookies. The kids, when they saw the size of the cookies, got wide eyed and couldn't wait to get their hands on them. Then I read some of the books that I took out of the library for them. Before you know it, they were ready for their nap, which they took without any fussing. While they were napping, Joey and I just sat and talked, but this time mostly about what we want to do with our lives when we grow older. I said that what I would like to do is to be able to brighten people's lives and becoming a nurse might enable me to do just that. I was telling him about all the different things that nurses do in their work that brings smiles to patient's faces. I had seen this a few times when I went, with my family, visiting my Uncle Carl's wife, my Aunt Ruth, who was sick at the time with acute indigestion. Of course you know Joey had to ask me what was cute about it. I guess if he didn't ask me that I would've thought that he was sick or something. He said that what I want to do is very nice and he hopes my dreams come true. He said as for himself, he also would like to help people make a better life for themselves, like all those people that we've seen in our textbooks, from all over the world who are very poor and in most cases go to bed hungry too. That, he said, is what he would like to do, help those people if he can. He also added that there are plenty of people in this country, who are poor and hungry that need help too, so if he can't get to travel around the world, he could just travel around this country trying to make people happy. Sometimes when he talks, from his heart, with the passion that he has for people, he gives me Goosebumps.

After the kids got up from their nap, Joey stayed around for a little while longer and then left. When Mom got home the kids left with Mrs. Bernstein and I helped Mom get dinner ready. I was a little tired after dinner, so I didn't go out to the park to be with my friends. I stayed home and took it easy by reading the newspaper and finally went to bed early. It was a very nice Saturday, even though I was tired early in the evening. I'll tell you about how today went tomorrow because it's getting late and again I'm tired. Good night dear diary.

Monday, June 18th, 1945

Dear diary, I got up early Sunday morning and helped Mom around the house for a little while. She was making a pot roast for Monday's dinner, her pot roasts are so delicious and I helped her with that. In helping her with cooking I'm learning how to cook myself, so that now I have something else to talk to Joey about, cooking. About noontime Heshy, who had been out with his friends trying to play a little ball in the rain again, came home for lunch and he brought Joey with him. Daddy was also home because most of his friends didn't want to come out in the rain. Mom made kosher franks and beans and invited Joey to stay for lunch and he accepted.

After lunch Heshy and Joey, who had just formed a softball team to play in the park league, were assigning numbered shirts to the different

113

kids to wear. Heshy and Joey both wanted to wear number three because it was Babe Ruth's number. Heshy argued that Joey should wear number five, Joe DiMaggio's number, because they are both Italian. Joey then asked Heshy what his connection was to Babe Ruth that he gets to wear his number. Daddy was sitting nearby taking it all in and I thought the two of us would fall out of our chairs when Heshy said that his Aunt Sherry's daughter, our cousin, is named Ruth and his Uncle Carl's wife's name is Ruth. Joey looked at him in disbelief and then said to Heshy that he's Jewish and Ruth is not. With that Daddy rose out of his chair to say something and Joey looked at him and quickly said, "Wait a minute, don't tell me, before I had the pig and dog circumcised you had Babe Ruth circumcised!" Now we all fell out of our chairs laughing with Daddy pointing a finger at Joey and saying, that's right, that's right. Mom in the kitchen had to run into the bathroom again.

The more I think about it, the more I think that one of the most important reasons why I like to see Joey come around to our house is, because he always seems to make my parents laugh and smile and I love to see them that way. Anyway, the rain stopped for a while and Heshy suggested that he would pick up Sarah and a few of the other kids and we could all go to the movies together. It sounded good to me, but I told him no war movies this time and he said okay and so did Joey. About ten of us went and this time it was a love story with a little bit of action in it and that satisfied the guys. After the movies we again went to the Old Brooklyn Malt Shoppe for ice cream, even though it was close to dinner time, but nobody seemed to care. When I got home, and I was able to get Mom alone, I told her about what a wonderful weekend I had and she seemed so pleased. After dinner I tried on my new bathing suit again, because I'm getting very anxious for the summer break to begin in a few more days. Although Mom and I both thought I looked good in the suit, I still didn't want Heshy or Daddy to see me in it yet. Maybe I'll try it on again tomorrow and let them see it on me, we'll see. Good night dear diary.

Friday, June 22nd, 1945

Dear diary, hooray, hooray, today was the last day of school and the weather is really nice and warm these days and that means that I will be going to the beach with the gang on Sunday. Most of them are going tomorrow, but I can't because I have to baby-sit for the Bernsteins. It seems that every Saturday I'll have to baby-sit for them during the day and once in a while on Saturday night or Sunday night. On this coming Wednesday I start to baby-sit for her during the day. I'll have to do that for the whole summer on Wednesday, Thursday, Friday and of course Saturday. That's not so bad because I'll still have three days a week when I can go to the beach and maybe more if I take the kids sometime.

Mom said that if I wouldn't be embarrassed, she would like to come to the beach with me and my friends on Tuesday. When I looked surprised she quickly added that she would bring a separate blanket and not interfere with us. There is no way that I could say no to Mom, so of course I said yes and that made her happy. Mom told us at dinner tonight, that some woman who she has waited on at the dress shop a few times and who has bought a bunch of stuff from her, told Mom that the reason that she is buying so many clothes, is because she just got divorced from her very abusive, rich husband and is planning on dating again. Mom said the woman told her that her ex-husband was physically abusive to her with regular beatings. She told Mom that before they were married and for a short time after he was the sweetest guy in the world and she never saw the dark side of him.

I asked Mom if there was any way that a girl could tell, before marriage, what kind of husband a guy will be. Mom said she didn't know for sure, but that they used to say, the old folks that is, that you can judge how a man will treat you, by the way he treats his mother. A big smile crossed my face when I said to Mom, "Oh really. just like the way Heshy treats you"? Mom said yes, that's exactly what she means. So then I added, "And like Joey treats his mom"? Trying to look serious but fighting to hold back a smile, Mom said to me, "Be careful young lady". She had never called me young lady before and then she told me just have some fun but don't get too serious, not just with Joey, but with any boy because I'm too young. When I asked Mom how old that most "beautiful girl" in her town in Germany was, when she got serious about that certain boy, she smiled, waved her arm at me as if to shoo me away and told me to be quiet. I just laughed, as did Mom and went into my room. Good night dear diary.

Saturday, June 23rd, 1945

Dear diary, I had another great day today. When I took the kids to the park this morning, all of my friends were gathering, getting ready to go the beach. I was a little disappointed, especially when I saw Joey coming into the park and I figured he was going to go with them. But I felt better when he told me he wasn't going to the beach today, even though it was a most beautiful day, because for one thing he was very tired from working late again last night at the pizza parlor, and for another thing he didn't care if he went or not today, because Heshy was working today and wouldn't be there either. So he said he would rather go to the beach tomorrow, when Heshy would be going too and besides that, on the radio they said that the weather tomorrow will be even better than today. Is he playing with me or what, waiting for tomorrow because of Heshy! I wondered to myself if Heshy did not go tomorrow and I did, would Joey still want to go. I may never find out, not this weekend anyway, because Heshy told me he couldn't wait to go to the beach, but not because of Joey, because he wanted to go with Sarah. I wondered what Joey would've said if I told him that.

Well I didn't tell him, because I don't like to start trouble and have Heshy and Joey mad at each other. Anyway, Joey stayed with me and the kids in the park, until after the whole gang left for the beach and the kids got to play on the swings and things. He said he couldn't stay for lunch with us because he had to do some things for his Mom. He didn't tell me what things and I didn't ask. But before he left he told me that if it was alright with me, he would come over to my house at about 2 or 3 o'clock. Of course I said it was okay. The kids were very disappointed that Joey was leaving us, but not nearly as disappointed as I was. At 2:30 Joey showed up while the kids were still napping and he brought a little surprise for the kids. He bought them each a cute little stuffed animal and some Italian cookies from his cousin's pizza parlor. I asked Joey what the occasion was, I mean it's not their birthday or anything, and he said that while he was at work last night, a nice man who has a toy store right next to the pizza place, gave him a very good price on the two of them. The pizza parlor, he said just got in a shipment of the cookies and Jimmy, his cousin, told him to take some home to his family and he did. He said he thought the kids would like them, so he brought some over for them. Is he some kind of wonderful or what, thinking of the kids like that.

Then surprise of surprises, he stepped out of the apartment for a second and came back in with a large stuffed squirrel and told me it was for me, but that I ought to hide it from the kids so they don't get jealous. I was speechless. Does this mean that he wants me to be his girlfriend, I thought. But when I asked him what the gift was for, he said it was just because he knows that I like nature and all the little animals. He added that he didn't go out looking to buy a gift for me, but when he saw it he just thought I would like it. He also said that he bought his sister Mary a stuffed animal too, a little Tiger. Oh really I said, in a snippy sort of way, "And did you get one for Barbara too"? I said she had told me that the both of them were like brother and sister. He just looked at me shaking his head and told me that while it's true that they were like that for a long time, they really don't hang out much anymore. Then he asked me if I was feeling well, because I'm acting very strange. I told him I was feeling fine, it's just that I was wondering if his gift had a special meaning, but now I see that it doesn't. He just gave me a bewildered look and said nothing. No matter what, I love it and the fact that he is so thoughtful for getting me and the kids gifts and I told him so. He seemed relieved to hear that. Then he asked me, if when the kids go home, I would like to go for a ride with his parents to his Cousins Jimmy's pizza place and maybe Heshy could squeeze in, maybe with Sarah too. To entice me into going, I think, he said that we would probably all get free pizza. I said yes of course, I mean I would've said yes even without the offer of free pizza.

We all managed to fit, including Sarah, into Mr. Balducci's jalopy and in about thirty minutes or so we were at the pizza parlor in Queens. Jimmy, Joey's cousin, welcomed all of us, even though it was very busy in the shop. I guessed maybe it was so busy because it was Saturday night, but Joey, hearing me say that to myself, told me that it is busy there on most nights. Sure enough, we all got to taste free pizza or whatever else we wanted, but because most of us had already eaten, we just had some pizza. It was very good too, but not quite as good, I thought, as the pizza that Joey made for us at Mrs. Green's house. When we left, Jimmy brought out a big pizza in a takeout box and gave it to Mrs. Balducci to take home and I thought that was so sweet. We went home just like the way we went there, Joey sat in the front with his Mom, while his Dad drove and Heshy, Sarah and I sat in the back. I had hoped that I could've been squeezed in next to Joey but there I go again, dreaming. When we got back to our neighborhood, Mr. Balducci dropped Sarah and Heshy off at her house and Heshy said he would walk home later.

Then I was dropped off at my house and as I got out of the car, Mrs. Balducci handed me the box of pizza and told me to take it for my parents. Before I could even tell her how nice I thought it was, she told me not to say anything to Sarah, because she didn't want to hurt her feelings. She went on to say that if she knew and was as close to Sarah's parents as she was to mine, she would've gotten a pizza for them too, even if she had to pay for it. I couldn't thank her enough. My parents were just delighted and after they reheated it and ate some, they really were glad to have gotten it. Mom said that the next day she was going to walk over to their house and thank them personally. I only hope that Joey doesn't think that I'm crazy, the way I acted with him today. I don't think so, but I'll know for sure tomorrow, by the way he acts with me when we all go to the beach. We all have to meet in the park at 10am. I still can't believe it, that I'm going to the beach without my parents and just with my friends. I'm really starting to feel all grown up. Good night dear diary.

Sunday, June 24th, 1945

Dear diary, I just have to tell you a few quick words about my day at the beach in my new bathing suit, hat and my almost matching, new beach bag. First, I must tell you that the weather was even more beautiful than yesterday and Joey, who had been lifting weights with Heshy in gym all school year, really looked great and in shape with his natural Italian tan, in his new yellow bathing suit. All the girls were looking at him and making comments about how nice he looked. I was proud and jealous at the same time. Secondly, I'm not ashamed to tell you, that while I was sunning myself on my beach blanket, two very good looking older guys walked past and one said to the other about me I think, that I looked very hot in my bathing suit. I don't think he was talking about the weather. Ha! Ha! I thought I'd get Joey a little jealous and told him what that guy said about me. Joey said the guy was right, I do look hot and then he added he wasn't talking about the weather. When I first took my clothes off and displayed my new bathing suit to everyone, Joey did tell me that I looked very beautiful. I was so flattered, I thought I was going to faint, but I just said that he was probably saying that because of my bathing suit. He added that the suit looks good too and laughed. Then, in a serious way, he said that the other day when we were talking about he and I getting taller and he said there was something different about the way I looked but he didn't know what it was. Well now he knows.

He said that now, I have the look of a beautiful young lady and not a little kid anymore. He had to add that I still act like a little girl once in a while, but he thought that was a good thing. I couldn't help wonder where he was going with this. Was he trying to tell me something that I've been waiting to hear for a long time, I don't know. I thought I'd put him on the spot, so I asked him if he was flirting with me after all the years we've known each other. Before he could answer me, I said I bet he told all the other girls on the beach the same thing. I could actually see him blush a little under his tanned face and he said no, that while there were a lot of very pretty girls on the beach, I was the only one that he spoke those words to. He then added, that all he was trying to do was tell me how nice I looked and that I should stop trying to read between the lines of everything he says, because there is nothing there. That hurt a little, I mean he wasn't mad or anything, well maybe just a little annoyed. After thinking about it for a few minutes, I guessed that I was asking for that comment from him.

However, the rest of the day at the beach and even on the way home Joey was, as he usually is, very nice to me, so I guess I ought to be happy and thankful for that. You know even though I used lotion and wore my new matching sunhat to keep from getting sunburned, I still managed to get a little bit of a burn as did most of the gang. It was for me a truly wonderful day at the beach or anywhere for that matter. When I got Mom alone, I told her everything that happened today including of course, Joey's comments. She looked at me a little disappointed, and told me that he again has told me everything I   needed to know about the way he feels about me, just by the things he says to me and they are, she thinks, wonderful things that he says. Again she told me to just be patient and be happy knowing that whenever I seem to need him to be around, he's there, that should tell me something. When he said that I should not read between the lines of whatever he says to me, she thinks he is just trying to cover up his true feelings. Mom always seems to make so much sense and sound so smart to me, that I once asked her if she had ever taken psychology in school. She told me that she hadn't, but that she had gone and still goes every day to the school of life and people, and that the advice that she gives me is what she has learned from observing people dealing with other people. See what I mean about Mom being smart. I hope that someday I'll be like her. Being out in the sun and ocean all day has made me very tired so I'll say good night dear diary.

Tuesday, June 26th, 1945

Dear diary, the weather today was not as nice as it has been for the past week or so, a lot of clouds in the sky and the threat of rain, but we all went to the beach anyway, including Mom. I never realized before just how beautiful Mom really is. She looked so good in her bathing suit that a couple of older men started to flirt with her. At first Mom seemed to be glad about the attention she was getting, but then she seemed annoyed and chased them away with words that I couldn't hear. When I asked Mom about it and what she had said to them, she laughed and said it was nothing, but she asked me not to say anything to Daddy because he might get upset and object to her going to the beach without him again. I thought only us kids acted that way. I was thinking about offering Mom some of the advice she always gives me, but I thought it would be better if I said nothing.

Even though Joey wasn't there I had a very nice day. Joey had to work with Sam Siegel, who also works at the Brooklyn Navy Yard, but on his days off he would do roofing repair jobs and sometimes Joey would help him. Joey thought that tomorrow he would be going to the beach and he hoped that I would be able to take Joshua and Sophie. When I told Mom about that she told me not to worry about it because if I didn't mind, she would like to go with us to the beach again and she would ask Helen if it would be alright. After dinner Mom took a walk around the corner to Powell Street to ask Mrs. Bernstein about taking the kids to the beach tomorrow and she said it would be okay. While Mom was on Powell Street she stopped in to say hello to Mrs. Balducci and she said she had a nice visit with her. Every time Mom has a chance to visit with Joey's Mom, she always comes home a little more impressed by her warmth, generosity and spirit. Now I have great expectations about tomorrow with both Joey and Mom going to the beach with me and the rest of the gang. It should be great fun, we shall see. Good night dear diary.

Wednesday, June 27th, 1945

Dear diary, a most wonderful thing happened today. This morning as the whole gang gathered again in the park, at least the ones who aren't working, not only was my Mom there, but Joey showed up with his Mom too. Joey asked us, if we minded if his Mom came too and of course we didn't. In fact my Mom was very happy that Mrs. Balducci would be there to keep her company while she helped mind the kids. To make a long story short, we all had a great time especially the kids. We really didn't have to do any babysitting because Joey spent most of his time with the kids and they loved being around him. He took them to the water's edge and of course I went with them because after all I'm still their babysitter. Being down by the water with Joey was a big thrill for me too, but I also love being around the kids when they're having fun. That's the good part about babysitting, not just the money I make, but the fun I get out of sitting for kids that I have a good time with. I've heard other girls who baby-sit tell stories about kids that they don't like because they say the kids are awful. I thank God I never had that happen to me. I can't believe that little kids can be that bad.

Anyway we all had a great day today and my Mom and Joey's Mom seemed to have a great time with each other and with the kids too. Mrs. Balducci seemed to really like Joshua and Sophie and was doting on them whenever Joey wasn't. The kids seemed to take to her too, just like they took to my Mom. I sensed that they were very happy and felt safe and comfortable with so many nice people watching out for them and playing with them. Joey's Mom loves the beach and the water. She wore a lovely black bathing suit that my Mom had gotten for her at Mrs. Bernstein's store, free of charge. I thought that was very caring and nice of Mrs. Bernstein and her sisters, and so did Joey and his family.

After we got home at about 5:30, I got Joshua and Sophie cleaned up and even fed them because they were hungry. I think the beach and the sun can make you hungry and tired. After the kids were gone and we ate our dinner, I just went to my room and thought about things in general. I think that it's wonderful, that in our neighborhood for instance, for as many people as there are in it, and with as many people around here who don't want to or can't get along with each other, the Balduccis, the Bernsteins, the Greens and so many others are like one big happy family. What a nice way to end a beautiful day, to think a beautiful thought. Good night dear diary.

Tuesday, July 3rd, 1945

Dear diary, the past week has been just as wonderful as it could be. I did the same old things as I did the week before, like babysitting, going to the beach, to the ice cream shop for Sundaes and Joey's cousin's pizza place. Today my Mom and Joey's Mom went to the beach again with Joshua and Sophie and me, Joey and the gang. Again we had a great time. I hope that Mom and Mrs. Balducci make going to the beach with us a regular routine, when the weather is good of course. Our friends all seem to really like Joey's Mom and my Mom. Joey's Mom only works a few days a week now because she says she feels a little tired lately. I hope she is not sick or something. Tomorrow is the Fourth of July and I don't have to baby-sit. The weather is supposed to be great and that means we will all be at the beach along with a million other people. We might stay for the fireworks afterward, I don't know for sure but we'll see. Good night dear diary.

Monday, July 30th, 1945

Dear diary, it has been another good several weeks since I've written. The babysitting has been the same and the weather has been nothing but beach, beach and more beach. Joey has been with us at the beach and the babysitting most of the time, so you know I've been happy. A couple of weeks ago I met Barbara in the park on a Saturday morning while I was minding Joshua and Sophie. She was just out for a walk she said, but I think she may have been looking for Joey because sometimes I think she likes to talk over some problems with him, if for some reason she can't get to talk with his mother or sister. Anyway, she told me about that guy Ronnie. He must have been madder than she thought or maybe he just wanted to impress the rest of the football team, because he told them that he had a wild time with her and did all kinds of terrible things to her. She said she can't wait to talk to Mrs. Balducci about this because whenever she gets angry about stuff like this, Joey's mom always knows the right things to say to her to calm her down. I told her that I hoped that she would be able to brush it all aside. She thanked me and then we just chatted about a bunch of other stuff and then she left. She is such a nice girl, I like her a lot and I feel so sorry for her. Oh well, I hope everything works out for her. I only hope Sylvia the "yenta" doesn't get a hold of this crazy and ugly story because who knows what she would do with it. We shall see.

Oh yeah, the Fourth of July was a very good day because weather was great and I didn't have the kids to watch so I was able to spend more time with Joey. We even walked along the beach for a short distance alone and that was the first time we ever did that. Later I gathered around our blankets with all the girls, while the guys all got together along the water's edge. After a short while Heshy and Joey came walking over to me and told me that there was a contest and that I was voted the girl with the cutest rear end on the beach. I must have turned many shades of red because I could feel my face burning. I was on the verge of tears when Heshy and Joey both put their arms around me and told me that it was supposed to be a compliment and that I shouldn't feel bad. Joey then gently held my face in his cupped hands and said that he wouldn't hurt my feelings for all the money in the world. Heshy then told me that I would be the envy of all the girls in our crowd. After listening to them I not only felt better, but I was a little bit glad that they all picked me, but of course I told them not to tell my parents, especially Daddy. I'm not sure how they would react to something like that. Then Joey told me that he was once voted the cutest rear end at the pizza parlor, but it's all "behind him" now. Heshy and a few others all started laughing.

Sylvia Roth, when she heard about the contest, came over to me and the guys and wanted to know why she didn't win, while sticking her backside out. The guys just ignored her because most of them don't like her. Then everyone came over to congratulate me, the guys and the girls, so I guess I'll just have to accept it and forget about it. I just hope my parents don't find out, because Mom and Daddy were with us not only for the beach but for the fireworks too, which were spectacular. All the days since then have been very good too. It was cloudy and overcast all day today but I still had a good day because Joey was always nearby. He even took the time to play with the kids. Most of the gang, including Heshy, Sarah, Joey and me, went to the movies tonight and then for ice cream again afterward. See what I mean about me having a good day. Well, good night dear diary.

Monday, August 6th, 1945

Dear diary, today all the talk is about the U.S. Air Corp. dropping a bomb, an Atomic bomb, whatever that is, on a Japanese city called Hiroshima and destroying the entire city. They estimate that maybe one hundred thousand people were killed by the blast from the bomb. One bomb! Wow! Oh, how terrible that is, was my first thought but someone said, I don't remember who it was, that it may make the Japanese surrender and that would save millions of lives on both sides. When I thought about it, in that way, I felt better about it although I still think it's terrible for so many people to die like that. We shall see.

Anyway, by now, after going to the beach so often, so far this summer, everybody in our circle of friends has a nice tan body, but Joey who is a little dark skinned to begin with, is now almost black and he looks great. Not just to me, because most of the girls all make nice comments about how good he looks. Again I get mixed emotions when I hear that coming from the other girls. My jealous side is showing again, oh well, that's just me being me again. By the way, Mrs. Bernstein, the other day insisted that because we know each other so well now, that I call her Helen. I felt a little funny at first doing that, but after a while it felt okay, so I don't even think about it anymore.

I don't know why or how it started, but Joshua and Sophie started calling me Aunt Esther and because it sounds so good to me, I didn't object. I was wondering if they would start calling Heshy or Joey "Uncle". They don't, but I thought they would because the guys spend almost as much time with the kids as I do. It makes me wonder why they don't, not that they should, but I just wonder what the kids' thinking is. Oh well, I've got to go now, but I hope because of the news today, that the war will be over in a matter days if not hours, maybe. Good night dear diary.

Tuesday, August 7th, 1945

Dear diary, a wonderful thing happened this morning as we were gathering in the park getting ready to go to the beach. As we were waiting for Joey and his mother to arrive, we saw them walking into the park with Arlene Green, her kids and Barbara. Mrs. Balducci asked Mom, after she introduced her to Mrs. Green, the kids and Barbara, if she minded them all coming with us to the beach. Of course Mom said she didn't mind and in fact she welcomed any friend of Mrs. Balducci. I was so happy we were all going to be together, I think I had an ear to ear smile on my face all the way to the beach.

When we got to the beach we all laid out our blankets real close together and the bonding going on between Mom and Mrs. Green and Barbara too, filled my heart with joy. I mean having most of the people I really like all together and liking each other is a great feeling. If we ever do this again and I'm hoping we will, I hope Mrs. Bernstein is with us too. It was great watching Alan and Adrienne looking after the other kids along with me, Joey and all of the adults. I felt so wonderfully happy today I hope it will last forever. Good night dear diary.

Monday, August 27th, 1945

Dear diary, since I wrote last, a few days after the first atomic bomb was dropped on Hiroshima, a second atomic bomb was dropped on a Japanese city called Nagasaki, with the same terrible results. This time though, a short time later, the Japanese surrendered. Finally the war is over thank God the killing has stopped. I hope for good. All over our neighborhood people were celebrating in the streets and block parties broke out all over the place. It was wonderful to see everybody happy all at the same time, except of course for the Balduccis and all those other families who have lost people in the war. Mom went over to see Mrs. Balducci, just as she did when the war in Europe was over. Mom said she went there to try to comfort Mrs. Balducci but Mom said she was the one who was comforted by Mrs. Balducci. She told Mom that everything is okay because she said she still talks to Buster everyday and just by doing that she feels better. What an amazing woman Mom says she is. I started thinking what an amazing guy Joey is too.

Well anyway the official surrender won't take place until next week sometime, on September 2nd, I think, the day before Labor Day and a few days before school starts. For me it has truly been a great summer, probably the best I ever had. Even though Joey has not asked me to be his girlfriend, or try to kiss me or even hold my hand on the few times that we walked alone, I still feel as close to him as if I were his girlfriend. I'm not complaining, I'm just going to do as Mom has told me so many times, and that is to take whatever he gives me and be patient. Everything, the babysitting and the hanging out in the park and at the beach with Joey and my friends has been so great, that I hope it never ends. But I had to think about going back to school next week, so I already did some shopping for clothes last week. One day with Mom and another day with some of my friends, so I got most of that done. My body may be in school next week but I think my heart and mind will still be at the beach. Oh well, as Mom always told me, I can't live in the past. She's always telling me to remember the past, but move on. I'm not exactly sure what she means by, move on, but I'll try to do it anyway. That doesn't make much sense, does it? Good night dear diary.

Monday, September 10th, 1945

Dear diary, last week was the official Japanese surrender on board an American battle ship and the pictures of it in the newspaper were very dramatic. We also started our last year of jr, high school last week and that is something we are all, my friends and I, looking forward to. The first few days as usual were spent getting used to our new classes and teachers, and preparing for our upcoming homework assignments, as well as covering our books and getting school supplies from the store. Just about all of the same kids from last year, are in all of my classes, including Joey, thank God.

Today we got our first heavy homework and as I hope will be the usual case Joey came over while we were getting ready to eat dinner. We were having kosher franks and beans and Mom invited Joey to have some and he accepted the offer. After we finished eating, while we were doing our homework, Daddy was telling Mom that the son of one of the women that work in the factory has just been discharged from the Army and joined the New York Police Department. Heshy looked up from his text book and asked Joey if he thought he would like to be a policeman. Joey thought for a moment and said maybe, because as a cop he can get to help people, so that might not be a bad idea. Heshy, started to laugh as he asked Joey if he did become a cop, would they call him "the wop cop". Joey holding back a laugh told Heshy that he should have a smile on his face when he says things like that. Heshy said that he was smiling and Joey said, "You call that a smile? It looks more like a gas pain to me!" We all laughed at that and then Joey asked Heshy if he ever became a cop would they call him, "the Jew in blue!" Heshy immediately told Joey that he should be wearing a smile when he says things like that and Joey said he was smiling. Heshy said it looked more like a gas pain to him and Joey quickly shot back, "I know, it must be the franks and beans we just ate!" Now we all howled. See why I love for Joey to be around our house.

I once asked his sister Mary if Joey was funny and made her family laugh like he did mine and she laughed and said, "All the time". He just has a great sense of humor, sort of a gift for making people laugh and feel good, and he seems to enjoy doing that too. While he was still laughing, Daddy again said out loud so we all could hear him, "Oh what a "Joey boy" he is, such a "Joey boy"!" That may not make any sense to a lot of people, but to our family Daddy is paying Joey a big compliment. That's the way my Daddy expresses himself. Well dear diary, the going to the beach is over for this year and now it's back to the old school grind for another year, but I kind of like that too. Good night dear diary.

Tuesday, September 18th, 1945

Dear diary, it has been a very nice week and weekend for me and that seems to be the norm for me lately. Thank goodness for that. Today I got a little bit of a scare when Sylvia Roth asked me, between classes in school, whether or not Joey was my boyfriend, because, she said, she always sees us together. She really took me by surprise, but I was able to answer her right away. I told her that Joey's not my boyfriend and the reason that it seems like we're always together is because Heshy and Joey are best friends and our two families are very close too. She looked disappointed at my answer, but then asked me if I wished that he was my boyfriend. Diary, I don't like to tell untruths, but I had to tell her a lie and said no. She then had to add that I'm one of the few girls in our crowd who doesn't have a boyfriend and was wondering why not. I laughed and pointed a finger at her and asked why she didn't have a boyfriend. She didn't answer me, but said that it was too bad I turned down her cousin Bobby because he and Ruth Brodsky are getting along great. I had to hold back my anger and told her that when the right guy comes along, I'll think about getting a boyfriend. Hey, I told her that we're only fourteen years old, so why the rush about having boyfriends. She kind of smirked and said she still thinks I should've gone to the movies with her cousin Bobby and then walked away. Believe it or not, even though she was very annoying to me today I still think she's a nice person and like her. A lot of our friends don't like the fact that she's such a "yenta". Joey, who likes almost everyone, while he doesn't hate her, is not crazy about her either.

My new babysitting duties are now when ever Helen has to be at the store, usually Wednesday through Saturday, Mrs. Balducci, who only works two days a week at Daddy's factory, will mind them, with a little help from my Mom, on her days off, and I will pick them up at her house after school and watch them until Helen gets home. It's not too bad and I'm able to make a little money to buy clothes for myself and birthday presents for others and stuff like that. I know a lot of girls in school who look, but can't find any kind of job to make some extra money. I guess I'm just a very lucky girl. Well good night dear diary.

Thursday, September 27th, 1945

Dear diary, today, in school, I got the shock of my life. Sarah Gold told me, before the English class started and no one was in the room yet, that Sylvia, "the yenta" Roth, told her a terrible thing this morning. She said that Sylvia wondered out loud to her, why Joey would vote for me as the one with the cutest rear end, on the beach this past July, unless she guessed, Joey had actually seen my bare behind. Sylvia told Sarah that she could understand Heshy voting for me because chances are, being that he is my brother and we live in the same house, he must have seen my rear end a few times, but Joey? I was so mad and hurt by those stupid, hurtful remarks that I started to cry but Sarah told me not to worry because she told Sylvia to go to hell for saying such nasty things like that. Sylvia, she said was speechless and then apologized for thinking and saying those things. She told Sarah that she wouldn't repeat those thoughts to anyone else. I stopped crying but I was still very angry. I can't believe that Sylvia is still thinking about that stupid contest.

I found out later from Heshy that Sylvia had told other people before she told Sarah, about her ugly thoughts and Joey found out about it. Heshy said while he was very mad, me being his sister, he had never, ever seen Joey so mad before. Heshy and Joey went looking for Sylvia and when they found her, they called her every nasty name they could think of. Joey then told her that if she ever again spread rumors, or even said anything bad about him and his family and me and my family she would be very sorry. Heshy said that Sylvia was crying, but he and Joey wouldn't let up yelling at her. Heshy said when he told Joey that he had never ever seen him so mad before, he said he didn't care what was said about him, it was all the talk about me that got him so mad. It took a while, all through gym class before they both calmed down and Joey was his usual easy going self. I think that shows that Joey really does care about me, in some way, anyway.

Joey didn't come over to our house tonight, so as soon as I finished my homework, I went to the park hoping I would see Joey, and I did. When I told him how sorry I was that he had to hear that garbage out of Sylvia's mouth, and about him getting so mad and upset, he walked me away from the rest of the crowd and sat me down on a bench. He looked at me, in deep thought for a minute and told me that I reminded him of his mother, in that I only choose to see the good in most people, even when there is not much there. That's a good thing he told me and hoped that I would always be that way, but sometimes I would have to be very careful around certain people and that Sylvia is one of those people. I started to speak and he put his hand, gently to my mouth to stop me and told me that Sylvia Roth is not only a "yenta" but a trouble maker. He said if I looked at the things she has done, I would know what he was talking about. She starts trouble because she enjoys it. I told him that I think I know what he was talking about and I would be very careful around her from now on. Then he told me the same thing Heshy told me about why he got so mad at her, because of what she said about me and that made my spirits soar. He quickly added that that is exactly the way he would've acted if Sylvia had said those things about his sister Mary. My spirits came down a little bit, but it was nice to hear. I'd love to tell Mom about what happened and what Joey told me about getting mad, even if it was only me that the bad things were said about, but I don't know. I'd love to hear what Mom would say about Joey's behavior. We shall see. Good night dear diary.

Wednesday, October 3rd, 1945

Dear diary, on this past Friday I met Sylvia, I should say I went looking for her, in the schoolyard as we were all gathering around before going into the building, and asked her why she had told everyone those stupid ugly thoughts that she had. She really didn't have an answer for me, other than she was sorry and it wouldn't happen again. Although I was still a little bit mad at her, I heard myself tell her that it was all right, as long as she never does it again. She repeated that she wouldn't and then I added that she shouldn't say things like that not only about me, but about anybody. She just nodded yes and I walked into school with my classmates.

Joey came over tonight to do his homework with us, as usual, and told us that he has a new job. A guy, who is not originally from the neighborhood, just got out of the Army, where he learned how to be a baker, and opened up a doughnut shop right around the corner from Joey's house. Joey will be helping him out after school for a couple of hours everyday and I guess that means he won't be able to hang around with me when I watch Joshua and Sophie. But the big part of his job is that he'll have to deliver a load of doughnuts every morning, on his old beat up bicycle that he hardly ever uses, to a new kind of big grocery store called a "supermarket". They're opening up all over and the one that Joey has to deliver to is about ten or twelve blocks away. He says he has to ride real fast in order to get back in time for school in the morning. I hope he gets back in time to walk with us to school as he always has. We shall see.

While we were doing our school work and talking too, Daddy, who was reading his paper and as usual, listening to us with one ear, heard Joey say that he has to leave a little early so he can clean up his room. Daddy, looking up from his paper asked Joey where his room was, because on the few times that he was at Joey's house, he didn't notice which room was his. Joey told Daddy that as you walk into the living room, his room is the one on the left, just past the living room. Joey explained that he used to share it with his brothers when he was much younger, but the room is all his now. Daddy then asked Joey if it was a big room and did it have a walk in closet. Joey, again put on a very straight face, so I knew something funny was coming, told Daddy that the room was a nice sized room, but it didn't have a walk in closet. He said he had a walk on closet. Daddy looked at Joey and asked what the heck is a walk on closet and Joey said that he throws most of his clothes on the floor and every time he walks into his room he walks on them. While the rest of us were laughing, including Mom from the kitchen, Daddy was mumbling, "He did it to me again! He did it to me again!" Then he told Joey that's the same kind of closet that Heshy has. As Heshy started to protest, Joey told Daddy that that is where he got the idea from and more laughter and more protests from Heshy that fell of deaf ears. I noticed that while my family does laugh a lot when Joey is not around, we're usually laughing about something that Joey, either said or did.

Daddy for the first time tonight, while talking to Mom, referred to Joey as "Yussie", the Yiddish way of saying Joey. I thought that was very nice, a sort of acceptance of Joey into our world. Of course I welcomed Joey into my world a long time ago. Well anyway, Joey starts his new job tomorrow morning and we shall see if I get to see his smiling face waiting for us as usual, on the way to school. I sure hope so. I don't care if he's late for school but I hope he's not late for walking with us to school. I know that doesn't make sense but hey, I'm only a fourteen and a half year old girl who has a huge crush on a guy who I think is a gorgeous person, so what do you expect.

So far, except for that stupid thing with Sylvia Roth, everything else is going the usual great way for me. When I baby-sit the kids I'm always being surprised by how well their brains are growing because they pick up things so fast and they're starting to really figure out little problems by themselves. I find it amazing. School is great too because most of my teachers are very good and of course Heshy and Joey are in all of my classes, so like I have said many times before, I feel like the luckiest girl in the world. Good night dear diary.

CHAPTER 7

Tuesday, October 9th, 1945

Dear diary, ever since I had that talk with Sylvia about spreading rumors about people, we have not really spoken to each other except to say hello and I feel bad about that. She looks so sad these days that I actually feel sorry for her. Most of our friends don't seem to want to talk to her either. You know diary I'm not mad at her anymore, but I have to do what Joey and Mom have told me to do and that is not to get too close to her. That hurts me a little but I just have to be on guard against people trying to take advantage of me in any way that they can, but I still don't like it. I just like being myself and friendly with everybody, that's all.

Well anyway, another week has gone by with my usual great days of school, babysitting, hanging out with my friends and of course Joey. Barbara asked me to fill in for her again, babysitting for the Green kids, on Friday night and I said I would. Because Barbara goes to high school now, I don't get to see her every day like I used to and I miss it. Barbara told me she heard all about the Sylvia Roth incident, wow word really gets around. She told me that she too confronted Sylvia about it. Barbara wouldn't tell me what she told Sylvia, but she said that I wouldn't be having any trouble with that little "yenta", as she put it, anymore. Barbara also told me that the reason she got so mad at Sylvia is because of all the nasty things, that weren't true, that was said about her and Arlene. When I told her that I heard, from my brother, that Joey was madder than he'd ever seen him, about what Sylvia had said, she said she thought it was probably for the same reason as hers.

Speaking of Joey, he had to give up that morning job of delivering the doughnuts to the supermarket, because the baker could never have them ready early enough for Joey to get back in time for school. I think that's great because now I get to see that smiling face the first thing in the morning again. Joey says he now has another job lined up with a couple of guys from the neighborhood, who recently got out of the Army and are starting their own business. If I heard Joey right, I think he said that they will be making cardboard spools for the people that make and sell all kinds of ribbons and things like that. That's going to be an after school and Saturday job, so I guess I won't be getting his help with the kids on Saturday mornings. Oh well, it was a lot of fun while it lasted. I know the kids will miss him almost as much as I will.

On Sunday, after I spent the morning in the park with the gang. I decided to go home for lunch and Heshy, Sarah, Joey and a few others tagged along with me. On the way there Joey asked what we were all going to eat for lunch and I told him I didn't know. He said that we should all go on to my house and that he would join us in a few minutes. He told me not to worry about lunch because he was going to get it. After about ten minutes, Joey showed up with two big grocery bags full of stuff and headed straight into the kitchen. I quickly followed him there and asked him what he was going to make and he said that he just learned, from his mother's friend Mrs. Klein, who lives up the block from him, how to make quick and easy blintzes. That's what he was going to make for all of us. He even invited me and Mom to watch and learn how it's done. When I told Mom, who was in her bedroom getting laundry ready, she eagerly stopped what she was doing and joined me and Sarah in the kitchen with Joey.

Joey took three large loaves of white bread out of the grocery bags and then with a sharp, big knife cut all the ends off the bread. Then he rolled each slice of bread flat with a rolling pin, and put them aside. He told my Mom to save the ends to make bread pudding or use as binding to hold meatballs together. Then he took a big mixing bowl out of the closet and pulled out of the grocery bags two large packages, one of pot cheese and the other of farmer cheese and dumped them into the bowl together. He next poured in two cups of sugar and two eggs and a little salt. He said that if we wanted to, we could put in a little cinnamon for flavor and color, but it wasn't necessary. He mixed everything that was in the bowl and set that aside. He asked me to get him a large deep dish and a pastry brush, which I did. He took the pastry brush, filled a glass with cold water. Then one by one he put some of the cheese filling that he had mixed up, onto the middle of each slice of bread, then brushed a little water on the edges of the bread and folded it over and sealed the edges. When they were all filled and sealed, there must have been close to sixty of them, he took two more eggs and cracked them into the big, deep dish. After he beat them for a minute or two, he added milk to the mixture just as if he was going to make French toast. With all that done, he next put some butter in a big frying pan, dipped the blintzes into the egg mixture and dropped them into the frying pan, again as if he was making French toast. After each step Mom would say in wonder, "Well what do you know. I never knew that!" In the meantime Daddy came home looking for lunch and asked what was going on in the kitchen, as he walked in. When Mom told him that Joey was making blintzes for everyone for lunch, Daddy said, as if in disbelief, "He cooks too? Are they any good?" Mom told him he will taste them when they're all cooked.

While they were getting a nice golden brown, he asked me to set the table and handed me, from out of the grocery bag, a large container of sour cream to put on the table. Before he could cook them all up people were eating the blintzes, almost as fast as he cooked them. Finally, they were all cooked and Joey, I and Mom sat down to eat the great looking lunch. Mom was very impressed with Joey's blintzes even before she ate a bite. When she started eating she was oohing and aahing as were everyone else. Daddy loved them too and kidding around, wondered out loud who was going to do the clean up of the kitchen and the dishes. Joey, without hesitation said everybody will and got a big laugh from all. Heshy, trying to be funny told Joey that someday he was going to make a good housewife. All he got were groans, but Joey quickly told him that the way he was putting down those blintzes, his body would be as big as a house some day. Everybody, except Heshy laughed and Daddy told Heshy that he should stop trying to get the last word on Joey because it can't be done. Everyone, including Heshy, laughed at what Daddy said. Do you see what I mean diary, about all the great days I've been having? I had a great Sunday and blintzes too! Well good night dear diary.

Thursday, October 18th, 1945

Dear diary, everything worked out fine for my fill in babysitting job for Barbara last   Friday night. Joey is not working for his cousin Jimmy at the pizza parlor right now because he was only filling in for someone who was out sick, so he was able to be with me, Heshy and Sarah. Joey did his usual great job with the kids and that made my job a whole lot easier, not that it was hard to begin with. I was a little tired on Saturday morning but I babysat Joshua and Sophie anyway and that was great too. Joey had to work on his new job Saturday but only in the morning, thank God for that. I didn't get down to the park until 11 and a short time later, while the kids, Heshy, Sarah, and I were at the playground area, Joey came walking into the park with Barbara and all the Green kids. Even though Joey was tired, he and Heshy put on a show for all the kids and us too. The kids all seemed to get along playing and sharing with each other and had a great time laughing at the way Joey and Heshy crazily read the kids story books. Barbara, Sarah and I laughed just as hard as the kids did.

At about 1pm, just when the kids and all of us for that matter grew hungry, Joey again marched us to the kosher deli for sandwiches, hot dogs, French fries and sodas, whatever anybody wanted and he even paid for it all. Heshy told Joey that he will never have any money if he keeps on spending it like he does. Joey just looked at Heshy and with a smile on his face told him that he would rather enjoy his life everyday than have a lot of money. Joey then said to Heshy that he should make all the money and he, Joey, would help him spend it. We all laughed, even the older kids who understood what Joey meant and the younger ones who laughed just because the older kids did. We took all the food out and ate it in the park. It's hard for me to find the right words to describe the great time we all had and to think that it had so much to do with Joey being there. After we all ate, Joshua, Sophie and Michael Green were tired and ready for their naps, so I quickly went up to the Bernstein's apartment and brought back some blankets, pillows and their favorite stuffed animals, the ones that Joey bought for them, and they napped on a bench in the park. While they were napping Joey, Heshy and Alan played catch with a rubber ball, a "spaldeen" as the boys call them. Barbara and I sat and talked and read books to Adrienne. It was truly a beautiful day and I'm not talking about the weather which was beautiful too.

Monday night Joey didn't come over to do his homework with us and on Tuesday morning on the way to school, he looked like he was mad about something. When Heshy and I asked him about that, he got us to walk a little slower than the rest of the gang until we were at the back of the pack and no one could hear us talking. He told us that the night before, while he and his family were eating dinner, Barbara came over looking very upset and angry. His mom and sister immediately got up from the table and embraced her and asked what was wrong. Barbara told them about the date she had with that football player, Ronnie and what had happened on the date, about how she had refused to do any funny stuff with him and how he was mad. She said because this Ronnie guy had gone away on vacation with his family shortly after their date, she only found out now that when he came back for football practice in August, he told the whole team that he had his way with her. She said that was bad enough, she could handle that, but as that story spread it got a lot worse. Monday, in high school she found out that the big mouth "yenta", Sylvia Roth is at it again. Now Sylvia is going around telling everybody, although I hadn't heard about it, that Barbara messed around with the entire football team on the same night on the fifty yard line of the football field. Joey said he got so mad when he heard that, he wanted to go out right then and there to look for Sylvia, but his family and Barbara stopped him. Barbara said her immediate reaction was to want to do the same thing as Joey wanted to do and look for her and beat up on her. Joey said, as she said that, while his mother was still hugging and comforting her, Barbara started to cry. Joey guessed that Barbara is not as tough as she thought she was. After listening to his mother and sister, and even his father offering some words of wisdom, Joey and Barbara calmed down and decided, as his mother told them, that Sylvia was not worth getting in trouble over and besides that, there aren't many people who believe her anyway. His mother also added that in a short time the story would go away and people, when they find out the truth, will like the "yenta" even less.

In school, the "yenta", I won't even say her name anymore, tried to make eye contact with me, but when she saw the hard look I had on my face for her, she quickly turned away and stayed away from me, Heshy, Joey and a few others. I never thought I could feel so negative about someone, like I do about her now and I don't feel good about it. I can't repeat the things that Joey said about the "yenta". I've heard a lot of the kids over the years in school, curse and use bad language, but I never, ever heard Joey talk that way in front of me. Oh I know that he can talk that way and does when he's with Heshy and the guys, or when he's playing sports and is arguing about whether a ball was fair or foul or something like that, but he never talked that way in front of me before. I didn't mind because I know he's not going to make a habit of it and also because I understand his anger at the "yenta".

When I told Mom about all that went on, she just shook her head and said, "That poor girl! That poor girl!" She again told me how dangerous rumors and untrue, ugly stories can be. Even though I think Mom would've understood Joey's bad language, I thought it would be better if I didn't mention it. In spite of all the grief from the "yenta", I still have to say that it has been a nice week or so, since I wrote last. I hope the good days will always be with me. We shall see. Good night dear diary.

Friday, October 26th, 1945

Dear diary, I heard some very interesting news tonight from Joey about Barbara. It seems that some of the high school faculty heard those nasty rumors about her and the football team and called in Barbara to question her about it. Naturally she denied everything and then they called in the entire football team, one at a time. When most of the players denied that any of the stories were true, Ronnie admitted that he made up the initial story and was promptly suspended for a few days. Barbara told me the other day that even though a lot of her classmates would whisper things about her behind her back, she did exactly what "Mama B.", as she calls Mrs. Balducci, told her to do and that is to walk with her head held high, because she knows that she did nothing wrong. It is nice to know that there is vindication in this sometimes crazy world. So Mom and Mrs. Balducci were right all along.

Today, in school we were told that we will have a Halloween contest this year and like last year, we can pool our efforts in groups of anywhere from two to ten people. Like last year, Heshy, Sarah, Joey and I, plus a couple of our other classmates, Evelyn Portman and Jonah Hochberg are joining together to work on a theme and costumes for this years contest.

At our first meeting, during the last ten minutes of our homeroom class, we discussed ideas but nothing was decided. We planned on getting together again in the park on Sunday morning at ten. We shall see what happens then. Good night for now dear diary.

Monday, October 29th, 1945

Dear diary, well yesterday in the park, our Halloween team got together and after a crazy round of wild ideas were suggested, we all decided on a very nice project. Because the war is over and everyone knows or has someone in their family who was in the military, we are all going to ask them for some old uniforms so the boys can dress up as soldiers and sailors just home from the war. The girls are going to dress up in some of their mother's clothes and play girlfriends and wives welcoming the boys home. That's what most of us started to do yesterday afternoon. Off course in a way I thought it would be a little sad and tough for Joey because Buster didn't come back, but he said he was alright with it. He said he could probably get some kind of uniform from one of the guys on the block just back from the war and was friends of his brother's. I don't know, I still think it might be tough on his mother seeing Joey dressed up in a military uniform. We shall see.

Oh yeah, today we also found out that the story about Barbara and the football players got back to our school. When the Principal, Mr. Goodman, found out that the "yenta" was the one spreading it around, he called her in to his office. When a bunch of the kids in school heard about it, they were all hoping she would get suspended too, but all she got, we heard afterwards, was a good talking to and a warning not to spread rumors again. You won't believe this diary, but I'm starting to feel sorry for her again, just a little bit. I mean she has so few friends left and a whole bunch of kids are talking about nasty things to get her for Halloween. Someone, I don't know who, left a toy broom on her desk with a note on it that said they hoped she had a nice ride home on it. When the rest of the class saw it they all started to laugh and she started to cry. I sure hope it wasn't Heshy or Joey who did that.

By the end of the school day the "yenta" started getting all sorts of homemade Halloween cards comparing her to a witch and worse than that. It got so bad that she ran crying to the Principal's office and complained to him about it. Of course by that time school had let out so we won't know what, if anything, Mr. Goodman will say about it. Do you see what I mean about me feeling a little sorry for her? I hope that doesn't mean that there is something wrong with me. I just don't like to be mad at anyone. Mom and Joey always tell me that is a good thing, so I guess maybe it is. I'll just have to be careful not to let anyone take advantage of me and hurt my feelings. Good night dear diary.

Wednesday, October 31st, 1945

Dear diary, yesterday Mr. Goodman called the entire 9th grade to the auditorium and told us to stop harassing the "yenta" if we all wanted to graduate next June. She just sat up on the stage with a weird looking smile on her face that made everyone even madder at her. Most of the kids stopped bothering her, but a few continued for a little longer. She didn't complain to Mr.Goodman this time because I heard she was warned not to. I hope that is the end of that nonsense.

Last night was "Cabbage Night" and so many kids were roaming the streets doing all sorts of pranks that it was a little scary for me. They were egging and chalking anything and everything in sight from cars to front doors of houses. In some cases even people got egged and chalked. I thought that was awful. I'm ashamed to tell you that Heshy and Joey did some of that stuff too, but they swore that they didn't do any of the really bad things. I believe them, I guess because I want to. Daddy was mad because some kids did a lot of egging and chalking all over the front of our house. After he came home from work today he expected to be cleaning it up but Heshy and I fooled him, we cleaned it after school so Daddy was pleasantly surprised.

Meanwhile the contest was great again this year, we didn't win but we had a lot of fun doing it. A lot of the judges, students and teachers liked our little skit about the men coming home to their women from the war, but again Gloria Rothenberg won. She dressed up to look like Kate Smith and sang "God Bless America". I mean how could she lose with the war so recently over and everybody still in a patriotic mood. I was right about Mrs. Balducci feeling bad seeing Joey in an Army uniform, but she understood and didn't ask him to not do it. She's a very strong and wonderful person alright, just like Mom says. When Joey hears me or my Mom say these things about his Mom, he always says don't forget his Pop, because, he says he's a great guy too. That is so nice to hear, because many times I hear other kids saying not so nice things about their parents, especially their fathers. I think that's awful, I don't understand it. Maybe it's because I'm so lucky to have such wonderful parents. Well like I always tell you, I'm just a very lucky girl. Good night for now dear diary.

CHAPTER 8

Friday, November 9th, 1945

Dear diary, everything seems to be back to normal these days, with school, babysitting and Joey. The "yenta" doesn't hang around with us, or at the park anymore. Now she has new friends, a bunch of girls and guys who are a year or so older than us and in high school. I'm glad in a way that she has some friends. The homework is on the heavy side, but the good part is that when Joey comes over to do his with me and Heshy, he has to stay a little longer to get it done. It seems, just like Mom always says, there is a good side to everything.

It's a little early, but the talk around my house has already started about Thanksgiving Day. Mom was wondering, out loud, how the holiday was going to affect the Balducci family. I can't imagine Joey talking about his mother making a giant meatball shaped like a turkey this year. Daddy asked if we were to invite them to our house for Thanksgiving, would they come. Mom and Heshy and I thought it was a good idea, so I think Mom is going to go over to their house to visit with Mrs. Balducci and invite them. If nothing else, if they should say no, at least Mom says she'll have a nice visit with her dear friend. In any case I think it's going to be an awkward situation, I mean I don't know how they will feel thankful for anything this year. Even though I always have so many things to be thankful for, it saddens me when I think about them. You know diary I wish we could invite Barbara and her Aunt, the Greens, the Bernsteins and Sarah and her family too. I know we can't because our house isn't big enough, but it would make me especially thankful if we were able to do that.

I've been babysitting a little more for the Green kids lately, because Barbara has been dating a lot more now than she used to. I hope it's not

141

because of her so called reputation. It should be because of her good looks, nice personality and good sense of humor. Arlene Green is such a nice person. I find the more I get to know her, the more I get to like her and she is really great with her kids. I'm getting to be almost as close to them as I am with Joshua and Sophie and that makes me feel good. I truly like to get to know people and get close to them, because it makes me feel as if I have a larger family. On those Saturday nights when I'm not babysitting, I sometimes go with the gang, including Joey most times of course, to the movies and the ice cream parlor. So no matter what I have to do these days, I always seem to be having fun and I love it.

Joey is still working for that company making spools, every afternoon for a couple of hours after school and Saturday mornings, and he looks a little tired some days. He says that his mother, although she won't admit it, is still not feeling well and she will not go to see a doctor. He says it's not the money, because she can go to the medical center that the union she belongs to provides for all their members. It's just a subway ride away in Manhattan, but she still won't go. Joey thinks she's just afraid she might hear bad news and when I mentioned that to Mom, she said that is a very common reason why some people are afraid to go to the doctor. I hope she'll be alright, but I noticed the last time I saw her that she looked tired, even though she only works two days a week now. We shall see. Good night dear diary.

Wednesday, November 21st, 1945

Dear diary, well tomorrow is Thanksgiving Day and along with my Aunt Sherry and her family from the Bronx, my Uncle Carl and his family from Queens and the Balduccis, a few other friends will be coming here too. Just like last Passover Seder night. I told Mom that I didn't know where everybody will sit and that it will be very crowded, but she told me, in her usual calm way not to worry. She said it's just like going to Coney Island on a very hot day in July. She said that no matter how crowded it is there always seems to be room for one more. She calls that "The Coney Island Mentality". She said that just like in every day life, no matter how much you have to do in any given day, there is always room for one more thing to do. I thought about it for a moment and again she was right. That always seems to be the case.

Anyway, Joey told my Mom yesterday, not to worry about dessert, because he said he doesn't have to work after school today and he will bake the apple and pumpkin pies, and make enough to go around for everyone. I thought that was so nice and sweet of him, that I offered to help and he said I could go over to his house after school today, and I did.

We made three apple, two pumpkin and two mince pies and they smelled so good cooking in the oven. This time I'm happy to say, I didn't burn anyone's feet with the juice from the apple pies. In addition to the pies, Mr. Balducci went to the Italian pastry shop and bought a big box of Italian pastries and special holiday breads. We are all going to put on more than a few pounds tomorrow, that's for sure. Joey said that his father is also bringing two gallons of nice wine to go with the dinner and this time it didn't fall off a truck. Do you see what I mean when I say he always makes me laugh? I feel so close to the whole Balducci family that I almost, because I really feel it, called Mrs. Balducci, "Mom", today. When I get close to people like the Baldacci's I feel like they're family to me.

In school today, in art class with Mrs. Shultz, we made Thanksgiving Day decorations. Turkeys, cutouts of Pilgrims, fall flowers and leaves and things like that. Between what Heshy and I made, it'll be enough to make our house look very festive, I think. At least I hope so. Last week in art class, I made a bunch of Thanksgiving Day cards for my family and some of my friends. This time I didn't play any games with Joey's card and signed my name. I just wrote in it, to a very special friend, my "brother", and signed it "your sister Esther". I'm anxious to see his reaction to it. I mean nobody can read anything into it, can they? I hope not. Good night dear diary.

Friday, November 30, 1945

Dear diary, the Thanksgiving dinner was wonderful and a little bit sad, but not too much because Mrs. Balducci wouldn't let it be. Daddy was trying to propose a toast and a prayer of thanks, at the same time, but interrupted himself to express his sorrow and sympathy to the Balduccis for their loss of Buster in the war. He even suggested that they don't have anything to be thankful for this year, but Mrs. Balducci stopped him and said a most remarkable thing. I don't remember what she said word for word, but it was something like this. She said that while it was true, that her heart is broken by the loss of Aneillo, (Buster's real name} she is thankful for a lot of things this year. For one thing, she is thankful she's still able to talk with him and that helps her get through the day. She said she is thankful because she can feel his presence around her all the time and that lifts her spirits and comforts her. She is especially thankful that the war and the killing is over and no more families will have to go through what her family and a lot of others have gone through. Then she said something that made me feel so proud. She said she is always thankful for the love and support of her family and many friends, especially the Abromovitzs. While some of the women, including Mom, were dabbing their eyes, the men all stood up with raised glasses and saluted her with a toast. It took my breath away it was so touching. The meal was fantastic and the dessert was great, especially the pies that I helped make. At the end of the meal all the men had to undo their belts to breathe and some of the women had to do the same with their dresses. I'm sure that most, if not all of the people that were there will be talking about that day for a long time, I know at my house we will.

Now for some horrible news, the "yenta" is back at it again. Now I'm not repeating a rumor or a little gossip, I'm just going to tell you what I saw with my own eyes and know to be true. In the other group of kids that the "yenta" pals out with now, there is a very nice girl named Marilyn. I think she is very nice, even though I don't know her too well, but when I do see her on occasion she's always friendly to me. I got the idea that she is a bit of a follower, just by the way she seems to always do what the other girls in her crowd do. Anyway, this part is what I heard, but you'll see in a minute why I know it to be true. Marilyn and all of her girlfriends were in one of their houses when their parents weren't home and they talked her into taking off all of her clothes, and took her picture, standing there naked. I don't know who, but one of her so called friends gave the negative to a boyfriend to develop and then made a bunch of copies and passed it out to everybody. I know this is true, because I saw the "yenta" not only showing the picture to everyone, but also giving copies to the boys who were interested in having it. I even saw the picture and I thought it was disgusting and mean, for not only the "yenta" but whoever else had anything to do with it. I hope Heshy and Joey don't want to get a copy of that picture, heck I hope they don't even get to see it, but as Mom says, boys will be boys. Another bad part of this story is that Marilyn had this nice, tall, good looking boyfriend and when he saw the picture and saw that a lot of kids also had the picture, he got mad and broke off with her. Now nobody has seen her for a while and the thinking is that she and her family moved far away from Brooklyn. What a shame and the "yenta" had a big part in it I'm sure. I don't think I could ever feel sorry for her again. Good night dear diary.

Friday, December 7th, 1945

Dear diary today is the fourth anniversary of the bombing of Pearl Harbor and everyone is talking about always remembering this day like we do the Alamo. I hope nothing like that ever happens again. The other important thing, for me anyway, is that Heshy asked me after dinner, when we were doing our homework and were alone for a few moments, if I liked Joey. He took me by surprise, but I told him that of course I like Joey, just like a brother, because after all he is like part of our family practically. Heshy said that's not what he meant. He said he was talking about liking Joey as a boyfriend. I was a little shocked, but I figured that it was time to confide in Heshy, but I first had to find out what made him ask me that. He told me that Herb Sackeroff, from Alabama Avenue, on the other side of the bridge over the tracks, asked him in gym today if I was Joey's girlfriend, because he always sees us together. Heshy said Herb was asking because he would like to ask me for a date to go the movies or something. I told Heshy, after I swore him to secrecy, that I've had a big crush on Joey for a long time, but I didn't want him to tell Joey or anyone else about it. I then asked Heshy if he knew if Joey felt the same way about me. He said that Joey would never want to talk about it whenever he would ask him. He added that he thought Joey really liked me a lot, but for some reason he won't admit it. Heshy said he didn't want to get Joey mad at him so he stopped asking him about it.

I told Heshy that we'll have to come up with a good excuse for me not wanting to go out with this Herby guy. We sat there trying to do our homework and at the same time, think of a good reason to turn Herby down. After a while Mom walked into the dining room from the kitchen, where she had been cleaning up after dinner. Daddy looked very tired at the dinner table and I think he went in to take a nap. Anyway, now that Heshy knows my little secret I felt I could now talk about it in front of both of them and I did. I told Mom what had just taken place with me and Heshy and the problem we were having in finding a way to say no to this Herby fella without getting anybody suspicious. Mom thought about it for a few minutes and came up with a beaut of an excuse. She told us to tell not only this boy Herb but also all of our friends that Mom and Daddy are old fashioned, being from Europe, and wont let me date for at least another year or so. She's so smart she's starting to scare me. I still don't know how to get Joey to tell me he likes me, if he likes me as a girlfriend I mean. I think he does, but I still don't know for sure. I'll just have to do as Mom always tells me and be patient.

Speaking of Mom, I asked her today if it would be alright if I got a Christmas present for Mrs. Balducci because she is always so nice to me. Mom thought for a minute and then told me that If I got a gift for her, I'd have to get everyone in their family a gift too. She thought it might be better if we all chipped in and bought a gift that their whole family could use and like. I asked her like what, and she said she didn't know yet but we have time to think about it. She's right again! I don't know why I bother to go to school. I could just stay home and learn from Mom all the really important things I should know about in life. I know I can't do that but it is an interesting thought.

Joey said on the way to school this morning that his mother is still not feeling well and won't go to see a doctor, but he made her promise him that if she didn't feel better by the first of the year, she would let him or his sister make an appointment with her union's medical center in Manhattan. Again, I hope she's alright. She's such a wonderful person, and why shouldn't she be if she's Joey's mother. Good night dear diary.

Friday, December 14th, 1945

Dear diary, Mom's idea of Heshy and I telling Herby and all of our friends that she and Daddy are old fashioned and don't want me to date yet, seemed to work like a charm. At first some of our friends looked surprised but soon accepted it. Some of them even mentioned it to their parents and their parents thought it was a very good idea. Now they're sorry not only that they told their parents, but also that Heshy and I told them. Well, like Heshy says all the time, you can't win them all but we did good. I think Joey is the only one of our friends who was a little suspicious of our story because, on the way home from school the other day, he said he knows Mom and Daddy so well and doesn't think they're that old fashioned. So Heshy and I had to tell Joey that we made up that story just so I wouldn't hurt this Herby guy's feelings. He laughed, shook his head in disbelief and said he was going to have to watch out for the two of us and our scheming ways. We all laughed at that and continued on our way home.

On Livonia Avenue, on the other side of the bridge near Georgia Avenue, there has been for as long as I can remember, a small but very busy and popular variety store called Schlossberg's. It had been closed for a while because they were making it into a very large department store and they had a big grand reopening last week. Joey quit his job with the spool making company because he got a better job that pays more at Schlossberg's. Joey is going to try to get Heshy a job there too. Heshy doesn't work for Helen, yes diary I call her Helen now, anymore because the dress shop is getting so busy, they had to hire a full time stock clerk. Mom and Daddy thought that a very nice gift for Christmas for the Balducci's would be gift certificates for the whole family from Schlossberg's. We all thought it was a great idea, but now we have to decide if we should get one big gift certificate for the whole family or get smaller individual ones for each member of their family. We have to think about it over the weekend and decide by Monday.

Well anyway, I have to baby-sit Joshua and Sophie tomorrow during the day and while Heshy may be around to keep me company, if he's not playing ball or hanging out with his friends, Joey has to work all day Saturdays on his new job at Schlossberg's Department store. I don't look forward to that but I'm sure I'll see him around tomorrow night after work in the park or someplace. I hope I'm right. Good night dear diary.

Wednesday, December 19th, 1945

Dear diary, on this past Sunday Mom, as busy as she is on Sundays preparing meals for the next couple of days, housework and things like that, found, or I should say made the time, to visit Mrs. Balducci.

Guess what? We, my whole family, the Bernsteins, Arlene Green and the kids and Barbara and her Aunt are all invited to the Balducci's this coming Sunday not only to see their Christmas tree but for dinner too. When Mom first told us about it, I wondered to myself out loud, where everyone was going to sit and Mom said that it's going to be a serve yourself kind of dinner. Everything will be laid out on the kitchen table and everyone will just walk up to it and serve themselves, that way there will be room enough to have chairs for everyone to find a seat. Mom said she was asked if we had any folding chairs to bring. The Bernsteins and Arlene and Barbara were asked the same thing and everyone will be bringing their own chairs. I think that's great, everyone pitching in to make a party, sort of. It reminds me of what we kids do sometimes when we have a little party or get together.

Mom also said that while Mrs. Balducci is feeling a little better she agreed to go to see the doctors in Manhattan in January on the 5th I think she said. I found out on Sunday, through Mom, that Joey's mother's first name is Angelina. I never knew that before. I'm not sure but I think Daddy said it means "little Angel". I'll have to ask Joey about that. If Daddy is right about what her name means, it fits her to a tee, because she is wonderfully nice to everyone. Anyway, Mom said that Mrs. Balducci made sure the doctors appointment was on a Saturday so that Joey and Mary, who are both going with her, don't miss any days of school. Is that being thoughtful or what? They, their whole family, always seem to be thinking about each other and looking out for each other. Do you see what I mean, when I say they are such a wonderful group of people? Now don't get me wrong, they have their differences from time to time, but they always work it out and as Daddy likes to say, at the end of the day, they're one big happy family. The more I think about it the more I realize that my family is very much like that too. No wonder we all get along so great.

Anyway, we decided to get the Balduccis separate gift certificates and bring them with us to the dinner at their house on Sunday and put them under their Christmas tree. Now we are trying to decide, mostly Mom and Daddy are trying, what to bring to the dinner with us, for a dinner present on Sunday. I think Daddy will probably visit the Italian pastry shop again, like he usually does and maybe also get them some wine or something like that. We shall see. I can't wait until Sunday gets here, because I love it when the people that I love to be around are together in one place, like one big happy family. I always feel so lucky at times like that. Actually lately I feel lucky all the time. Good night dear diary.

Sunday, December 23rd, 1945

Dear diary, oh what a wonderful, fun filled and happy day I had today. The serve yourself dinner at Joey's house was fantastic. The food was simply the best. I don't know how Mama B, everyone including me calls her that now, does it and neither does Mom. I know she got a lot of help from the rest of her family, but I think they must have been up all night preparing the food. It was so delicious. I think I'll be tasting it forever. Of course, the fact that most of my favorite people in the whole world were all together, I'm sure had a lot to do with me having such a great time. Oh yeah and the seating worked great too. Everyone brought chairs and there was plenty of room for all. Not just me, but everyone seemed to be enjoying themselves and got along with each other nicely. The Bernsteins, the Greens and Barbara and her Aunt Becky all seemed to bond even more so, than those few days we spent at the beach together this past summer. It was so wonderful that I can't seem to be able to stop talking about it. It almost seems like a warm, wonderful dream.

At one point, Joey invited everyone to join his family tomorrow night to go church for Midnight Mass. He said he thought we might all enjoy it. Of course he first asked if it would be alright with them and not conflict with anyone's religious beliefs. Everyone said it would be okay. When Joey first asked us, his mother and father and sister too joined in inviting everyone. They said that even though it will be very crowded, as it usually is on Christmas Eve, there always seems to be room for one more. Mom and I looked at each other and started to laugh. Mom had to explain why we were laughing and about Mom's "Coney Island Mentality". Almost everyone seemed to know what she was talking about and smiled while nodding in agreement. The only problem was what to do with the younger children and it was decided that Mama B, would stay home and watch the younger kids, because she really wasn't up to being in a very crowded church. The younger kids would stay the night at Mama B's house, because Helen and Arlene both agreed, that it would not be a good idea to wake them up and move them to their own homes at 1 or 2 am.

Just like last year, the Christmas tree is beautifully decorated and looks lovely. There were lots of gift wrapped presents under the tree too and Mama B was very upbeat today. She told us while we were eating, that a wonderful thing happened to them yesterday. She said that all the boys from around New Lots Avenue that Buster used to hang out with, came over to visit her and the family and she was thrilled. She said she felt like they were all her sons too. A lot of them just returned from military service and were really heartbroken about her Aneillo, like the whole family was. But she said she felt the joy of family coming together with their presence and that made all of us feel good. Now I have another great day to look forward to tomorrow night. Sometimes, because I have been having one great day after another and feel so lucky, I have to pinch myself to make sure I'm not dreaming. If I am dreaming, it's a great big, warm and wonderful dream. Good night dear diary.

Thursday, December 27th, 1945

Dear diary, the Midnight Mass on Christmas Eve was very beautiful and interesting. Before we left our house to walk over to the Balducci's, we were listening to music on the radio and Bing Crosby was singing "White Christmas". At that moment I just happened to look out the window and saw snow flakes gently falling. It was so beautiful and made me feel as if I was in a Hollywood musical or something. Walking through that light snowfall to Joey's house gave us all a very warm feeling, even though it was kind of cold out. Mr. Balducci, through the taxi company that he works for, arranged to have one of his friends drive half of us in a taxi, to and from the church while he drove the other half in his car. The entire Mass was spoken in either Latin or Italian, which I couldn't understand but it was beautiful anyway. Of course I couldn't even tell the difference between the Italian and the Latin, but Joey at times told me which was which. All of us non Christians were very impressed with it and really enjoyed the experience.

When the older kids found out that the younger kids, Sophie and Michael were going to sleep all night at Mama B's house, they all wanted to sleep there too. Of course at first they were told that they couldn't, but Joey, Mary and Mr. Balducci all said that they had some cots and other things at their house, so that if the kids really wanted to and the parents didn't object, they could stay the night there too. Joey said if he had to, he would give up his bed to one of the kids and he would sleep in the bathtub. When everyone first laughed and then protested, Joey said, with an exaggerated serious look on his face so I knew something funny was coming, that yes he would do it even though he didn't like sleeping in the tub, because every time he does he wakes up feeling drained. He got a few laughs and lots of groans with that one, but I loved it anyway. The parents finally said okay, so now the older kids were happy too.

I can't wait to tell you this. The next morning, Christmas day, I got up early to go to Joey's house to see if I could be of some help with all the kids being there and of course to see Joey too. Here's the beautiful part, when the kids got up they all found presents, beautifully gift wrapped for each of them, under the tree. Not only that, but there were presents for me and my family too. I never saw the kids so happy and surprised like they were that morning. Alan and Joshua got new baseball gloves, Adrienne and Sophie got beautiful dolls and little Michael got a little toy train set. Joey said that he and Mary must have spent ten minutes wrapping each present and the kids took ten seconds to tear the beautiful paper off. But he said he and Mary did the same thing when they were their ages. Anyway, I got a lovely makeup kit in a beautiful carrying case. Heshy and my parents weren't there yet to open their presents but Joey told me and showed me what they were getting. Joey, through his cousin Jimmy, who knows a guy who collects baseball things, got Heshy an autographed picture of Babe Ruth posing with some other Yankees and their bats. Joey said that he and Heshy didn't care about the other Yankees, because they are both Brooklyn Dodger fans, but they like and admire "The Babe", as he is called. Because of his cousin Jimmy, he didn't have to pay too much for it. Mr. Balducci has a steady rider in his cab, who deals in what he calls "Biblical Art" and got my parents a big, beautiful painting of Moses coming down the mountain with a large stone tablet in each arm and the Ten Commandments written on them. I know Heshy and my parents are going to love their presents.

Everyone who was at the Midnight Mass got an invitation to come to Mama B's for breakfast, if they felt like getting up early on Christmas morning and by about 10am everyone was there. I got there tired but early, about 8am, so I was able to help not only with the kids who were wild over their gifts but also with the making of breakfast. I was glad to see that Joey and Mary didn't let Mama B do any of the cooking and were treating her as if she were a Queen or something. Once more I enjoyed the thrill of cooking with Joey. Joey made something special for the kids that they loved so much. Some of us big kids asked for the same thing too. He made jelly omelets. He made it just as if he were making a cheese omelet only instead of cheese he used jelly for the filling. You know we were all asking for seconds and got it too.

I didn't know this until my Mom got there, that Mama B had a special present for her. She had asked Mary to look for and buy a big, lovely Italian cook book for my Mom and my Mom loved it. All of the Balduccis liked their gift certificates from Schlossberg's Department store. The beautiful thing about the whole morning was that everyone felt so comfortable and at home with the Balduccis and that to me, made their whole house seem filled with love. I feel so good about the kids all having a warm loving place to go to, besides their own homes and my house too, of course.

Today Heshy and I went with Joey to Schlossberg's, to see what he would buy with his gift certificate. We shopped around for a good while until he finally decided to buy himself a nice dress shirt and because he works there part time, he got a little discount off the price. I thought that was great. Of course Heshy will get a discount too on anything he buys there. The shirt cost less than the certificate amount so Joey took the difference back in cash, which wasn't much, a dollar and change I think. On the way home we went to the soda shop and Joey used the money he got back from his present to buy the three of us sodas. Is he something or what?

Oh, I almost forgot to tell you something incredible that I found out today. While we were in Schlossberg's, I saw Mrs. Schultz talking to someone on the phone, in the telephone booth in the front of the store. Here's the funny part, she was speaking in Yiddish! I couldn't believe it, so I waited outside the booth while Heshy and Joey went shopping. When Mrs. Schultz came out of the booth I said hello to her and asked her if she was Jewish. She looked around to make sure nobody could hear her, and then whispered to me that yes, she was. She explained that in the mid thirties, it was getting dangerous for Jews in Germany, so her family moved to a small town in another part of the country and pretended not to be Jewish. She said that because there were so many Nazi spies every where, even in this country, and she still had family living in Germany, she had to keep pretending. She said she is still not sure about what's going on in Germany today so she asked me to please not tell anyone until her family really feels safe. Of course I said I wouldn't and I didn't say a word about it to Joey or Heshy. To think that somebody started that stupid rumor about her being a Nazi.

When I got home you know I had to tell Mom about it, because if anyone can keep a secret, she can. Mom said she heard about some Jewish families doing things like that to survive, but it was a very tough thing to do, because Germans are very good record keepers and it was very hard to change your background. A lot of those families were caught and were never heard from again, she said she was told. Then of course she told me again about listening to stupid, untrue stories that people make up. But of course, she said in this case it probably worked in Mrs. Schultz's favor, because if there were some Nazis spying on her and they heard those rumors, they would think that for sure she and her family weren't Jewish. I thought to myself that is very interesting. Then I told Mom that maybe that is why she didn't seem too upset, when those rumors were being spread around. Mom said maybe I was right and then added that maybe she was the one who started those rumors in the first place. Wow! I never thought of that. Boy, if she did, she is one smart lady and a nice lady too.

Well, anyway Heshy and I told Joey what a great couple of days we all spent with him and his family. He told us that his family is still talking about the wonderful time that they all had with us being there. You know I forgot to mention that Sarah also went to the Midnight Mass and came over for breakfast on Christmas morning. Mary did a very beautiful, unselfish thing that morning. When she found out that Sarah was going to be there too, she quickly took one of the nice things she had gotten for Christmas, a lovely scarf that Joey had given her and quickly gift wrapped it for Sarah and put it under the tree. Joey just looked at her and gave her a loving smile that to me told her that he understood and that it was alright. I find it so hard to believe that someone would do something so wonderful and caring like that, but then again she is Joey's sister. Do you know they even had gifts for Helen and Arlene and Barbara and her Aunt Becky too? Thank God for people like the Balduccis.

I found out today that Sarah is having a New Year's Eve party again at her house and this time Joey said he will come, but he probably won't stay until midnight. I don't care as long as I get to see him, even if it's only for a little while. Wouldn't it be something if he wears his new shirt and tells everybody that my family bought it for him as a Christmas gift? I bet he'll look great in it too. I'll have to ask Mom and Daddy if it's okay if I use my new makeup kit that the Balduccis gave me, when I go to Sarah's New Year's Eve party. Mom did ask me a while ago not to wear makeup or use perfume until I was at least fifteen. I only have about five months to go. I wonder if that's close enough? If they say yes, and I'm pretty sure they will, and he wears the new shirt, then we will be wearing each others gifts. I'd love that. Now I can't wait to see what happens. Oh well, we shall see, we shall see. Good night dear diary.

Saturday, December 29th, 1945

Dear diary, it has been a great holiday season so far and there's more to come. I forgot to tell you about the nice presents I got from my parents and Heshy for Chanukah. Mom and Daddy bought me a new warm winter jacket, probably Daddy got it free from work, but I don't care about that and Heshy got me a years subscription to a movie magazine called Stars. It promises to "dish the dirt on who's who and what's what" in Hollywood. Most of the girls my age in school read it and talk about it a lot and it's a nice gift, but I think I would have liked a magazine about Nature or something like that. Of course I'll never tell Heshy that because I wouldn't want to hurt his feelings, after all I'm sure he meant well and thought I'd really like it. I mean I do, but I just don't like to hear or read about a bunch of gossip, especially since I heard all those nasty stories that the "yenta" told about me and some of the people that I like so much.

Anyway, today was a good day for me babysitting Joshua and Sophie, even though Heshy and Joey both had to work at Schlossberg's, as they have most of this past week and couldn't be with me in the morning, but they did show up around 1pm. In the morning I was nicely surprised when Barbara came into the park with all of Arlene's kids and we all had a good time. The kids were so happy to see each other again and you know how happy that makes me. Barbara and I enjoyed each other's company as we always do and so the morning went by fast. By the time Heshy and Joey showed up we were just finishing eating our lunch which we bought from the Deli. The kids, all the kids, were so thrilled to see Joey and Heshy, they were jumping up and down and yelling and cheering at the same time. Joey was so funny he made believe that he was mad because we didn't have any lunch for him or Heshy. He did it in such an animated way, with his arms flailing about with a big brown paper bag that he held in his left hand and yelling that he was so hungry after working so hard all morning, that he could eat a skunk. We all had to laugh and again I was hoping that the kids didn't wet their pants. Thank God they didn't.

Then Joey said that he was only kidding, that he and Heshy had already had their lunch and then he gave the kids a big surprise by opening the big brown paper bag he was holding and pulled out giant chocolate chip cookies. He had one for every one of the kids plus enough for us big kids too. When I asked him how he knew enough to get cookies for everyone, he told me that he had seen Barbara on the way to work this morning and she told him that she had to watch the kids this morning, because Arlene worked very late last night and was tired. He added that she told him she knew that I liked to take Joshua and Sophie to the park on Saturday mornings, when the weather was nice and she thought she would bring Arlene's kids there too.

Well as usual Heshy and Joey put on one of there crazy shows for the kids and this time it was about a baseball game that they made up as they went along. Joey made believe he was a pitcher, pitching an imaginary ball at Heshy who was swinging an imaginary bat. What none of us knew was that Joey had a "spaldeen" in his jacket pocket and when Heshy took an imaginary swing with his imaginary bat at an imaginary ball, he made a cracking sound with his mouth, like a bat hitting a ball and Joey reeled and bent over as if he was hit in the face by the ball. As he had his back to us, he took the real ball out of his pocket and put it in his mouth and then turned around quickly for all of us to see. Then he started making these funny noises like he was trying to speak and breathe but couldn't because of the ball in his mouth and he couldn't get it out. He was getting frantic about it too. Well this time I'm sorry to say the kids did wet their pants, the younger ones that is, they laughed as hard as we all did. Then Joey threw his imaginary ball and Heshy pretended he was hit in the groin and fell to the ground, making believe he was in pain and when he got up he made believe he couldn't walk. All the while Joey is jumping up and down yelling that there goes his no hitter. Barbara and I had to run to the ladies room before we had an accident, because we were laughing so hard. The older kids had to do the same.

Although the weather for this time of year has been very nice, it still is a little on the cool side. After I took Sophie home to change her wet pants and Barbara did the same with Michael, we all went to the soda shop for nice hot chocolates for everyone. The kids really liked that. Whenever any of the kids started to get to excited or unruly, Joey would just talk to them in a very firm but nice way and they would listen to him. I think they are all crazy about him and Heshy too. I know that I am, but you already know that. Ha! Ha! Because of Heshy and Joey being there, the afternoon went by very fast and it was now way past the kids nap time so we all left to go to my house for the kids to take their naps. When we got there, only Sophie and Michael napped as the older kids are getting to be a little past napping, I think. Anyway, they didn't want to nap but I sure felt like I could use one. So I laid down just to close my eyes for a little bit and asked Heshy, Joey and Barbara to just watch the kids for me for a few minutes and to wake me in a little while if I dozed off.

The next thing I knew Mom was waking me up and telling me it was time for dinner. I couldn't believe it. I must've slept for two hours because now it was a little past 6:30, but I felt very refreshed and wide awake and that felt good. All the kids and Joey and Barbara were gone and it was very quiet in the house except for Mom moving around setting the dinner on the table. I apologized to Mom for not getting the dinner ready and she told me that Heshy, Joey and Barbara all pitched in and got it ready. She told me that they all just left about ten minutes before she woke me up. After dinner Heshy and I went to the soda shop to meet our gang of friends, it was getting a bit too cold now to be hanging out in the park, although my new winter jacket keeps me nice and warm wherever I go. We decided to go to the movies on Pitkin Avenue again and see a movie and a live stage show. We had a good time at the movies and then we again went to the ice cream parlor. It seems to be a nice habit that we're getting into. I know that I like it very much and I think most of the other kids like it too. Well I can't wait for Monday night, New Year's Eve to get here so I can see Joey at Sarah's party. Good night dear diary.

Monday, December 31st, 1945

Dear diary, even though it's late and I'm tired I have to tell you about what happened tonight, while it's fresh in my mind. It seems as if the surprises and good times never end for me. Joey came over to our house earlier in the evening and asked us if we would all like to ring in the New Year at his house by coming over at about 10 or 11pm. When I asked Joey about Sarah's party he said that he was going there too but he was going to leave about 11pm. He then asked me and Heshy if we would leave with him because he and Mary thought it would be good for Mama B. to have people around her at this time of year. I said I would leave with him but Heshy said he would have to talk it over with Sarah first, because after all it's her party and she couldn't leave her own party, could she? Joey then asked Heshy if he was sure he wasn't married yet. Mom and Daddy laughed the loudest and so did I but Heshy just smiled and groaned at the same time. My parents, after talking it over for a second or two said yes, of course they would come over. Joey then told them not to worry about bringing anything over because they already had everything they needed for this little get together. What a beautiful turn of events I thought to myself, another gathering at Joey's house.

Sarah's party was just like last year's except the "yenta" and her cousin Bobby weren't there and my Joey was. What a lovely change. There must have been about twenty or so kids at the party and of course I knew them all. It was almost like the way we gather in the school yard before entering the school in the mornings, except that now we had drinks and snacks and no teachers to worry about. Sarah was sorry to see us leave early but she said she understood about Mama B and even told Heshy that if he wanted to go too, she wouldn't be mad at him and it would be okay. Poor Heshy couldn't make up his mind, because he said he wanted to be with Sarah at the stroke of midnight to kiss her and welcome in the New Year and at the same time it would be nice to be with family too. I suggested to him that he stay with Sarah until after midnight and then he could come over to the Balducci's. He brightened up with that idea and said that's exactly what he would do.

Joey and I left Sarah's party at 11pm and walked alone together to his house. Did I love that or what? I was thinking to myself that maybe tonight I might get a kiss or maybe a little hug from Joey for the New Year. Actually I was praying that I would. Mom and Daddy were already there and everyone greeted us warmly. It feels so nice to be welcomed like family. Everyone was sitting around talking and enjoying drinks and food that the Balduccis prepared for the get together. At about 11:30 Mary turned the radio on to listen for the official stroke of midnight. In addition to my parents and me, Helen was there but not her husband who was too tired to go out, so he stayed home and watched the kids. Arlene had to work tonight, Barbara said it's one of her busiest nights and she makes the most money, on tips and commissions, tonight. Barbara was there with the kids, who are staying over and Aunt Becky was there too. It was just a nice small group of close friends, who seem to me to be getting closer every day, getting together and enjoying each other's company.

At midnight everyone was hugging and kissing each other, but all Joey would do with me is put his arm around me and give me a tight squeeze, wish me a Happy New Year and walk over to Mary and the rest of the people there and do the same thing. It was very nice I suppose, but I didn't get anything special because he did the same thing to everyone else as he did with me. Oh well, I'll have to do as Mom always tells me and as I've said before, be patient, just be patient. Sure enough when I mentioned it to Mom after we got home and were alone for a few moments, that's exactly what she told me to do, be patient. If I were Joey, I probably would've told Mom that if I had any more patients I'd be a doctor. I think Joey is rubbing off on me.

At about 12:20 or 12:30 Heshy arrived with Sarah and everyone was surprised to see Sarah. Mom asked Sarah why she left her party so early and she said that most of them had to be home by 1am and no later, so it didn't make much difference if they left at 12:20 or so. When she took off her coat we could all see that she was wearing the beautiful scarf that Mary had given her and it really looked good on her. When I mentioned that to Joey, he whispered in my ear that yes it looks very nice on her, but it would've looked nicer on Mary. Later, when I told Mary what Joey said, she laughed and took me to her room, where Michael and Adrienne were sleeping, and showed me a gorgeous looking sweater that Joey went out to buy for her, when he saw what she had done with his first present for her. Diary, I don't think I like Joey anymore, no, now I think I love him like crazy. How can that be, I'm only fourteen and a half years old. I'm too young to be in love with any guy. But wow! What a guy this guy is! At about 1am Helen had to leave. Joey and his father, because of the late hour, walked her home. Do you see what I mean about the Balduccis and the way they treat people. Wow again!

Well it's 1946 now and I'll be going back to school in a couple of days and back to the old routines. At the Balducci's tonight a lot of the talk was about how everyone is now on a list to get telephones in their homes, so I'm looking forward to that, I think. I guess it'll be nice to be able to talk to my friends on the phone and not have to leave the house, especially in the winter and on cold days and nights. Of course I think it's nicer to be able to talk to people face to face, but we shall see. Now I'm getting too tired so I have to say good night dear diary

CHAPTER 9

Monday, January 7th, 1946

Dear diary, well it was back to school on Wednesday, after our Christmas break. Although it was a ten day break, it seemed much shorter. I guess it's just like Arlene says, when you're having fun time flies. That's a whole lot better than if I didn't enjoy myself the entire break. Most of the kids in school on Wednesday were talking about all the things they did over the Holidays and all the stuff they got for presents. Me, I didn't say too much, but I believe I had the best time and got the best gift of them all. In addition to the warm jacket, make up kit and other things, I got the gift of a warm, loving and expanding family and I think that's the best present of them all. It's amazing and wonderful to me that Helen, Arlene, Barbara and her Aunt Becky and Mama B all, not just find the time, but make the time to look out for and watch each other's kids. Of course Joey, Heshy and I do our part too and that makes me feel proud.

Well on Saturday, the 5th, Joey and Mary went with Mama B to visit the union doctors in Manhattan and it was discovered that Mama B has diabetes. Now she has to have Insulin shots regularly. Mary didn't think that she could give them to her mother, so Joey volunteered to do it. He has to practice by injecting the needle into orange peel. That's right orange peel, because the texture is very much like human skin. He was taught at the medical center how to draw the Insulin from the bottle into the syringe and how to do the injection itself. But the first thing in the morning, after she wakes up, Mama B has to give Joey a urine sample for him to test. Joey has to insert a specially treated paper strip into the urine and if the strip turns a certain color, then he has to give her the Insulin. If it doesn't turn to that color then she doesn't get

160

the Insulin. Now if she does need the Insulin, then Joey has to get her breakfast and make sure she eats it. If she gets Insulin and doesn't eat, she could fall into what they call "Insulin shock." That doesn't sound good to me at all, so I hope she always eats her breakfast and never goes into any kind of shock. I think she has had enough shock in her life already, don't you diary?

I guess all of this means that on some mornings I won't be seeing Joey's smiling face on the way to school. In fact, he may even be a little late for class. He told me that on many nights Mama B doesn't sleep well, so he doesn't like to wake her up if she didn't get much sleep. He waits around for a little while until she wakes up by herself and if it means he's a little late for school, he didn't care. He said he feels that his mother comes first. Of course Mama B doesn't like him doing that, because she doesn't want him to miss any part of school. She asked Joey to tell his teachers what he's doing for her, so that he won't get into any kind of trouble. Mary of course helps out when she can, so no matter what, Mama B is getting plenty of loving care and attention. Of course the extended family is there for her too, like my Mom, Helen, Arlene, Barbara and Aunt Becky and a few others on their block. In this sometimes crazy world, this seems almost too good to be true but it is true, thank God. I may miss seeing Joey's face first thing in the morning sometimes, but I also feel so good knowing what he's doing for his mother. Good night dear diary.

Wednesday, January 16th, 1946

Dear diary, this past week has been good for me, because except for one morning, I saw Joey's smiling face every day on the way to school. On the one day when he wasn't able to walk with us to school, he was only a few minutes behind us and caught up with us in the school yard, so that was a good morning too. Everyone was asking Joey about how it felt to be giving injections to someone and all the other things that he has to do for Mama B. He was being treated like he was some kind of hero or something, which in a way I guess he is. I mean, I've felt for a long time now that he was my hero, but I think you know that, don't you diary?

All the talk, or I should say gossip, in school since we came back from the holiday break, is that no one has seen the "yenta", I have to say her name again, Sylvia Roth, since the last day of school before the break. All kinds of rumors are being spread around about her that I wouldn't repeat to anyone else except you dear diary. The story that's being told the most is that one of the football players that got in trouble over the untrue stories that she was spreading last year, got her in trouble, if you know what I mean and her family sent her away to live with relatives until the baby is born, some where in Canada or out in the mid west or some place like that. My first reaction to that story was, that poor girl, what she must be going through. I couldn't believe I was feeling sorry for her again, but I was. I don't know why, when I know all the trouble she's started for people, including me. I guess that's just the way I am. Joey and Heshy both said that if the stories about her are true, she's just getting what she deserves, but I don't know about that. If I tell them that I'm feeling sorry for her again, I'm sure they will be unhappy and disappointed with me, so I'll just have to pretend to agree with them.

When Mom went over to help Mama B mind the kids yesterday and today, Mom said that since Mama B has been getting the Insulin shots, she feels and looks better too. That's great to hear and it means that Joey is doing a good job of taking care of his mother. So far the arrangement for watching all the kids is working out just fine. I'll be going over there tomorrow and Friday right from school to help out too. Between me, Joey, Barbara, Arlene and sometimes Heshy too, Mama B doesn't have to work too hard. Of course these kids are really not too much trouble to watch, but they are kids and like Mom always says about boys being boys, I have to say that kids will be kids no matter how good they are. I think the most important thing about this arrangement is that the kids are so happy with it and really love not only being in Mama B's house with her, but also each other's company. I noticed that Alan, Adrienne and even Joshua watch over Michael and Sophie just as if they were all brothers and sisters. It's just so wonderful to see and I hope they will always be this way with each other when they get older. They seem like such happy kids together and I believe, as Mom once told me, that usually happy kids grow up to be happy adults. And happy adults I think will not only make a better world but also will raise happy kids themselves. Maybe that could spread around the world like a virus or something. Wouldn't that be great, but there I go dreaming again. I wonder what I would be like if I weren't such a dreamer?

Oh yeah, yesterday a lot of people in the neighborhood, including us, had telephones installed in our homes and almost immediately my friends and I started calling each other as soon as we exchanged phone numbers. Our phone number is Dumont 5-1650 and Joey's number is Dumont 5-3434 and that's the only phone numbers that I care to remember right now. Mom and Daddy keep telling me, and Heshy too, "don't make too many calls because they cost money". Heshy is on the phone almost as much as I am, talking to Sarah. Mom says it's a nice thing to have, because now she can talk to her sister Sherry in the Bronx. While she said that's good, she thinks she would much rather talk to people face to face. I'll have to think about that for a while to see if she is right. What am I talking about, she's always right. Well most of the time anyway.

The homework has been on the heavy side and with helping to watch the kids I don't have much time to hang out with my friends or for that matter to write to you every night dear diary. I'll just keep you updated when I can and I'll try not to leave out anything important. I'm only able to write tonight because I was a little overtired, as Mom likes to say, and couldn't fall asleep, but now I'm getting tired and sleepy, so good night dear diary.

Thursday, January 31st, 1946

Dear diary, I've had another two good weeks since I last wrote to you. Joey has been greeting us, Heshy and me, almost every morning with his gorgeous, smiling face and he is his usual friendly, wonderful self every day. He only comes over to our house to do his homework with us one night a week, because he and Heshy have to work three days a week after school until 8pm. When he does come over, usually on Wednesday night, I make the most of it and make sure I don't hide in my room. Last night when he was over and in the middle of doing our homework, Daddy asked Joey, if everyone calls his mother Mama B, does anyone call his father Papa B? Joey looked up and quickly said to Daddy that no, nobody calls his father Papa B and nobody calls him a Son of a B either! The laughter started with us in the dining room and quickly spread to Mom who, this time didn't have to run into the bathroom, because she was already in there. We could hear her laughing

163

from where we were sitting. Even Daddy who looked a little stunned at first, started laughing too and told Joey that was a good one.

One of our friends, Herman Novatny who we all call Herm, lives in the building next to where the "yenta" lives, on Christopher Avenue near Livonia Avenue. He told us that he saw her father the other day and asked him where Sylvia was, because he hadn't seen her in school for a while. He said that her father got a little angry, because he felt that all of her friends turned on her and spread untrue stories about her. Her father told Herm that she felt so bad when almost all of her friends stopped talking to her, that he sent her away to live with his relatives in another state but he wouldn't say where. Can you imagine that! We spread rumors about the "yenta"! I hope he really doesn't believe that. Well anyway I hope that it's true, that she just went away because she felt bad and not because she was pregnant.

The weather on Saturday is supposed to be very cold and a heavy snowfall is forecast, so I'll have to entertain Joshua and Sophie in my house all day. With Heshy and Joey both working in the morning I'll be on my own until about 1pm when at least Heshy will be home. Maybe if I'm lucky Joey will be with him when he gets home. If it snows a lot I don't think I'll be going out on Saturday night and I know I'm going to miss that, especially the trip to the ice cream parlor. I think I'll buy some ice cream tomorrow so that on Saturday night I won't miss the ice cream parlor. I'll probably miss being with my friends though, but I guess it's like Mom tells me sometimes, I can't have everything. Someday I'm going to ask her why not. Good night dear diary.

Tuesday, February 5th, 1946

Dear diary, the weather forecast for last Saturday turned out to be a little wrong because it started snowing about 10 o'clock Friday night. It snowed all Friday night and into Saturday all day long and it was heavy snow and pretty cold too. Because the weather was so bad, Mom and Helen didn't go to work because Helen and her sisters decided not to open the store. Heshy called Joey on the phone to see if he was going to work and Joey told him that he had just called their boss at Schlossberg's and was told that the store would be closed, but he and Heshy should come to the store in the afternoon as soon as it stopped snowing. They will be needed to help out with snow shoveling so the store could open on Monday morning or maybe even on Sunday for part of the day.

I was disappointed and relieved at the same time, because all the snow meant that I would be stuck in the house all day and probably wouldn't get to see Joey or any of my friends. Plus, I wouldn't make any babysitting money or see the kids. Well I still had the telephone and if I couldn't see Joey or my friends or the kids, I could call them and talk to them and that's just what I did. Daddy said the telephone company would be making a lot of money that day.

About ten o'clock in the morning, at the worst part of the storm, the door bell rang. I went to open it and was I surprised to see bundled up like an Eskimo, Joey. He was standing there all covered with snow and he looked half frozen. I just stood there with my mouth wide open for a few seconds looking at him with surprise and he finally blurted out to me, "Well aren't you going to let me come in?" I was so surprised and happy at the sight of him I could hardly speak, but I heard myself stammer to him, oh, of course Joey, come right in. Now listen to this, he brought with him a box of hot chocolate mix, that he had in his coat pocket and a bag of rolls and coffee cake that he had just bought from Finklestein's bakery. He told us he just dropped off a big bag of goodies at his house too. Wow! What a nice surprise. My parents, who already think the world of Joey, couldn't get over how thoughtful he is. We all sat down and enjoyed the hot chocolate and coffee cake and later Heshy bundled himself up like Joey and the two of them went out in the middle of the storm to build a snow man and have a snowball fight. Mom and Daddy told them they thought they were crazy for going out in the storm, but they went anyway.

A short while after they went out I looked out of the window, into the dark stormy day and in the midst of the wind blown snow that was coming down heavy, I saw the outline of two figures. It had to be Joey and Heshy of course and they were building what I guessed to be a great big snow man. While I was watching them I saw a few more figures join them and then another one. When the snow man was finished they started building something else. I couldn't figure out what it could be, but then it hit me. A snow fort! They were building snow forts. They were getting ready for a snowball fight. I quickly got bundled up and over the protests of Mom and Daddy, went outside to join the gang. I was happy to see, when I got out there, that Sarah and Rhoda Berlin, a friend of Sarah's from the other side of Stone Avenue, were part of the snow fort builders. When the snow forts were finished we chose sides and began a snowball fight. The rules were that only softly packed snow was to be used and definitely no ice balls. We didn't want anyone to get hurt we just wanted to have some fun.

About one o'clock Mom called us in to have a nice hot lunch of homemade chicken noodle soup and some of the nice rolls that Joey had brought over in the morning. All seven of us came in and really enjoyed the soup and rolls. We even had some of the left over coffee cake. We were all sitting there, rosy cheeked from the cold wind and having so much fun. As usual Joey and Heshy made everyone laugh, including Mom and Daddy, with their stories and antics. If Helen's and Arlene's kids had been there I'm sure they would have been laughing their heads off. It's moments like these that make me feel so special and lucky.

It didn't stop snowing until late Saturday night, so Heshy and Joey didn't have to go to work until early Sunday morning. They told me when they got home about 2pm that they worked at the store until noon time, shoveling all the snow from in front of the store and all the sidewalks around the store. They said they had a lot of help from the other guys who also worked there. On the way back from work they made about five bucks apiece shoveling snow off peoples' sidewalks and stoops. Sunday was a beautiful, sunshine filled day and a little bit warmer, at least when I was standing in the sun it was. Joey stopped at his house first to check up on his mother before he came over to my house. When he came over he brought with him a gift of a big bag of Italian cookies that his father had gotten from his Cousin Jimmy's pizza place. Joey said that his mother thought that we might like some and she also sent some over to Helen, Arlene and Barbara and her Aunt. The goodness around her never seems to end, thank God. Good night dear diary.

Monday, February 11th, 1945

Dear diary, last Thursday it snowed again, but not nearly as much as the Saturday before last, whose snow is still piled high along the sidewalks and curbs. While it still remains a bit on the cold side, I think it's getting warmer. I don't really know if it's getting warmer or if it's just that my body is getting used to the cold. The good thing is that we didn't lose any school time because of the snow. I mean, I like a day off from school just as much as the other kids, but I don't like to have to work twice as hard to make up for it.

The weather this past Saturday was cold, but very sunny, so I bundled the kids up good and took them to the park for a little while and then to the library, where I met Barbara who was with Arlene's kids. The kids were very happy to see each other as were Barbara and I, but they all said they missed seeing Heshy and Joey. They kept asking me when they were going to get here and of course all I could tell them was, sometime in the afternoon. At noon Barbara suggested that we all go to Arlene's house for lunch, because she said Arlene should be back from her grocery shopping. She said that she was sure that Arlene wouldn't mind if we all came over for lunch. I suggested that maybe we should bring something in for all of us, including Arlene, from the deli. Barbara said that while it was very nice of me to make that offer, she thought that Arlene would really enjoy not only us coming there for lunch but making it too. So naturally I offered to help her make the lunch and Barbara laughed and said that we can both help her.

When we got to Arlene's house I asked if I could use the phone to call my Mom and I did. I just wanted to tell Mom where I was in case Heshy and Joey went looking for me and Helen's kids they would know where to find me. Sure enough it wasn't long after I called Mom that in walks Joey and Heshy. The kids were so happy to see them. I was too of course, but you knew I would be, didn't you diary? Arlene let us help her a little in making baloney sandwiches with our choice of white or rye bread and with mustard or ketchup. She even had pickles and potato chips if we wanted them. Joey got up, said he'll be right back and left. Everyone was asking why he left and where did he go. To myself I said, I bet he went out to buy some surprise dessert for all of us, especially the kids. I just didn't know what kind of surprise dessert he was going to get.

Well I was right, he came back with a big bag and box and put them on top of the ice box while the kids were all screaming at him to tell them what was in the bag and box. Joey then did his magic again with the kids, by getting them to calm down by just talking to them in his usual soft but firm way. It really is something to see. They are all so crazy about him, as everyone in Arlene's apartment at that time is, especially me. When everyone had finished eating their lunch, Joey brought down the box and bag from the top of the ice box and placed it on the table. The kids were all so anxious they couldn't sit still and were fidgeting about. Joey opened the bag first and pulled out about a dozen big assorted cookies and told the kids not to fight over who wants which cookie because, he said there are enough cookies for everyone. He again told them that ladies always go first, so Sophie and Adrienne picked their cookie first and when Michael started to pick out his, Alan told him to wait because Barbara, Arlene and I are ladies too and have to go first. That was too cute for words. All of us older kids and that includes Arlene too, were grinning from ear to ear. After everyone picked out their cookies, Joey then opened the big box and it was filled with all kids of fresh doughnuts that he had bought from that guy he used to deliver them for. You should've heard the kids yelling and carrying on about all the nice goodies Joey bought for them. I really believe he's spoiling them, and me too for that matter, but I don't care because it's so great to have someone around you who is always thinking about you and your family. Do you see why I feel so lucky all the time? I know I keep saying that, but that's the way I feel, because It's true.

Sunday's weather was just like Saturday's and we all met in the park for a while and then a bunch of us, in the afternoon went to the movies. Of course on the way home we stopped at the ice cream parlor. Before I went to the park I did help Mom with some of the cooking and the housework and that made me feel good. I think Mom liked the help too, but I don't know for sure, because Mom always gives me loving smiles. Well anyway, I got home about 4:30 in the afternoon and was a little tired so I lay down for a little nap, or as Mom would call it, "my beauty sleep." During dinner Mom was telling us about a woman, a rich woman who spoke with a very heavy foreign accent, but Mom could not tell from where she came. The woman was talking bad about America and especially about New York City and how she hates it here. Mom was saying to us that if she didn't like it here she should just go back to wherever it is that she came from. Daddy, shaking his head said she is probably, like a lot of people in other countries, just jealous of this country. Then he said something that I never knew before and if it's true is really remarkable. Daddy said that one of the reasons that this country is so great is that we have the best people from all over the world living here. Now here is the remarkable thing. Daddy said that living in New York City and the surrounding areas are more Jews than in Palestine, More Italians than in Rome, more Greeks than in Athens, more Irish than in Dublin, more Germans than in Berlin and probably more Puerto Ricans than in San Juan. And then he added that Brooklyn is not only famous because of the Dodgers, but also because it's known as the "Borough of the Churches". I never knew these things before. I'll have to ask about them in school tomorrow.

Speaking of school, today in Mrs. Schultz's art class we started preparations for making Valentine cards and Joey is making a bunch of cards and one particularly large card. I asked him who the large card was for, hoping of course he would say me, and he said it was for his mother. I wasn't and couldn't be disappointed with that, could I? When I asked him if I could see it when it was finished, he said yes if I promised not to laugh at his drawing or his poem that he was going to write in it. Of course I said I wouldn't laugh. I mean how could any one laugh at someone who is so sincere. I decided this year to sign my name to the card I'm making for Joey. I'll just use the same kind of words that I use for the rest of my family. Do you see what I just wrote diary? I wrote like the rest of my family just as if he was really a family member, so I guess in a very large sense he is. I hope I don't get another unsigned card this year like I did last year, because I still haven't figured out who gave it to me. We shall see, good night dear diary.

Thursday, February 14th, 1946

Dear diary, today Joey made me cry. No, he didn't do or say anything hurtful to me, I don't think he could or would ever do anything like that. He let me and Heshy and only us, read the Valentine card that he made for his mother. I thought the artwork he did on the front of the card was very nice, but it was what he had written, a poem on the inside that touched me so much that I shed a few tears. I think even Heshy was a little choked up, it was so beautiful and Jocy let me copy it. His poem went like this,

To my Mom,

> Your name is Angelina, that means Little Angel in Italy
> but everyone here calls you "Mama B"

I want you to be my Valentine forever

because you have always been an Angel to me.

I will love you always, Mom

When I showed Mom what Joey had written to his mother, Mom wiped away a tear and said she wondered where this boy comes from. I was puzzled and asked Mom what she meant, and she said that he just seems so perfect that maybe, she thinks he came from another world or something. I started to laugh and after a few moments so did Mom. Then she said she was only kidding, but he is a very unusual boy. He has so much feeling for his family and friends and kids and people that he likes. She said it's a very good and wonderful thing to be that way. She asked me if I noticed that nothing seems to phase him. He seems to be able to find the solution to every and any problem. Isn't that wonderful, she asked me and of course I said it was. I mean I would've said he's wonderful even if he couldn't fix any problem, but hey that's me.

Mom asked me to show it to Daddy and I did. Daddy read it to himself and then said, "Joey didn't write this, it's too professional looking. He must have copied if from a book of poems or something". Mom and I assured him that Joey had written it all by himself and Daddy started muttering that, "he writes poetry too, he writes poetry too". Mom then laughingly told Daddy that he is not the only poet around here, with his "Hannah get me a banana". We all laughed at that even Daddy. Heshy then mockingly said to me, "Esther, please don't pester." They all laughed except me, because I couldn't think of anything to rhyme with Heshy. A little while later I came up with one for Heshy. I told him that If I could, I would trade him in for "another brother". Heshy said that his was better than mine, but Mom said that mine was not bad at all and Daddy was just sitting there saying to himself, "What did I start here? What in the world did I start?" We all laughed at that and then started to clean up the dinner dishes.

Anyway I received beautiful Valentine Cards and I'm happy to say that every one of them was signed, even the one from Joey. He made me a very nice card and this time he didn't mention me as his sister. Now we're getting somewhere. He signed it, "your long time friend"

170

and I'll accept that, for now anyway. I got the usual lovely cards from Heshy and my parents and from a few friends. I gave Joey the card that I made for him and he seemed to like it very much. As a matter of fact, Heshy remarked to Joey that the card I made for Joey was nicer than the card I made for him, and then laughed. Actually they both laughed about it. That's the way they are with each other, always teasing about everything and anything. Most times I love it. I think you could tell by the way they tease and kid around with one another that they really are very close friends. I've got to go sleepy bye now, so good night dear diary.

Thursday, February 28th, 1946

Dear diary, I've been having so much fun lately that the time is really flying. I can't believe that tomorrow is the first of March. I have also been so busy with my school work and babysitting and at least one afternoon a week going over to Mama B's house to help out with the kids. But I'm doing everything that I love to do, so I'm not complaining. It seems that most of our friends are taking it for granted that if Joey and me are not now girlfriend and boyfriend, we will soon be. Of course you know that I already knew that, but it won't come soon enough for me. We shall see. I'll just have to keep on being patient. In the meantime, I'll also keep on enjoying every minute of seeing him wherever it may be. Being that he's Heshy's best friend, he's always around so I thank God for that.

Joey still comes over to do his homework just on Wednesday nights and on Wednesday night of last week, when he was over he and Daddy were at it again. Daddy was commenting on the lovely Valentine's Day card that Joey had made for his mother and asked him if he was sure he made by himself. Mom was a little annoyed with Daddy for questioning Joey like that, but Joey said that it was okay and told Daddy that he did indeed make the card by himself. Daddy told him that he thought the words inside, the little poem were very touching and beautiful and asked Joey where he found the words. Joey told Daddy that the words came from his heart, but he didn't know how they got there. Daddy then said that maybe Joey had read them somewhere and forgot about it. Joey said no, he didn't think so. He said he wasn't one hundred percent sure but he believes that God put the words there. Daddy looked at Joey very seriously and asked Joey if he was trying to convert him. We each held our breath at that surprise question, and Joey put on his exaggerated serious look and told Daddy that yes he was trying to convert him, from a Jewish office manager to a Jewish comedian. He quickly added before anyone could start laughing, that he needed an awful lot of work. Then the laughing started from everyone and when it died down Mom told Daddy that he should know by now not to start in with Joey, because he'll never win. Joey never fails to make us laugh and mostly at ourselves.

Daddy's company last year had to make the switch from making military clothing, mostly coats, to civilian clothes. Daddy told all of us that he is going to get us new spring outfits in a short while. That's the first time he was ever able to get us whole outfits. He used to get us a coat or something once in a while and even then it was for one of us at a time. It probably has to do with the fact that he was promoted to a vice president of something or other. Whatever it was I think it's great and I'm looking forward to getting the new outfit. Daddy said that one day after school, when Mom isn't working, we can all come to the factory and pick out what we want. The owners of the company, Mr. Sol Cohen and Mr. Sal Giacamo, have always been very nice to not only Daddy but also to all the people who work for them. Mama B always says nice things about them, but then she usually says nice things about most people. Daddy says between one of them called Sal and the other called Sol, it gets very confusing around there at times.

Heshy and Joey are still working out with weights in their gym class and it's really showing on their bodies, well I've only seen Heshy with his shirt off around the house. I haven't seen Joey that way since last summer at the beach. Now, because of the discounts they get at Schlossberg's Department Store, they have each bought a set of weights so they can work out at home. I can't wait to see how Joey's body is going to look by this summer time. Of course I always thought he looked great no matter what. I suppose if he is going to have a great looking body, to go along with his great looking face, I can expect to see all the girls flirting with him. I know I'm going to hate that but I guess I'll have to learn to live with it. Mom is finally getting through to me. Good night dear diary.

Friday, March 15th, 1946

Dear diary, this past Monday was Joey's fifteenth birthday and like last year Heshy and I chipped in and bought him a present together. I let Heshy pick out whatever he thought Joey would like and just like I thought he would, he picked out something to do with sports. We bought Joey a Brooklyn Dodger baseball hat and a new basketball. Of course, because of Heshy's discount at the department store, it didn't cost us too much money. Mom even baked a small birthday cake for him and Joey loved the presents and the cake. He told us that he got a lot of nice stuff from his family, Barbara, Arlene and even her kids. Joshua and Sophie even got him a little gift and I think he especially liked the gifts from all the kids. We were invited by Mama B to come to their house on Monday night to help sing "Happy Birthday" to Joey. I couldn't help but notice how Mama B would look at Joey with such love and pride in her eyes. It really moved me.

The weather has been living up to the old saying of March winds and maybe it will for April showers too. It has been very windy the past few days. The wind was so strong that ash cans were being blown all over the streets, store front awnings were being ripped apart and windows were not only rattling but in some cases blown out. Thank God none in our house. When Joey came over on Wednesday night he told Daddy he started out for our house the night before and just got here because for every step he took forward he was blown three steps backward. He said that after eight hours of walking that way he wound up in Boston and had to take the bus back. When Daddy looked at him in disbelief and shaking his head, Joey asked Daddy if he thought that maybe he should have walked faster. Daddy is getting pretty quick with his responses, because he immediately said no, because he might have wound up in Vermont. Joey not only laughed but told Daddy that he was getting real good. Daddy just sat there looking very pleased with himself.

Even though I know that the farmers need the rain I hope that April doesn't live up to it's reputation like March is doing. It was really hard for me trying to walk to and from school the last couple of days. It was a good thing that I had Heshy and Joey on either side of me or I don't think I would've made it. The funny thing about it is, that most of the girls, including me and many of the boys all arrived at school with their hair blown all over the place. We all had a good laugh pointing fingers at everyone with messed up hair and they were pointing at me and laughing. On the way to school we saw a pair of men's underwear that had probably been blown off somebody's clothes line, stuck on a branch high up on a tree and waving in the wind like a flag or something. It looked so funny. When we all got to the school yard and talked about how windy it was, Joey told everyone that the wind was so strong it blew his underwear right off him and they landed and wrapped around a branch high on a tree, but left his pants on him untouched. Of course nobody believed him so he told everyone to go look up at the tree on Sackman Street. He then said that every time he passes that tree his underwear waves hello to him in the breeze. Everyone went crazy laughing at that. He makes every one of my days so enjoyable. Even when I don't see him I have to laugh and smile to myself, just thinking about all the things he says and does.

We are all getting ready for Passover which falls on Wednesday, March 27th this year. I think Joey said that Easter Sunday falls on April 6th. Joey told us that he already bought his new Easter suit at Schlossberg's, because he gets a nice discount. I think Heshy might do the same if he doesn't see anything he likes at Daddy's factory. Oh yeah, we are all going to the factory next Wednesday, March 20th, a week before Passover. I can't wait to see what kind of outfits they have. Mom and Daddy couldn't invite the Balduccis to the Seder this year because it's not at our house. We are all going way up to the Bronx to Aunt Sherry's house for the Seder. Not only did the Balduccis understand when Mom explained it to them, but they invited all of us to join them for a pre holiday dinner on the Sunday before Passover, the 24th. Mom and Daddy accepted of course. They didn't want to hurt their feelings. Then Mom and Daddy had a good idea and invited them to come to our house this coming Sunday for dinner and they accepted. So now I have more wonderful things to look forward to. My good luck continues like I hope it always will. Good night dear diary.

Monday, March 18th, 1946

Dear diary, we had a wonderful time with the Balduccis coming over for dinner early yesterday evening. Mom served some traditional Passover dishes, just like a Seder night. Being that it was also Saint

Patrick's Day yesterday, Mr. Balducci, Daddy calls him "Big Joe" now, brought some Irish soda bread for us to try, even though nobody at the table was Irish. Of course he also brought his usual wine that "fell off a truck". The soda bread was delicious and everyone enjoyed it. Mama B seemed to really enjoy the evening and she looks as if she is feeling so much better. She still is not going to go back to work and Daddy keeps telling her that she has a job anytime she wants to go back to work. Oh yeah, I forgot to tell you Joey came walking into our house wearing a big green hat, I think it's called a topper, and singing with an Irish accent, "When Irish Eyes are Smiling". Is he something or what? We were all delighted in seeing and hearing him do that, it was so funny. Daddy said only in America can you hear an Italian boy singing an Irish song walking into a Jewish man's house. Everyone laughed and agreed with Daddy, but Joey had to add that on Saint Patrick's Day everyone's a little Irish. No one disagreed with him.

Come to think of it, we do have an Irish school mate actually we have a few but only one that we are very friendly with, in school anyway. His name is Kenny Kerwin and he lives on Stone Avenue near New Lots Avenue and he hangs out mostly with his friends in a little park near there. In school everybody calls him Kay Kay, but Joey sometimes kidding around, calls him Ka Ka. I thought that wasn't nice of Joey until I heard Kenny call Joey, Baldy. Because Heshy and Joey talk a lot in class but only Heshy is caught and is always being hushed up by the teachers, every once in a while if Heshy calls Kenny Ka Ka, Kenny calls him Hushy Heshy and they all laugh at each other. I guess that's just the way they get along. There never seems to be any serious fighting going on between any of them, so I like that.

While we were doing our homework with Joey last night and Heshy was saying, loud enough for Daddy to hear him, that it wasn't fair that every time he and Joey get caught talking in class, the teachers always only hush him and not Joey. Joey, trying to sound very adult like, with a deep voice said, "Harry Abromovitz let this be one of life's very important lessons for you, always know when to talk and when to stop." Daddy looked at Joey and asked him how a fifteen year old boy can sound as smart as a much older man. Joey told Daddy that being best friends with Heshy has aged him. Heshy didn't know whether to laugh or be mad, so he asked me if that was a compliment or an insult. I told him to laugh and forget about it, because Joey would never say anything bad about him. Mom and Daddy were both smiling and shaking their heads in agreement.

Mom told me something very interesting tonight when we had a few minutes alone. She said when she was doing the dishes last night Mama B came in to help her. Mom washed and Mama B dried. While they were talking, Mama B mentioned that she thought that Joey and I sometimes act as if we were boyfriend and girlfriend and that she thought we liked each other more than just friends. Wow! And I thought Mom was very perceptive. She went on that Mama B asked her if that were true, would there be any objection from either Mom or Daddy. Mama B said that as far as she is concerned if two people really like each other, let it be as long as they are happy with each other. She also said that in our case we're too young for anyone to get too excited about yet. Mom said that she agreed with her, but told her Daddy might have strong objections and Mama B said she understood. Then she told Mom a story about Buster that probably explains why Joey doesn't ask me to be his girlfriend.

Mama B said that when Buster was about sixteen he started to hang around with those boys from New Lots Avenue, the ones she now calls her other sons. Most of them have Spanish sounding names because they are "Sephardim", the Jews who came from Spain and Portugal many, many years ago. He met and fell in love with a Spanish Jewish girl and because his name is Italian and sounds very much like it could be Spanish, her parents thought that he was a Sephardim too, like all of his friends. Mama B didn't know how, but when they found out that he wasn't Jewish, they wouldn't let the girl see Buster anymore. Mama B told my Mom that Buster came home and cried like a baby and that hurt her to see him that way. More then once she said she told Joey that story and she wouldn't want to see Joey go through the same pain, as young as he might be. She assured Mom that if it came down to that, it wouldn't affect their friendship one little bit. Mom told me she told Mama B not to worry because she wouldn't want to see me in any kind of pain either.

Mom said they then gave each other a big hug as Daddy came walking into the kitchen and asked what's going on and what's all the hugging about. Mom told him it was nothing but just two mothers talking about their children. Daddy said he came to help her with the dishes. Mama B was drying the last dish when Daddy said that, so Mom told him that his timing was perfect, because all the dishes are now done. He just smiled and said in a mocking way, "Oh really! That's too bad because I was looking forward to drying dishes tonight". Mama B laughed as Mom picked up a dish towel and threw it at him, in a playful way of course. Mama B said that men are really like little boys, just a little bit taller. Now I know where Joey gets his sense of humor from. Mom told Mama B that she would do whatever she could to keep Daddy from interfering. Is that great news or what! I've got Mom and Mama B on my side. Now it's all up to Joey. Mom again told me not to get my hopes up just yet and to be patient, because Joey will get around to telling me how he feels about me, in his own time. Good night dear diary.

Monday, March 25th, 1945

Dear diary, yesterday's holiday dinner at Joey's house was just as wonderful as I knew it would be and there was also a little surprise. There was a very nice looking guy there who I had never seen before. His name is Biaggo Bongiorno, but everyone calls him Benny. I remembered who he was after I heard his name. He's the twenty one year old guy, who recently got out of the Navy and works in the Brooklyn Navy Yard with Helen's husband. Mr. Bernstein not too long ago asked Joey if he thought Mary would like to meet him, because he is a very nice guy. He had told Benny all about this nice Italian girl he knew. I didn't know that he met Mary only this past Friday night and they hit it off right away, so she invited him, with Mama B's permission of course, to have dinner with them yesterday. He seems like a very nice guy and Mary and the whole family seem to like him a lot. We shall see what happens with these two. Now if only Joey would ask me to go to the movies or something with him, just me and him. We shall see about that too.

Well like I said, the dinner was wonderful and I think I'm getting spoiled because now, every time we get invited to Mama B's house for dinner or anything, I expect it to be wonderful. Anyway, I noticed that Joey and Mary are keeping a close eye on Mama B to make sure she doesn't eat any of the pastries or too much bread and pasta. She has such a sweet tooth, that it must drive her crazy watching everybody eating all the desserts and other stuff that were there. I could tell that she was trying very hard to be good about it, but at the same time I would notice her looking at some of the goodies as if she was ready to reach out and grab some. She didn't do it thank God.

When we got home, we were all talking again about what a good time we had and what a good cook Mama B was. Without thinking, I said out loud that we shouldn't forget that Joey probably helped and he was a good cook too. Mom quickly added, after giving me a surprised look that Mary must have helped a lot too. She told me later that she didn't want Daddy to think that I always have Joey on my mind. Boy, Mom is not only perceptive and smart, but a quick thinker too. You know I really believe that Daddy knows how I feel about Joey, but for some reason he doesn't say anything about it. I don't know for sure, but I'll have to ask Mom about that.

This morning before we left our house for school, I was remembering how we, Heshy and I, talked so glowingly about having the great dinner we had at Joey's house last year and everyone pestered Joey about when they were going to be invited. I reminded Heshy about that on the way to school and said we shouldn't say anything about it to anyone and he agreed. Of course when we were walking to school and I felt sure that nobody could hear me, I told Joey in a very low voice, what a great time we all had and thanked him very much. He just smiled at me and told me I didn't have to whisper, because he didn't care if the other kids knew about it and started asking for their invitations. As a matter of fact, he said that last night after we left, he asked his parents if one Saturday or Sunday after the holidays, he could invite a bunch of his friends over for an Italian dinner. He told me he even offered to cook it himself. Of course they said yes, but knowing his family, I'm sure that they will all help him prepare the dinner.

While I'm looking forward to seeing Aunt Sherry and her family Wednesday night at the Seder, I'm not looking forward to the long subway ride up to the Bronx and back again. I wonder what time we'll get home that night. Aunt Sherry is a good cook but Mom is much better. I'm sure we'll all enjoy the food because I think who you're eating with, has something to do with how much you enjoy the food. Maybe I'm wrong but that's what I think.

Oh yeah, I forgot to tell you, but last Wednesday after school, Heshy, Mom and I went to Daddy's factory to pick out our new outfits. I pick out a beautiful navy blue dress that had a pleated skirt, a three inch wide belt with a big brass buckle, three quarter length sleeves, white buttons down the front and a vee neck with a slim white collar. It came with a matching blue vest with white buttons and trim. All I need now is a white hat and I'll look like a sailor. Mom picked out a lovely spring looking flowered dress that came with a matching wide brimmed hat and like my dress, a wide belt with a big brass buckle. When she tried it on she looked so beautiful that when Daddy saw her, he just stared at her and couldn't speak. When he did, he told her she looked just as beautiful as the day they first met so many years ago. As they hugged, Mom had a few tears in her eyes and so did I. Heshy just kept saying that he didn't see anything he liked. He finally picked out some pants and a nice looking sweater and they both looked very nice on him. The next day Heshy bought a good looking suit for himself at Schlossberg's. With his employee discount it didn't cost too much and that made him very happy.

Daddy told us that he wished he could've asked Joey to come over to pick something out too, but he didn't want his bosses to think he was trying to take advantage of them. But a funny thing happened when Daddy introduced us to his bosses, Sal and Sol. While we were talking, or as Mom would say "chit chatting", Sol told Daddy to bring Mama B's son Joey and daughter Mary around to pick out something too. His partner Sal agreed and said the same thing also. Wow! What nice people Daddy works for. At the dinner at Joey's house yesterday, Daddy mentioned it at the table and they were all excitedly happy at hearing that. Mama B said that they were, including Daddy too, wonderful people to work for.

You know diary I'm always telling you, well at least most of the time, what wonderful things that are happening to me and going on in this neighborhood, but there are a lot of bad and ugly things happening too, that I don't like to talk about too much. For instance, a bunch of boys a few years older than me, from around the corner on Powell Street got caught stealing cars, just to go, as they say "joy riding". Some other guys, also a little bit older than me got arrested for selling drugs and there are also the bookmakers and gamblers all around us. But it seems that all of the people that I like and am very close to just seem to be able to live their own lives and try to always do the right thing. So while we know that we don't live in a Paradise, we are always trying to make a Paradise out of where we live. You know how I know all this?

Who else but Mom and Daddy have told me and Heshy these things many times and in many ways. The point they tell us they're trying to make, is that we should always stay focused on the positive things in life. That makes a lot of sense to me. Now I'm really getting tired dear diary, so I have to say good night.

Saturday, March 30th, 1946

Dear diary, Wednesday turned out to be a sunny and kind of warm day and evening, so our trip up to the Bronx, to Aunt Sherry's house for the Passover Seder, was a little nicer than if it was cold and windy. The Seder was very nice, but not as nice as last year at our house, when the Balduccis were there. All of our relatives were at Aunt Sherry's house. I don't know how Uncle Carl and his family did it, coming all the way from Queens. I think my Aunt Ruth said it took them a little over two hours, changing trains and all. Like I said before, it was a very nice Seder, but I just missed seeing Joey, Mama B and the rest of their family. Somebody said, I don't know who, that they missed drinking wine that "fell off a truck", everyone looked at me and started laughing, me too. I was so glad that they remembered the Balduccis, even if it was just for the wine. Well anyway, it must have been 1:30 in the morning when we got home and not just me, but everyone was very tired.

The next morning we all slept a little bit late and I don't know about anyone else, but I was still a little tired. I think we all were a little tired because we seemed to be moving in slow motion, almost. After we ate breakfast and got dressed, Heshy and I went to the park to see our friends. Daddy did the same to be with his friends. It was a little warmer than Wednesday and everyone was dressed up in their best clothes and looked nice. Joey again didn't go to school, just like last year and he said that he didn't think that the teachers really expected him to. He wasn't dressed up in a suit, but he did have on a nice looking sweater and jacket over a nice pair of slacks and to me he looked great. Of course, I wasn't paying too much attention to him, so I really didn't notice exactly what he was wearing. Ha! Ha!

The weather was so nice that the park was crowded with people. I was so happy to see Helen and her family, Arlene and her kids and Barbara there too. It was really nice to be around most of the people that you like, in the same place at the same time. Heshy, Joey and I walked over to where Daddy was, because Joey wanted to say hello to him. Daddy greeted Joey warmly, as he usually does and Joey told Daddy to have a Happy Passover. Daddy thanked him and then Joey asked Daddy if he had heard about the bomb threat at the George Washington Bridge. When Daddy said he hadn't, Joey told him that the New York and New Jersey Police were stopping and searching everyone trying to walk across the bridge. A New Jersey cop stopped a guy who was trying to cross the bridge and was carrying a big square box under his arm. The cop asked the man what was in the box. When the man said matzah, the cop said, "Okay, pass over." All of Daddy's friends started laughing and Daddy laughing too, told them that he is such a "Joey boy".

After a long time of talking to and playing with the kids, they all left with their parents. Joey, Heshy, me and a bunch of other kids went to the Chinese restaurant on Sutter Avenue for lunch. It was crowded there too, but we all managed to find a table after a short wait. When we finished lunch we all walked over to Saratoga Avenue to the ice cream parlor for some dessert. It seems that when ever we eat Chinese food, we get hungry again about an hour later, so by the time we got to the ice cream parlor, we had plenty of room for the ice cream. It has been a very nice holiday for me for the past two days. Sometimes diary, when I have such nice days like these I wish they would never end.

Yesterday and today have been raining and cooler. It looks like April showers have come a little bit early because it's still March, but I managed to enjoy them too with a little help from Heshy, Joey and some of my other friends. Heshy suggested yesterday, that a nice thing to do on a rainy day is go to the movies and a bunch of us, including Joey thank God, did just that. We went to the Premier Theater on Sutter Avenue and saw a double feature. The main feature was a mystery love story called "Spellbound" with Ingrid Bergman and Gregory Peck, and was very good. As usual the second movie was a western "shootem up" as the guys call them. "Dawn on the Wild Plains" or something like that was the name of it. The boys enjoyed that one more than the girls did. By the time we got out of the theater it stopped raining, for a while anyway.

This time we didn't go to Saratoga Avenue for ice cream, we went to our local candy store for desserts. It's not as good as The Olde Brooklyn Malt Shoppe, but it's very good anyway and we all enjoyed it. Like I've said before, the company probably had a lot to do with it. By now it was getting to be about 4pm and I was getting a little tired, so I went home to take a little nap before dinner. Being that I had to baby-sit starting early this morning, I didn't think I'd be hanging out with the gang last night. I just sat around the house after dinner and helped Mom with a few things, before going to bed early.

Everyone went back to work today, so I had the kids by myself, but everything worked out okay. Because it was only raining softly, I asked Helen before she left with Mom to go to work, if it was okay with her, if I took the kids to the movies this morning to see a couple of kiddies movies at the local movie house on Livonia Avenue, called the "Deluxe Theater". Everybody calls it "The Dump". She said it was okay. I bundled the kids up and we got to "The Dump" at nine and spent the next three and a half hours laughing and giggling through the two Walt Disney movies plus cartoons. It was twelve thirty by the time we left the movie house and the kids were hungry and had to go to the bathroom.

On the walk through the park to go to my house, I met Heshy and Joey just coming home from work. Again Joey had a big bag and a box in his hands and a big smile on his face when he saw us. I would love to believe that the smile was for only me, but I know it was for the kids too. Of course Heshy had a big smile on his face too. Joey asked us all if we'd like to have hot dogs and fries for lunch and you know the kids were all for it, so Heshy and I had to go along with it too. He told us to go on to my house and he would bring the dogs and fries there in a few minutes. Heshy told me that they both had to work a little longer this morning and didn't have their lunch yet. When he got to my house and set the food down on the table, the kids wanted to know what Joey had in the big bag and box that he was carrying. Joey told them that they would have to wait until after they finished eating their lunch. If I had told the kids that, they would be pestering me constantly to show them what was in the bag and box, but when Joey tells them to wait, they just seem to listen to him. It amazes me, the way he's able to do that. Heshy in the meantime had this big grin on his face every time the kids mentioned the box and bag, so I had to believe that he knew what's in them.

I was very curious myself, but I keep hearing Mom's voice, whenever I'm in situations like that, saying to me to be patient, so I am. When the kids tried to eat faster than they should, Joey just told them in his firm but gentle way to chew their food slowly and to take smaller bites, again they listened to him. Finally they finished their lunch and Joey opened the box first and inside was what I thought would be there, fresh doughnuts. He bought a baker's dozen, which means thirteen delicious doughnuts that we all love, especially the kids. Again when the kids started to dive into the box Joey had to only tell them once, in fact he didn't speak the words, he just looked at them sternly and they knew right away how they were supposed to behave.

After the kids, I should say we, all had our fill of doughnuts, we all wanted Joey to tell us what was in the bag. With a big grin on his face, Heshy was grinning too, Joey slowly opened the bag, peeked inside and said, "mmm, let's see what we have here" and he pulled out a beautiful little rag doll for Sophie, as he said ladies and princesses first and handed it to her. He then told us that he forgot to mention, that Heshy had joined him in getting all the goodies. Then he peeked into the bag again, stuck his hand in and pulled out a beautiful stuffed little puppy and handed it to me, again with a ladies first and then added that it was for a very special lady and babysitter. The kids both cheered when Joey said that about me, but poor Joshua was getting very anxious by this time. Joey pulled out the last thing from the bag it was a big colorful picture book, all about baseball that Joshua was wild about. Of course as he handed it to Joshua, he said it was for a prince.

Diary, here is the very best part and it's not even about me, it's about Heshy. The presents by the way, which everyone including me got, was for no special occasion. Joey later explained to me, that he just happened to see these things on sale and thought we would all like them. Then he pulled out of his pocket six tickets to a Dodger's game at Ebbetts Field and handed them to Heshy. He said that because Heshy was his best friend and because all of the Abramowitz's make him feel like a part of their family, he wanted to get these tickets for all of us. Heshy looked so surprised he didn't know what to say. Joey quickly told Heshy that the tickets are for him, Sarah, me, Joey, Joshua and Alan and they are for Sunday, May 5th against the Boston Braves. Joey then added that the fact that he was able, through a friend of his Cousin Jimmy's, to get the tickets for nothing didn't hurt either. Heshy, when he got his tongue back asked Joey if he thought that maybe Warren Spahn would be pitching that day for the Braves and Joey said he didn't know, but it would be an extra bonus for us if he was.

After Sophie played with her new rag doll for a short time, she laid down for her nap. Joshua just continued looking at the big color pictures of different ballplayers from all the different teams in the major leagues, in all kinds of poses. He would slowly turn the pages and study each picture intently. Every once in a while he would ask either Heshy or Joey to explain something in a picture to him, and of course they did. While Sophie was napping and Joshua was looking at the pictures in his new book, Heshy, Joey and I just sat around and talked. We talked about school, about their jobs, about our families and whatever else came into our heads. It made the afternoon go by so fast, that before I knew it was almost 5pm.

Sophie napped longer than she usually does. When I looked over at the couch where Joshua was sitting and looking at the book, I saw Heshy sitting next to him and the two of them were sleeping. I motioned to Joey to take a look. When he did he just shrugged his shoulders and said it must be the rain or the dark day that has everybody tired, because he said he was feeling a little sleepy too. So after Sophie woke up, Joey was good enough to watch her for me, while I started to get dinner ready for when Mom got home. Joey was so funny, he took her rag doll and made believe it came to life by making it do all kinds of crazy things. He almost was able to use it as a hand puppet. Her giggling and laughing so hard sounded to me like the sweetest music I ever heard.

After Mom got home and the kids left with Helen, she invited Joey to stay for dinner with us. Joey accepted, but he first wanted to go home to see how Mama B was doing and if she needed anything. I told him to use our phone and call her to see how she's doing, but he said that he likes to see her and wants her to see him. He said he knows that doing that makes Mama B feel much better. After about 30 minutes or so Daddy got home and Joey returned a few minutes later and sat down with us for dinner. Daddy was telling us that now that the war is over, the automobile companies have stopped making tanks and other military vehicles and are now starting to make cars again. He was saying he heard that because the backlog of orders for new cars is so big, some people are going to have to wait, in some cases up to a year for a new car. Because of his promotions in the company and the increases in his salary that went along with them, he thinks that in maybe six months or a year he would be able to order a new car. He added that when the time comes we will all have a voice in picking out the car model and style and of course the color. Wow! That's going to be something. I can't wait for us to have a family car and go on Sunday drives out to the country and maybe even a picnic.

It was a very tiring day for me and I really didn't feel like going out tonight, so Heshy asked Sarah to go to an early movie with him and told me he would bring her back here afterward with ice cream for all of us. Joey said that he would stay a little while longer and then go home, because he was felling a little tired too. It sounded great to me, but then Heshy and Sarah surprised us by coming over here shortly after he went to pick her up. When Sarah heard that I felt too tired to go out tonight, she said she felt tired too. She had been working all day, in the woman's clothing department of Schlossberg's, where Heshy had gotten her a job. So instead of going to the movies, they went right to the ice cream store and bought enough for everyone and brought it over right away. Joey then decided to stay for some of the ice cream. What a pleasant and delicious surprise. By ten o'clock I was really pooped and everybody left and I went to bed, but as you can see I probably got myself overtired and couldn't sleep so I decided to write to tell you what's been going on with me. I'm glad I did, but now I think I'm ready for sleepy bye, but before I go I just want to ask you, if you see what I mean about being able to turn a rainy, dreary day into a beautiful, happy day? Good night dear diary.

CHAPTER 10

Monday, April 1st, 1946

Dear diary yesterday was Palm Sunday and it was a windy but very sunny and warmer day. Joey had gone to church with his father and Mary. Mama B still doesn't like to be in crowds. Afterwards, Joey met us in the park. Mr. B, that's what I call him now because said he doesn't mind, was in the park too, talking with Daddy and his friends. Joey and his father were still dressed up in their, as Joey likes to say," Sunday going to meeting" clothes. They both looked very nice and had little crosses made out of palm, pinned to their lapels. Mr. B invited Daddy and our family to come over for a little lunch and so we all did. It was more like an early dinner than a lunch. There was no fussing with a lot of cooking this time, they just went to the Kosher Deli and brought in a lot of nice corned beef, tongue and other goodies. It was all very delicious and just being together with them all made the day so special.

In school today and even afterwards in the park, everyone was trying to pull an April fools trick on everyone else, including the teachers. Some of the tricks and jokes were pretty good, but the best one I thought was pulled on Daddy tonight, by Joey. Because Joey and Heshy work every night until about 7pm, except for Wednesday, the night Joey usually comes over, we didn't expect to see him tonight. When Heshy got home at about 7:20, who should pop his head in the door unexpectedly but Joey. He said he just wanted to say hello to everyone before he went home to have his dinner. Daddy gave him a big hello and asked him what was new. That was a big mistake on Daddy's part, as you will see in a minute.

Joey very excitedly told Daddy, that he just saw a man in a car run over himself. Daddy, in complete disbelief looked at Joey as if he was crazy or something and told him that he didn't know what he was talking about. He said there is no way anybody can run over themselves in a car. So Joey explained, that he and Heshy stopped at the candy store on Riverdale Avenue, and while Heshy went in to buy some candy for a snack, he waited outside. A man drove up, double parked in front of the store and called him over. Daddy was listening very intently as Joey said the man asked him, if he would run over to the store and buy him a pack of cigarettes. Joey said when he told the man no, the man ran over himself, April fool. Daddy sat there stunned for a second, then pounded his fist on the table and yelled out that he did it to him again and then started laughing. Of course Mom had to run into the bathroom again and I almost had to follow her. It isn't always what Joey says, that's so funny, so many times it's Daddy's reaction to it that's really so funny.

Heshy was taken by surprise too and was doubled over laughing. When the laughing eased up, Daddy asked Joey if he just came over to fool him with that story and he said yes. He said it was worth it for him to be a little late for his dinner. Daddy then asked Joey what he would do, if he didn't have him to kid all the time. Joey immediately went into a crazy dance and pointed at me, Heshy and the bathroom door where Mom was still inside and started singing a crazy song that he was making up as he went along. He sang, "I'd have Heshy, Esther and their mother too if I didn't have you, to pick on for fun, 'cause you're not the only one, I like to make laugh and kid, and that's what I did but you're not the only one". It was something like that I think, a little silly and crazy, but so funny that Daddy yelled out to Mom who was still in the bathroom to please hurry because he had to get in there. Mom, who heard every word of Joey's crazy song, because she was on her way out of the bathroom when he started singing, had to rush back in.

After Joey left, Mom and I were talking in the kitchen and she said that she thought, after watching him do his crazy dance, he almost looked like a puppet on a string or something, that he is probably a very good dancer. I told her that I didn't know because I've never danced with him. Mom then suggested that I go to the next school or "Y" dance. I told her that Daddy always says that I'm too young to go to dances. She just smiled and told me that she doesn't think I'm too young anymore and that she will talk to Daddy about it. She went right into the living room where Daddy was sitting reading the newspaper to talk to him about me going to dances. I thought that was great, Mom sticking up for me again.

I couldn't hear everything that was being said, but I could hear Daddy every few minutes say, "My Totala wants to go dancing?" and "My Totala is old enough to dance with a boy?" Finally after about five or ten minutes Mom came back and told me I could go to the next dance that comes up. It's hard to believe that last summer I was allowed to go to the beach with my friends, but I couldn't go to a dance. I think Mom and Daddy are trying so hard to be up to date with the way things are done in America today, but they still have a lot of the "Old World" culture in them. I guess it must be pretty tough on them at times, trying to figure out what to do with Heshy and me, but I think they're doing great. Maybe I think that because they're my parents, I don't know, but anyway that's what I think. Good night dear diary.

Monday, April 7th, 1946

Dear diary, the big news these days is television. I don't understand how it works and I find it hard to believe that pictures of people, just like in the movies, can be sent through the air and come out on a screen in a little box in your house. I've seen it in the front windows of radio and now television stores, but I still find it hard to believe. It's a little strange to see a small crowd of people gathered on the sidewalk outside one of those stores watching a TV show or ballgame or something. Right now most of the people in this neighborhood don't have TVs because they're expensive, but Daddy says that the prices will be coming down soon and then we'll be able to afford one. It's kind of fun to walk to school or when we go anywhere to see TV aerials going up on rooftops one by one and people saying, "Oh there's one. Oh look they have a TV over there in that house." It seems that every day, little by little, more and more people are getting them.

Yesterday, Easter Sunday, was a very beautiful day. We all spent the afternoon at Mama B's house just like last year, except that this time we only had a light lunch. Mom asked Mama B to please not fuss and spend the whole night cooking for us. If fact Mom cooked the turkey and Daddy sliced the breasts, carved the rest of the bird, and we brought it over to Mama B's. Arlene and the kids and Barbara and her Aunt Becky were there too. Arlene brought a big pan of macaroni and cheese and Barbara made a three bean casserole that she learned how to make in cooking class in school. There were nice Easter breads and pastries that Mr. B got from the Italian bakery, plus the wine of course. Daddy was telling Mr. B that the big supermarkets had their own bakery departments and were selling Italian pastries, along with their other baked goods. Mr. B and Mama B made frowning faces at that and said they don't taste anything like the real Italian bakery pastries.

It was another happy occasion for me to be in such a warm family like gathering. Joey and all of his family looked so nice in their new Easter clothes. Off course Mama B still wears only black, so whenever Mom or Helen see anything in black that comes into the dress shop, they usually put it aside for Mama B. I shouldn't call it a dress shop anymore, because for a while now they have be selling a whole line of women's clothing, not just dresses. Many times Helen gives them to Mama B for free and when she does have to charge her, she only charges her the wholesale price. Daddy does the same thing for Mama B with the clothes from his job. Of course Daddy's bosses know and like Mama B a lot, so they don't mind giving her a break on the price and sometimes don't charge her at all. Mom says because Mama B is such a proud person, she doesn't like to take advantage of people like that and likes to pay her own way, as she says. For me it's such a joy to know and be so friendly with people like that.

Today's weather was just as beautiful as yesterday's and the rest of the week is supposed to be the same. What a great week to have off from school. Tomorrow, a bunch of us are planning to go to Prospect Park in the afternoon and have a picnic. Heshy and Joey are supposed to work all day all this week but Heshy told me that Joey asked their boss to let them just work in the mornings. He said okay, but only if they start at 7am every day this week and work until noon. So even if we all go to Prospect Park before noon, Heshy and Joey can meet us there. Heshy is very happy because Sarah was able to take this whole week off from her job at the store, so she'll be at the picnic too. Joey is so great, he told Sarah and me not to worry about making any food for the picnic because he was going to make the sandwiches tonight, along with some other goodies and bring them to the picnic when he and Heshy go there. Hey, did I pick the right guy to like or what? Now I can't wait until tomorrow. I think it'll be a beautiful day, even if the Sun doesn't shine, don't you dear diary? Good night.

Monday, April 15th, 1946

Dear diary, last Tuesday's picnic in Prospect Park was so beautiful and wonderful, that I can't say enough about it. Except for Heshy and Joey, we all met in the park about 11am and walked to the train on Livonia Avenue and went to Prospect Park. Heshy and Joey were to meet us at the boat house, at the Prospect Park Lake at around 12:30, but they were able to talk their boss into letting them leave a little bit earlier so they got there at noontime. Joey and Heshy were each carrying big bags of picnic food for us. Joey said he was up until 11pm making the sandwiches and Mary helped him with everything. He didn't make sandwiches for everybody, just for the four of us plus a few extra, he told us just in case somebody didn't have anything to eat. If he wasn't so thoughtful, I guess he wouldn't be Joey.

He went to Finklestein's bakery he told us about 10 o'clock the night before and bought, at half price of course, a bunch of pastries. He said he saw Frances and in fact she waited on him. He invited her to join us at the picnic, but she told him she had to work at the bakery. I hope he doesn't have his eye on her. Thinking things like that get me crazy. Oh well, anyway on the way to meet us, Heshy and Joey said they stopped at the grocery store and bought some cold drinks for us, but of course by the time we got to drink them they were on the warm side. The drinks tasted good anyway. Joey did think about the sandwiches staying fresh, so he put them in his icebox surrounded by ice the whole night and until he took them out right before he came to meet us, so they were nice and cold and fresh. He made tuna salad, egg salad, kosher salami and baloney and corned beef sandwiches. Everybody thought they were delicious. He even thought to throw candy bars into the bag for snacks in case any of us got hungry later on in the afternoon.

When we walked through the park to the zoo, or to the baseball fields or just walking down the beautiful flower lined paths, we were walking four abreast, Sarah, Heshy, Joey and me. I didn't care what anyone might say, I just loved it. Of course it would've been great if we were holding hands, but I didn't want to push it. I could hear Mom's voice telling me to be patient. Joey, knowing how much I love nature and the outdoors, would stop and point out a woodchuck or a field mouse or a beautiful wild flower or a colorful bird to me. He made me feel so special and happy. During those moments I didn't know how it would be possible for me to ever be happier, except of course if he held my hand and told me he would like me to be his girlfriend. There I go again.

After we all ate our picnic lunch, we talked about renting rowboats for an hours ride on the lake. Because not everyone had enough money to do that we decided to go down to the lake and sit along the water's edge and just watch the ducks and geese swimming along leisurely and couples rowing past in their boats. It was so peaceful and serene that I hoped at that moment that it would never end. But of course it did and about 5 o'clock we left Prospect Park to go home, but what a wonderful memory to take home with me. Again I felt like the luckiest girl in the world, but I didn't know that the best about that day was yet to come.

In our neighborhood park after dinner we all gathered again, as we usually do when the weather is nice. Joey was not in the park when Heshy and I got there but he got there a short time later. As we were all talking about what a lovely day and picnic we had, Joey said that he enjoyed the day so much, that when he got home he just had to write something about it. I knew that he liked to write down his feelings, sometimes in a poem and sometimes not, about things that happened to him, or to people and things around him. When everyone asked him what he had written, he pulled out a piece of folded up paper, unfolded it and started to read it to us. It went like this:

I saw a butterfly in front of me take flight

What beautiful colors, what a beautiful sight

I heard birds chirping early in the morn

Telling the world that a new day is born

I saw squirrels chasing one another up a tree

I heard a crow shouting loudly, was he shouting at me?

All of these things and much, much more

I saw in my backyard and my neighbor's next door

I didn't have to travel very far or wide

I just went to my window and looked outside

For the best things in life are truly free

They're there for you and they're there for me

A pretty flower or a beautiful tree

All you have to do is open your eyes to see!

Everyone thought it was beautiful, but someone had to tell Joey
that he didn't have a backyard and neither did his neighbor, and we
were in Prospect Park in the afternoon, not the morning, so what was
he writing about, they asked. The question didn't seem to bother him a
bit, although it bothered me. Joey simply said that it's true, that he and
his neighbors don't have backyards and yes it's true, that he wasn't there
in the morning, but because he was so inspired by the day we spent in
Prospect Park yesterday, he was using "poetic license", just as most poets
do and then laughed, and everyone else did too. Just thinking about
the things that Joey says and does gives me Goosebumps sometimes.
Maybe that's why he told me a few times that I was a silly goose, he saw
my Goosebumps. Ha! Ha!

I did get to do some babysitting last week, but not too much. I just
went over during the day a few times to help Mama B with Joshua and
Sophie but she did have some help from Arlene and Barbara. It's a lucky
thing that their kids all like each other and get along so well. I know
that I seem to only tell you about the good and wonderful things that
are going on around here, but believe me there are plenty of not so nice
things going on. I might have told you about a few of them before, but
there is so much more. Albert Jackowitz, who was on the high school
football and basketball team, he was such a good looking guy too, got
into drugs and the last time I saw him he looked awful. He was walking

around like he was in a daze and he could barely hold his head up, all because of drugs. Joey, who knows him pretty well, because they live on the same block, told me that Albert's new philosophy about life is that he can end it any time he wants to. Is that a horrible thing to think and say or what? Just thinking about him makes me not want to say anymore about the bad things that are going on around here. I'll tell you some more about these things at another time. Just thinking about it gets me a little depressed. I can't write anymore tonight so I'll just say good night dear diary.

Tuesday, April 16th, 1946

Dear diary, it's been a sad day today, not only for Mama B and her family, but for all of us who are their friends, because today is the one year anniversary of the death of Joey's brother, Buster. The whole family has been very sad today and that's understandable. I hope they get back to their usual selves soon, because it hurts me to see them that way. Not just me but all of us. Mom went over to visit with Mama B tonight after she got home from work and stayed there for quite a while. Mom said that although Mama B is hurting and sad right now, she thinks they will all be alright in a short while. I hope Mom is right, as she usually is. I can't write anymore right now, because you know that sad things bother me, so I'll just say good night dear diary.

Monday, April 22nd, 1946

Dear diary, we got great news today about Heshy. I forgot to tell you about a month ago, that Heshy entered a national essay writing contest about the Stock Market, free enterprise and capitalism. When we got home from school today he got a letter telling him that he won the contest. None of us could believe it. I mean, it involved the whole country and he won. I remember how hard he worked on it every night after doing his homework. He would stay up sometimes until midnight until it was done just the way he wanted to present it. I think it took him about two weeks to finish it because he had to do a lot of research on the subject. We are all so proud of him. He gets to spend a whole day at the New York Stock Exchange in Manhattan and also will ring the opening bell, whatever that means. Here's the best part, he's going to get a sample, I think it's called a portfolio, of one stock from ten of the biggest companies in the country. Is this great or what? I mean he's not even fifteen years old yet and as Daddy says, now he's a stockholder.

I think Heshy said that he goes to pick up his prize on Thursday, May 16th. I know he can hardly wait and neither can Mom, Daddy and I. Joey and Sarah are also very proud of him. Daddy told him that he now has to go and buy a brand new suit so he will look good for the occasion and Mom and I agreed. Joey came over after the news spread around the neighborhood and pretended to be mad and demanded that he get half the prize because he said he helped Heshy with most of the essay. Of course he didn't, but he got a good laugh even from Heshy. Joey couldn't stop telling Heshy how proud of him he was. Heshy couldn't stop beaming the whole night, he was so happy. Can you blame him? I wonder how he'll be greeted in school tomorrow. Like a hero I suppose. I hope it doesn't go to his head and make him a different person. If it does I guess Mom, Daddy and I will have to bring him back down to earth. I'm sure Joey won't let his best friend get a swelled head either at least I hope he won't. We shall see tomorrow, but for now, good night dear diary.

Thursday, April 25th, 1946

Dear diary, all of my concerns about Heshy getting a big head over winning that contest were for nothing. He was greeted in school on Tuesday like a hero alright but he didn't let it go to his head. In fact he told Joey and me on the way to school that morning that even though he worked very hard on the essay, he felt that he was very lucky to have won. The whole school, teachers and students were all proud of him, as were many of the people in our neighborhood.

When Daddy came home from work on Tuesday night, he told us that his bosses, Sal and Sol both live in big houses in New Jersey. In a town called Tenafly. I never heard of it before and I'm not even sure how to pronounce it. Anyway, Daddy said that we were all, including the Balduccis, invited over to Sal"s house this coming Sunday, the 28th, to spend a day at his pool, if the weather is warm enough, and, have a cookout. Daddy said that on the way home from work he stopped at the Balducci's house to tell them about the invitation. He said they were very pleasantly surprised and said they would love to go with us.

Mr. B said that through one of his bosses at the taxi garage where he works, he was able to buy a new eight passenger station wagon and he is picking it up on Saturday. He said it's going to work out perfectly. Is this great or what?

We're all looking forward to not only going to the cookout on Sunday, but also to riding in Mr. B's new car. Do you see why I'm always saying that I'm the luckiest girl in the world? Daddy and Mr. B are trying to figure out what to bring with us to give to Sal as a "thank you" present, even though Sal said that we didn't have to bring anything. Knowing Mom, Daddy, Mama B and Mr. B, I'm sure we'll be bringing something. Heshy said that at Schlossberg's they are having a sale on picnic tables, chairs and stuff like that. He said he saw something that Sal might like. It's an apron, chef's hat and outdoor cooking utensils, all in a set. Joey added that with the sale and our employee discount, it won't cost a lot. Everybody thought that was a good idea, but Daddy thought we should get something else too. Mr. B and Mama B agreed with him and suggested maybe some wine or pastries, or maybe both. Everyone looked at Mama B when she mentioned the pastries, you know because she's not supposed to have any of that stuff. She quickly added that of course she couldn't eat any of them. We all smiled and shook our heads in agreement. We shall see. Good night for now dear diary.

Monday, April 29th, 1946

Dear diary, wow, what a great time we all had yesterday at Daddy's boss, Sal's house in Tenafly, New Jersey. First of all he lives a very big and beautiful house with a huge backyard, with a swimming pool. The trees and the flower beds that surrounded the house all reminded me of Prospect Park. Although the weather was warm and full of sunshine, Sal said that the water in the pool was still too cold for us to go swimming in. Although Heshy, Sarah, Mary, Joey and I brought our bathing suits just in case, we were not at all disappointed, because it was so lovely just being there. Sal immediately put on the apron and hat and also used the big cookout fork and spatula. He seemed to love that gift and the wine that Mr. B brought and also the different kinds of Italian breads and pastries that Daddy brought. He cooked on a big beautiful stone outdoor grill. He cooked enough food to feed an army.

He cooked chicken, steak and fish too. He even grilled some of the vegetables. I never had that before and they were delicious.

Sol and his family joined us after a while and ate with us. I can't begin to describe the beauty of the inside of the house, with fireplaces in some rooms and it even has a library. Sal called it his study, but it looked more like a library to me, with bookshelves lined with books on all the walls. That room had a fireplace too. It looked so cozy and I thought to myself how warm that room must be in the cold weather, with a fire going in the fireplace. Mom's jaw dropped as she took the tour of the house too. Mama B just looked around and said everything looked so nice and that Sal and Sol both deserve what they have, because they not only worked so hard, but they are so good to people. She said they never seem to forget that they once had very little too.

Heshy looking around the house kept saying to himself, but out loud, that someday he would have a house like this and maybe even bigger and better. Joey on the other hand just admired all the fine work that the people who built the house had done. He looked closely at the mouldings on the ceilings and said that whoever did this kind of work are truly artists. Sol and Sal heard him say that and they both agreed with him. Not only that, but they thought that Joey had a "good eye" for art, like a lot of people do who usually go unrecognized. They compared him to some of the people that work for them, who not only design but work out the details of making the clothes they sell.

As we were getting ready to leave for home, Sol invited us to stop by his house for a few minutes, which was very close to Sal's house and looked every bit as lovely. I found myself getting a little jealous, but then I thought about the little poem that Joey wrote, about the best things in life being truly free and I wasn't jealous anymore. On the drive back home we were all talking about the beautiful homes that they both lived in and Daddy was saying that he didn't think he would ever be able to afford to own a house like that. Mr. B said that he didn't think that he would either, but Mama B said that having a nice big house isn't important. She said that having a loving home, no matter what kind of house you live in, is what's important. After a moment of silence we all agreed that she was right.

On the way to Sal's house and on the way back, when we were crossing over the George Washington Bridge, we noticed a large boat crowded with people on the Hudson River. In the morning it was going north up the river and on the way home we saw the same boat going south down the river. Joey and I at the same time asked if anyone knew what that boat was. Mr. B said it was the Hudson River Line that goes on day trips up to Bear Mountain on just weekends this time of year, but every day during the summer months. He said he had driven people there many times in his taxi cab and that's how he knew. Heshy, Sarah, Joey and I thought that would be a great thing to do, so we decided to arrange to go on that trip the following Sunday, May 5th.

So today we asked a few others to join us on Sunday for the boat ride up to Bear Mountain and spend the day up there. We found out that there is a big lake up there and picnic grounds, softball fields, horseback riding and a lot of other stuff. One of our teachers, when he heard us talking about it, said that if we liked Prospect Park, we'd love Bear Mountain Park. To our surprise about ten other kids wanted to go too. I only hope that the weather will be good and warm, but we were also told that even if it rains, we will enjoy the boat ride and they do have some other things to do in the park where we won't get wet. We shall see. I can't wait. I have another good time to look forward to. Good night dear diary.

CHAPTER 11

Sunday, May 5th, 1946

Dear diary, I'm so tired tonight and I'm also the happiest that I've ever been in my life. I really should go to sleep, but I can't wait to tell you about the most beautiful day I've ever had. Joey said that he would again make the sandwiches for our trip to Bear Mountain Park, like he did for our picnic in Prospect Park a few weeks ago, but I told him that I wanted to make them this time, because it wasn't fair for him to always make the lunch for us. He reluctantly said okay and that's what I did. I told him if he wanted to, he could bring the drinks. He said how about he brings the drinks and the dessert too. I couldn't say no to him again, so I said okay. Sarah was going to make some stuff too and we, the four of us were going to share it all. Of course, just like Joey did, I made some extra sandwiches in case someone didn't have enough. Joey is starting to rub off on me I think.

We all met in the park at 7:30 this morning and took the subway into Manhattan and then walked over to the pier where the Hudson River Line boat was. We got there a little early and had to wait a few minutes before we could go aboard. Joey all this time carried the big bag of food and the drinks that he bought, while Heshy carried the food that Sarah made and the drinks he bought. From the beginning of this trip, I kind of felt like we were two couples in the midst of a bunch of other couples. At 9am on the dot the boat left the pier and we started our trip up the Hudson. Thank God it was a warm and sunny today, although on the water it was a little on the cool side, but not really cold.

We were told that the trip takes about two hours, so we should all just enjoy the ride and the scenery on the way up there. They played nice music on the boat, but dancing was not allowed. After about half an hour or so, while I was standing with Heshy and most of the gang, I noticed Joey hanging over the guard rail staring at the water. I quietly walked up to him and stood right next to him and in fact leaned my left shoulder to his right side, touching him. He didn't notice me at first, but when I touched him with my shoulder he was startled for a second. When he realized it was me, he gave me a smile that I had never seen on him before. I gave him a smile right back that I think came from the depths of my heart. We just smiled at each other for what seemed like a long time, but I'm sure was only for no more than a minute. I don't know but there seemed to be magic in the air or something, because he seemed to me to have a glow about his face when he looked at me. I don't know if I was blushing or not because I felt warm all over. I was wondering if he felt that way too.

When the boat passed under the shadow of some very tall buildings close to the river's edge, it suddenly felt cooler and I must have shivered, because Joey asked me if I was cold and put his arm around me and pulled me close to him, to give me some warmth, he said. As soon as we were in the sunshine again he took his arm away but still stayed close to me. I couldn't believe what was happening to me, I thought that maybe I was dreaming or something. We stayed close by each other the rest of the way up to Bear Mountain Park and nobody said anything, although we did get some curious looks from some of the gang. I don't know about Joey, but I didn't care what anyone thought.

When we got off the boat Heshy, Sarah, Joey and I walked four abreast again, just like in Prospect Park. Joey was carrying our lunch bag in his right hand and I was walking on his left side, when I gently took hold of his hand and without missing a step, he held my hand gently but firmly. He looked to his left and down at me as I looked up at him and there was that glow on his face again. I know that they say the eyes are the windows to the soul, but I swear I could see Joey's loving heart in his smile. We just walked that way, looking and smiling at each other and not a word was being spoken. Not with our mouths anyway.

Because we all got up and ate breakfast early, and it was now 11am, we were all hungry, so we decided to go to the picnic grounds first. We just followed the signs and in no time we were there. I'm not sure, but I think Joey and I holding hands all the while we were walking made the time go by so much faster. I couldn't believe that my dreams were coming true. I think there must have been a silly grin on my face all through lunch. I know Joey was smiling the whole time and people were just looking at us and smiling too. Besides our gang being there, the park was very crowded because it was the first really beautiful weekend of the spring, but I didn't notice anybody except my Joey.

After we finished eating we all decided to walk to the zoo area. It was very lovely along the path, with wild flowers blooming, colorful birds singing, squirrels and chipmunks and rabbits and other small animals scurrying all around us and being surrounded by the tall beautiful trees. But the best part of all was, that Joey and I were walking together holding hands. The zoo reminded me a lot of the Prospect Park Zoo and was very interesting. Joey was his usual funny self around the Monkey House, making faces at the monkeys and then he started walking around like one. He had everybody laughing. When Heshy tried to do the same walk he almost fell over and that too made everyone laugh, I think the monkeys did too.

From the zoo, we walked over to the boathouse at the lake. Unlike our trip to Prospect Park, everyone brought enough money, so we all could rent rowboats. Soon we were all on the lake with the guys doing most of the rowing. Joey pointed out to me the beauty of the tall trees around the water's edge that were mirrored in the water. It was very beautiful. This lake is much bigger that the Prospect Park Lake. It wasn't long before I realized that we were very far from any of the other boats and as we went around a bend in the lake, Joey headed the boat toward the shore, behind some tall trees and underbrush. Because we couldn't see any of the other boats, I guess Joey thought that no one could see us. He pulled in the oars and came over to my side of the boat and sat down beside me. At this point my heart was racing so fast I thought I was going to have a heart attack or something. I felt sure that Joey was finally going to kiss me. I think I even started to purse my lips, when all of a sudden we heard Heshy's loud booming voice yelling out for Joey and me. He didn't just call out once, he kept it up until Joey quickly went back to his side of the boat, put the oars back in the water and rowed out to where he could see us.

Joey looked a little mad and embarrassed at the same time. He then looked at me, smiled and then we both started to laugh. Sarah all this time was yelling at Heshy for calling out to us and as she said, bothering us. Joey and I both lied, but it was a little white lie and said that Heshy didn't bother us at all. The hour on the lake went very fast and then we just walked around and admired all of nature's wonderful creations that were everywhere to be seen. As Joey said in his poem, "all we have to do is open our eyes and see". Of course throughout all of our strolling through Bear Mountain Park, Joey and I held hands, tightly and yet gently. Not a word passed between us about why we were holding hands and we just seemed to speak to each other with our eyes and the touch of our hands. It was so beautiful.

As we lined up, all of us waiting to get on the boat for the trip home, Joey let go of my hand and put his arm around me, drew me so close and tight to him and leaned over and kissed me. It was a steady and gentle kiss and took me by surprise, but when he pulled his head back from the kiss, I stood up on my tippy toes and kissed him right back. I don't know if there were any fireworks going off in the park or on the river but they were sure going off in my head and heart. Everyone seemed to leave us alone on the boat during the entire trip home and Joey and I, it seemed to me were hugging and kissing for most of the trip. Of course we weren't but the magic of the moment made it feel that way to me. We talked a good part of the time and when I asked Joey if this meant that we are now boyfriend and girlfriend, he looked surprised and then shocked me. He said that we have been boyfriend and girlfriend for a long time it's just that he never told me so in so many words. I couldn't believe it! So I asked him how I was supposed to know that if he didn't tell me. He laughed and said that he told me many times and in many ways and he thought I picked up on that.

He told me that today was absolutely the best day of his life and he would never ever forget it. When I asked him why he never told me how he felt about me before today, he started to tell me the story about his brother Buster and how he had his heart broken because he was not Jewish and loved a Jewish girl. I stopped him and told him that I knew about that story, because his mother had told my Mom about it. He was a little surprised at first, but then went on to tell me that all he was waiting for was, to try and get Mom and Daddy to like him enough, so that if I liked him as much as he liked me, they might not object to him being my boyfriend. I said, like him, they love him. He said that while he likes them almost as if they were family and he thinks they like him probably the same way, he still wasn't sure that they would like him to be my boyfriend. After listening to him, I now have some doubts about how Daddy is going to feel, even though I think he knows how I feel about Joey and he never says anything to me about it.

When I got home tonight Mom looked at me with a funny looking smile on her face and asked me if something good happened to me today. Is she perceptive or what? So of course I told her everything that happened and everything that Joey and I said to each other. She gave me an "I told you so look" and said, "I told you so". She laughed and told me she was so happy for me, but she wasn't sure how Daddy would react, so she told me not to make a big announcement about it in the house or anywhere for that matter. Because she said It is not Daddy that would object, because he likes Joey very much, but it's what some of the "yentas" at the temple might say. Besides, she said she and Daddy have talked about me and Joey before and he didn't get angry at the thought. She thinks Daddy accepts Joey for the good guy that he is. Isn't that funny, because that's just what Joey wanted my parents to do, accept him for the person that he is and nothing else. I'm praying that everything will be alright now that my dream seems to be coming true. Oh well, we shall see. I can't believe it's almost midnight and I'm very tired so good night dear diary.

Monday, May 6th, 1946

Dear diary, on the walk to school today, for the first time ever, Joey and I held hands and nobody seemed to either notice or mind. That's exactly the way I wanted it to be. When we got into our home room class, before the teacher took attendance, Joey handed me a piece of paper and told me to read it when I was alone. He said it was personal and private and only for my eyes to see. He then added that if I liked it, I could show it to anyone I wanted to. On the way to my English class I went into the girls room, into a stall and read it. It almost brought me to tears. It was a very lovely little sentiment that he felt and put down on paper, entitled "The joy of holding hands" and here is what it said:

THE JOY OF HOLDING HANDS

As our hands touched, just a split second before they clasped, a warm wonderful sensation passed from our fingertips, through our bodies and went down to our toes and gently warmed our hearts. We both breathed a deep sigh as our hands firmly, but gently locked onto each other. We turned our heads toward each other, giving each other a loving look, kind of kissing with our eyes. As our hands were interlocked in their own special embrace, so too were our hearts, minds and souls. Through the touching of our hands, our hearts were filled with the warmth of how we feel about each other and at that moment we only felt joy. At that moment we were not aware of anybody around us. Even after we unlocked our hands, the feeling of oneness lingered, until we got into another Heavenly hand lock. It all began with a touching of our fingers. It's just another lovely way of saying, "I care".

I was on cloud nine all day in school and all the way home. On the days that Joey and Heshy have to work at the store, like today, they go there right from school and I missed having my hand held by Joey. I couldn't wait for Mom to come home from work so I could show her what Joey had written, about what our holding hands meant to him. I did my homework as soon as I got home from school, so that I could have a nice talk with Mom and maybe still have time to hang out with the gang in the park. Maybe, if I got lucky, I'd see Joey and Heshy when they got home from their jobs.

After we finished eating and cleaning up, I was able to be with Mom alone for a short while and I showed her what Joey had written. When she finished reading it, she held it to her heart, wiped a tear from her eyes and said, "What a sensitive heart he has". I added what a loving heart too. Mom said, yes that too and told me not to make too big a fuss about it, because when the word got around the neighborhood, there will be trouble from the "yentas". All of a sudden my joy turned to worry and when Mom saw that on my face, she told me not to worry, because she said we can deal with whatever happens and that she will let no one or nothing hurt me. See what I mean when I say I have the best Mom in the world? Well maybe Mama B's just as good to Joey.

When I went to the park to see my friends, for the first time some of them told me, that they thought it was great that me and Joey are a couple, as they put it. They also said that they knew for a long time that this was going to happen just by the way Joey was always hanging around me and Heshy. And the way he would always help me when I babysat the kids, and how mad he got when the "yenta" Sylvia said all those nasty things about me. A couple of them said they wished they had someone who would be as protective of them. It felt so good hearing that. Some of the girls said that Joey was very lucky to have a girlfriend like me, but most of the others thought that I was the lucky one to have him for my boyfriend. I don't know if Joey feels lucky or not, but I sure feel like I'm the lucky one. I think Daddy would probably say that Joey is the lucky one, but Mom would say that we are both very lucky. I think I'll agree with Mom.

Just as I had hoped, Heshy and Joey came walking into the park at about 8:15 and Joey came straight over to me and gave me a big hug and a kiss. I was on top of the world. I felt like a princess, like someone very special. That's how he's made me feel for a long time, only now much more so. Heshy and Sarah greeted each other the same way, but not nearly as eager as Joey and I were to embrace, if you know what I mean. We were just standing around with the gang, our arms around each other, and I asked Joey if he was going to go home to have his dinner and he said he was and asked me to come and sit with him while he ate. Of course I jumped at the chance and went with him. In the meantime Heshy went home to have his dinner and Sarah went with him, so I guess Joey and I are just like an old couple now. After all, it's over a whole day now that we became officially girlfriend and boyfriend. Good night dear diary, with Joey by my side, I know that all my tomorrows will be great.

Wednesday, May 8th, 1946

Dear diary today is Heshy's and my fifteenth birthday and Joey made the most beautiful card for me with a most lovely message inside. My only hope is that I make him feel the same way.

If there's a more beautiful girl in this world, than you Esther,

I don't know who she could be,

You are the only girl in this world for me,

You have the bluest of eyes,

Bluer than the bluest skies,

You have a radiant smile and a heart so true,

That's why I, with all of my heart wish you,

A MOST BEAUTIFUL AND HAPPY BIRTHDAY.

It almost had me in tears it is so beautiful. He makes me feel so lucky and special

He told me that Mrs. Schultz, the art teacher helped him with making the artwork on the front, because he told her the card was for me. He told me that Mrs. Schultz likes me very much. I told Joey that I liked her very much too. Joey didn't know what to buy me for my birthday, so he asked Heshy what he thought I might need and Heshy told him to buy me a gift certificate from Schlossberg's store. He said with the discount I would get more for the money and I can pick out whatever it is that I liked. That sounded very good to me. Guess what? Heshy gave me the same thing. I love that too. Now I can really feel like I've grown up by shopping for myself and by myself if I want to. But you know I'm going to ask Mom to come with me, to help me shop and If I have any money left over, I'll buy something for her too. My parents bought me another new outfit to wear for the spring and the summer. I love it. Joey, my Parents and I chipped in and bought Heshy two tickets to see a Broadway show, "South Pacific" with Sarah. Then to our surprise my parents got two extra tickets for me and Joey, a matinee, because they didn't want us to be in Manhattan by ourselves late at night. They also got Heshy a nice sport shirt and a pair of slacks that he liked very much.

The past few days have been glorious for me. Every morning I walk to school holding hands with Joey and most of the time he carries my books too. On the days he doesn't have to go to work, we walk home the same way. Of course, we are always with Heshy and Sarah, who are also walking and holding hands too. It may look a little strange to some people I guess, me and Joey holding hands, but like I said before, I don't care. In the school yard in the mornings waiting to enter the school, Joey and I are usually still holding hands and sometimes maybe even hugging. Some of our teachers have seen us and a couple of them, because they're Jewish I think, have looked at me in a disapproving way. "Yentas", I said to myself, I don't care what they think, because I don't think I'm doing anything wrong. I mean, I don't think Mom would let me do anything wrong, would she? Of course not, not my Mom.

Tonight when I was in the park with the gang, Barbara came strolling in and came over to me. She had a big grin on her face and told me she heard all about me being Joey's girlfriend and she said she thought that was great. I couldn't believe how fast news travels around here, especially since "yenta" Sylvia isn't around anymore, and I told Barbara that. She told me she knew it was going to happen for a long time just by the way we acted when we were around each other. I never realized that I was so obvious when I was around him. Then she said that she thought we were both very lucky, because we were the nicest of all the kids in our age group, in our neighborhood. What a nice thing for her to say. She said she thought that Joey got his nice thoughtful ways from Mama B. I asked her if that's true, and I think it is, what did he get from Mr. B? She asked me if I meant besides his external plumbing. Even though I was a little shocked by the question, it was so funny that I had to laugh and so did she. I told her that she is so naughty, but so nice. She said she was only kidding, but the truth of the matter is, that both of Joey's parents are very nice and thoughtful, giving people so Joey is the way he is, because of both of them.

You know diary, after I thanked Joey and Heshy for the nice and thoughtful gift, I told Joey when we were alone, that the best birthday present I ever got was when he told me we were boyfriend and girlfriend and have been for a long time, although I didn't know it for a long time. Then he told me the sweetest thing. He said that almost from the time we first met in grammar school, he thought I was a special person and that even though as we grew older, he became friendlier with people, he always still thought of me as being very special. I always knew that he liked to kid around with everyone, but sometimes I told him, I thought he had a special interest in some of the girls he kidded around with. He looked at me a little surprised and then asked me if I had Goosebumps. I told him no and when I asked him why he wanted to know that, he said because I was acting like a silly goose. We both had to laugh at that.

I then asked him how he would've felt if I had gone to the movies with Sylvia's cousin Bobby, whatever his name is. He said that of course he wouldn't have liked it, but he never asked any other girl to go anywhere with him and in fact, when he was asked a few times to go somewhere with a girl, he always turned them down. Now I was surprised, because I never knew that any girl had ever asked him to go anywhere with her. And I thought I knew just about everything that was going on around here and everything about Joey. Where was Sylvia the "yenta" when I needed her, I thought to myself. I told Joey I was sorry and that I would never be jealous again. He told me that there was nothing to be sorry for, but he said that I shouldn't be surprised if I ever feel that way again because, he said I am a woman. A woman! I said I'm not a woman, I'm a young girl! He laughed and said that he meant to say a young woman, because that's what I really am, a young woman. I thought about it for a second and then had to agree with him, I am a young woman. After all, I can now go shopping for my clothes all by myself if I wanted to, so I guess that makes me a young woman. What a guy he is. He can make me laugh, feel so special and sometime he teaches me a thing or two.

Wednesday, May 15th, 1946

Dear diary, Joey and I are old news around here now. We still walk either holding hands or with our arms around each other, but no one seems to notice or say anything about it anymore. That's good because that's the way I like it. Even Daddy doesn't say anything about us holding hands when he sees us in the park together. I wasn't sure if that was good or bad, so I asked Mom and she said it was good, so I'm not worried about it anymore. He and Joey still kibbutz with each other and they both seem to love it. In fact last week Joey told me and my family that Mrs. Klein, Mama B's friend from up the street on Powell Street, showed him and Mama B how to make Chicken noodle soup and he brought some over for us to sample. It was very good, but of course not as good as my Mom's, but then again whose chicken noodle soup is. Well tonight when Joey was doing his homework with Heshy and me, Daddy asked him if he learned any new recipes. Joey put on that serious face again so I knew Daddy was going to get it, and he told Daddy that he in fact did. He said he learned how to make Gold soup. Daddy said, "Gold soup! I never heard of Gold soup. How in the world would you make Gold soup?" Mom was so curious she came into the dining room from the kitchen to hear Joey's answer. Joey, with a very straight face looked Daddy right in the eyes and said that first you start out with fourteen carrots.

Daddy in exasperation said, "I had to ask him! I don't know why I bothered to ask him!" Mom, laughing more at Daddy's response than at Joey's joke I think, ran into the bathroom again. Joey then added that if you wanted to make a richer gold soup you could use eighteen carrots. Again we all laughed and Daddy trying to get the last and best word in, asked why you wouldn't use twenty four carrots and Joey snapped back that it would make it too soft and mushy. Daddy laughed and said he gave up and that Joey had won that one.

I think I'm coming down with a cold or something because I didn't feel just right all day so I'm going to go to bed now and maybe a good night's rest will make me feel better in the morning. Oh yeah, tomorrow Heshy is going to get his prize for winning that essay contest. Mom and Daddy are going to go with him. If I feel tomorrow like I felt today then I'm glad I'm not going too and besides I don't want to miss any school days so close to the end of my Jr. High School days. I asked Mom to take a camera with her so she snap some pictures and I can see them later on. Good night for now dear diary.

Thursday, May 16th, 1946

Dear diary, a terrible thing happened in school today, but first let me tell you that when I woke up this morning I didn't feel good. In fact I felt a little worse than I did yesterday and when Mom saw, by the look on my face I guess, that I wasn't feeling well she said that she was going to stay home with me and not go with Daddy and Heshy to the stock exchange. I protested and told Mom that I was going to go to school today and that I thought I would be alright and besides I said, if I didn't feel any better in school I would come home and go right to bed. That seemed to satisfy Mom and she went with Heshy and Daddy to Manhattan. Heshy looked so great and grown up in his new suit, I felt so proud of him.

I was feeling lousy when I started to walk down Sackman Street but when I got close to the corner of Riverdale Avenue and saw Joey's smiling face I seemed to perk up and feel a little better. Even Joey by just looking at me could tell that I wasn't feeling well and asked me if

I was okay. I told him I thought that I was just coming down with a cold or something, some kind of a bug. I went to hold his hand but he put his arm around me instead and held me tight and so close to him that the two of us had to walk slowly. I didn't care at that moment if we were late for school because his holding me so close felt so warm and wonderful. We managed to get to school on time.

Our home room teacher just finished taking attendance when I suddenly felt very sick. I felt so faint that I thought I was going to pass out. At the same time I started to feel nauseous and I thought I might throw up too. When some one yelled out that I looked like I was going to throw up, all the kids sitting near me quickly moved away and at that moment I felt a pair of strong, familiar arms around me, lifting me out of my seat and half carrying and half walking me to the door. Then I heard Joey's voice comforting me with words of assurance that I was going to be alright. He never said a word to the teacher and she didn't stop him. Once we got into the hall I did throw up a little and Joey quietly told me not to worry and sat me down on the bench in front of the Guidance Counselor's office and went into the boys bath room, came out with a fist full of toilet paper and cleaned up the little mess that I made.

I don't know how Joey did it, but he half walked and half carried me out of the school and we headed toward my house. Joey wanted to take me to the nurse's office but I begged him not to because I was afraid she might call for an ambulance to take me to the hospital and I don't like the idea of riding in an ambulance, it scares me and it always has. Joey is amazing, I mean he just got me out of the classroom without even asking the teacher if it was alright and nobody stopped him. On the way home, I was still feeling very sick and as we were nearing Livonia Avenue I saw Mrs. Epstein, she's the grandmother of one of the kids we go to school with, Lenny Kahn. Anyway, she was coming down the long stairs from the "EL" and was loaded down with packages. She only lives a short distance from my house and in fact we had to pass it on the way to my house, so I asked Joey to please help her with some of her bundles. I mean she looked like she wouldn't be able to make it home carrying all that stuff. Joey gave me a, "are you kidding me look" and then asked her if she would like a little help and she thanked him and said yes.

So there was Joey half carrying me home with his right arm holding me up as I walked and with his left arm loaded down with Mrs. Epstein's packages. Joey breathed a sigh of relief when we got to Mrs. Epstein's house and he was able to unload her stuff, and we continued to my house. Joey was so good to me. When we got into my apartment he told me to go right into my bedroom and get undressed and get into my bed. I knew what he wanted me to do but I jokingly made believe I was shocked by what he told me to do and asked him what he had in mind. He knew I was kidding and told me that this was no time for jokes and he made me a cup of hot tea while I made myself comfortable in my bed. Before he brought the tea in he came over to feel my head to see if I felt warm and then asked me if we had a thermometer because he wasn't sure if I felt a little warm to him or not. I told him that I thought we did but I didn't know where it would be. I felt like such a dope for not knowing and I told him that. He said I wasn't a dope because unless I had a reason to know before, then I wouldn't know. The next time, he said, I think I have a fever I'll know where Mom keeps the thermometer. After he felt sure that I was going to be alright he went back to school. Before he left he took my house keys and told me that he would be back, if not at lunch time then right after school. As sick as I felt, I also felt like the luckiest girl in the world.

I didn't know what time it was when I was awakened by some noise in the kitchen and I sleepily called out to whoever it or whatever it was making the noise. There was music in my ears when I heard Joey's voice answering me. He came into my room and told me he didn't mean to wake me up, but he was glad that I was awake. He said that on his way back to school this morning he stopped at his house and after telling Mama B that I was sick he asked her to make some escarole and chicken broth soup for me and that he would pick it up at noon time. Today in school right before the lunch break we usually have gym class and Joey told me that he asked Mr. Lewis, the gym teacher, if he could leave early because I was sick. Mr. Lewis told him that he couldn't authorize it, but if Joey left while he was looking the other way then he wouldn't know the difference. Of course, he told Joey if he got caught out of school at that time he would claim that he didn't know anything about it. So that's what Joey did and thank God he didn't get caught. Joey thinks Mr. Lewis is a very nice man for understanding the way that he felt about me being sick.

Joey was heating up soup when I heard him in the kitchen. He asked me if I felt well enough to come to the dining room table and if not he would serve it to me in bed. Before I could answer he asked me if I would like to have some toast with it. I answered yes to both questions and I got out of bed and put my bathrobe on and walked into the dining room. Joey set out the bowls of soup. He fixed some for himself too and went back into the kitchen to get the toast. Before sitting down he came over to me and felt my forehead to see if I had a fever and said I felt cool now. He fussed over me so that he reminded me of Mom. After I had the soup I felt a little better and was even talking about going back to school with him but Joey wouldn't even let me talk about it.

At about six o'clock Mom, Daddy and Heshy came home from Heshy's big day at the stock market and I told them what happened to me today in school. Mom immediately rushed over to me in the bed and asked me if I felt feverish at the same time she was feeling my head. Joey, who was still there with me, since after school, told Mom that he was checking up on me all day and he didn't think I had a fever. He told Mom that I had the soup that Mama B made for me and also some toast that he had made for me. Mom couldn't thank Joey enough and also told him to thank Mama B. I told Mom that I slept most of the afternoon and was feeling a little better. She kept saying that she knew that she shouldn't have gone into the city and that she should have kept me home from school and stayed with me. I tried to assure Mom that I was okay and that all I had was probably some sort of bug or something. Mom just said that if I didn't feel better in the morning she wasn't going to work and she was going to call Dr. Morris Gold.

Mom thought that a little of her chicken noodle soup might do me some good and heated up some that was leftover from a couple of days ago. Before Mom and the rest of them got home tonight, Joey's sister Mary brought over a loaf of home made Italian bread so I had a piece of it with the chicken noodle soup. They both tasted very good and again made me feel a little better. I still felt very tired and a little light headed and as soon as I finished the soup I told everyone that I just wanted to go to sleep. Joey hugged me, gave me a kiss on my forehead and told me he hoped I felt better in the morning. He also said that he would call me on the phone in the morning to see how I felt and if I needed or wanted anything. Mom and Daddy thanked him again and

Mom gave him a hug and he left. I don't know what I would've done if he wasn't with me most of the day. Just knowing that he was there for me really made me feel a little better, but I still felt and still feel sick, if you know what I mean.

I woke up a couple of hours later and got up to go to the bathroom. Mom asked me how I was feeling and checked my head again. She then asked me if I would like a nice cup of tea and when I said yes, she fixed a cup for me and it hit the spot. I then went back into my bed and started to read the newspaper and Mom came into my room and sat down on the bed and we just had a nice talk about how Heshy's big day went. She told me that after Joey left earlier and I had gone to sleep, Daddy told her that he was so glad that I had such a nice fella like Joey here looking after me. Hearing that really made me feel good but I knew that something was going through my body. After Mom went to bed I decided to write to you dear diary but now I must say good night.

Friday, May 17th, 1946

Dear diary, this morning I felt much worse than I did yesterday except I didn't throw up, so Mom stayed home from work and called Dr. Morris Gold and asked him to please come over to look at me. We have to say Dr. Morris Gold because he has a brother who is also a doctor in the same office and his name is Dr. Andrew J. Gold. Joey called me at 7:30 this morning just like he said he would, to ask how I felt and if I were going to go to school or needed anything. He is so sweet, even Mom said so when he called. He told me he would try again to come and see me at lunchtime. As sick as I felt I was looking forward to seeing him at noontime. I bet he'll bring his lunch and maybe even something for me and Mom and sit and eat it with us, I told myself.

While the doctor was examining me Joey showed up and just like yesterday he was a little out of breath from running all the way over from school. Joey quietly waited in the dining room while the doctor finished checking me over. Dr. Gold said that he thinks I probably have a bug of some kind and he gave me a shot of Penicillin and also a prescription for some pills that I will have to take every three hours for a few days he said. He also said that he wanted to take some blood from me to send out to a lab to check out a few things just to make sure there is nothing else wrong with me. After he left and while we were eating our lunch, by the way I was right about Joey bringing something for Mom and me to eat, I was saying that the blood test business scared me a little bit. Mom and Joey both told me that there is nothing to worry about because it's just a routine thing that they do just to make sure that everything is alright. I was a little relieved. The doctor said that he would know the results of the blood test by Monday or Tuesday at the latest but he would call me over the weekend to see how I was feeling.

Joey was going to rush back to school for his afternoon classes but he decided to stay with me and Mom for the afternoon. After he called Mama B to see how she was and to tell her that he wasn't going back to school so that he could be with me, he went down to the drug store to get the prescription for the pills filled. Even though Mom told him that he didn't have to take off from school this afternoon I think she was glad that he did. I know I was. Joey said that if I wasn't well enough to go to school by Monday, he would ask all of our teachers to give him make up work for me to do at home and between Heshy and himself helping I shouldn't be behind in any of my schoolwork. He then added that the last time he was a little behind was when he was a baby and of course you know he had me and Mom laughing. I really needed one at that moment because I was still feeling sick and that laugh picked me up a little. Joey told me that in school this morning everyone, kids and teachers alike, were asking how I was feeling and what was wrong with me. Of course he didn't know exactly what is wrong with me, but since he did call me before he went to school this morning, he told them that I was feeling a little better but not well enough to go to school today. He said everyone wished me well. That was very nice to hear.

A few minutes after Joey left to go home to have his dinner and to see how Mama B was doing, Daddy came home from work. After he first greeted Mom he came straight into my room and asked me, with a big smile on his face, how his "totala" was doing. I told him everything that happened today, from what the doctor said, and the blood that he took from me to test, and the Penicillin shot he gave me. I also told Daddy about how nice it was of Joey to run over to the drug store to get my prescription for some kind of pills filled and Daddy said, mockingly that Joey ran over himself and he doesn't even own a car. Daddy's jokes are getting funnier. I think Joey is rubbing off on him. Daddy sat down on the bed, gave me a big hug and asked me if he could get anything for me. I told him that between Mom, Heshy and Joey I'm being very well taken care of. He said that's very good and got up to leave but when he got to the door he turned around to me and said that Joey not only cooks, writes poems and tells jokes, now he's a nurse too. Then he said something that almost made me fall out of the bed. He said that Joey is some fella that I've got.

About eight o'clock tonight Helen came over to tell me not to worry about babysitting tomorrow because Barbara and Mama B said that they would mind the kids. To tell you the truth I had forgotten about watching the kids tomorrow because I was feeling so sick I could think of nothing else I guess. Now that I don't have to worry about tomorrow, which I forgot about anyway, that's a relief I guess. Helen said something interesting about me and Joey. She, just like Daddy did, referred to Joey as "my fella". She didn't say "my guy" or "my boyfriend", she called him, "my fella" and I really like the sound of that the best, "My fella". That has such a nice ring to it, doesn't it? The Penicillin shot Dr. Gold gave me at noontime and the pills I have to take every three hours must have made me very tired and sleepy so dear diary I'll have to say good night now.

Sunday, May 19th, 1946

Dear diary, except for yesterday when he had to work at Schlossberg's in the morning, Joey has spent most of yesterday and today with me and getting me whatever I would ask him for. I know he's spoiling me, but I love it. Actually I love the fact that he cares so much for me that he wants to make me feel better and comfortable. When Heshy asked Joey, after they came back from work yesterday if he wanted to go to the park to play a little softball or shoot some hoops, as they call playing basketball, he told him to go on ahead and that maybe he'll join him later. Joey never went to the park, instead he stayed with me and we listened to the radio, played cards, I beat him playing "gin", and just talking. Of course a couple of times I dozed off and for a little while, when I felt a little better I got up and we sat at the dining room table. I just remembered that he did walk through the park but that was to go to the deli to get me a hot dog for lunch and also made me a cup of tea. You know he did a very kind thing when he went to the deli, he had forgotten to ask Mom if she wanted anything so he got her a hot dog too and some fries. Mom loved it and remarked about how thoughtful he is. Hey, that's "my fella"

I was starting to feel a lot better by last night, after all the medicine I was taking, but still felt tired and lightheaded. Joey had gone home about five o'clock to have his dinner and again to see how Mama B was doing. You know he always likes to check up on her to see if she needs or wants anything. Very often Mr. B drives the taxi long hours and doesn't get home until late and now that Mary is going out with that nice looking Italian guy Benny, Mama B is alone. That's why Joey likes to go home to see if she's alright. He's not a mama's boy or anything like that, he is just a loving, caring person and that's probably one of the many reasons why I'm so glad he's "my fella".

Joey came back to my house about eight o'clock last night. He waited, he said until his father got home so that Mama B wouldn't be alone. He told me that he helped her make dinner and how nice it was for the two of them to cook together and talk and laugh while they were cooking. He makes everything he does sound so nice. I know everything he does with me always feels so nice. Daddy was sitting in the living room as usual, reading the newspaper when Joey came back. After greeting him, Daddy said that considering the fact that nobody knew too much about him before, President Truman is doing a pretty good job so far, and then asked Joey if he thought that way too. Joey just looked at Daddy for a second and said," That's true man. That's true man". Daddy, trying to hold back a smile and laugh, mumbled something about "Joey's still at it". I was so tired and sleepy that Joey left at ten o'clock and I fell asleep soon after.

Even though Mom woke me up a few times during the night to give me my pills, I did get a good night's sleep and by the time I got up this morning I felt much better. I guess the Penicillin and the pills are working but it still has me a little drowsy and lightheaded. Mom told me that Joey came by our house before I woke up and brought us a bunch of stuff from Finklestein's Bakery. She said that because I was still sleeping he left to bring some fresh rolls and stuff to his family, but he'll be back later. He also told Mom that she should make sure that Heshy doesn't eat all of it by himself and she should save some for me. We all laughed at that, except Heshy of course. True to his word, just as I was having one of the fresh rolls with butter and a cup of tea, Joey came back. When Mom asked him if he had his breakfast yet, he said he had a little but that he was saving his appetite so he could have breakfast with me. He not only gives me Goosebumps, I think Mom gets them too whenever Joey says things like that.

It was such a nice sunny and warm day today that I told Joey he should go to the park and enjoy playing ball with his friends. He looked at me and asked me if I was kidding, and before I could answer he told me that being with me, wherever I'm at is all the sunshine and enjoyment he needs. Without thinking that maybe he could catch the bug that I have, I opened my arms wide and invited him to come give me a hug and he did. When I realized what I was doing I quickly pulled away from him and told him I was sorry, but he told me he didn't care because he said if it was my bug, it couldn't be too bad. Besides, he said that he thought he read somewhere that once you take Penicillin after a few days, nobody can catch the bug from you. I didn't know that. Oh, did I tell you that he is "my fella" and that's why he's so smart? Mom who was sitting at the table with us drinking her coffee, heard what Joey said and agreed with him so now I know for sure it's true.

Because it was such a nice day Joey suggested that after lunch I should sit in front of the house for a while in the fresh air and sunshine. He said it might make me feel better and when I looked at Mom she nodded in agreement. After a nice lunch of Mom's chicken noodle soup and fresh rolls that Joey had brought over this morning, we went outside to sit in front of the house, Mom too. It was so nice and kind of quiet too. From where we were sitting the park looked crowded and I was glad I was not there because I still feel headachy and lightheaded and I don't think I was able to stand the noise of everybody talking and playing and yelling like they all seemed to be doing in the park. The warmth of the sun on my face really felt nice and I was glad that I came outside like Joey suggested.

We were sitting there for only a few minutes when Joey got up and said he was going home for a minute and that he would be right back. For me it seemed like a long time but I know it was only about ten minutes or so and Joey came back with a nice surprise for me and Mom. He brought Mama B with him and Mom and I greeted her warmly. Mama B bent over to hug and kiss me and asked me how I felt. Before I could even answer she handed me a shopping bag that had a big container of escarole in chicken broth soup, a loaf of fresh baked home made Italian bread and a box of cookies. She said she hoped that I felt better and maybe the soup and bread will help. Mom gave Mama

B a big hug and thanked her so much for being so kind. Joey went into my house and brought out another chair for his mother to sit on and we all spent the next couple of hours just sitting and talking. Joey at one point, after asking my Mom if he could, went into my house and put on a pot of coffee. Of course for me he made a cup of tea with honey. I even opened the box of cookies that Mama B had given me and we all, except for Mama B of course, had some. They tasted so good with the hot tea I was drinking. Joey gave Mama B some sugar free cake that he brought from their house. That's all she eats now and only puts saccharin in her coffee and tea. It was a very beautiful afternoon and again I'm not only talking about the weather.

Tonight, after we had just finished eating dinner and Heshy and I were helping Mom clear the table, Dr. Gold called and apologized for not calling sooner, but he said he and his brother, Dr. Andrew J. Gold had gone to Caldwell New Jersey to visit with their sister and her family on Friday night and just got back this evening. He said he stopped by his office to check on his mail and some other things and he saw that the results of my blood test had come back. He said that something didn't look right but that they are not sure what the problem might be, so he wants me to go to Kings County Hospital first thing tomorrow morning for some further testing. He thought that if everything tested okay I'd only have to stay for a couple of days. He said he already called the hospital and set it up so they are expecting me at eight o'clock tomorrow morning.

Wow! I'm so scared. Mom, Daddy and Heshy were all trying to reassure me that everything will be alright but I'm still so scared. I had to call Joey right away to tell him because after all he is so close to me and my family and I know he cares about me so much. Joey said nothing for just a split second and then told me to just sit tight and he would be right over. As soon as he got here he took me into his arms, gave me a big hug, then gently stroked my forehead and hair and told me not to worry and that everything will be alright. He looked around the room where my whole family was sitting watching us and said for me to look at all the people here who will not let anything happen to me, ever. I felt a little better but I was still scared and I am right now too. Then Joey told me that everyone in his family and every one of their friends are all praying for me to be alright, so he knows that with so many prayers being said for me that I'm going to be okay. I know he was just trying to keep my spirits up and he did a little bit, but as Mom told me later it's only natural for people to always think the worst when they don't know the answers to certain questions. She said that people have been doing that for as long as there is history. It just seems to be a part of the way people think and behave, but she said for me to just have faith in God and that will give me the strength to get through the hospital stay for the testing.

Mom told me that she will call Helen and tell her that she won't be able to go to work tomorrow too and she will be with me at the hospital the whole day. That felt good to hear. Joey said that he had to go to school tomorrow but he will go to the hospital right after school. Mom and I both tried to talk him out of coming to the hospital but Joey insisted. Of course inside of me I was glad to hear that he would be coming too. Daddy was trying to put on a brave front by smiling at me most of the time tonight, but I could tell he was worried about me just like I was. I know that he will be at the hospital with the rest of my family and Joey too, so that made me feel a little better. I'm so scared that I don't know how I'll be able to fall asleep tonight, but I have to try, so good night dear diary.

CHAPTER 12

Thursday, May 30th, 1946

Dear Diary, there's so must to tell you about, that I don't know how much I'll be able to tell you tonight. I couldn't write to you sooner because as you may remember I had to go to the hospital the Monday before last, for testing for a few days. Well I just got home today and I'm tired and still in shock from what the doctors told me last week. On Monday I underwent a few tests and later that evening, while my whole family, including Joey was there, Dr. Gold came into my room with another man who he introduced as Dr. Edward, a blood specialist. They both looked very serious and that kind of scared me right away. They started to lead my parents to a corner of the room where I couldn't hear them, so I protested and said I wanted to hear what's wrong with me too. I surprised myself by being so outspoken, but after all it's me and my body that they're talking about. I figured I had a right to know. The doctors looked at Mom and Daddy, who both nodded that it was okay, and walked back to the side of my bed. Joey was standing there holding my hand as Dr. Edward said that the tests have confirmed what the original blood test had found, that I have Leukemia!

I was stunned! I was so frozen with fright I couldn't scream or even cry even though I felt like I wanted to. Joey immediately hugged me and turned white as did Mom and Daddy. Heshy just stood there and I saw tears well up in his eyes. Dr. Edward seeing everyone so upset finally said, "While Leukemia is a very serious disease, there are treatments that do help some people". Then he added, "The medical researchers are making some nice breakthroughs these days and they expected more good things in the near future". I was still so stunned and scared and frozen, I mean I was like a statue or something. Mom asked them what they could do about it now and they said that first there were a few more tests to do to determine the exact kind of Leukemia that I have and then they will start treatment and keep me in the hospital for a while to see how I respond to the treatment.

I heard a voice ask if this means I'm going to die and before anyone answered I realized that it was my voice I heard. I was asking the question and didn't even know it at the time. Dr. Gold who I've known since I was a little child, came over to the bed, held my hand and said that everyone is going to die in time, it's just that none of us know exactly when that time is. I said that he knew what I meant, am I going to die now, soon, in six months or a year? Dr. Edward said that they couldn't be sure because right now a person with my illness and my age and the tools they have to fight it can survive anywhere from six months to two years or maybe even more. The longer I live he said, the more chance there is that new things will be discovered and developed to help me live a longer, more normal life. He went on to say that he didn't want to give me false hope, but some people do survive from it. The trouble is that not enough of them do and that is why the research is going on around the clock. He looked me right in the eye and told me that he and the other people involved in taking care of me are going to do everything they can to make me better. Then he added, that new and better medicines and a lot of prayers are what is needed right now. He smiled at me and said that he believes a positive attitude on my part and the people around me wouldn't hurt any either.

After the doctors left, Mom and Daddy came to me on one side of my bed while Joey was still holding my hand on the other side. I think Heshy started to cry because he quickly left my room and I saw and heard him standing in the hallway just outside my door. Daddy had tears in his eyes as he leaned over to hug me while calling me his "tottala" a few times. Mom was able to hold back her tears but I could see that they were there. Like I said before, Joey turned very pale when he heard what the doctors said and I think that he too was so stunned that he couldn't even speak. It took a little while for every one of us to settle down and then we were all able to speak a little bit. I told everyone that I was very scared and I got up out of bed. I just felt like walking around for a little bit, but Mom stopped me and hugged me as she told me not to worry because she felt that I had a good chance of beating this thing. Daddy more or less said the same thing and at that moment Heshy came back into the room, red eyed and quiet and he hugged me too.

Joey never left my side or said a word for a long time. I think that he felt every bit as bad for me as anybody in my family. When he was finally able to speak he told me that he hoped and prayed that I will be alright. He asked me if he could get me anything, if there was anything that I wanted or needed. I just hugged him tightly and told him that I couldn't think of anything. He hugged me back and told me that he never wanted to let go and that's when I started to cry. When he saw me cry, he started to cry too. Mom and Daddy seeing us in tears started to cry too and it was only a couple of seconds before Heshy started again too. I couldn't stand it any longer so I asked everyone to please stop crying because it only makes me feel worse and gradually they all stopped. I said that I was very tired and wanted to go to sleep. They all hugged and kissed me as they said goodnight and left, and I went to bed. Even though I was given something to make me sleep, I had a hard time sleeping that night. After what seemed a long time, I finally cried myself to sleep.

The next couple of days I spent getting tested and treated. They gave me a drug called Methotrexate, or something that sounds like that. The Penicillin that I had been taking helped me get rid of that bug I had, whatever it was, and I was feeling better although still very tired. Now the new drug was making me feel a little sick to my stomach, so they gave me something to help me with that. Mom shook her head at what was going on with me and the medicines. She said it seems that sometimes the cure hurts more that the sickness. I had to agree with her. God bless my Mom, she has been by my side every minute of every day, except when she goes home for some sleep and a change of clothes. It seems to me that her face is the last one I see at night before I fall asleep and the first one I see in the morning. I didn't know how she did it, but today she told me that Mr. B offered to take her to the hospital in the morning and bring her home at night.

I found out from Mom, last Thursday I think it was that Joey asked his boss at the store if he could take a few weeks off so that he could come to the hospital to see me every day. When the boss said no, Joey quit. When Heshy found out about it, he quit too. I was wondering how they were able to come here every afternoon and evening too. I had too much other stuff on my mind to ask them about it. I know you can understand that. When they came over after school that day, I asked them why they quit their jobs like that. They both said that they can always get another job. Joey said they would never, ever find another Esther like me. Heshy then said that I was more important to him and Joey than any job. Do you see dear diary why even though I've got this terrible disease, my family and Joey make me feel like a very lucky girl?

It seems as if it took me about a week or so to regain some of my composure, and even then I spent a lot of time crying, mostly at night when I was trying to fall asleep. I kept feeling sorry for myself. I was thinking about all the things I will never be able to do if I can't beat this thing. It's at these times I start to think about Joey and I never being able to get married, or have children some day. And of course my dream of becoming a nurse may not come true. I even found myself saying to myself, "Why me? Why not some one else? I mean I've always tried to be a good person, why would God let this happen to me?" After a little while of thinking about it, I came to my senses and put those thoughts and questions out of my head. That made falling asleep easier. I did pray to God and asked Him to take care of me and make me better, and all the other sick people in the world.

It seems that the news of me being in the hospital has gotten around the whole school and neighborhood too. I've been getting all kinds of cards wishing me well. Some from people I don't even know. It's unbelievable. Mama B, Helen, Barbara and even Arlene all came up to see me, at different times of course. Helen brought home made get well cards from Joshua and Sophie. They were so beautiful and they both signed their cards with, "lots of love". That really moved me. On top of that, they sent me a little stuffed dog, because, they wrote, they know I love animals. Arlene's kids also made cards for me that are just as beautiful, and they too sent me a stuffed animal. An elephant with great big ears that is so cute. I love those kids very much they're such beautiful and thoughtful kids. Like I've said before, I've been so lucky to baby-sit such good kids. Helen and Arlene gave me lots of nice words of encouragement and they both said that I will be in their prayers too. That lifted my spirits. They told me that they worked out the babysitting with Barbara and Mama B so that I shouldn't worry about that. I know I'm going to miss sitting for those kids, but there is nothing I can do about it right now. You know what I always say, we shall see.

On Saturday, Sarah Gold came up to visit me and as hard as she tried to smile at me and not cry, she couldn't. After I begged her, through tears of my own, to please stop because crying made me feel worse, she finally stopped. She told me how much she loved me and prayed that I would be okay and get better. I was really moved and touched by that. I mean, I knew that she liked me a lot but that was the first time she ever told me she loved me. Wow! I heard myself tell her that I loved her too, and at the time I wondered if I just said that because she said that to me first, or what. After I thought about it for a moment, I realized that I did feel that way about her. It's funny how in a time of trouble, you find out about how you feel about some people.

On Sunday afternoon Barbara came to visit with me. Everyone else was there too. When she came into my room and saw me, she started crying and bent over to give me a big hug. She wouldn't let go right away and through her tears, said in a very angry way, that she was mad as hell at God for making me so sick. She asked why, He would do that to me, who she thought was such a good person, and let a mean person like the "yenta" go unpunished. She said she felt like she was a jinx to the people around her that she cared so much about. When I asked her what she was talking about, and why she felt that way, she said because of what happened to her parents, Buster and now me being so sick. I found myself trying to comfort her by telling her that she was not jinxed and it was not God's fault. I heard myself telling Barbara that God was just putting us, me and her and our families and close friends to the test to see how we would react and handle the situation. I don't know where that came from except that it must have come from my heart and I'm sure only God put it there. I think I'm starting to sound like Mom and Mama B now. I guess that's not too bad.

The biggest surprise I got was when I saw Joey come into my room the other night, and he brought Mama B and the rest of his family too. Mama B gave me one of the biggest and longest hugs I've ever gotten in my life. While she was hugging me she spoke some words in Italian that I didn't understand but sounded very nice and comforting. Then she said, through tears, that she loved me and was praying very hard to Jesus and the Blessed Mother Mary that nothing bad was going to happen to me. Then she looked at Daddy and asked him if he minded her doing that. Mom and Daddy said they will take all the help they can get. Mama B was hugging me like she didn't want to let go. I started to cry a little bit, not because she was hurting me but because of her sweet concern and the warm feelings she has for me. When she stopped hugging me, she started kissing me on my cheeks and saying something in Italian again. I found out later, from Joey, that she called me "beautiful face" and "my beautiful child". Believe it or not she brought me a big container of her escarole in chicken broth soup. I mean she brought it right into the hospital and right into my room. She said I could maybe ask one of the nurses to heat it up whenever I felt like having some.

She also brought me some cookies hoping, she said, that I would be able to eat them. Mary gave me a big beautiful bouquet of lovely spring flowers with a nice card wishing me well. Mr. B, after he and Daddy finished hugging each other, gave me a beautiful sweater that was made in Ireland, with Irish wool. He said it was in case I felt cold in the hospital. Mr. B promised me that it didn't fall off a truck. That made me laugh and when everyone saw that they all laughed too and that made me feel good. Mama B and Mom went out into the hall and from what I could see, before the door closed, were hugging and crying. I didn't like to see that.

Joey has been at the hospital every day after school. He and Heshy have brought me school work that they have gotten from the teachers. They said they didn't want me to fall behind in my school work, and that I would be able to graduate with the rest of the class. After dinner the three of us would do our homework together just as if we were at my house and that really made me feel better. Joey every day, many times a day, would tell me that I was going to be alright and for me not to worry. It's funny, but as close as I've felt to Joey before I got sick, I feel that we're even closer now. Joey has gotten over his shock of hearing that I have Leukemia, and now has a big smile on his face when he comes into my room every day. No matter how I'm feeling, and I am feeling better the last few days, I always find myself giving him a big smile in return. I think it's kind of catching because I notice Mom and Daddy smiling a little bit now too. Joey and Daddy don't kibitz like they used to but I think, at least I hope, they will again soon.

Anyway, a funny and wonderful thing happened. I think it was the second day I was here in the hospital. A nurse came into my room to take some blood from me, and said that there were too many people in the room. She asked Joey who he was, and when he said that he was my boyfriend, I wish he would've said "fella", she said he had to leave because he was not a member of the family. Mom and Daddy, who were sitting near the bed, immediately jumped to their feet and told her that Joey is part of the family. The nurse just looked at them and without saying a word left the room. Nobody has asked Joey to leave since then. I just loved the way Mom and Daddy both said that Joey was family, not like family, but family. Isn't that great? I don't know diary, with all that's wrong with me I still feel like a lucky girl.

I think this is probably one of the reasons. I don't remember the exact day, but one day when Joey came to see me, after school I think it was, he presented me with a folded piece of paper and asked me to read it. I looked at him for a moment and then read the paper slowly to myself. While I was reading it, I was shaking my head in agreement with everything that Joey had written. When I finished reading it I told Joey that it was beautiful and made a lot of sense. I also said that I would always try to remember his words. This is what he wrote.

"HOPE SPRINGS ETERNAL"

When there is life there is hope and when there is hope there is life. Hope should always "Spring Eternal". A life without hope is like no life at all. With hope in your life you will always know love. The scent of spring flowers is sweeter. The sound of birds singing is more pleasant to your ears. With hope and love in your life, children playing and making noise will not be annoying, but rather the loveliest music you ever heard. When "Hope Springs Eternal", your whole life is worth living. You live your life to the fullest. You welcome each day like the precious gift that it is. Yes, when there is hope, there truly is life. Hope is also very contagious. If you wear hope on your face, just like a warm smile, you can give it to some one else. "Hope Springs Eternal". So always count your blessings and keep hope and love in your heart. You will never feel lonely, you will never be alone. You will always know love and you will always appreciate and experience life to the fullest. Hopelessness is just like a disease that can always be chased away and cured with love. So never give up on hope and never give up on life! "Hope Springs Eternal"! Always.

It is a very uplifting message and I told Joey that I really love it. I asked him how some one his age could speak with such wisdom. Before he could answer, I told him that he sounded like a person who has lived for a long time. He sounded a little bit like Daddy or one of his friends in the park. Joey answered that he knows all these things because he always listens when he is around older people when they start talking about their life's experiences. Joey has said for a while now, that he thought, in order to be a good speaker, you have to be a good listener first. Do I have some kind of "fella" or what?

The good news was that today, after about ten days in the hospital, Dr. Edward said I could go home. He said that if I felt up to it, I could go back to school on Monday. He warned me not to get fooled, because sometimes the disease goes into what they call, remission, but that's only temporary. The disease, he said will usually come back. There is a small chance that it won't and that's what he's hoping and praying for. He added that if I start to feel tired, I should just take it easy and rest, until I feel a little stronger. He also explained that the drug they will be treating me with may cause me to have some side effects. I asked him what kind of side effects. He said that it may cause soreness of the mouth and diarrhea. Sometimes he said, nausea and vomiting may occur. Or maybe, he added, I won't have any side effects at all. I hope he's right about the last part, no side effects at all. That's what I'll be praying for. That and of course a cure. He told me to come back to see him in two weeks, unless I feel really bad. Then I have to see him right away. He said I will have to come back to the hospital every month for treatment, and stay for about a week, or maybe a little less.

Mr. B is such an Angel. He has changed his work schedule the past ten days so he could take Mom to the hospital in the morning, and pick up the whole family at night. Today he did the same thing. As soon as he found out yesterday, that I might be coming home today, he took the day off from work so he could drive me and Mom home. What I didn't know was, because I was coming home at about four in the afternoon, after school let out Joey had all of my friends gather outside my house to greet me. When he told Mrs. Schultz, the art teacher, that I was coming home today, she had one of her classes make a big huge banner that said, in what looked like four foot high letters "WELCOME HOME ESTHER" As I stepped out of Mr. B's car everybody that was gathered there let out a big cheer. Joey told me later that I had a grin from ear to ear. That all made me feel so wonderful. Mom too, was very surprised at the reception I got. I know that she had a grin on her face that went from ear to ear, and she looked so happy for me and so beautiful, as she usually does. We both knew that it was Joey who organized the whole thing. When we told him that, he just gave us a sheepish smile and said it was nothing.

Tonight after dinner, Joey ate with us too, we did our homework together just like we always did and that felt so good. I know that being able to sleep in my own bed tonight, is going to feel so good. Mom and Daddy are so glad that I'm home. They told me they invited Joey and his family, to come over for an early family dinner on Sunday afternoon. Then, as an after thought, they asked me if that was okay with me. Of course it was and I'm looking forward to it. After we finished our homework, Joey handed me a piece of paper and said welcome home Esther. On the paper was written words that I know came right from his heart. He said:

WELCOME HOME ESTHER AND WELCOME TO MY HEART

WELCOME TO MY LIFE OF WHICH YOU HAVE BECOME A PART

ON THE DAYS THAT YOU DON'T FEEL WELL

I DON'T FEEL WELL

AND WHEN YOU FEEL GOOD

I FEEL GOOD

THAT'S THE WAY IT WILL ALWAYS BE

ME ALWAYS FOR YOU

AND YOU ALWAYS FOR ME

SO WECOME HOME ESTHER AND WELCOME TO MY HEART

Well I'm getting tired now dear diary so I'll have to say good night, but before I go I just want to tell you, that it feels so good writing to you again. Good night.

Monday, June 3rd, 1946

Dear diary yesterday was almost like Thanksgiving Day and Christmas Day, rolled into one for me. Because Joey and his family, Aunt Sherry and her family from the Bronx and Uncle Carl and his family from Queens, all came over for dinner. Mom was up and busy cooking very early in the morning. By the time I awoke, I could smell the wonderful and delicious foods cooking. There was a big turkey already in the oven by the time I walked into the kitchen for breakfast. Of course you know Mom stopped what she was doing, greeted me with a big good morning kiss and hug and made breakfast for me. After I got dressed Mom let me help her a little bit in preparing the dinner, but she warned me not to get myself too tired. Heshy and Daddy pitched in too. It felt really nice, the whole family working together like that.

When the guests all got here they came loaded down with gifts for me and of course Mr. B brought some "fell of the truck" wine and Italian liqueur. Joey carried in what he called a "get well" cake. It was just like a birthday cake but the inscription said, "Get well soon Esther". When I asked if it was from Finklestein's, he said no, it was from the Italian pastry shop that his father likes to go to once in a while. Mary gave me some nice books to read, mostly love stories and one on little known poets and their poems of inspiration. Mama B, through Mom and Helen got me a very beautiful comfortable looking bed jacket. She told me she thinks I would find it useful when I have to go to the hospital and at home in the cold weather months. Mom later told me, she often wonders where the Balduccis come from because she never, ever met such giving and thoughtful people in her whole life. I told Mom that I too, often wonder about that.

My aunts, uncles and cousins all gave me lovely presents too. I got everything from a wonderful make up kit, [yes another one] house slippers, stuffed animals, [my favorite] and some clothes. Of course, I also got very lovely get well cards, with beautiful words of well wishes. I wish my aunts and uncles, and their families lived closer to us so that I could see them more often. Even though we don't see each other as often as we all would like too, we are still a very close family. I guess it's just like Mom says, we don't have to be close geographically to be a close family. Well anyway, everybody being there, and all the cooking that Mom did is what made me feel like it was a holiday. Like Thanksgiving or something.

The meal that Mom made, with just a little help from the rest of us, was great. Before we started eating, Daddy offered a prayer and thanks to God, for all of us being together to have this nice dinner. He also mentioned the close friendship of the Balducci family with ours. When he finished, Mama B asked if she could say a prayer too. She had us all hold hands as she prayed to God the Father to watch over all of us, especially me in my time of need and for us all to have the strength to fight this problem together. It was very touching and we all thanked her for offering such a lovely prayer. The dinner was enjoyed by everyone and the cake was delicious too. To me, the best part was all of us being together and that really made me feel good even though I was starting to feel tired. It seemed to me that for a few hours we all forgot my problem and I think that is a very good thing too. I felt so good about the day I had no trouble falling asleep last night even though I was a little excited about going back to school today.

This morning, bright and early, before Heshy and I left for school, Joey came to our house. He said he just wanted to walk with me and Heshy from our house to school to make sure I was alright. That's the first time he ever did that and I loved it. All the way to and from school today, I was sandwiched by Heshy and Joey. That really made me feel good, I mean I felt pretty good when I first got up this morning because I didn't feel tired and weak, and was anxious to go to school. I felt like a princess being guarded by Heshy and Joey all the way to school and even in school they never ever let me out of their sight. That felt very comforting, knowing that they were there for me every minute of the day. They both asked me, what seemed to me like every other minute if I was alright and if I needed anything. At one point Joey apologized for asking me so often and wanted to know if he was annoying me or anything like that. Of course I told him he wasn't bothering me at all and neither was Heshy. In fact I said I felt very lucky to have them look over me like that.

The welcome I got in school today was so wonderful and warm from everybody, my friends, the other students and even the teachers. In my homeroom and art class they made and hung up, big banners that said, "WELCOME BACK TO SCHOOL ESTHER". I was speechless. I just nodded my head and all I could say was "Thank you all so much". I hadn't even brought in a doctors note yet, but I was excused from gym class, without me even having to ask to be. Everyone seemed to be going out of their way to make me feel welcome and comfortable. I hope I don't get spoiled by all the attention I'm getting. When I mentioned that to Heshy and Joey, they told me not to worry because, they said they would make sure I don't become a spoiled little girl. We all laughed at that thought.

Thanks to all the schoolwork Joey and Heshy brought home for me to do in the hospital and at home, I found myself very close to being up to date with what has been going on in school. That was a big relief to me, knowing that I wasn't falling behind in my schoolwork. When I told Heshy and Joey that I was only a little bit behind in my schoolwork, Joey said that's good, because he hasn't been a little behind since he was a baby. As we started to laugh Heshy told Joey that he didn't think he was a little behind even back then, and we laughed a little louder.

Just before dinner time, Heshy got a telephone call from his old boss at Schlossberg's Department store. He wanted Heshy and Joey to come back to work and he apologized for making them quit. He even asked how I was doing and hoped I would be alright. Heshy is going to be a good business man I think, because he played a little hard to get and managed to get a ten cents an hour increase in pay, for himself and Joey. It seems that the boys they got to replace Heshy and Joey were not as reliable or as good as Heshy and Joey. Heshy even got the boss to allow them to start a little later after school, just so they can walk me home from school and as Heshy said, make sure I'm okay. I know that they are both glad to be making money again and working together too.

It sure felt good, all of us doing our homework together in my house after dinner tonight. When Joey came over he was very happy to hear that Schlossberg's wanted them to come back to work at the store. When Heshy told him that he got them a raise in pay too Joey just shook his head and told Heshy that he was going to be a great negotiator someday. Heshy asked Joey what he meant by someday, what's the matter with right now? Joey laughed and agreed with Heshy and told him he was one right now. I'm getting a little tired now so I have to say good night dear diary.

Friday, June 7th, 1946

Dear diary, it has been a pretty good week for me so far. The attention that I got on Monday, my first day back, has died down a lot but, there are still so many people looking out for me in and out of school. A lot of the teachers looked me over as I entered their classroom to make sure I was alright. Like I said on Monday, I don't have to attend gym class and I spend the whole period sitting in the guidance counselor's office. I spend the time doing some of my homework and studying. On Tuesday, in History class I got myself all worked up inside. The class was separated into groups of four and five kids to work on a project. Each group had a different project, but they were all about the American Revolution. Because I missed school the day the project started, I was assigned to a group that didn't include Heshy or Joey. Joey was in a group of four that had Heshy, Sarah, himself and big chested Thelma Herzog. Boy did that make me jealous, because she was sitting right next to him. I could hardly concentrate on my project but I didn't say anything to Joey about it when the class was over.

That Joey is pretty perceptive. On the walk home from school, it was just the two of us, because Heshy and Sarah went to the library to work on their project. Joey asked me if I was feeling well, because I was so quiet. He said I looked like I was mad at him or something. I wasn't really mad at him, I was just a little hurt that I wasn't sitting next to him, working on the same project as he was. I think I might have sounded a little mad, when I answered that I couldn't help notice him and Thelma looking very cozy, sitting so close together in class. He started to protest, but I cut him short and told him that all she has going for her, besides her pretty face, is her big chest, that she keeps sticking out all the time. He started to speak again, but I interrupted him again, and said that she always wears tight sweaters and almost runs wherever she goes, just to make herself bounce all over the place. Just to get the attention of all the boys. He started to speak again and when I started to stop him this time, he wouldn't let me.

He said, "Listen Esther, let me tell you something. Please let me talk for a minute. In the first place, I didn't pick the group I was going to be with, except to say that I would like to be in the group with Heshy. Sarah said she would like to be in the group with Heshy too and the teacher picked Thelma to join us. I didn't pick her. In the second place, as far as I'm concerned it's not the size of a girl's chest that's important it's the size of the heart that beats within her chest that really matters." I was about to say something but again he stopped me and said, "Please let me finish. In the third place, Thelma wears tight sweaters and runs a lot because she gets more bounce to the ounce and she has more ounces to bounce." I was startled at first, but then I asked what he meant by more ounces to bounce. I think, but I'm not sure I stuck my chest out as I said that. Of course by this time we both started laughing.

Wednesday after school, Joey and Heshy both had to work at Schlossberg's, so Joey didn't come over until about eight o'clock, to do homework. I had already finished mine, because I had done a good part of it in school, during the gym class. While Joey and Heshy were working on theirs Daddy, who had been sitting and reading his paper as usual, looked up and asked, of no one in particular, if Schlossberg's has what is called a "Lay-away" buying plan. Heshy answered that they did but Joey said that they have a "Lay-awake" plan. Daddy looked up from his paper and said that he never heard of a "Lay-awake" plan. Then he added that Joey must mean a "Lay-a-way" plan. Joey said that no, it's a "Lay-awake" plan, because after you buy it, you lay awake all night trying to figure out how you're going to pay for it. Daddy couldn't help but laugh and said that Joey was right, because he knew that feeling well.

I was so glad to see that Daddy, Heshy and Joey are kidding with each other again. Tomorrow, if I feel up to it, Joey said that he will take me to Prospect Park for a little while so that I can enjoy the beauty of the park at this time of year. The weather is supposed to be very nice tomorrow and in fact for the whole weekend. Joey said of course he will take care of getting lunch, either making it or buying it. If I feel tomorrow as well as I felt today, I'll be very happy and we'll go to the park. I'm looking forward to it. Heshy, Sarah, Mom and Daddy all have to work so Joey arranged to take the day off just so he could be with me, but he'll have to work an extra day during the week. Now dear diary I'm getting tired so I'll say good night.

Sunday, June 9th, 1946

Dear diary yesterday was a most wonderful day for me, in spite of the fact that I felt a little tired after a while, walking through Prospect

Park. Joey made the lunch for us and it tasted so good. He made roasted turkey breast sandwiches on pumpernickel bread and he even put jellied cranberry sauce on them. We also had Kosher Pickles and he bought a container of potato salad too. I mean he thinks of everything. He told me he stopped at Finklestein's bakery early in the morning for the pumpernickel bread and also got a couple of cheese Danishes for dessert. He saw Frances and she sent well wishes for me. I thought that was very nice of her and then I felt a little guilty, for being jealous of her, because she used to be so friendly with Joey.

Although we didn't go out on the lake in a rowboat, we spent a little time sitting on the edge of the lake, and dipped our bare feet into the cold water. He's so cute. He thought he'd scare me by telling me that a fish might bite my toes, but I told him that his smelly feet would keep the fishes away. He pretended to be hurt, so I started to call him "sweet feet", to soothe his feelings, which weren't really hurt in the first place. We laughed and hugged, it was so beautiful and lovely that I wished the day would never end. Even though I know that I'm sick with a very serious disease, being with Joey like I was on Saturday makes me forget all of my troubles. I love him so much. Some people might want to call it "puppy love" but I don't care what anybody calls it, I just know that I love him. Of course I've never told Joey that I love him and he has never told me that he loves me either. We just tell each other how much we like and care for each other. Maybe someday soon, we shall see.

Today was a very nice and warm day. I got up a little later than usual this morning, I don't know why, I was a little tired I guess. After breakfast I just sat around the house talking with Mom. Daddy and Heshy had already gone to the park to be with their friends. I asked Mom if she thought I was too young to know what true, real love was, and she said no, she didn't think so. She said maybe that would be true with some girls my age, but she didn't think I was. Mom said that she thought I was a little more mature than a lot of my friends are. She also said that she thought Sarah is very mature for her age too. Then I asked Mom what she thought was going to happen to me. She looked at me with her love filled eyes, put her arms around me and told me she didn't know, but that she hopes and prays that I'll be alright. She said it's all in God's hands right now, and there's nothing more we can do about it, except do as the doctors tell us. With that she kissed me on my forehead and told me not to worry about it and to try not to even think about it, even though she knows it's hard to not think about it. I hugged her very tight, told her how much I loved her and tried very hard to hold back my tears, but I couldn't. Mom started crying a little and told me she loved me very much too.

After we settled down Mom asked me to have another cup of coffee with her and I did. Even though it was so beautiful out, I didn't feel like going out to the park right away. Mom and I just sat at the kitchen table, drinking our coffee and holding each other's hand while we talked some more. It was for me, such a precious time that I didn't want to cut it short, even though I was anxious to see Joey. Before I could leave for the park, Joey came to the door and wondered if I was alright. He greeted me and Mom with warm hugs and I left for the park with Joey. Before we left, Joey told Mom that it's so nice out she should come out to the park with us. He added that his mother was thinking about coming to the park with Mary and Mary's boyfriend, Benny. Mom brightened up when she heard that and said that she will be there soon.

Not too long after we got into the park, Mama B, Mary and Benny came walking in. When I saw Mama B and she saw me, we just opened our arms, smiled big warm smiles and hugged each other. She seemed so happy to see me it made me feel so special. Mary gave me a big hug too and she also seemed so glad to see me. It wasn't long before Mom walked into the park and greeted Mama B and Mary like long lost relatives or something. I loved watching it all happen. Joey and I had already spent some time with our friends so we were very content to spend the rest of the afternoon with Mom, Mama B, Mary and Benny. Benny seems to be a very nice and shy guy. Mary, I think is crazy about him and he's crazy about her too, or so it appears. They make a very nice couple, almost as nice as me and Joey. Ha! Ha!

My lovely day ended in a nice quite way this evening. Joey went home to have dinner with his family and after that came back here and spent a couple of hours sitting and taking with me and my family. It was so very nice I couldn't help but feel good, even if I was feeling bad, if you know what I mean. On this coming Thursday, right after school I have to go to see Dr. Edward for a checkup and probably a blood test. I think he'll tell me at that time, when he wants me to go back into the hospital for my next treatment. I'm not really looking forward to any of this, but I've got to do what they tell me to, if I want a chance to get better. Thinking about it gets me down, so I'm trying to put it out of my head, especially after the wonderful day I had today. That's what I'll do, just think about today and forget about everything else. I'm sure that will make me get some sleep, faster and better. I hope so. Good night dear diary.

Friday, June 14th, 1946

Dear diary, my visit to see Dr. Edward yesterday went well. He told me that so far I checked out okay, and he took some blood from me to test. He asked me if I had felt any of the side effects that he told me about on my first hospital visit. He was very happy to hear that I felt none of the things he described to me. So was I. Anyway, I'll find out the results of the test when I go to the hospital next Wednesday, the 19th of June. I was a little worried because graduation day is June 21st, and I was afraid I wouldn't be able to graduate if I wasn't there. Today I went to talk to the principal, Mr. Goodman, and he assured me that I will graduate with the rest of my class. He said that I was a very good student and that I had already completed every thing that was required of me to graduate. That was no nice to hear and it took a load of worry off me.

Since most of our school work has already been done, we don't have homework to do, except for some review work, which is very easy. In spite of that, Joey still comes over every night and you know I love it. Now we all sit around and talk about and wonder what high school is going to be like. Mom told us that we sounded just like we did when we were getting ready to go from grammar school to jr.high school. She said that the difference is that there is no difference. We asked her what that meant and she said we're wondering and worrying for nothing, because we've already had one year of high school studies. All we're really doing is changing buildings and teachers, the studies should be the same, only a little more advanced, that's all. That seemed to make sense to all of us and we all told Mom how smart she is. She said she already knew that and laughed. We all did too.

When Daddy came home from work tonight he told us that his bosses, Sal and Sol invited us out to their homes this weekend for a special treat for me. Daddy said that he always tells them how much I love nature and trips to Prospect Park and stuff like that. They told Daddy that a new bird and animal sanctuary has been created in their town of Tenafly, N.J. and they are among the founders. They have invited all of us, including the Balduccis to come visit with them this Sunday and Mr. B will drive us there. Afterward, they will take us down to the boat marina on the Hudson River, where they keep their company boat, for a picnic. I don't care too much about the picnic, but I can't wait to see the sanctuary.

Daddy also told us a very nice and interesting story about his bosses. At work today, Sal noticed that Daddy looked like he was worried about something, besides me being sick and asked Daddy if anything was bothering him. Daddy told him that he didn't know how he was going to pay the huge hospital and doctor bills that keep coming. Sal went into Sol's office and after a short while he called Daddy in. The two of them told Daddy that their corporation has an insurance policy for themselves and all the other senior management people. They told Daddy that they were not only going to put him on that list, but also back dating it so that he would have the full coverage from the very beginning of my illness. When Daddy asked them if that was legal, they told him not to worry about it because they said, he should have been getting that insurance a long time ago and that it was an oversight on their part. They also told him that normally the insurance pays for most of the bills and Daddy would have to pay the rest, but because they know and appreciate that he's been such a good and loyal employee, they will pay whatever the insurance company doesn't pay. Can you believe there are people so good like that? Daddy always thought the world of them before, but now he says that on Thanksgiving Day he will say a very special thanks for them. Daddy and Mom both said they thank God for lifting that burden off their shoulders. Heshy said that if God would make me better, he would really have something to be thankful for. Is he sweet or what? I'm getting tired now so I'll say good night dear diary.

Monday, June 17th, 1946

Dear diary, the trip yesterday to the sanctuary in New Jersey was so wonderful that I wished I could've stayed there forever. It is so peaceful, quiet and beautiful. There were all kinds of birds, even wild turkeys walking around. All kinds of small animals and some one even said they saw a deer walking through the woods. We all had to be very quiet so as not to disturb the wildlife. We walked along a few of the many paths that went through the wooded area, and then we sat very still in an area near the entrance and just watched the birds feeding in the many bird feeders that hung everywhere. It was fun to watch some of the squirrels trying to get at the bird feeders. Most of them were content to hang around beneath the feeders and eat the seeds that the birds dropped. It was almost like watching a Walt Disney movie come alive in front of my eyes.

After what seemed to me like only a few minutes, it was actually about an hour or so, we all went down to the Hudson River and Sal and Sol's boat. The name of the boat is "Sew What". I didn't get it at first but Joey told me it's called that because they're in the clothing business. Joey said that is his kind of a joke. It's a big and beautiful boat and they took us all on a tour of it. We ate our lunch on it and it was so lovely with a nice cool breeze coming of the river. That felt so good because the day was very warm. They didn't take the boat out on the river because, they said, they didn't want to take the chance of me getting seasick. That was very thoughtful of them I thought. What made the day extra nice was that most of the people that I care the most about were there with me, especially Joey. I know I say that a lot but that's only because it's true and that's me just being me.

Mama B and Mom loved the "quiet beauty" of the sanctuary, as Mom put it. Mom told me later, that she thought the reason she and Mama B were especially fond of the place, is that they have been through some troubles and turmoil in their lives. Peace and quiet always feels good after you've been through some hard times, she added. Then she said that it's like going through a rough, cold and long winter, makes a lovely spring feel so much lovelier. I had to think about that last part of what Mom said. Then I understood what she meant, I think. Whatever, the most impotent thing is that we all had a great time. Good night for now dear diary.

Tuesday, June 18th, 1946

Dear diary, a most wonderful thing happened to me today in school. A special assembly was called this morning for the whole school. When I walked into the auditorium I got the shock of my life. Hanging across the stage was a hugh banner that read in large capital letters, "BEST

OF LUCK ESTHER AND GET WELL SOON". I couldn't believe it! I started crying immediately. Everyone there started applauding students, teachers and to my surprise Mom and Daddy were there too. They even took up a collection for me and gave me a two hundred dollar gift certificate for one of the big department stores in downtown Brooklyn. Mr. Goodman called me up onto the stage and then he and a few of my teachers got up and said so many nice things about me that made not only me, but even Mom cry. I can't remember all the things that were said but I know they were all nice. I was even handed my diploma and was told that I just graduated, two days early. Everyone in the auditorium cheered, even the kids I didn't know. I can't begin to tell you how wonderful and special I felt at that moment. Then I was told to take the rest of the day off from school.

I walked home with Mom. Daddy had to go to work. Mom hugged me all the way home and I loved it. It felt so comforting. Mom said she felt so happy for me and the nice things that everyone said about me. She said she always knew and felt that way about me, but to hear it come from people who are not in our family, made her feel very good. When we got home, Mom told me to just take it easy and rest up for my trip to the hospital tomorrow. After we had lunch, I did just what Mom told me and relaxed on the sofa. It wasn't long before I fell asleep for a couple of hours. It felt good too. After I awoke Mom told me that Mr. B again arranged his work hours so that he can drive us to the hospital in the morning. Mom said she will stay with me all day and Daddy and Heshy will have dinner at Mama B's house. Mr. B will then drive them to the hospital and stay with us until they want to go home. Now you know why, when Mom and Daddy talk about family they include the Balduccis. I'm sure that Joey will be with me tomorrow, at some time, at least I hope so.

I wont be able to write anymore until I come home from the hospital and I don't know for sure when that will be. When I do write again I know I'll have a lot to tell you about. I know I'll miss writing. I've got to go to sleep now, so good night dear diary, please wish me luck.

Monday, June 24th, 1946

Dear diary, I just got back today from my stay at the hospital. I got my treatment on Wednesday when I went into the hospital. They call it "infusion". That's probably the worst part, getting the needle into my arm. That hurts if they don't find the vein right away, but after that it's not too bad. The next day my stomach ached a little, and they give me some other kind of medicine for that. After that, they just wanted me around the hospital for a few more tests and to make sure I'm alright. I really got home earlier that I thought I would. I figured I'd have to spend at least a week there, but thank God I didn't. As nice as they are to me in the hospital, I'd much rather be home, sleeping in my own bed.

Joey told me at the hospital, that I probably would feel better sitting on my own "throne". I didn't understand what he meant at first but then I got it and gave him a disapproving, dirty look. All he could do was laugh and say he was sorry. What could I do but laugh too. Joey then hugged me tightly and said it made him so happy to hear me laugh, knowing how sick I am. He has a way of touching my heart, if you know what I mean. It was at that point I told him how very scared I really am, especially at night when I'm all alone in my bed and start thinking about my illness. He kissed me, then told me not to be scared because there are so many people rooting and praying for me to get well, that he was sure that I will and that made me feel a little better until I tried to go sleep that night. I started thinking the worst things again. I finally was able to think only of what Joey told me and fell asleep right away.

It has rained every day this past weekend and today too. Starting tomorrow the weather is supposed to be nice beach weather for three or four days. Most of my friends, who aren't working or going away, are planning to go to the beach tomorrow. Joey said that if I felt up to it and if it was okay with my parents, he would take the day off and go with me to watch over me. That sounded very good to me and when I asked Mom about it she said that she'll come with us too. Now I was really looking forward to tomorrow and the beach. I only hope I feel good enough in the morning. Poor Mom she had to stop working since I've been sick, except for a few Saturdays, but Helen and her sisters told Mom that she can come back to work for them as soon as she wants to. Helen told me not too long ago, that she and her sisters like Mom and the good work that she does, very much. That was very nice to hear about my Mom. Well good night dear diary.

Friday, June 28th, 1946

Dear diary, Tuesday I woke up feeling pretty good so I decided to go to the beach with Mom, Joey and some of my friends. It was a very warm and sunny day but at the beach it was a little cooler. The breeze coming in off the ocean made it feel just right. Mom and Joey insisted that I don't stay in the sun too long so Joey rented a big beach umbrella for me to sit under. I really enjoyed watching a bunch of little kids playing in the sand and around the water's edge. Mom packed a lunch for us, including Joey of course and he brought the drinks. Me, I just brought myself. Everybody's starting to spoil me by doing everything for me. I wish sometimes that they would let me do something too, so I can feel useful again. When I said that to Mom and Joey, they told me that they didn't realize that they were doing too much for me, and they will let me do something's for myself. That was good to hear.

I usually start getting tired by late afternoon but being on the beach, by the water, salty air and a little bit in the sun made me feel tired very early in the day. After we had eaten the nice sandwiches Mom made, I asked Mom if she would take me home. It was only two o'clock but of course she said yes. I told Joey he could and should stay at the beach longer, but I knew he would insist on coming home with us. I'm really glad that he did. I mean, I enjoyed going for a short walk with him along the water's edge and getting our feet wet, but I just all of a sudden got so tired. You know that on our little walk through the water I had to call him "sweet feet" and that made us both laugh. He always walks with his arm snugly around my shoulder. He's Strong enough to hold me up if I was too weak to walk, and yet very gentle so as not to hurt me. That's the way we walked to the subway, with Joey holding me like that with one arm while helping Mom carry some of the stuff we brought with us. As tired and weak as I felt, I still felt good about being with Mom and Joey.

After we got home I took it easy for a while and it wasn't long before I started to feel a little better and stronger. Joey stayed with us for the rest of the afternoon and in fact even did a little shopping for Mom at the grocery store. What a guy! He went home to have or help fix dinner for Mama B and came back here afterward. By that time Daddy and Heshy were both home too. We sat around the dining room table and talked for a while until Sarah came over. Then the four of us decided to play cards, Gin Rummy. It seems that I won almost every hand and I still don't know if I really did win or if they let me win. Every time I won a hand I'd say. "I can't believe I won again" and they would all start laughing. When I asked them if they were letting me win they all swore that they weren't, so I don't know. Anyway, it was great fun and it took my mind off me being sick for a short while and that's something good.

Wednesday was another beautiful beach day but I didn't feel like going so I just stayed home with Mom. Joey had to work in the morning but when he came home in the afternoon he took me out to the park and we just sat around and talked. Again he made me wear my beach hat from last year, with the big floppy brim to shade my face. The way he watches over me, I started calling him my very own, "mother hen". He laughed and said in the first place he's not a hen, he's a rooster, and in the second place he only lays eggs when he's telling jokes. He is so cute and funny! I hope he never stops making me laugh. While we were talking, I again confided in him how scared I was and he again reassured me that he thought I was going to be alright. I sure hope he's right. Mom, Daddy and Heshy keep telling me the same thing that I'm going to be alright. I hope that they really believe that and it's not just wishful thinking.

I got a wonderful surprise while in the park when Barbara came walking in with all the Bernstein and Green kids. When they saw me, they all came running over to me and gave me hugs and kisses. Of course you know my "mother hen" Joey made sure they didn't all jump on me at the same time. The kids being so good listened to everything Joey said. Barbara gave me a very loving and tender hug. I know she was trying very hard to not hurt me by holding me too tight. Little thoughtful things like that always impress and move me. They all asked me how I was feeling and told me how much they loved and missed me. Sophie gave Joey a very playful look and asked him to read her a story but they didn't bring books with them. Joshua told Joey to make up a story and that's just what he did.

He was at his best that afternoon. He told the kids that they were going to help him make up a story. First he asked them for suggestions for what the story should be about. Little Michael wanted a story about the zoo. Joshua wanted to be about a gorilla. Allan told Joey to make it a white gorilla. Adrienne giggled as she said make him trying to find a girlfriend. Finally Joey pointed to Sophie and asked her what she wanted the white gorilla to do. She looked so cute as she put her little finger up to the corner of her mouth as she was thinking. Then she said make him picking flowers for his girlfriend. Now Joey went to work.

First he announced, just like a circus ringmaster, that he was going to tell the story of "The Vanilla Gorilla", a rare white great ape. Right away, we all started laughing at the gorilla's name. Then he bent over at the waist, bent his knees and started prancing around just like a gorilla. He made up a whole story about this poor lonely gorilla who spent all of his time looking for a girlfriend. He was narrating and acting the gorilla all at the same time. At one point he pretended he was picking flowers and sniffing them first. A few times he made believe the flower he just picked smelled bad. He put on this scrunched up face and keeled over. We were all hysterical. This time none of the kids wet their pants, thank God. Joey made a wonderful afternoon even better.

Wednesday night was spent the same way as Tuesday night, sitting around, talking and then playing cards. The only difference was, I didn't win most of the hands that were played, but if was fun anyway. When Heshy left to walk Sarah home, I was feeling tired so I told Joey that I just wanted to relax on my bed. Joey got up and said he was going to go home, but I asked him not to leave and invited him to sit in the chair next to my bed for a while. I just sat on my bed, propped up by a pillow and Joey and I talked. I asked him when he first started liking me and his answer really surprised me. He brought me back to the time when we were in grammar school. He said he always thought that I was so beautiful and a very nice girl too. He told me he liked me the best of all the other kids in our class, girls or boys. He thought I was different from all the other girls because, he said, I never talked behind anyone's back or gossiped about anybody. He laughed as he told me that he loved to hear me giggle when I was a little kid. Then he added that he still loves it when I do that. I loved hearing that, but I was getting very tired and told Joey that I wanted to go to sleep. He gave me a smile, a kiss and a hug and left. I went to bed right away and slept pretty good.

Yesterday was a rainy, depressing kind of a day, if you know what I mean. I wasn't feeling that well when I woke up in the morning and was feeling pretty lousy all morning. Then I started thinking about me and this disease that I have, and I started feeling worse. I stayed in bed most of the morning crying and I guess feeling sorry for myself again. I got up to eat the lunch Mom made for me and then went right to bed. Not long after that Joey came over and Mom told him I wasn't feeling well and that I was in bed. He asked her if it was okay if he went in to see me and she said yes, but first she asked me if I was decent. I heard Joey tell Mom that he thought I was the most decent person he has ever known. I had to smile even though I didn't feel well and I also heard Mom laugh. I tried to fix myself up a little bit, but when he came into my room he saw right away that I had been crying. He sat on the bed, held my hand and asked me what was wrong. I didn't answer him. Instead I asked him, through tears if he still liked me and wanted me to be his girlfriend. He gave me a look of disbelief and said, of course he still wanted me to be his girlfriend and as far as liking me, he said no. Now, he said, he would have to say that, he not only likes me but that he loves me!

He loves me! I couldn't believe it. He loves me. I told him not to say that to me unless he really meant it. He said that if he didn't mean it, he wouldn't say it. I was still sniffling when I told him I felt the same way about him that I loved him and have for a long time. We hugged and kissed and then we heard Mom making some noise, working in the kitchen, so we stopped the kissing. I still felt sick, but a whole lot better knowing that Joey feels about me, the same way I feel about him. When I told Joey that, he said that he wished he could cure me and make me well with just a kiss. Wouldn't that be wonderful? I thank God I never get any soreness of the mouth that Dr. Edward thought I might get. I mean if I did I don't know if I'd be able to let Joey kiss me, or me kiss him. Now that would be really bad, for me anyway.

Joey stayed with me the rest of the afternoon and right through until he left at about nine o'clock last night. He did call Mama B at dinner time, to see if she needed anything and if she was alright. Mom and Daddy never seem to wonder at what a thoughtful guy Joey is. Of course I always knew that. Heshy always says that if he had a brother he would want him to be Joey. Not like Joey, but Joey himself. I'm so lucky that everyone in my family loves Joey, because I know a lot of the girls in school, have boyfriends that their families don't like. There are a few girls who even have to sneak around, because their boyfriends aren't Jewish. I'm so glad that I don't have to do that. In fact when I once told Joey about Vivian Sigmond having to do that with Vinnie Cottone, he told me that he would never let me do that. He said that he wouldn't want to tear apart the nice, close family that I have, no matter how much he cared for me. I'm still not sure how I feel about that, if that's good or bad.

After Joey left I told Mom when we were alone, that Joey told me he loves me, and that I love him too. Mom looked at me with surprise and said that a blind man could see that Joey loved me. Now I was looking at her with surprise and asked her how she knew that. She said just by the way he treats me, talks to me and the beautiful words he always writes about me. I asked her if she meant that I was the last person to find that out. Mom laughed and said that's right. I asked her if she thought Daddy knows too. While they haven't spoken about it, she thought he probably does. Wow! I asked Mom if she thought Daddy would be upset and she said that if he hasn't said anything by this time, she didn't think that he would, but she didn't know for sure. Knowing that Joey loves me made me have a very good night's sleep.

Today I still wasn't feeling great and when Joey came over to see me after work, he gave me a piece of paper with the following written on it:

AS I SIT HERE LATE AT NIGHT, I THINK ABOUT WHAT I
COULD WRITE,
ABOUT THE PAIN I KNOW YOU FEEL
BECAUSE WE ARE AS ONE, EVERYTHING THAT IS DONE,
TO YOU, I EXPERIENCE TOO
AND TO ME YOUR PAIN IS REAL
INSIDE OF ME I CRY FOR YOU 'CAUSE I KNOW YOU
DON'T FEEL WELL
AND WITH YOU IN YOUR PERSONAL HELL, I ALSO DWELL
OH, I MAY TRY TO BE FUNNY AND CLEVER,
TO TRY AND PUT A SMILE ON YOUR BEAUTIFUL FACE
BUT I ADMIRE YOU 'CAUSE I KNOW, THOUGH YOU'RE
SCARED
YOU FACE THE TASK AHEAD WITH STYLE AND GRACE
YOU ARE SO MUCH MORE THAN MY GIRL AND BEST
FRIEND
YOU ARE THE ONE I ADORE AND I'LL ADMIRE YOU
ALWAYS WITHOUT END
I WILL ALWAYS WALK BESIDE YOU, HOLDING YOUR
HAND
EVERY STEP OF THE WAY

I WILL ALWAYS TRY TO CHASE AWAY THE PAIN INSIDE
YOU
THIS I WILL ALWAYS PRAY
MY LOVE FOR YOU WILL GROW DEEPER AND STRONGER
EACH AND EVERY DAY
I WILL LOVE YOU FOREVER, MY ESTHER

After I hugged and kissed him, I wiped away my tears and called Mom to come into my room. I showed her what Joey had written to me and after she read it she didn't say a word. She just went over to Joey and gave him a big hug. Holding the paper to her heart, she bent over and hugged me. She quickly left my room wiping tears from her eyes. I could hear her murmuring something but I couldn't make out what it was. Later on when I asked her what she was saying, she said it was nothing. She said she can't get over what a sensitive and caring young man Joey is. I think that's the first time Mom had ever called Joey a young man. I mean sometimes when she's scolding Heshy she may say, "Young man you better clean up your room or something like that, but never in the sense that he wasn't a kid anymore. I guess it's true what Mom sometimes tells us, that we are coming of age.

When Daddy came home from work tonight he told us that his boss Sol owns a summer bungalow up in the Catskills and if we'd like, we can use it for a week or so at the end of July. Sol and his wife are going away to Florida for a few weeks and won't be using the place at that time. I told Daddy that I don't know yet when I have to go to the hospital for my next treatment. He told me that's what he told Sol, but we don't have to let him know right away. I don't know how that would work out even if I was able to go. I wouldn't want to go that long without seeing Joey and I don't think Joey would want to come with us. Mama B's not feeling that great right now plus he still has to give her insulin in the mornings. I don't know what to do but as Mom always says, things have a way of working out so there's nothing to worry about. We shall see. Good night dear diary.

CHAPTER 13

Monday, July 8th, 1946

Dear diary, I know I haven't written in a while and that's because I've been very tired lately. It seems that not long after I have my dinner, I fall asleep and stay asleep for most of the night. Mom thinks it might be because of the medication, or maybe my body is trying to fight my Leukemia by making me rest. I don't know, it's very confusing. I have to go to see Dr. Edward this coming Thursday, the 11th. Maybe he can explain it to me. I honestly believe, that if it wasn't for the support and love that I get from my family and Joey and his family, I'd be feeling a lot worse. I hope I never find out for sure.

Last Thursday, on the Fourth of July, while most of my friends, including Heshy and Sarah went to the beach, Joey and I just stayed home. For a short while we went to the park in the afternoon. We just sat on a bench, in the sun and talked. I reminded Joey of what he told me last week, about thinking I was so beautiful in grammar school, and asked him if he still thought I was beautiful, as sick as I am. He looked at me with so much love in his eyes I could've cried. He put his arm around me and told me that I'm more beautiful than ever. He said that when he looks at me he sees my beautiful heart and soul and that's all that he sees. He added that when I smile he sees a reflection of my heart and that's how he knows it's beautiful. He doesn't know for sure what anybody else sees, but he said, judging from the way my friends and neighbors have responded to my being sick, he thinks they may see the same thing he does.

I asked him why he never told me these things before, and he said, because he was shy, quiet and preferred to listen and not talk. He said he learned a lot by listening to older people talk about different things and

246

life in particular. He did tell me that he wanted to tell me many times over the last couple of years how he felt about me, but he was always afraid that I would laugh at him and tell him to get lost or something. I hugged him as tight as I could and told him that I would never, ever tell him to get lost. Then he confirmed what Mom thought was holding him back from telling me that he liked me. He told me again, the story about what happened to Buster when he was about sixteen or seventeen years old. Of course I already knew the story but I let him tell it to me anyway, because I love to hear him talk. When he asked me why I never told him I liked him before, I said that boys are supposed to tell girls first. He said, says who and I said it's an unwritten law. Of course I never heard of that law and he knew it so we both started to laugh.

Mama B is not feeling well and she looks very bloated. Mom says it's probably water retention, which is a common thing with some women. She went to see the union doctors in Manhattan with Joey and Mary on Saturday. They gave her some pills to take to make her get rid of the water and if that doesn't work, then she'll have to go into the hospital where they will have to "extract" it out of her. I sure hope that the pills work because the word "extract" sounds painful to me. Joey told me that yesterday Mama B was going to the bathroom a lot so maybe the pills are working. Good night for now dear diary, I'll write again after I see Dr. Edward on Thursday.

Thursday, July 18th, 1946

Dear diary, I saw Dr. Edward today and he said that so far so good, as far as my progress goes in fighting this disease. He wants me to go into the hospital next Thursday, for my next treatment. He said that Mom was partly right, when she said that I feel tired because my body is telling me to rest, so it can fight the disease. The disease itself is making me feel tired too, so he told me to get as much rest as I can. He also said I should try and enjoy being out in the fresh air with my friends for a little while, whenever the weather permits. I asked him if I could go to the beach or Prospect Park or even the movies once in a while. He told me to not get too much sun and if I go to Prospect Park, or any park like that, I should keep myself covered as much as possible. He also said I should try to avoid getting bitten by insects, because while I'm fighting Leukemia, I'm very susceptible to other diseases. That doesn't sound as if I can have much fun does it? Well at least he didn't say I have to stay away from Joey, so that's good. I guess my "mother hen" Joey, was right when he shielded me from the sun.

Mom told Daddy tonight, what Dr. Edward had told us and we all decided that it wouldn't be a good idea for us to go to the Catskills and use Sol's bungalow. It really did sound nice, but like I said before, I didn't want to spend any amount of time without seeing Joey. When Heshy and Joey found out about my next treatment starting next Thursday, they said they will have to work it out with their boss, to get the afternoons off if they can. Joey said that he felt sure his father will make similar arrangements, so he will be able to take Mom to and from the hospital. Joey also told us, that Mama B is getting bloated again and she's going to see Dr. Gold this time, because she doesn't think she can make the subway trip into Manhattan. She's going to see him tomorrow, as soon as Joey gets home from work. His office is only one block away on Powell St., near Livonia Ave., so that's not too bad. Joey said that if she had to climb all those stairs, to get to the subway train, she'd never make it. He also told me that Mr. B offered to drive her into Manhattan in his cab, but they would have to leave very early in the morning to not only beat the rush hour traffic, but also because in the middle of the morning and on, he's very busy. They might just do that. We shall see. Good night for now dear diary.

Wednesday, July 24th, 1946

Dear diary, we got bad news today. Dr. Gold had given Mama B new pills to take and she didn't get any better. In fact, now she's bloated bigger than ever. Joey said she looks like she going to have a baby. He said Mama B laughed when he told her that and she said she wished that was her problem. She is in such discomfort that she couldn't even walk down the stairs, so Mr. B could drive her to the hospital. They had to call for an ambulance to take her to the hospital. Joey said that the ambulance workers had to put her in a chair and carry her down gently with the chair and all. They took her to Kings County Hospital, the same one that I'm going to tomorrow. I hope she'll be in the same wing as me, so that maybe I can visit with her. I sure hope so, but we shall see.

Now Joey had two reasons for making the special arrangement for having the afternoons off. Joey calls it a double header for him. Heshy does too. Everything revolves around baseball with these two guys. Joey told me not too long ago, that when we became boyfriend and girlfriend, he felt like he hit a grand slam. I remember asking him why not just a home run and he said he felt like he hit a home run every time he saw me in the morning on the way to school. Now he feels like he not only hit a grand slam, but that he's won the game. Now that comparison to baseball I really like. Mr. B has taken off from his job for as long as Mama B is in the hospital. Joey told us not to worry because his father will take us to the hospital tomorrow morning and he'll stay there for as long as they let him and if he has to, he'll come back to pick up Mom and whoever else needs a ride home. I sure hope and pray that Mama B will be okay.

On my last visit to the hospital, in the middle of June, Joey said I inspired him to write a beautiful poem for me. One night, before Joey left to go home, I was feeling a little down, and I suppose a little sorry for myself. I asked Joey why he still wanted me to be his girlfriend, why he feels, as he always tells me, that he needs me. He told me to stop talking that way and just accept the fact that he does want and need me. Then he kissed me and went home. The next afternoon he came to the hospital right from school. After he greeted me with a kiss and a hug, he handed me another piece of paper. He told me to read it and never again ask him those silly questions, like I did the night before. I read it and as usual with anything that he writes for me, I got all choked up but I managed to keep myself from crying, thank God. I handed the paper to Mom and she read it and walked quickly out of the room. Here is what he had written.

WHY I NEED YOU

My body needs water, food and air to survive,
My soul needs only your love to feel alive.
For you make every day feel like spring,
You and you alone, can make my heart sing.
Knowing you love me makes me swell with pride,
You fill my heart with love, I cannot hide.
Of all the lovely things you say and do,
The loveliest, is when you say to me, "I love you".
These are only some of the reasons why I need you!

After a few minutes Mom came back into my room and said she was sorry but she had to go to the bathroom in a hurry. I'm not really sure it that was true or if she didn't want us to see her reaction to Joey's little poem. When I asked Mom how she liked the poem, she said that most people, who would read his poems and sentiments, would not believe that they came from a boy not yet sixteen. Joey just looked like he was a little embarrassed and said nothing. I told Mom that I didn't care if Joey was sixteen or sixty I still love what he writes for me. Mom said that she loves what he writes too, but it just seems a little hard to believe, that it all comes from him. She quickly added that she knows it does, but it still a little hard to believe. I still don't care I hope he never stops writing these nice words for me. Good night for now dear diary, I'll write again as soon as I get home from the hospital.

Wednesday, July 31st, 1946

Dear diary, I arrived home from my treatment at the hospital, at about three o'clock this afternoon. I received my infusion of medicine last Wednesday and I've been in the hospital since then undergoing some tests and mostly observation. I got a little sick to my stomach and remain tired as usual. Mama B was still in the hospital when I got there and I did get a chance to visit with her before she went home. She was in the same wing as me and the nurses let Mom and Joey take me to see her, but only if I sat in a wheel chair, which I did. Joey was so funny, he told me as we were going to see Mama B that he knew someday he would get to push me around.

Mama B was very glad to see me and Mom, as we were to see her. She had the water removed from her stomach the day before our visit, and she looked her usual self to me, because I've never seen her bloated. By the way, they don't call it "extracted" anymore, now they call it "tapped", as if they stick a water spigot in her and the water comes out. Just like you would tap a water pipe I suppose. That sounded just as painful to me as "extracted" did. I was right, because Mama B told us all about how they did it and also about what happened afterward.

She said that it hurt her so much that she called out Aniello's name, in Italian, and the pain would seem to go away. When the doctor asked her what she was doing, Mama B told him all about Buster and that when she called out to him, he would stop the pain. The doctor didn't say anything about to her at the time, but a few hours later he came back with another doctor, who was Italian and spoke the language. This other doctor started asking her questions and in a few minutes, she realized that he was a psychiatrist. The doctors thought she was crazy or something, because she was talking to her dead son. I have never seen Mama B get mad at anybody, but she said she got so mad at the doctors, that she chased them away. She said she even cursed at them for thinking that there was something wrong with her talking to Buster. In telling the story to us, she was getting mad all over again and Joey had to calm her down. Then Mom told her that they probably can't understand how her son, who is no longer living can take away her pain, when the doctors with all that they think they know, can't. That seemed to make sense to Mama B. I know it made a whole lot of sense to me.

While we were there, the doctor who "tapped" the water from her came back and told Mama B that if calling out to her dead son, helped take the pain away from her, she should continue doing that. Then he said, "We doctors don't know everything". I couldn't believe it. It was a wonderful thing to hear, coming from a doctor. Mama B just smiled thanked him and said that is just what she was going to do. Joey just stood there looking at Mama B while in deep thought and then finally said that there is a very good lesson to be learned from all of this. When I asked him what it was, he said he wasn't exactly sure, but he knew that it was there. I looked at Mom as if to ask her if she knew what Joey was talking about. She just looked at me and shrugged her shoulders. She didn't know either. He got me wondering about it. I was getting tired by that time, so I asked Mom and Joey to take me back to my room. We all said good night to Mama B and left.

When we got back to my room, I asked Joey if he figured it out yet what lesson he learned from Mama B's experience. He said he's working on it. He then added that when he figures it out, he will write it down on paper. After thinking about it for a few more minutes, Joey said he thinks he knows what part of the lesson is, because he heard Mama B say it a few times. Joey said that Mama B thinks that as long as you keep some one in your heart, they are alive, no matter what. He thinks that is living proof of what happened to Mama B, when she was getting her stomach emptied of water. Some day, he said he will write it all down, but not right now. I wonder what's going through his mind, what he is thinking about. Oh well, we shall see.

Joey seemed unusually quiet so I asked him if everything was alright. He looked at me and smiled his usual beautiful smile and said that everything is fine. I asked him why he was so quiet and he said he was just thinking about some of the news he's been reading about in the papers lately. "What news", I asked and he told me about a lot of people who have come into contact with the Russians near the end of the war who have all disappeared. He was wondering, he said, if maybe that might have happened to Buster. I asked him how that could've happened to Buster and he said that at the time he was supposed to have been killed in action, the American and Russian Armies were getting very close. Maybe he and his buddies saw something they weren't supposed to see and were taken prisoners. I told him that is a very interesting theory, but I thought it's a little bit of wishful thinking on his part. Of course, I told him I hoped he was right. He told me that I was right, it probably is wishful thinking on his part, then kissed me and hugged me and said good night and left. I'm getting very tired again so I'll say good night, dear diary.

Thursday, August 15th, 1946

Dear diary, I haven't written in a while because I didn't have much to say. I have been taking it easy, just like Dr. Edward told me to and resting a lot. I think I'm beginning to feel a little bit stronger, because I don't get as tired as I used to. In fact, I saw Dr. Edward this morning, at his office. He told me, that I seem to be going into a little remission period. While everything isn't quite normal with my blood tests, they are looking a little better. I still have to go for another treatment next Thursday, the 22nd. He said I should be out of the hospital in plenty of time to start my high school year. That was good news for me to hear. Now I'll have to start my shopping for back to school clothes, maybe tomorrow. I'll have to see how I feel and when Mom can take me.

Joey has been over to see me every day. Between coming to see me and taking care of Mama B, he told me he was going to quit his job. I begged him not to, because I thought he was going to do it mostly for me, but he insisted that it was mostly because of Mama B. When I asked what he was going to do for money, he told me he has saved up enough so that he really doesn't have to work for a while. Then he said the sweetest thing. He said that as long as he has enough money to buy me a present once in a while, he was happy. When I said that because I haven't been able to baby-sit in a while, I wouldn't be able to buy him or anyone else anything, he said that my love for him is the only gift he needs. He always makes me feel so special. I know I've said that a few times before, but I can't help saying it because it's true. At times his words almost make me cry and sometimes they do.

I don't know if I ever told you about the first time Joey made me cry, and I think Mom too. It was when I first got sick. I think it was the day after he half carried me home from school. He came over after school to see how I was feeling and he brought me a beautiful rose in a lovely little vase. As he walked into my room with Heshy, Mom was standing behind him, in the doorway, he held up the vase and said that the difference between that beautiful flower and me was, that the beauty of that rose would soon fade, but the beauty of me, would last forever. Do you see what I mean? Mom wouldn't admit it, but Heshy and I both think she was wiping away a tear from her eye when she walked back into the kitchen. Well I have to go to sleep now, so good night dear diary.

Monday, September 2nd, 1946 [Labor Day]

Dear diary, I went shopping with Mom for my back to school clothes, at Schlossberg's, a few days before I had to go into the hospital for my treatment. I didn't feel up to going to downtown Brooklyn, where the big department stores are and the ride to Daddy's factory is even further away. Plus, using Heshy's discount, we got a nice break in the price at Schlossberg's. Mom and I picked out some very nice things and I used some of my own money, to buy Mom a little present. She didn't want me to, but I insisted because I just wanted to show her that I appreciated all that she does for me, and I told Mom that. She said that she knows I love her as much as she loves me and that's all we have to give each other, our love. I'm not sure if she starting to sound like Joey or if he's starting to sound like Mom. They both touch my heart every day and in every way. Now I'm starting to sound like Joey.

On the 22nd I went into the hospital for another treatment and it went as usual. Dr. Edward said that my blood tests show that I continue to be in remission, and that made me feel better. He said that in addition to my regular treatment, he was going to give me a small dose of a new drug, one pill a day for five days that might help me even more. I asked him if the new drug would make me feel sicker than I usually do after getting my medication and he said that he didn't know, because the drug was so new. He said it might have a few side effects, but he wasn't sure what, if any. He told me not to worry, because he said, he wouldn't give it to me if he thought is might do me any harm. He has such an assuring way about him, that I wasn't worried about it. He also told me, that he would be testing me every day, to see if the new drug would have any effect on me and that meant that I would have to stay in the hospital a whole week, or maybe a few days more. Oh well, what can I do about it? Nothing.

Mom, as always was with me almost every moment that I was awake. On Sunday, the 25th, she told me she had a surprise for me. She opened the door to my room and in stepped Mrs. Schultz, the art teacher. I was so happy to she her because, as I've told you before, I like her very much. She told me she was very sorry that she hadn't been able to come to see me sooner, but she was away visiting relatives in Ohio. Then she told me how happy she was to see me. After we chatted for a few minutes she said that she met Mom about a month or so ago, while shopping in Schlossberg's. Mom goes there a lot because Heshy gets that discount, you know. Anyway Mrs. Schultz said that because she had done some calligraphy work, you know that fancy printing stuff, for people for their wedding invitations and things like that, Mom asked her to do something for her. Sarah Gold has talent and does calligraphy too, but Mrs. Schultz is the best. She told me that Mom gave her a poem that Joey had written, titled, "A Most Beautiful Thing" and asked her to copy it in calligraphy, so Mom can have it framed to give to me. Before I could say a word, Mrs. Schultz said that when she showed the poem to her husband, who is a woodworking shop teacher at Boy's High School, he made a frame for it in the little shop he has in the basement of their home.

Then she handed me this picture frame, that was wrapped in beautiful paper and told me to open it. I very carefully unwrapped it and was left speechless by the sight of the most beautiful, hand carved, picture frame I had ever seen. Sure enough there was the poem that Joey had written for me, right after that boat trip to Bear Mountain.

Mrs. Schultz did a gorgeous job of printing. Mom told Mrs. Schultz that she loved that poem because it reminded her of when she and Daddy first fell in love as teenagers in Germany. Mrs. Schultz said that it reminded her too, of her and her husband, when they were young kids in Germany. To me, as beautiful as the picture frame and calligraphy was, the most beautiful part was, the words Joey had written. Of course I didn't say that out loud to anyone. After Mrs. Schultz left I told that to Mom and she agreed with me, but she still admired the lovely work that the Schultz's did.

Then Mom told me that Mrs. Schultz won't be coming back to teach this year, but she didn't know why. She is also going to have to sell her house in E. Flatbush and move away. When I asked Mom if the Schultz's were going to move to Ohio with their relatives, Mom said no, she didn't think so. She said that the truth of the matter is that she doesn't have any relatives in Ohio. Mom said that through friends of theirs from Germany, she found out that Mr. Schultz, before the war had worked for the Nazis, on some very secret projects. Then she really shocked me and told me that Mr. Schultz is not Jewish, but Mrs. Schultz is. In fact, Mom said Schultz is not their real name. Mom didn't know the rest of their story, but she finds out about them a little more every time she gets a letter from one of her old friends in Germany, or meets one of them right here in Brooklyn. Mom said that to this day, when they meet, they all talk in hushed voices, when they talk about the Schultz's.

The next day, Mom told me that by coincidence, she met someone she knew back in Germany, in the lobby of the hospital, and he asked her if she had seen Mrs. Schultz lately. This man, who is not Jewish, was a minor official in the local Nazi party back in 1935, the year we all left Germany for England. She said that although she hadn't seen him since, she recognized him by the scar or his cheek that ran down to his chin and his very crooked nose. She didn't know how he knew the Schultz's, because they weren't from her part of Germany. Mom seemed very scared by meeting this guy. When I asked Mom if he had been mean to our family she said no, not when we were there. She heard later on, a couple of years later on, that he was part of the crazy mobs that did awful things to Jewish people, including our family, that were still living there. What the heck is going on here, I thought to myself. I thought the war was over.

That evening, after I had just finished eating my dinner, two men in dark suits came into my room and very politely asked to speak to Mom. They went outside into the hall for about five minutes and then they all came back into my room. One of the men, he seemed to be the one doing most of the talking, asked me how I was feeling and then wished me well. He even told me that he would keep me in his prayers. I was surprised by that, but I thanked him for it and thought it was very nice of him to say that. Mom was just standing near him with a serious look on her face and said nothing. The man told me his name was Higgins or something like that, I don't remember exactly. My heart was beating rapidly, because I didn't know what was going on and who these men were. He then told me that they were from the government, an agency that he was not at liberty to say. I blurted out," The FBI" He turned to his partner who nodded okay and then looked at me and said I was right, it is the FBI.

I looked at Mom with eyes that asked her if everything was okay. She must of read my fears perfectly, because she told me not to worry and that everything is okay. She said that these men were our friends and that they just wanted to explain something to me. The man doing the talking, Mr. Higgins, looked at Mom, then at me and nodded in agreement. Then he told me a little bit about what's going on, but first made me promise not to say anything to anyone about what he was going to tell me. Of course I promised not to. He said for national security reasons, he couldn't tell me everything and the only reason he's taking a chance and telling me some of the details, is because he knows I'm sick with Leukemia. He said he was worried that if he left me wondering and worrying about what was going on, I might make myself worse. He seemed to be a very nice and kind man and I told him so. He thanked me and said that he has a daughter my age and a couple of younger kids too. Anyway, he started to tell me this story about the Schultz's and the man Mom met this morning in the hospital lobby.

He said that Mr. Schultz's real name is Helmut Von Holstein and he was a leading scientist on a very secret project, to develop and produce an atomic bomb for the Nazis. What the Nazis didn't know was that he was working as an agent for the British. His mission was to keep the British up to date with the progress the Germans were making and if they were getting close to developing the bomb, he was to somehow delay the progress. The British said that he did a great job at both tasks, but the Nazis were getting on to him. While he was doing his work, he somehow discovered a link, with certain Nazis and Gestapo agents, to the Russian KGB. Mr. Higgins said that Mr. Schultz, that is Von Holstein, found out too much about them, from one of his co-workers, who was working as an agent for the Russians. His co-worker was having a lot of trouble and stress doing what he was doing and eventually killed himself. Because he was close to this poor fellow, he became suspect. The British felt that he might be arrested, so they made arrangements to have him come to England under the name of Schultz.

That was in 1938 and after telling the British everything he knew, about the project he was working on and what his co-worker had told him, they let him come to America. Over here, he had to tell the FBI the same things he told the British. Then he worked with the American scientists on developing the atomic bomb. When he started having health problems, because of the very long hours of work, he was allowed to leave that program and become what he always wanted to be, a woodworking shop teacher. Woodworking had always been his hobby in Germany and he always said that he loved to teach. That's how he and Mrs. Schultz came to live in Brooklyn.

In the meantime, Mr. Higgins said, many Gestapo agents went to work for the KGB, in the Russian occupied section of Germany and wanted to settle old scores. Through some of their own agents working in England during the war, they found out about Von Holstein working for the British and tracked him all the way to Brooklyn. They sent the man that Mom met in the morning in the hospital lobby and a few others to try and confirm that Schultz is really Von Holstein. However the FBI had been watching them closely and were about to move the Schultz's to a safer location, when the Schultz's got very scared and ran off on their own. Mr. Higgins said that he is trying to find them before those German/Russian agents do.

At that point I asked him what that had to do with me and my family. He said because that man approached Mom, that very morning in the hospital and Mrs. Schultz had given me that picture frame with something hand scripted on it, that we somehow might be involved. In an unknowing way, he quickly added. Mom asked him, with great surprise in her voice, how he knew about the picture frame and poem that was hand written in calligraphy on it. He told us that he was over the Schultz's house a few days ago, to warn them about the danger that they were in and that he wanted to move them to a safer place. While there, in their basement, he said he asked Mr. Schultz what he was working on and Mr. Schultz told him. Now he thinks there may be a clue or two in either the hand carvings on the frame, or in the very fancy calligraphy that the poem is written in. Then he looked at me, smiled and said that it was a very nice poem. He wanted to know if I wrote it. When I told him that it was written by my "fella", Joey Balducci he said, "Balducci, is he related to Aneillo Balducci?"

Buster! You know about Buster? I asked loudly in disbelief. Again I asked how he knew about Buster. He looked at me and asked if that was Aneillo's nickname and I said yes. He grew a little solemn and said he knew about Buster Balducci, because of something else that's going on. He asked all of us in my room, Mom, Daddy and myself, Joey and Heshy were not finished working yet, to be sworn to secrecy. He said it was a matter of national security. He even said that if his bosses found out he was telling us, what he was about to tell us, he would be in big trouble. He said the reason he is telling us, is because his kid brother, who was only twenty four years old at the time, was reported killed in the same area that Buster and fifty four other soldiers were reported missing or killed, mostly missing. The recorded history book of the 1st Army, of which their divisions were a part of, lists no major battles on the day that Buster and his brother were reported killed, he said. Yet the Department of the Army records say that they were killed during an attack on a city in the western part of Germany.

He continued and said at about that same time, the Russian Army was very close to the American lines. Through an old Fordham collage classmate of his, who had gone right out of collage into the Army Intelligence Department, he found out some very interesting things about the time that Buster and those other boys were killed. He suddenly changed that to "reportedly killed". He found out that on the 16th of April, 1945, as the American Army was getting deeper into Germany, the Russians were moving very close to the American lines. At that very same time there were a lot of German scientists, who had worked on the German rocket ship program, along with a convoy of trucks full of their rockets and equipment, heading toward the American lines. The Americans were informed of this and sent out those four patrols to find them. Neither the Germans nor the Americans wanted them to fall into Russian hands.

From a few eyewitnesses, they've pieced together a picture of what happened. The Russians were aware of that convoy trying to get to the west and were racing to cut them off. They caught up with them at the same time as out patrols reached the convoy. A brief fight broke out and the Americans, being greatly outnumbered, were surrounded and had to surrender. What was left of them surrendered. That was the last that was seen or heard of them since. All that was found was some of the bodies. Most of the civilians who witnessed this were either killed or taken prisoner. However a few managed to escape and told their story to the Americans. When the Government, the State Department and the Department of the Army found out about it, they said that for "national security" reasons that information is classified "Top Secret". That every one of those soldiers in those four patrols be listed as "killed in action" or missing. He said he believed that the missing soldiers, about forty of them might be alive and held prisoners of the Russians.

He asked us specifically, not to say anything to any of the Balduccis, because he didn't want to give them any false hope, that Aneillo might still be alive. He said that he hasn't even told his own mother, in case he is all wrong about them maybe being alive. I heard myself say that Joey told me not too long ago, that he thinks the same thing might have happened to Buster. Mr. Higgins seemed surprised to hear that and said that Joey must be a pretty smart kid. He said with a laugh that maybe Joey should come to work for the FBI. We all laughed at that and then Mr. Higgins said that he just doesn't think the Russians are to be trusted. I couldn't believe it. I mean Daddy and Mr. B have always said that.

I couldn't believe I was hearing all this. I mean, here I am fighting a disease that could be fatal to me and now I'm in the middle of an international spy mystery, or something. I still didn't know what the point is, of all this stuff that Mr. Higgins was telling us. By the looks on Mom's and Daddy's faces, they didn't know either. I asked Mr. Higgins why he was telling us all of this. I told him it was all very interesting, but why was he telling us. He said because he thought we should know, so that we might understand some of the things that are going to be happening with people around us. Mom asked him what people he was talking about and he said The Schultz's for one and Sylvia Roth for another.

Sylvia Roth! Sylvia Roth, the "yenta", I asked with shock in my voice. What does she have to do with all of this I asked, she doesn't even live around here any more. Mr. Higgins said it's very complicated, but her father was a double agent working for the British and German governments before the war started and also had contacts with the KGB. Mr. Higgins said that the FBI is bringing Mr. Roth back to live in our neighborhood again, to see if he can identify the German agents who are now working for the Russians. The same man who spoke to Mom that same morning, is one of them. When I told him that he should be careful of what he says in front of Sylvia because she is such a "yenta", a gossip. He said he knows all about her and he's counting on her to gossip and be a "yenta" as I put it. I couldn't believe what he said, so I asked him why and how, is he counting on her.

He is going to tell her some phony story, about the Schultz's and also why she and her family moved back to Brooklyn. He's going to tell her not to say anything to anybody about it. He knows for sure that then she'll definitely tell everyone and everybody. That German agent and some of his fellow agents have been quietly asking questions all over the neighborhood, about the Schultz's and where they came from and how long Mrs. Schultz has been a teacher in our school and things like that. He said here's where we come in. The first thing that he going to tell Sylvia is, that Mrs. Schultz is not Jewish. The second thing is that she has been teaching in the New York City school system since 1934. He has already arranged it with the Board of Education, to alter her records to show that. He said that he wants us to back up the story as soon as Sylvia starts telling it. If we should be approached again by that same man, or any other person asking about Mrs. Schultz, he told us to just tell them what he told us.

Joey and Heshy arrived just as Mr. Higgins and his partner, whose name I never got were leaving. Heshy and Joey, at the same time, asked who they were. Heshy said that they looked like cops or something. Mom, the quick thinker that she is, said that they were from the hospital administration department and were just asking routine questions, about what we think of the hospital services and the treatment that I'm getting. I had all to do to keep from telling Joey about what Mr. Higgins told me, about Buster maybe still being alive. I felt so proud of myself at being able to keep a secret, but at the same time I felt bad, that I couldn't share what might turn out to be good news for him. After what seemed like a long time to me, of talking with everyone, I told them all that I was getting very tired, so they all left and I fell asleep.

It seemed to me like it was the middle of the night, maybe two or three in the morning when I was awakened by the sound of two men in dark suits standing on either side of my bed. It was dark in the room and I couldn't make out their faces. They were trying to take me out of my bed and I started screaming for them to stop. I heard myself yelling out for Mr. Higgins and for Mom, but nobody was coming to help me. Finally I started screaming at the top of my lungs, first for Mr. Higgins and then for Mom. I thought the men in the dark suits were trying to inject me with something and one of them said to the other, with a foreign accent, "Try and hold her still and calm her down." I yelled for them to stop, that I knew nothing that would be of any help to them, but they wouldn't listen. I must have passed out or fainted or something, because the next thing I knew, I was tossing and turning and saying something. Mom was sitting by the side of my bed, holding my hand and softly talking to me, in a very soothing way. I kept hearing her tell me that it's alright, everything is alright.

When I opened my eyes, I looked around the room and asked Mom where Mr. Higgins was. She asked if I meant Dr. Higgins, the one who is in charge of testing the new drug I was taking. I said no, Mr. Higgins from the FBI. Mom laughed and said that I was having a bad dream. She said that the new drug they gave me for the last four days was causing me to be very sleepy, groggy and have dreams. She told me that on Sunday, after being on that new drug for just four days, I started to fall asleep, right after Mrs. Schultz left my room and I've been half asleep and half awake ever since then and that it was now Tuesday. The doctors were a little worried about me, because they didn't expect a reaction like that, but everything looks fine now. The doctors agreed that I won't be having any more bad dreams. I insisted that there was a Mr. Higgins from the FBI and that the Schultz's were in a lot of danger that they are hiding out somewhere. Mom laughed even louder and told me that the Schultz's were not in any danger that they will be moving to Australia. I said Australia, why Australia? Mom said that Mr. Schultz's brother has started a business there and wants to make Mr. Schultz a partner. Mom stroked my forehead and told me not to worry because they are not in any danger.

I asked Mom about the man she met in the lobby of the hospital yesterday and she told me that he was arrested for coming into this country illegally. It seems that he met Mrs. Schultz years ago in Germany and had what Mom called a, "fixation" on her for all these years. After he sneaked into this country, he somehow found out that she was here, and where she worked and lived. When she went away to Ohio for a few weeks, he was looking all over for her and must have overheard somebody say, that she was coming to see me. Here in the hospital. You mean it was all a bad dream that I had, I asked Mom. Mom said yes, she was sitting next to me for quite a while and I was talking about the Russians and the British and the FBI. She said I even mentioned Buster's name many times, and Joey's too.

When I was fully awake, I told Mom everything that happened in my dream, even about what Higgins said about Buster maybe being alive. Mom just looked at me and said it would wonderful if it were true, but we can't pin our hopes on just wishful thinking. I told her that is just what I said to Mr. Higgins in my dream. Mom just laughed again and said that everything is going to be alright. She said that the doctors aren't sure yet, whether or not the drug was of any help to me, so they are going to discontinue it until they know for sure. I don't know, that dream seemed so real to me, it's still hard for me to believe that it was not. I couldn't wait for Joey and Heshy to come over later that day, so I could tell them all about it. I was hoping they wouldn't laugh at me too much.

When Heshy and Joey came over, they both breathed a huge sigh of relief, when they saw me awake and taking to Mom. Joey held me so tight and yet so tenderly. He told me that the doctors were so worried about me the past couple of days, that he was getting worried too, along with the rest of my family and his family too. Joey said that he couldn't sleep the past few nights, thinking about me and the way I was acting. He wasn't sure if I was ever going to wake up, and that got him very depressed. Even though the doctors were a little concerned about me, they felt sure that I was just reacting to the new medication. Mom said that no one in the family got much sleep while I was having that reaction.

Heshy laughed his head off when I told them all about my dream, but Joey just laughed a little and then hugged me, bent over and kissed my forehead and told me that it's okay to have dreams. After awhile, I looked at Joey closely and told him I didn't like the way his eyes looked. He told me I should like the way his eyes looked, because they're only looking for me and at me. I told him that I meant they looked so tired, and he said that his eyes will never, ever get tired of looking at me. I pulled him closer to me, hugged him and told him he was a silly goose, but I loved every word he said. Then I noticed a piece of paper sticking out of Joey's shirt pocket and asked him what it was. He looked surprised and sheepishly said that it was nothing. I asked him if I could see it and he was very hesitant about showing it to me. Well you know that made me want to see it even more, so he handed it to me and I read it. I was so breathless after reading it I couldn't even cry or speak for a few moments. Joey explained to me while I was reading it, that when he wrote it, he thought I might not be waking up again. That's why he wrote it. He titled it,

"NEVER HAVING TO SAY GOODBYE"

WHEN ONE OF US IS FIRST TO LEAVE,
TO GO TO THAT BIG BEAUTIFUL PARK IN THE SKY,
THE OTHER WILL NEVER HAVE TO GRIEVE,
NEVER HAVE TO CRY,
BECAUSE WE WILL FOREVER BE TOGETHER
WE WILL NEVER HAVE TO SAY GOODBYE,
WE WILL ALWAYS LIVE IN EACH OTHER'S HEART,
WE WILL NEVER, EVER DIE,
WE WILL NEVER, EVER BE APART,
WE WILL BE TOGETHER, FOREVER,
THERE'S NO NEED TO GRIEVE OR CRY
WE WILL BE TOGETHER, FOREVER,
WE WILL NEVER HAVE TO SAY GOODBYE,
I WILL LOVE YOU ALWAYS AND FOREVER,
MY SWEETHEART,
MY ESTHER,
MY LOVE,
YOUR FOREVER FELLA,
JOEY

When I did start to cry, Joey told me he was so sorry, because he didn't mean to make me cry. He said all he wanted to do, was tell me how much he felt about me, and how we are going to be together, always. When he bent over to hug me, I handed the paper to Mom. When she finished reading it, she immediately left my room with the paper still in her hand and Heshy following her out the door. I could see and hear her crying in the hall as she handed the paper to Heshy. After a moment or two I saw the two of them hugging each other. When Mom and Heshy returned to my room, both of them red eyed and sniffling, Mom asked Joey where he came from. I don't know if Joey was trying to be cute and funny or not, but he told Mom that he comes from Powell Street. Mom just looked at him for a few seconds before she gave him a big hug, laughed and told him to never change the way he is. Heshy, with his hand on Joey's shoulder, nodded in agreement. To me it was a very beautiful and tender moment to see.

The rest of my stay in the hospital went without any more problems with my medications and I came home on Thursday, the 29th of August. I was feeling pretty tired the first couple of days home from the hospital, but I think Mom's cooking has made me feel a lot better and stronger. I don't think I'll have any problems starting school this coming Wednesday, the day after tomorrow. I'm all prepared for it you know new clothes, new school and all that. I really believe that I'm mentally and physically ready for it too. I hope so. I feel good knowing that Heshy and Joey will be my "book ends" walking to and from school again, just like this past spring in jr. high school. Of course on some days on the way back from school Heshy will only be able to walk with us as far as Schlossberg's, because he has to go to work. Joey, as I told you before, quit working to take care of Mama B and to come over to see me when we were both in the hospital. I still think he did it mostly for me. Am I flattering myself? I don't know, but that's just what I think. It's a good thing I started writing this early today, because I had a lot to tell you. Now that I've told you just about everything, I'm getting tired and have to say good night dear diary.

CHAPTER 14

Friday, November 29th, 1946

Dear diary, I am sorry that I haven't written in so long. I started school on September 4th like I told you I would. So far I have been able to keep up with my schoolwork, but it's been very tough on me. I get very tired, sometimes in class, but almost every night I'm just about able to finish my homework. That's why I haven't written in so long. I'm writing now because it's only 11am and I'm on Thanksgiving break. I have so much to tell you, that I don't know if I'll be able to tell you it all today. I might have to finish writing about it tomorrow, we shall see.

Everyone in the high school, the principal and all the teachers, all know about me and what I've been going through. I'm excused from taking gym classes again and when I'm not able to attend school, they'll all send work home to me, with Heshy and Joey. So far I've been able to attend class every day except for the days I have to go to the hospital. It all makes me very tired. It's a good thing I can sit in the study hall during my gym class, so I can get a head start on my homework. I say head start, but what I really mean is that on most days I get most of it done. That's a good thing too, because by the time I finish eating my dinner I can only do a little bit more before I get very tired. Joey comes over here almost every night now to do homework with us and it's a good thing. Between him and Heshy helping me, I have managed to so far get my homework done. Like I've said so many times before dear diary, they make me feel so lucky.

I had to go back into the hospital Thursday, September 26. Everything went so well that I was able to come home on Tuesday October 1st. I only missed four days of school, but Heshy and Joey did bring me work to do on Friday and Monday, which I did while in the hospital. Thank God for that. That means that I didn't fall behind the rest of my class. The weather was getting cooler by that time and the bed jacket that Mama B gave me, really came in handy, not only in the hospital, but at home too. It keeps me so warm and comfy. Mom, Joey and everyone, always tell me how nice it looks on me.

Just like Mom said a while back, high school work is not much different or harder than what we did in jr.high. I've also made some new friends, although I still stay very close to the friends I kind of grew up with. Two of the new kids I met are sisters, Sherry and Suzy Gonzalez. Sherry is a year older than Suzy, who is my age. I think they said that their father is Puerto Rican and their mother is from Trinidad. I think that's such an interesting combination. They are so beautiful too. They attract so much attention from the boys that a lot of the other girls are jealous of them, but not me. After all I've got my "fella", my Joey, and I know he always looks only at me. Anyway that's what he keeps telling me and I believe him. Speaking of Joey, he is so funny. We were all talking in front of the school one morning before classes started and Joey looked at Suzy, who wears braces, and told her she should never kiss Jimmy Teagno, another boy in our class who also wears braces, outside in the middle of a lightning storm. He said they might get struck and their braces fused together. He added that they'd have to spend the rest of their lives locked in a kiss. Everyone laughed but Suzy said that because Jimmy is so cute, she didn't think it was such a bad thing, to be locked in a life long kiss with him. More laughter as we all walked into the school and our classrooms.

The teachers seem to be all very nice. Of course some of them are better than others, but like I said, they all seem to be nice. The walk to and from school is much longer than the walk we had going to jr.high school and that gets me very tired. Mr. B is such an angel. Joey must have said something to him about that because, almost every morning he shows up at my door, with Joey in his taxi and takes us all to school. When he can, he also tries to be at the school at three o'clock in the afternoon to take me home. I told Joey that I hope his boss doesn't find out about this. I was worried that he might lose his job or something like that.

Joey told me that there is nothing to worry about, because his father has already worked out some sort of deal with his boss, to buy one of the cabs and taxi license. Wow! I told Joey that was great news. I said

I guess that means he will be his own boss. Joey said yes and no. He said he has to pay off the boss over a long period of time and also be responsible for all the things that it takes to keep a cab running in good order. Plus, he said that Mr. B will be working longer hours to make the money to pay off the boss, but he can work any hours he chooses. Now I know how he's able to pick me up every morning to take me to school, but not every afternoon to take me home. Anyway just taking me in the morning is a great help to me and I think it keeps me from getting tired sooner than I do.

On the way to school Mr. B talks to us, Heshy, Sarah, me and Joey just as if we were all his kids. Sarah even remarked about that to me when we got out of his cab one morning, so it's not just me that noticed it. He still makes himself available to us whenever we have to go any place, so much so, that he has us spoiled. When we tell him that, he always says, "That is what family and friends are for, to help each other out". Joey always says that when there is food around, Heshy wants to help him out too, out the door or window so he can have all the food to himself. Joey seems to find something funny in whatever some one says or any situation. I think that's good, but now he's got me wondering where he came from.

On Friday, the 18th of October, I went into the hospital for my treatment again. Just like last month I only had to miss four school days. I came home on Wednesday, the 23rd, with the usual problem of being very tired, but Mom's chicken noodle soup had me feeling stronger again. I was glad I didn't have to stay in the hospital so long, that I would miss Halloween this year. I always have a good time getting ready for it. Of course working with Joey had a lot to do with it and I'm sure it will be the same way this year too. We shall see.

Halloween worked out very well for all of us. Just like in jr.high, the high school held a costume contest and a sort of parade. Again we were allowed to work in groups or by ourselves. This year Joey and I teamed up. I was able to get, from one of the nurses at the hospital, an old uniform, cape and hat that didn't fit her anymore. She even let me borrow a stethoscope for the contest. Joey bought a bunch of bandages and got an unwanted crutch from someone on Powell Street. He wrapped his head up in bandages and his left leg too. He even put some ketchup on his head bandage, stuck the crutch under his left armpit and hobbled along in the parade. All the while I was holding his left arm and the stethoscope in my ears I pretended to be checking his heart. We got a great reception and I thought we might have a chance to win.

Heshy had Daddy get one of the women in his factory sew together a look-a-like Babe Ruth uniform, that looked very real. He borrowed Mr. Bernstein's Babe Ruth autographed bat and walked around with it on his shoulder. Sarah wore one of her mother's really tight fitting dresses and a fake fur stole over her shoulders. She walked beside Heshy with her arm in his and they paraded in front of the judges that way. I thought for sure that they might win something, because they looked so good.

I was wrong about any of us winning anything. I mean we were better than most of the other kids, but some of them really went to great lengths to win. The big winner was a kid who made himself up to look just like Hitler, mustache, military uniform and all. The "clincher", as Joey and Heshy would say, is that this kid had a large bullet sticking out of his head, half of it sticking out of one side of his head, and the other half sticking out of the other side. The judges and everybody else loved it. I was wrong about us not winning anything, Heshy and Sarah did manage to win an honorable mention. I guess that's better than nothing. The best part is that we all had fun working on it. Of course I had to have my picture taken of me in that uniform and with Joey too, so I could show the nice nurses at the hospital. They are all so very good to me.

The nurse who let me use her uniform, her name is Ann Marie, is a very friendly lady. Lots of times when she can, she takes the time to sit and talk with me. I often confide in her just how scared I am at times. She is so understanding and helpful to me. She told me one time, that in spite of my illness, she thinks I'm very lucky to have such great support from all of my family and friends. She said that there have been a lot of children, of all ages that she has seen in the hospital who very seldom have visitors. When they do have them sometimes, they don't stay very long. I asked her if I could, when I feel up to it, go over and visit with some of them. She said she thinks I could, but I'll have to have someone with me, in case I start to feel weak or something. Of course I said I understood and I did visit with them a few times.

After one of my visits with some of the younger patients, I asked Ann Marie how she is able to handle it when one of her young patients loses their battle with cancer. Because, I told her that I felt terrible when

I would not see one of the kids that I had seen the day before. She told me that is the toughest part of her job. She said in order to be a nurse you have to condition yourself to face up to these unpleasant, sad things that happen. That's part of the job, she said, the part she hates the most but one that has to be done. Sometimes, she told me that she goes home to her family feeling very down but when she thinks of the kids that she has to care for the next day, she gets over her doubts. What keeps her going is that there some happy endings, just not enough of them. Then she looked at me and smiled and said that she has high hopes that I will be one of those happy endings.

She admires Mom for all the time she spends with me at the hospital, and for that matter she said, my entire family. I felt so good when she told me that all the nurses are crazy about Joey. Then she told me they love all the things he writes for me. I couldn't believe that she knew about the stuff that Joey writes and I asked her how she knew about them. She laughed and then got serious when she thought she said the wrong thing to me. She asked me in a very nice way if I minded that she had read some of them, because she explained, that Mom had showed them to her. I told her I didn't mind and I really didn't. Then I told her that she was right, I am very lucky because of my family and friends who all seem to love and support me. I really surprised myself when I heard myself tell her that I was so crazy in love with Joey and he loves me too. I couldn't believe I told her that. She then surprised me a little when she said that everyone who has seen us together knows that. The ones who did read some of the things he wrote to me know it even more, she added. Here's the great part, she told me that everyone of them wish they had somebody who loved them the way that Joey loves me and shows it in every way that he can. That makes me feel so lucky but scared sometimes especially when I think about those kids that never got better, but lucky.

November went by fast and I had to go back into the hospital on Friday the 22nd and I was worried that I would have to spend Thanksgiving Day in the hospital. Thank God they let me go home on Wednesday the 27th, the day before Thanksgiving. I was so glad that I was going to be home with my family on Thanksgiving Day, although I know they would've all, including Joey I'm sure, been there with me in the hospital. It just feels so much better being home. I was wondering what Mom and Daddy would say about what they had to be thankful for this year. Then I remembered last year when Mama B gave that little talk about why she was thankful even though Buster was killed earlier in the year. I still remember how moving it was for me to hear her talk about it. That kind of made me think about what Mom always has told me, count your blessings for the little things you get out of life, because no one is guaranteed anything. Now dear diary, I'm getting tired so I'll have to finish writing about my Thanksgiving Day tomorrow. Good night.

Saturday, November 30th, 1946

Dear diary, Mom must have been up all night preparing the feast that she set out before us, on Thanksgiving Day. It was all so delicious and there was so much of it. I think we'll be eating the left overs for at least a week. My Aunt Sherry from the Bronx couldn't come because one of her kids, my cousin Irving, is sick with the Flu or something like that. Daddy's brother, my uncle Carl and his family were there. Joey came over later and was just in time for some dessert. I think he tasted a little bit of all of the desserts. Watching him eat like that made me wonder why he doesn't get fat. I mean Heshy is starting to put on some weight but Joey eats as much as Heshy does, maybe even more and he stays nice and slim. I don't get it. Joey told Heshy that if he puts on any more weight he'll look like twins all by himself. As we all giggled at that, Heshy told Joey that he resembled that remark. They slapped each other on the shoulder and laughed the loudest of all of us. I love to see them that way. I'm so glad that my brother and my "fella" are best friends.

The rest of the Balduccis didn't come over because Mama B is not feeling well. She's retaining water again and has trouble climbing stairs. I was thinking that Joey ought to watch what he eats now, so he won't have the same problems later on that Mama B has now. I mean I'll love him no matter what. When I mentioned that to Joey, he said that if I didn't love him fat I didn't love him thin. I had to think about that for a minute, to figure out what he was trying to tell me and I finally did. When Joey and Heshy are together, kidding around like they mostly do, they're just like any other boys fifteen and a half years old. When Joey is with just me or my parents, he sometimes says things that make him sound like a person who is very wise and much older. Daddy once said about Joey being that way, that he has met in his travels a few people like that, but not many. They were perfectly normal for their age but at times seemed to know more about life and what's going on around us, than everyone else. Mom agreed with Daddy and said she didn't know why that was, but that we should just accept it as a fact of life. They both agreed that Joey is a very special person. Mom looked at me and Heshy and added, he's special just like we are.

Anyway, let me get back to Thanksgiving Day. I know that sometimes I wander away from what I'm talking about, but I can't help it, that's just me. Even though the Balduccis couldn't come over to our house, they were invited of course, Mr. B and Mama B sent over some "did not fall off the truck wine" and a nice platter of Italian cookies that everybody loved. Mary gave Joey a little gift to give me. It was a lovely little glass or ceramic I think, statue of a squirrel eating a nut. It was mounted on a pedestal. On the base of the pedestal she had inscribed, "Just like Esther, this is one of God's beautiful creations". I don't know if Mary has a heart just like Joey's, it wouldn't surprise me if she did, or if Joey wrote it for her. When Mom saw it she just smiled, hugged me and then Joey. She looked at Joey, shook her head and asked Joey where his whole family came from. Joey immediately replied that they originally came from Italy. Mom just turned away, laughed and said, "I give up! I'll never get a straight answer from him".

Heshy did a very nice thing for me on Thanksgiving Day. Even though it's not Chanukah or my birthday, he gave me a gift. He said that because I have so many papers with the things that Joey has written and continues to write to me and for me, he wanted me to have something to keep them in. Then he handed me this beautifully decorated three ring binder for the papers, and a three hole punch, to make all the papers fit into the binder. He said he wanted to do that for me for a long time, but just didn't get around to it until the other day. He saw some of the papers lying around the house and thought it was time to get those things now. I think Joey must be rubbing off on Heshy because, Heshy said that he wanted to give me something on Thanksgiving Day, to show thanks for having me not just as a sister, but a twin sister. See what I mean when I say I'm the luckiest girl in the world? Someone said, I don't know who it was, that we sure don't look like twins, and Daddy said that's because we are fraternal twins and Joey quickly added that he thanks God for that, because he didn't know what he'd do if I looked like Heshy. Everyone, even Heshy had to laugh at that. Then Heshy said I'd look even more beautiful than I do now if I looked like him and everyone laughed louder, including me.

Tomorrow is December 1st and now I have to start thinking about what to get certain people for Christmas and Chanukah. I don't even know if I have enough money to buy everyone a gift, but we shall see. I think I figured out how I can get my shopping done if I feel too tired to go myself. I'll ask Mom to get me the presents for Heshy, Daddy, the Balduccis and whoever else I have money for. Then I'll ask Mary or Helen, or maybe even Arlene, to get me something for Mom. I think a woman would pick out a better gift for Mom than a man can. I hope I'm right. We shall see.

Good night for now, dear diary.

Friday, December 27th, 1946

Dear diary, I just got home from the hospital this afternoon. I went in on Monday, so that meant I didn't miss any school days because of the Christmas break. That's a good thing. Everything went pretty well and I had no more bad or wild dreams, thank God. Anne Marie, the nurse who let me use her old nurse's uniform, loved the pictures of me in costume on Halloween and with Joey too. She said that all of the other nurses, who saw the pictures, liked them also. I missed going up to Joey's house to see his Christmas tree but I hope I can go see it sometime this weekend. The biggest surprise for me was, when all of the Balduccis came to visit me on Christmas day and brought me all kinds of presents. Mom and Daddy were there too. Mom arranged to have us all go into a lounge area on my floor and eat a delicious turkey dinner that Mom and the Balduccis helped make. It was almost as good as being home. I asked the nurses, if some of the other kids could come and have dessert with us, and they said they will have to ask one of the doctors. The doctor, I don't know which one it was, said yes.

I don't know how or why the Balduccis knew to bring a bag full of little inexpensive gifts for any of the kids that they saw, but they did. Mr. B said that he goes to a place on the lower east side of Manhattan where they sell everything cheap, sometimes below wholesale. He said Mama B told him to try and pick up some nice little things for the sick kids in the hospital and that's what he did. It's almost magical the way they seem to make people around them feel good.

The last time Mama B and I were in the hospital together, I think it was last month she was in a large ward with about thirty or forty beds in it. While Joey and I were there, a woman who had been brought in and placed in the bed next to Mama B. was carrying on like a crazy woman. She was yelling at the young intern who was attending her, that he was not a doctor, he was an intern. She made so much noise about it that the doctor in charge had to come over to her and settle her down. He was a little stern with her and told her that the young intern was indeed a doctor, and that he knew what he was doing and was a very good doctor. Mama B didn't say a word she just sat up in bed and watched. The woman was still very agitated when we left.

The next day Joey took me to see Mama B again, and when we walked into the ward, we got a big surprise. There was the woman, very calm and sitting up in bed and Mama B was standing next to her bed brushing the woman's hair. As we got to Mama B's bed, the woman, whose name we found out is Doris Zuckerman, told us what a very special person Mama B is. Joey and I couldn't believe it. Mama B, just by talking to the woman calmed her down and made the woman feel comfortable. The woman seemed delighted to have Mama B brush her hair. See what I mean about how special the Balduccis are, especially Joey of course.

Yesterday, the day after Christmas, the nurses and the kids were still talking about how nice Mama B is for trying to think about everyone, and put a little joy in their lives. In the afternoon, Barbara and her Aunt Becky came to visit me bearing gifts for the holidays. I was wonderfully surprised and happy to see them. Barbara filled me in on what's going on with all the kids and Helen and Arlene, or as Joey would call her "lean, mean, teenage queen, Arlene". She told me that the kids are always asking her about me and how I'm doing. They told her to be sure and tell me, how much they love and miss me. I wasn't sure if Barbara would be a little hurt if they didn't tell her that they loved her too, but she did tell me later, that they always tell her they love her. I was so glad to hear that. You know diary, I don't know why but I feel very close to Barbara and sometimes I think of her like I would a sister, if I had one. Do you know what I mean? I hope I'm not confusing you.

Mom said that if I felt well enough tomorrow, we'll go to see the Balducci's Christmas tree and bring them their presents. I had given Mom a list of people and my last sixty dollars, to buy presents for them. By the size of the pile of wrapped gifts, I know she spent a whole lot more than the money I gave her and when I mentioned that to her, she just waved her hand at me and told me to forget about it. That's my Mom. Of course Mom wasn't on the list I gave her. I gave Joey my last twenty dollars and asked him to ask Mary if she would be kind enough to pick out something nice, that she thinks my Mom would like, and she did. I still haven't seen some of the gifts I paid for with Mom's help, that she picked out for me, but I guess I will tomorrow.

The things I got for Heshy, Daddy and Mom were given to them last week on Chanukah, before I went into the hospital. Like I said before, Mom did the shopping for me and picked out everything all by herself. They were very nice things too. I got Daddy, I mean Mom picked out for Daddy, a very nice grey cardigan sweater. It had real leather patches on the elbows and real leather buttons down the front. When I told Daddy that should keep him nice and warm this winter, at home or in the office, he said just knowing it came from me will keep him warm no matter where he is and no matter if he's wearing the sweater or not. I told him he's starting to sound like Joey and he smiled and said he'll take that as a compliment.

Although Heshy and Joey are Brooklyn Dodger and Babe Ruth fans, they also admire Joe DiMaggio of the Yankees. They're always saying they wished he was playing for the Dodgers. I asked Daddy if he could maybe ask the same woman, who made the Babe Ruth uniform for Heshy, is she could make a Joe DiMaggio uniform for him too. I mean, that Babe Ruth look-a-like uniform is now Heshy's pride and joy, so I figured he might love one of Joe DiMaggio. Actually they wear the same uniform but the numbers on their back is different. Heshy and Joey both collect all kinds of baseball things, like old ticket stubs to Dodger games and baseball cards and things like that. Besides, I figured it wouldn't cost me anything and that way I'd have enough money to get everyone on my list a gift. Anyway, the woman did another great job of making that uniform and Heshy is just crazy about this one too.

Mary did a very nice, but sneaky thing. She went into Manhattan, to Helen's ladies clothing store, on the Saturday that Mom was working.

Because Mary is the same size as Mom, she pretended she was buying something for herself. Mary told me later on, that she kept asking Mom if she like this dress or that outfit until Mom told her which one she really thought looked great. Little did she know she was picking out her own gift. Because Helen was in the store at the time too, Mary told her what she was doing, when Mom couldn't hear her of course. Helen told her that there would be no charge. Is that great, or what. Anyway, you should have seen the look on Mom's face when she opened up her gift. Her jaw just dropped. She yelled out that was the outfit she helped Mary pick out. A beautiful outfit it is too, a very smart looking navy blue dress suit with a double breasted jacket and white buttons down the front of it. Mary even had Mom pick out a lovely white blouse to go with it. Mom tried the whole outfit on and she looked absolutely gorgeous.

While she still had her new outfit on, she picked up the phone and called Mary. When she got her on the phone, Mom started laughing and told Mary that she fooled her good. Mom told her that she was very sneaky for doing that, but she understands why. Mary must have told Mom that Helen was in on it because I heard Mom yell out in surprise, "She didn't! You really mean that Helen knew about this? Mom was still laughing and in disbelief after she got off the phone. I asked Mom why she hung up the phone so soon, because I wanted to talk to Joey and she said that Mary told her, Joey was on his way over here and he had something for me.

A few minutes later Joey was at the door. As soon as he walked in he gave me a warm embrace and a kiss and handed me a twenty dollar bill. The same one I had given him to give Mary, to buy Mom's present with. He quickly turned around to look at Mom in her new clothes and told her how great she looked in it. Mom asked Joey if he was in on the deception too. He laughed and said no, but he wished he was. When Mom asked Joey why he wished he was in on it, he said if he had anything to do with picking it out, he would've picked something with a shorter skirt, because, he told Mom, she had great looking legs. I immediately yelled to Joey that he's talking about my Mom and at the same time Daddy yelled out that he was talking about his wife. Before Joey could respond, Mom looked at me and then Daddy and asked if we didn't think she had nice legs. Heshy said, in a very serious way that Mom does have very nice looking legs. Daddy suddenly looked over at

Mom's legs and said, "Yes, she does have great looking legs, doesn't she". I sheepishly agreed but added that Joey wasn't supposed to notice them. Joey then tried to explain himself out of it by saying, what he meant was that I had nice looking legs and I must take after Mom. Then he added that even though Heshy is my twin brother and also Mom's son, he had legs that belonged on a piece of furniture. Heshy lashed back at Joey by saying that he had legs that a dog wouldn't stop to pee on. Joey yelled out that he resembled that remark and then said, "Who are you calling a peon?" We all laughed at that and sat down for a little coffee and cake. Good night for now, dear diary.

Wednesday, January 1st, 1947

Dear diary, HAPPY NEW YEAR! Well it's new year's day today, 1947. I hope that as good as last year was, and it was very good in so many ways, this year will be a lot better. I think you know what I mean. Anyway, this past Saturday we all went to visit the Balduccis to see their tree. It is beautiful as it always is, and we again had some of their holiday treats and a taste of home made wine. I couldn't believe all the presents that were under the tree for me and all of my family. The Balduccis are unbelievable. When Mr. B started handing out the gifts to us, Daddy asked him if he was trying to convert us or something and that made everybody laugh. We all loved the presents we got and the Balduccis seemed to really love the things we got for them.

As we were leaving their house, we met Barbara and the Green kids. They were all excited to see me and I was excited to see them too. I couldn't stand outside too long because it was very cold out, but we did speak to each other for a few minutes. Everyone was bundled up to keep warm and little Michael looked like an Eskimo, he looked so cute. I had to get home because I was starting to feel tired. Joey came home with us and I was very glad about that. He wrapped his arm around me and that kept me warm all the way home. Daddy was very funny. He told Joey not to hold me so tight, because he might break me. Mom said that she thought Daddy was getting a little jealous of somebody holding his little "tottala". Off course Daddy said no, that wasn't true but he did say that since Joey came into our lives, I pay more attention to him than anyone else in the family. I said I didn't think that was true, but if it was, I asked what was wrong with that. No one answered me and we just kept on walking home. Joey didn't say a word and he just kept on holding me tight. It felt so good.

Last night, New Years Eve, I was feeling pretty good, so Joey, Heshy, Sarah and I went to a party at Sandra Einhorn's house, just a few blocks away. After a couple of hours, at about 10:30 I was starting to feel tired so I asked Joey to take me home. Heshy and Sarah wanted to leave with us but I told them to stay and enjoy the party and they did. Joey decided to stay and ring in the New Year with me, Mom and Daddy in my house. He did call Mama B as soon as we got to my house, to see if she was alright and then again right after midnight, to wish her and Mr. B a happy new year. Mom bought some snacks and cold cuts earlier in the day so we had our own little party. I really felt more comfortable in my own house because, when I felt tired I could just lay down on the couch and also because I was with Mom, Daddy and Joey. Daddy even let me and Joey drink a little bit of wine to toast in the New Year. It was a very nice, cozy and quiet way to celebrate. Joey went home about 1am and I was so tired by that time I went right to bed and fell fast asleep.

I got up late this morning, as we all did, at about 10:30. Mom made breakfast for us and now it's almost noontime. I think Joey will be either coming over or calling me soon, at least I hope so. Knowing him as I do, he'll probably stop at Finklestein's Bakery and come here loaded down with all kinds of goodies. I know Heshy will be happy if he does show up that way. Because of Mama B's diabetes, I know he won't by bringing much sweet stuff home to tempt her. Of course Mr. B and Mary can eat that stuff, and they do, but usually not in front of Mama B. See what I mean when I say that they are all so thoughtful about each other and other people too. That's why I feel so lucky that Joey's my "fella". The phone's ringing and I think it's Joey so I have to say so long for now, dear diary.

Friday, February 14th, 1947

Dear diary,

Suddenly, Heshy heard a noise and felt like there was a light shining in his eyes. He opened his eyes and looked up and saw Idrig, the housekeeper for his apartment. She had just pulled open the drapes and was looking down at him and saying that she was sorry, because she didn't realize that he was sleeping in his chair. He asked her what time it was and she told him it was 7:15 am. Heshy quickly jumped up and said that he didn't realize that he had fallen asleep reading. He asked Idrig if she could make some coffee and maybe a couple of poached eggs on toast for him while he got in the shower. She said sure and went into the kitchen. On the way into the shower, he told himself to be sure to bring Esther's diary with him, because he's going to be spending, at least the next few nights with Sarah and the family at their estate. He'd finish the diary later on that night, he thought to himself. He showered, got dressed, ate his breakfast and went on to work.

On the ride to work, sitting in the back of his limo, Heshy reflected on what he read in Esther's diary the night before. He couldn't get over how it brought him back to those early days of so much fun, joy and sadness too. He actually felt like he was reliving all of those precious moments as he was reading Esther's words. He heard himself say out loud, "And they said you can never go home again. Baloney! I just did!"

CHAPTER 15

At 7:30pm, Friday, Joey stepped out of the limo that had just pulled up in front of the huge double doors of the grand main house, at the Sackman's estate. Heshy rushed out from the doors to greet Joey. Vigorously shaking Joey's right hand with his and patting Joey on the back, gently with his left hand Heshy said, "Welcome to my home Joey, I'm so glad you made it. You're just in time. Everyone else is here and we are about to sit down for dinner." After telling Heshy how honored he was at being invited, Joey and Heshy walked through the huge front doors into the house. Just inside the house, in the spacious foyer, Joey asked Heshy if he read Esther's diary. Heshy told him that he had read most of it but fell asleep, not too far from the end and that he'll probably finish it later that night. He told Joey about his thoughts and feelings about reliving those early days in every page of the diary that he had read so far. Joey told Heshy that he had read it many times over the years and every time I've red it I can hear Esther's voice speaking. Heshy said now that you mention it that is just how I felt in reading it last night. Joey than added, that he just wanted Heshy to have it because after all she was his sister. He said he felt sure that Esther would want Heshy to have it. Heshy said, "Thank you so much Joey. You know Joey this is the same diary that I gave Esther on our thirteenth birthday years ago."

Heshy led Joey into the largest formal dining room he had ever seen, that surrounded the biggest and longest dining room table he had ever seen. Joey thought to himself, fifty people could sit comfortably around that table. He told Heshy that his family could've used a table as big as this when his family joined Heshy's family at their house for the Passover Seders and Thanksgiving Day dinners. He added that while we all managed to find a seat at the table back then, this table

279

would've been perfect for those occasions. Heshy laughed and told Joey he was right. The ten or twelve people sitting at one end of the table were dwarfed by the immenseness of the room and table. As Heshy led Joey toward the table he started introducing everyone to Joey and Joey to everyone. There were Selma and Ira Hirsch, Ellen and Barry Engle, Rhoda and George Barth, Elaine and Irv Glick, Phyllis and Seymour Cole and Sid and Vivian Christopher. Heshy explained to Joey that his two children would be coming, with their families to stay with him and Sarah for a few days. He said they should've been there already. Joey told Heshy that the traffic was very heavy and moving slowly, and that's probably why they're late.

When he saw Sarah, he knew her right away and she knew him too. They hugged each other, with much affection. Sarah even had a few tears in her eyes. Joey told her that she hadn't changed a bit and looked just like she did when he last saw her. They chatted for a few moments, remembering how they, with Esther and Heshy, would spend so much time together when they were young teenagers. Most of the others seemed to remember Joey. Joey told them that while he only had a fuzzy recollection of what most of them looked like, he remembered most of their names. He felt sure that the longer they sat and talked, the sharper his memory would become. So as they all talked through dinner, about the "good old days" of their youth, the more Joey started to remember about them.

After a while he almost felt like he was back in Brownsville, Brooklyn in the forties. Finally, Selma Hirsch, who was not from Brownsville, and didn't know about Esther and him, asked Joey about how his relationship with Esther got started. Joey proceeded to tell his story, of how he came to know and love Esther Abromovitz. Everyone at the table stopped talking as Joey started to speak.

"I had known Heshy and Esther since elementary school. I guess as long as I've known some of you here." Most the people sitting there, including Heshy, nodded or voiced their agreement. Joey continued. "We were all fast friends. We played together, did our homework together and even went to the movies together. We often visited each others homes. I'm sure most of you remember that. In fact, I now remember, I think it was in Barry Engel's apartment, that we had to be real quiet because of, ah I think it was your mother's brother or someone like that, who lived with you because he was sick. Am I right Barry?"

Barry smiled as the memory came back to him, and said that Joey was right. "I wonder if any of you remember coming to my house one time, for some good homemade Italian food, that my mother cooked for all of you. My sister and I helped her prepare it too.

"Well anyway those events are becoming clearer to me now, but what I'll never forget is, and let's see if any of you were there to remember it too, about what we did, a week or so before Esther got sick in class. About ten or twelve of us went on a boat ride up the Hudson River, to spend a day at Bear Mountain State Park. Well anyway for a long time, since I was twelve or thirteen, I knew that I had feelings, of what I would call, "puppy love", for Esther. Of course up to the time of the boat ride, while I was no longer shy, I wouldn't even think about telling her that I liked her and wanted her to be my girlfriend. I mean, what if she would've laughed at me and said, "No"? I really would have been embarrassed. Well anyway, on the boat trip up the Hudson River that morning, and it was a beautiful morning, I was standing with my arms on the railing of the boat, looking down at the water when I felt someone standing very close to me, and it was Esther. She was so close that our shoulders were touching. Well actually her shoulder was touching me, a little bit above my elbow. I turned to look at her and she was looking at me, with a most beautiful, big smile. I don't know if I was blushing or not, but I can remember to this day, how warm and wonderful I felt. I felt so full of joy, that I know I smiled the happiest smile I've ever given to anybody, up to that point in my life.

"Now, if you remember in those days, I don't know about today, when we all went to the beach, Brighton or Coney of course, the girls almost always made the sandwiches, or whatever for lunch and the boys would mooch a free lunch every time. This boat trip was no different, except that the night before, Esther said she thought, that because I liked to work with food so much, I should make some of the lunch. When I told her that I gladly would, she told me she was only teasing me and she would make it. As we started to leave the boat at Bear Mountain, I automatically picked up the big bag of goodies that Esther brought and in fact I think I brought a couple of bottles of soda, that I added to her big shopping bag.

"Now I don't remember if there were any official boyfriend girlfriend couples in the group, besides Heshy and Sarah, but everyone seemed to pair off and I just paired off with Esther. As we were walking together down the path, I think it was to the zoo or maybe it was the picnic area, I don't remember exactly, I was carrying the goodie bag in my right hand and Esther was walking beside me on my left. Suddenly, and I can feel it as if happened five minutes ago I felt something touch my left hand. Before I could even look down to see what it was, I realized that it was Esther's right hand gently, but firmly clasping my left hand. We turned our heads to look at each other and we smiled. At that moment I felt like I was thirty feet tall. I had never held hands with a girl before and it was absolutely wonderful. Esther made me feel like I was the only boy in the world who ever experienced such joy.

"For the rest of that trip, we held hands wherever we went. We went to Bear Mountain Lake and I rented a rowboat and took Esther for an hour boat ride, which as I recall at the time, I thought was way too short. During the rowboat ride, Esther squealed with joy at the sight of the little fishes swimming about in the water. She put her hand in the water to see if she could pet the fishes as they swam by, but quickly pulled her hand out if a big fish came close to her hand. She loved to watch them but was afraid she might get bitten by one of them. Then while we were in the middle of the lake, we were attacked by a swarm of gnats. Esther started to flail at the little buggers, all the while screaming her head off. I laughed so hard at her antics that she finally had to laugh too. I rowed into what I thought was a remote area of the lake and I pulled the oars out of the water and moved over to her side of the boat. We smiled at each other and I put my arm around her. Just as I was thinking about kissing her, I heard your big booming voice Heshy, call out to me. You had seen me row the boat out of your sight and you weren't sure exactly where we were, so you just called out my name. I mean really loud calling. I quickly forgot about kissing Esther, well not really, I just put that thought aside for the moment. I put the oars back in the water and rowed back to where you could see us Heshy.

"I think Esther suspected what I was going to do, because when she heard you start yelling out my name, she started to giggle and laugh. Maybe I was blushing, I don't know but I started to laugh too. As we got to the middle of the lake, Esther looked around at the vastness and beauty of the lake, with the reflections on the water, along the shoreline, of the big trees that surrounded the lake. I remember she breathed a deep sigh and told me how beautiful the whole scene was, and that the best part was knowing that living in the midst of all the forests around us, that we can't even see, were God's little creatures scurrying all around. And knowing that we were all a part of this wonderful scene filled her heart with joy. I smiled at her and rowed back to the boat landing, feeling pretty good inside myself. I think the two of us were humming and singing some song, about the beauty of spring or something like that. That's how our adventure on the lake ended.

"We all, if any of you who were there remember, ate our picnic lunches at the picnic grounds. It was really very nice, eating surrounded by all those trees and the birds singing and the squirrels scampering around. It was beautiful, especially for me being with Esther. Esther loved the beauty and wonder of nature. It was such a joy for me, to watch her admire the lovely colors of a butterfly or a bird. She told me how serene she felt, when she could harmonize with nature. Although I had never thought about it before, I had to agree with her, because I felt it too. When it was time for us to board the boat for the trip back home, I remember standing in line with my arm around Esther and I leaned over and kissed her. She was just a little bit taken by surprise, but a split second later, she reached up on her toes and kissed me back. The world to me at that moment was wonderful and has been so ever since. The one complaint that Esther had that day was that she felt unusually tired. At the time none of us thought too much about it, but of course now, in retrospect, we know it was probably the beginning of her terrible ordeal. On the boat ride back to Manhattan, the whole gang joined together in song and Esther, as tired as she felt, joined the rest of us and she loved it. She wore a grin from ear to ear. I loved just looking at her being so happy.

"On the day, in class, that Esther got sick, Heshy you were at the New York Stock Exchange, getting your award for that national essay contest you won. You know Heshy, we were all very proud of you for winning that thing, and I mean everybody. From everyone who knew you in school, the teachers, the students, everybody in the neighborhood, your friends and family and especially Esther. Well anyway, on that day in class, when Esther got sick, she was feeling nauseous and in fact started to throw up a little. Everyone sitting near her scattered, but I just rushed to her side and by that time she started to cry a little bit. It hurt me so much to see her cry. I don't know why I did, but I just put my arms around her and walked. or maybe carried her a little bit is more like it, out the classroom door. I told her I was

283

going to take her down to the nurse's office, but she begged me to take her home instead, which I did. Esther was afraid that the nurse might call an ambulance and she didn't like the idea of that.

"A very telling thing happened, as we walked along Sackman St. and crossed Livonia Ave. Esther saw Mrs. Epstein, you know I think she was the grandmother of that kid who used to hang with us, what's his name, eh I think it was Lenny Kahn, or something like that. Well anyway, Esther sees that Mrs. Epstein is loaded down with packages and coming down from the El, so as sick as she felt, she asked me to please help Mrs. Epstein with her bundles. Can you imagine that? Here's Esther not feeling well and as sick as a dog, I mean I had to half carry her and she feels sorry for Mrs. Epstein with her packages. So there I am, with one arm around Esther, trying to hold her up and my other arm loaded down with packages.

"I really didn't mind, Mrs. Epstein only lived a couple of blocks away, on the way to your house Heshy, but I was so impressed with Esther's concern for other people, even when she herself didn't feel good. I got Esther home, made sure she was settled in and feeling a little better and went back to school. That's how Esther and I got to be girlfriend and boyfriend."

At that point Ellen Engel asked Joey if he would tell them about he reacted to the news about Esther's illness and how he coped with it for the following two years, while she was fighting for her life. Joey said he would and when he started to speak, again everyone listened with great interest.

"When word got around that Esther was sick with Leukemia, a life threatening sickness, everyone was in shock. I was devastated of course, as was her family and my sweet Esther, was like a frightened little kitten. After a few days went by, I gathered up some school work from some of her classes and asked a bunch of her friends to join me in going over to your house Heshy. I'm sure some of you here might have been among the kids that I asked. I was sure glad I did that, because Esther's face lit up like the Fourth of July fireworks, when she saw all of her friends. She was beaming, she was so happy to see everyone. Seeing her so happy made everyone in her family happy too.

"After that day, I would go to see her every day after school and we would just sit around and talk or she would help me with my homework. Many times we did our homework together, whenever I brought school work home for her. Sometimes we would play cards or listen to the radio, but most of the time we would just talk. One day, when we were talking, she asked me, with tears welling up in her eyes, if I still liked her and wanted her to be my girlfriend. I couldn't believe she asked me that. I asked her why she would even think that I didn't like her anymore. She said she thought that because she was sick with such a terrible illness, that is probably fatal, I might have changed my mind about us.

"I looked at her for a minute and told her that I had changed my mind about how I felt about her alright, because now I didn't just like her, but I loved her and I wanted her to be my girlfriend forever. "Forever Joey"? she asked. I searched my heart for the right words and I told her that I believed, with my entire being, that she and I would be together forever. She looked at me for what seemed like a long time, but it probably just a few seconds, hugged me so tight, that to this day I can still feel it, told me she loved me and then the tears started flow like a water fall. Now I know that it might be hard for some of you to believe, fifteen year old kids are capable of love, but I truly believed it then and I believe it more so now.

"Well, Esther looks at me with her beautiful puppy dog, tears stained eyes, and her mouth quivering a little bit, tells me that is exactly how she felt about me. Wow! I was in Heaven. We hugged and kissed until we heard someone moving about in the kitchen. At that time I always liked to write. I'd write just about anything, poems, stories or just expressing a point of view or sentiment. So naturally, I wrote a lot of stuff about Esther and how I felt about her. Please don't ask me to show you any of the things that I wrote for her, because I can't. I gave them all to Esther and I know she put them all together in a loose leaf book that if I remember right, you bought for her Heshy. Anyway, I haven't seen that book since about a month or so before she passed on and I don't know what ever happened to that book. Maybe Heshy knows. Do you Heshy?" Heshy shrugged his shoulders and said that he didn't know where that book was.

"Anyway, on the days when Esther felt good of course, she attended classes with the rest of us, and because she did all of the school work that I brought home for her, she was able to keep up with the rest of the class and graduate from jr.high school on time. When school was out and the weather was nice, and Esther was feeling up to it, I would take her to where ever it was that she would like to go, or do whatever it was she wanted to do. I think once or twice, that first summer of her illness, we even went to the beach, only this time I made the lunches. I remember one nice day we went to Prospect Park. Again I made and packed the lunch. We visited the zoo and the lake, but we didn't go out on a rowboat that day.

"We just sat by the edge of the lake, took off our shoes and socks and dipped our feet into the cold water. We didn't like it at first, but after a few minutes the water felt just fine. It was very relaxing. I started to tease Esther about her toes getting bitten by a fish. She started to panic, in a mocking sort of way, then stuck her feet back in the water and said that my "smelly feet", would keep the fishes away. I put a phony look of hurt on my face and exclaimed, "Smelly feet"! You think I have smelly feet? She grabbed me in a hug and said, "You silly goose, I'm only playing with you. If anything, you have sweet feet. I'm sure your mother told you at one time in your life, that you had sweet feet." My mother told me I had sweet feet? How do you know that? Did she tell you that? I asked her in quick succession. Esther laughed and giggled at the same time and I loved it. She said, "You know, I have babysat for a lot of people since I was about eleven years old, and I would often observe young mothers at play with their young babies. It was beautiful to watch. The baby would be on it's back and the mom would sometimes hold it's hands or feet and "baby talk" to her baby. She would tell her baby how sweet his or her feet were and pretend to nibble on the babies toes. The babies always reacted the same way, with a giggle or a laugh. I 'm sure your mom did the same to you. My mom told me that she did it to me. Does that answer your question, sweet feet"? she said with a big laugh. The only thing I could do was laugh with her and for a long while, that was her nick name for me, "sweet feet", but only in private, of course.

"We ate the lunch that I brought as we sat at a picnic table, and then we just strolled through the park, holding hands, admiring all of nature's beauty and telling each other how much we loved each other. It was like heaven to both of us. As you may be able to imagine, Esther was having feelings of depression, anger and lots of fear about her situation. Of course, that was understandable. Even though I felt, to some degree the same way, I could never let Esther know it, or see it in my face. Every day that I came over, I always had to make myself upbeat, cheerful and put a smile on my face for her to see. When Esther would see me smile, then she would give me one of her lovely smiles right back. It seemed to brighten her day and she certainly did the same for me, in spades.

"Very often she would want to talk about the future, our future, if we in fact had one. I never wanted to go there, but after a while it became a little easier to talk about. I always tried to reassure her, that we had a wonderful and loving future ahead of us, no matter what direction her illness took. I told her time and time again, that no matter what, we would be together forever. That I will be with her, and loving her always and I knew that she will be there for me, likewise. After a while it began to sink in to her, that what I was telling her was true and at that point she was able to face, we were able to face, whatever it was that life had in store for us.

"Many times after that we would just look at each other, smile and tears of joy would well up in our eyes. Seeing the way we were together, seemed to have a positive effect on her family as well, for they all seemed to smile a whole lot more and take on a more positive outlook on the situation. Even Esther's doctors were amazed that she was, after about a year with the sickness, not as sick or weak as most people with Leukemia. In fact, they were a little surprised that she had survived as long as she had, and was still pretty strong. Of course, the prognosis was still the same. They did not hold out much hope, but Esther and I still thought that there might still be a long shot chance, that it would go into remission. Although we were hoping for a miracle, in our hearts we believed that the miracle was the love that we have for each other and that we would be together forever. That knowledge gave us the strength to face what ever it was, that was going to happen.

"Well on March 11, 1947, I turned 16 and on May 8, of the same year, Esther and Heshy did the same and she still felt pretty good, all things considered. We were both in high school now, and just like in jr.high, she went to class when she felt strong enough and when she didn't, Heshy and I would bring school work home for her. One day when I came over to see Esther, she looked as if she had been crying. When I asked her what was wrong, she told me that her father was getting a lot of grief from some of the elders in the Temple, about his daughter having a boyfriend who is not Jewish, so he intended to speak to me that evening, about us not seeing each other any more. She also told me that her mother was on our side and very angry at her father for listening to those busybodies, those "yentas", as she called them, at the Temple.

"I don't recall exactly what it was that I said, but what ever it was it worked, because he dropped his objections to our relationship and that made Mrs. Abromovitz very happy too. I remember that Esther was listening to our talk from her bedroom, and when I walked in after I talked it over her father, she had tears streaming down her beautiful face and a gorgeous smile from ear to ear. After that, we all, my family and Esther's, came closer together, if that was possible. I remember telling my mom that Esther was not feeling that great, because her stomach was bothering her. So the next day, my mom whips up a big batch of homemade escarole, in chicken broth soup. Esther and her mom were so surprised. Esther said she felt better after having some of the soup and they both said it was delicious. My mom was sure glad to hear that. The following week, Mrs. Abromovitz made a big pot full of chicken noodle soup, for my family. My family was also very surprised and we all thought that soup was delicious too. We all spent a beautiful day at Prospect Park one lovely spring day, when Esther was feeling better. Every one bonded with each other so well. Do you remember that day Heshy?" Heshy, smiling at that memory, nodded yes.

"In the late spring of 1948 it became obvious that Esther was not going to get better, but every day, even though I was crying and hurting so bad on the inside, I had to maintain an upbeat exterior for Esther's sake. Every time I came over and greeted her with a smile, an "I love you" with a kiss and a hug, she seemed to brighten up quite a bit, and even managed to smile back at me, though I know she was hurting so much. Many nights as I was leaving her room, I had to fight the tears in my eyes, and by the time I got home I could no longer hold them back. My mother tried to comfort me, but I was so angry at God for not making my Esther well, that I would rave and rant at Him. I realize now, that all those reassuring words about our never ending love that I always spoke to Esther about, came from my heart, the spiritual side of me. All my anger was coming from my head, the human side of me. Esther knew what lay ahead for her and she tried so hard to be strong for all of us. Am I right Heshy?" Heshy, choked up with emotion at the memory, just nodded yes.

"She was so brave. I think we all drew some strength from her. To the very end, I told her in every way that I could think of, how much I loved her. I never stopped writing all kinds of things to her and when she could no longer speak or see, I would whisper what I had written for her, in her ear. I think she heard every word because the very last time I did that, she smiled as if she heard me and then stopped breathing." By now Joey was somewhat emotional, and leaned back in his chair to regain his composure. Joey continued, "I'll never forget the date, August 17, 1948, because my mother always told me that 17 was an unlucky number. I always thought that it was my mom's personal unlucky number, but I found later on in my life that in Naples, Italy, where my mother came from, 17 is everybody's unlucky number. That's another reason why I could never forget it."

George Barth, who was a close boyhood friend of Joey's, asked what happened to him after Esther's demise? Where did he go, because he said, "You just seemed to vanish from the neighborhood. Over the years many people have brought up your name and wondered what ever happened to you. You know Joey you were a very popular guy back then, not just with the girls but with all of us. I really mean that." Joey thanked George for the nice words and continued.

"Well, as I just mentioned, I was overcome with anger and grief, and I didn't want to see anybody. What I couldn't understand for a long time was why after constantly telling Esther to be strong because we were going to together forever, no matter what happened in this life, at the moment she passed on I completely lost my grip and went pieces. To this day I don't fully understand it. Anyway, my poor mother tried so hard to make me feel better, but I was just so crazy that I didn't go out of our apartment for about two weeks. I knew that I was not going back to high school, but I didn't know for sure, exactly what it was that I wanted to do. I finally decided to join the army. Of course I was only seventeen so I needed my parent's permission. My mom wouldn't hear of it at first, because you may all remember that I had a brother who was killed in WW2, right near the end of the war in Europe. He was not even nineteen at the time. Because there was no war going on at this time, and she knew how much I was hurting, my mom, with great reluctance, agreed to sign the papers for me to enlist in the military. My father didn't want me to go either, but as long as my mother went along with it, he did too. So off I went, on the day after Labor Day, into the U.S. Army. I was so filled with anger and a feeling of being lost and adrift, that I didn't care what happened to me. Shortly after basic training, I volunteered for the airborne and after much training, I became a paratrooper. I would, on occasion come home on leave or a weekend pass, but I would arrange to either come home at night, or meet my parents at my sister's house in Canarsie. I was still so screwed up, that I didn't want to see anyone who might bring back, what I believed at that time, were terrible memories. Like I said, I was really messed up.

"Army life was pretty good and I earned a couple of stripes after about a year and a half or just about the time the Korean War broke out. It happened so fast and the American response was so quick that before I knew it, I was on my way to Korea. I knew that my mother was going through great pain about me going to a battle area and I felt bad about that, but there was not a thing I could do about it. I was involved in a few skirmishes and made Sergeant. I was slightly wounded early on, but I was able to return to duty after a short time. Then I was involved in a big battle and was seriously wounded, so much so that I spent a bit of time in Japan, before I was able to travel to the Walter Reed Hospital in Washington D.C. Up to that time, I was still filled with a lot of anger about Esther's passing. While at Walter Reed, my family came to visit me and my mom was so glad to see me that she cried during most of the visit. She couldn't keep her hands off me and kept calling me Italian names of endearment. I was very taken by my mom's display of affection at that time. I don't know why, because after Esther died, my mother spoke to me the same way and it didn't affect me like it did at the hospital. After my family left the hospital and I lay in my bed trying to sleep, or maybe I was asleep, I don't know for sure, but I don't believe I was dreaming, I heard Esther's voice. I remember her exact words because they are etched in my heart.

"Joey! My precious Joey I'm here to help you, me sweet love." Her sweet voice called to me. I was overjoyed and startled at the same time. I asked, if it was really her, why she didn't come to me before this, when I really needed to hear from her. She replied, " Oh my Joey, my poor Joey. I have been with you, beside you always, trying to get into your heart and thoughts but you were so full of anger and despair, I could not get through to you. I have been trying to tell you that everything will be alright with you, with us. Just keep the love that we have for each other in your heart and remember some of those wonderful words of encouragement and wisdom that you spoke to me, in my time of need and you will be alright, with yourself and all those around you. I know, and you should know too, that our hearts still beat as one and will always. Joey, I want you to know that I heard and loved every word of that last thing that you wrote and whispered to me, just as I moved on to the next step of our journey. I want you to remember too, the best part of your message, "we will be together, forever, every step of the way." Always know in your heart that I love you and look forward to you moving on with me, when your time comes. So don't let your heart be troubled anymore, for I am still with you as I will always be. I love you as always, only more so. Any time you wish to speak to me, please do so. I am always here for you and with you. Good night my sweet and sleep well, for the world awaits the Joey that I fell in love with, the Joey with the good heart and wonderful soul. Good night, I love you."

"I awakened early the next morning after the best and most restful night's sleep that I had in almost four years. Even though I had a long rehab ahead of me, I felt like a new man. My aches and pains while still there, were not as severe. I started to care about life and people again, about living again. After many months in the hospital, I was returned to active duty. I served two tours in Viet Nam and picked up two more Purple Hearts. I was not hurt too bad either time and finished my army service at the end of 1968, after twenty years as a soldier. After my discharge, I lived with my sister Mary and her family for about a year, while I tried to figure out what I wanted to with my life. I joined the Merchant Marines and shipped out on a bunch of old cargo ships for a few years and then left. Then I traveled with a group of migrant workers, picking all sorts of crops, from California to New Jersey to the far west. I got to know these poor folks real well. I still have many friends among them that I keep in contact with. In fact, I was talking earlier about that terrific boat ride that we were all on, to Bear Mountain, well I have a print of a very famous Renoir painting called "The Luncheon of The Boating Party" that always reminds me of our boating party. I have that hanging in a small house that I own in Florida. I only live in that house for a short period of time every year, maybe two or three months most years. I let some of my migrant worker friends live in it the rest of the year. Sometimes, even when I'm there they stay with me. They take wonderful care of the place for me. They're really nice hardworking people. About 1975 or so, I started to work with horses around the race track. As a "hot walker" at first, then mucking out stalls, as they say, and then I became a groom, and finally an assistant trainer, which is what I am today.

"In every job that I did and do, and every place that I go and went to, I always keep Esther on my mind and try to do what she wants me to do, and that is to help people who are less fortunate than myself. In a way I'm being selfish, because helping others makes me not only feel better about myself, but I also sleep better because of it. Of course I can't always help everyone's financial need, because of my limited recourses, but I try to always make people feel a little bit better about themselves. If nothing else, I always try to put a smile on their faces and some hope in their hearts. In my conversations with Esther, she tells me I'm doing the right thing. So there you have it. Any questions?"

Seymour Cole asked Joey about his wounds and if he had gotten any medals. Joey responded by saying that his wounds were all healed a long time ago, although he's getting a small disability pension on top of his regular one and yes, he did get awarded some decorations, but he does not like to talk about them, because he accepted them reluctantly. Seymour then said, "You know Joey, if my memory serves me right, I think I read about you, in the old Brooklyn Eagle newspaper. It said something about a local boy being a hero or something like that. I think you got some big medal or something." Suddenly, Irv Glick yelled out, "The Medal of Honor! The Congressional Medal of Honor! That's what he got. I remember it now." Before they could go on Joey stopped them. He said, "Look, medals are not important. In the heat of battle you never know how you're going to react. Sometimes, when you see your comrades getting killed and maimed, you do whatever it is that you have to do. That doesn't make one a hero. You just do the job that you were trained to do. A lot of guys have done heroic and courageous things on the battlefield and have not gotten any medals for it. That's why I say that medals are not that impotent to most of the individuals involved in fighting a war.

"I honestly couldn't tell you whatever it was that I was supposed to have done, because I don't remember. Things happen so fast in battle and I was hurt pretty bad, that's why I don't have a recollection of what happened. Besides, one of my sister's boys, or maybe all of her boys, she had four of them, have those medals. I couldn't even tell you what they were because I never saw them or wanted to see them. When my family visited me at the hospital, I was still a little bit out of it, so my sister, with my permission she said later on, I don't remember, took them home with her for safe keeping. It never mattered to me because like I said before, I didn't want them anyway. I really don't like to talk about those things, so I hope you don't mind if we skip past the subject."

By this time several of the woman were dabbing their eyes and one of them said, "Oh Joey I bet you miss Esther so bad?" Joey looked at her directly and then glanced around at all of them and said, "I missed Esther for about the first four years that I thought she was gone, but I don't miss her anymore." As jaws dropped and looks of disbelief spread around the table, Joey explained. "You see I don't miss Esther because she is always with me. Every time I see or hear one of nature's wonderful moments like a sunrise, a rainbow or people smiling from their hearts, I think of Esther. Or if I hear a bird singing early in the morning or any time of day, or hear a child giggle or laugh, then I hear my Esther. I am surrounded by her presence." Heshy, surprisingly asked, "Joey do you mean to tell me that over the years you never had a desire for female companionship?" "Heshy I am a man, so of course the physical part of me has had certain urges and I addressed them when I had to in a way that I know did not offend Esther. After all I'm not a priest or anything like that. The best way to describe it is, the sweet scent of Esther's existence is with me always so those urges were few and far between, as they say.

"That's why I don't miss her, because I always have her with me. You see, as long as I keep Esther in my heart and I always will I'm never alone. Of course I look forward to the time, as Esther put it, I move on to join her for the rest of our journey together, through eternity." As Joey finished his explanation, the tears were flowing freely at the table and Joey apologized for causing that, but he said he was merely answering the question the best and most honest way that he knew. Heshy at that point mentioned to everybody that Joey had sent him Esther's diary yesterday. It is the same diary, he just remembered, that he had given his sister for a present when they both turned thirteen. Rhoda Barth asked Heshy if it is a very sad book. Heshy said that he started to read it the night before, but he hadn't finished it yet. Joey had told him, he said, that there were some very personal and emotion filled entries in it, so he should read in private, when he's alone. That's what he said he did. He said he will read the last of it that night. Then he told Rhoda that maybe Joey should answer that question of whether it's sad or not. Joey, again looked around the table at everyone's face and said he didn't think it was a sad story at all, because he said, it is really only a story about two people who love each other so much, that they can overcome anything. With everyone's eyes glued on him, Joey told them that over the years, people who have heard about him and Esther and the great love they shared, would call him and Esther lucky or special, or even say that their kind of love is rare. Leaning forward in his chair, Joey told them that while Esther always made him feel special, there shouldn't be anything rare or special attached to their love for each other. In his opinion, he continued, that kind of love should be the norm, for everyone.

With a slightly pained look on his face, he went on and said that the fact that today, a lot of young people can't or don't seem able to understand this, is a very sad comment on the lack of real progress that we've made as human beings. Then his face brightened as he told them that he was very happy to see that for the most part, almost every couple at the table were together for fifty years or more. He said that they set or should have set a very good example for their children and grandchildren. He again said that he thought that the love that he and Esther shared was the way it should be for everyone, and that it saddens him, because it seems that in this day and age, with the vastness of the media, the media should be getting the right message out, but it doesn't.

Then Sid Christopher asked, "Joey, do you ever regret leaving the neighborhood when you did? I mean if you had stayed, you would be very wealthy today along with the rest of us. Heshy took us all along with him on the climb up the financial ladder." Joey thought for a moment and then answered, "No I don't regret it at all. I have all the money I need to get by, but let me ask all of you guys a couple of questions. I noticed that most of us, myself included, are carrying around some extra pounds, some more than others but we all carry extra weight. So my first question is this, would your wives love you any more if you were thinner than you are right now? Don't answer yet, let me ask the second question first. Would your wives or children and grandchildren love any of you any less if you were not wealthy? You don't have to give me your answers, just give them to yourselves and I feel very confident, that then you'll all understand why I have no regrets about leaving when I did.

"Now don't misunderstand me, money has it's rightful place and I don't begrudge any of you your wealth. As a matter of fact, when I was fourteen, fifteen and through to seventeen, I felt that I was rich because I had Heshy, Esther and their parents as friends. Also because of my own family I felt I was very rich, the only thing we didn't have back then was money, but I think we all felt rich anyway. Heshy, am I right? Do you remember those days, Heshy?" Heshy nodded yes, that he did remember those days and yes he now understands what Joey is talking about. With that Joey got up out of his seat and explained that he had to leave, because he had to get up early to get about twenty or so horses ready to ship out by Sunday morning. He told them that they were going to stop at Finger Lakes race track for a short stay and then proceed up to Canada for some races. From there he thought they might go to Saratoga for a short stay in August and then maybe he would see some of them again in the fall at Belmont Park.

It wasn't too long after Joey left that the rest of Harry's guests all left too. As soon as Harry's wife Sarah and the rest of his family turned in for the night, Harry went to his library, turned on the light over his favorite easy chair, sat down in it to finish reading the end of Esther's diary. He opened the diary and flipped to the page where he had left off. Before he could start reading, his thoughts went back to that period of time when Esther first got sick and everything that happened to her up until the time she died. He felt tears start to well up in his eyes as he thought about what his sister and parents went through and himself too.

Then he thought about what Joey had told everybody earlier that evening, about not missing Esther because she is always with him. He then realized that all these years he had been grieving and suffering for Esther and never knew it. Then it dawned on him that Esther has always been with him all these years too, not just with Joey. His parents too, have always been in his heart. It was like a wonderful awakening for Heshy. At that moment the words of what Joey had written to Esther, about never having to say goodbye, were very real and true. He knew then, that the rearranging of his priorities the last couple of days was the right thing to do. He felt even more euphoric thinking about it. He slowly wiped away some tears that had started to fall and started again to read Esther's diary.

CHAPTER 16

Friday, February, 14th, 1947

Dear diary today is Valentine's Day and I hand made cards for everyone, just as I've been doing for the past few years. I wasn't able to make them as well as I used to, because I get tired so easily, but they were very nice anyway. As Joey has often said, it's not the beauty of the card, but the beauty of the words inside that really mattered. Everyone seemed to like their cards and that made me feel good. I got very nice cards too, from my family of course and also from all of the Bernstein and Green kids. I was a little disappointed that I didn't get a card from Joey in school today. He told me that he made one for me but left it home and he would bring it over this evening when he came over to do homework with us. When he walked me home with Heshy, he even left his school books here to use when he came over later.

As soon as we finished eating dinner the door bell rang. I was sitting closest to the door so I opened it and what a shock I got. There was Joey wearing a four or five foot high cardboard Valentine's Day card. I thought he looked a little foolish at first, but after he came into the house and I got a closer look at him, I changed my mind. I thought he looked beautiful. The front of the card was covering his chest and the back of the card was on his back. The front of the card had a big red heart and said "WILL YOU BE MY VALENTINE ESTHER". I looked at him and told him that of course I will. When I opened the card I saw a smaller red heart pinned to his chest that said,

> "The only present I can give you is my heart,
> full of love for only you, forever.
> From your forever "fella", Joey".

Mom, Daddy and Heshy laughed, but I was speechless for a moment. It was so beautiful and lovely. Of course I couldn't get close enough to him to kiss or hug him no matter how I hard I tried. Joey finally told me to wait a minute while he took the "card" off. While I was hugging him he asked where I was going to keep such a big thing like that and I told him not to worry, because I would find a place in my room. Joey explained to me that because he hasn't worked in a while he couldn't afford to get me anything for Valentine's Day. He said the only thing he could think of was what he gave me along time ago and that is his everlasting love. I told him that it was the only present I needed and we kissed each other again.

Well anyway, I have to catch up with you on what has happened since I wrote last. It hasn't been a whole lot, but I have to tell you anyway. The first three weeks of the New Year were pretty good as far as me being able to go to school. I did have to go to the hospital again on Friday, January 24th, and I didn't come home until Thursday, January 30th. That means I missed five days of school this time. Heshy and Joey brought me school work in the hospital as usual and as usual they did their homework with me in my room. I think that's great every time they do that. I'm able to keep up with school that way and that makes me feel good.

Mr. B again arranged his schedule, so he was able take me to the hospital and home again too. He again took Mom every morning to visit me and picked everybody up in the evening. Mama B still retains water, but some new pills the doctor has given her, is working a little better than the other ones she was taking. She doesn't have to go to the hospital to have her stomach "tapped" to remove the water as often, but she still has to go once in a while. I love her so much, in fact her whole family too. Of course you knew about Joey. Didn't you? Ha! Ha!

Everything else has been just about the same, except Suzy Gonzalez, you remember her don't you? Sherry's sister. Well, guess what? She and Jimmy Teagno are boyfriend and girlfriend! Joey now always reminds them not to kiss if there's lightning in the area, and laughs his head off. Of course they all laugh with him. I mean how can anyone get mad at my Joey? No way. Oh yeah, there's one more new thing, I might have to try some new drug the next time I go into the hospital. That will be in a couple of weeks on Friday, February 28th. The doctor also told me that they will be trying to get something for me that may keep me from getting so tired all the time. We shall see. Speaking of getting tired, I'm getting tired right now so I have to say good night dear diary.

Tuesday, March 11, 1947

Dear diary today is Joey's sixteenth birthday. Mom was good enough, as usual, to arrange with Daddy for me to get an allowance a while back. I saved most of it, for me to be able to get presents for Joey, Heshy and whoever else has a birthday. I asked Mom to shop for me and get a nice gift for Joey and she did. She picked out two nice things with the twenty dollars that I gave her to spend. The first is a lovely sky blue pullover sweater with a vee neck, and the other is a great baseball board game. I made a card for him that he really liked. He said he loved the words of love that I wrote on the inside. He tried on the sweater and he loves it and looks great in it too. Ah, but the baseball board game. He almost did flips over it, and Heshy did too. I now know that's probably what the two of them will be doing in their spare time. They'll probably make sure they have plenty of spare time too. I hope I'm not sorry I got him that, but we shall see.

I went into the hospital on Friday, February 28th, like I told you I would before. Dr. Edward explained to me that he wanted me to try a new medication, but this time he would give me a small dose, and then watch me closely for a negative reaction to it. He asked me if that would be alright with me, and I thought that was very nice of him to ask me. He further told me that normally, a new drug would be tested for a very long time before they would give it to patients. However, because for so many Leukemia patients, the disease is not curable, doctors like himself, are trying to speed up the process of getting the new drugs to them. I asked him, in a half joking way, if he that meant I was going to be a guinea pig and Mom was nodding her head in agreement with me. He looked at me for a second and said that in a way that was true, but he felt it was a worthwhile and necessary thing too do. He added that he was leaving it up to me and my family to decide if we wanted to go ahead and try it.

Mom asked if we could wait until we had a chance to discuss it with Daddy when he comes to visit after work, and he said yes, of course. He went on to tell us he was going to give me another new drug that has been proven to work well in keeping patients from feeling tired and

298

weak. If we did decide to go along with using the new drug, he would start it the next day. When Daddy came over later on that day, we all discussed it and it was agreed that I should give it a try and if I had a bad reaction to it, we'll discontinue it immediately. The other new medicine, to keep from getting tired and weak, will take a little while longer to see if it works or not.

Well I'm happy to say that the new therapy drug to fight my Leukemia didn't make me sick, so Dr. Edward decided to increase the dosage, a little bit at a time, until I get the dosage that they feel will do me the most good. The other medicine he gave me, to keep me from getting tired and weak, seems to be working. I'm starting to feel a little bit stronger each day, so that's a good thing. Right now all we know about the new Leukemia drug is that my body is tolerating it, but we won't know for a while if it is working on the Leukemia. I told Dr. Edward that I can't wait to find out and he said that he can't wait too. I hope and pray that it works, not just for me but for everybody who has Leukemia.

I didn't come home from the hospital until Friday, March 7th, because of the new drugs and testing that I had to undergo. I thank God I got home in time for Joey's birthday. His family had a little party for him with a cake and all. I didn't go because even though I'm feeling a little less tired and weak, I still don't think I should be climbing stairs yet. Of course, thank God in school they have elevators. Mama B sent a piece of Joey's birthday cake for me and my family, so when Joey came over to my house, we all sang "Happy Birthday" to him again. Joey loved it so much he had a grin on his face from ear to ear. Heshy got Joey two tickets again for a Dodger game at Ebbets Field. Of course you know who Heshy wants Joey to take with him. It's not me or Sarah I can tell you that.

Well I missed a whole week of school so I have a little bit of catching up to do. Thank God for Heshy and Joey, who not only bring me work from school, but also help me a lot in getting it done. I hope and pray that I will be promoted with the rest of my class in June. Today in school, I was called into my guidance counselor's office, and he told me that he was very happy that I'm able to keep up with my studies, and wished me a lot of luck. He also said that if I ever get to the point where I'm having trouble getting my school work done, to come in to see him and he will help me in any way that he can. That was great to hear. I really appreciated it. Now I'm getting tired, dear diary so I'll say good night.

Sunday, May 8th, 1947

Dear diary, well today is Heshy's and my birthday. I'm "sweet sixteen" and many times kissed. Ha! Ha! Everybody was fussing over me and Heshy at our house. Mom made a very nice dinner for us and Joey came over afterwards with a big beautiful birthday cake for us. The biggest surprise of all was that Mom had invited the Balduccis, the Bernsteins, Barbara, Arlene, her Aunt Becky and all of the kids to our birthday party. Was I surprised! What a party it was too. Everybody gave us presents, even the kids. Joey, who started working a little at his Cousin's pizza parlor a few days a week, bought me a lovely necklace with a heart shaped locket. Inside the locket was a picture of the two of us that was taken last year on the boat ride to Bear Mountain. On the facing side he had inscribed, "All my love, always and forever". The card that he made himself was just as beautiful. On the front of the card he pasted a picture of a guy and a girl on the beech that he cut out of a magazine or newspaper or something. He said that it reminded him of us. On the inside of the card he had written the following;

You are all of my yesterdays and all of my tomorrows,
The most beautiful thing I can say,
Is that because of you, I shall never know sorrow.
Because we love each other in every possible way,
Our love will always be here to stay,
For all of our todays,
And all of our tomorrows.

HAPPY BIRTHDAY ESTHER
From your forever "fella" Joey!

Joey is absolutely the best present I ever got for any occasion. I'm sure that anybody who reads all the beautiful things that he has written to me would have to agree with that. I also think that if I'm going to get better, it will be because he is the best medicine for me. I mean my family's love for me too, of course.

All of the other gifts I got were wonderful, but I find myself thinking only of that locket. Although Mom and I have come to expect these special expressions of love for me from Joey, they still take our breath away. Like I've said a few times before, he always makes me feel so special. I hope that feeling never ends. When I mentioned that to Joey, he told me that his love for me will never end so I shouldn't worry about it. Whenever I feel worried and frightened about what will happen to me, he always tells me that we will be together forever. He says that he feels and knows that to be true, in his heart and soul. Now whenever I'm frightened I think about what Joey keeps telling me and that helps me not to be as scared. To tell you the truth, just like I've said before, he is the best present I've ever gotten, for a birthday or any day.

The kids were all so cute and loving. They all seemed to be so happy to be giving me gifts, if you know what I mean. Right now it's hard for me to remember who gave me what, but I did get a lot of lovely things. I got a very nice pair of earrings from Barbara, and a most comfortable pair of slippers from her Aunt Becky. Arlene gave me a very professional looking makeup kit, which I know I'll put to good use. Her kids told me that they all chipped in and bought me a beautiful pair of sunglasses, that they said I could use when we all go to the beach again this summer. They were smiling from ear to ear as they gave it to me, I could've cried tears of joy. Helen and her husband gave me a big, gift wrapped box that had me wondering what it could possible be. I carefully opened it and opened the box and found a beautiful sun suit just what I wanted to have, even though I'm not allowed to be out in the sun too long. I love it. At the bottom of the box were two Frank Sinatra albums. I love Frank Sinatra. Joshua and Sophie handmade a big birthday card for me and one for Heshy. They also picked out a set of three fancy handkerchiefs for me that are lovely. Of course they weren't as special as the ones that Joey had gotten me a couple or so years ago, but they were very nice anyway.

Heshy got a lot of nice things too, but I can't remember what they all were. I do remember that Joey got Heshy a set of baseball cards that they both said will be worth a lot of money someday. I don't know why, but that's what they said. Mom and Daddy got Heshy a pair of binoculars that they said he would love to use at a baseball game. Joey said that Heshy would probably love to use them at the beach this summer. Daddy said, with a laugh, that it's not a bad idea, and wanted to know if he could borrow them from Heshy once in a while. Everyone laughed and someone, I don't who, asked Mom why she didn't seem to mind what Daddy said. Mom said that if Daddy wanted to look at young girls in bathing suits, let him look. She said that Daddy looking at young girls is just like a dog chasing a car, if the dog caught the car he couldn't drive anyway, so let him look all he wants too. While everyone was laughing at that, Daddy wanted to know what she meant by that.

Mama B and Mr. B are always so thoughtful, and they were for my birthday too. In addition to buying the cake, they bought me a beautiful folding tray that will fit right on my lap when I'm too tired to get out of bed to eat or to play cards or whatever. How thoughtful is that? Now I can wear the beautiful bed jacket Mama B gave me last year and use the tray in bed too. Mary is so loving too. She got me a sterling silver bracelet that she had inscribed, "To Esther, the sweetest girl I know. Happy sweet sixteen" I think I will wear it everywhere. Actually it was from Mary and her boyfriend Benny. He couldn't be here tonight because he was working late.

I told you at the start of this writing about my birthday and the best present I got. Now I have to tell you about the most wonderful present I got from Mom and Daddy. Actually it is for both me and Heshy. They gave us a big twelve inch television set. Wow! We got a television set. Daddy even said that there's a long waiting list to buy a TV set, but through his boss Sol, who knows a distributor very well, he was able to get one quick and at a reduced price. Daddy said that on the days that I would be too tired to come out into the living room to watch it, he would move it into my room. Heshy said that he wouldn't mind if Daddy did that. I asked Mom last week to shop for a present for Heshy, for me and of course she did. I thought she picked out something very nice too. It is a very nice matching beach jacket and swim trunks. Heshy loved it, and he should, because it will look great on him I bet. I wish I had gotten Joey that for his birthday in March. Oh well, anyway that's how our birthday went.

And now for other news. I went back into the hospital on Friday, April 25th, the same day that Mama B had to go in also. She had to have her stomach "tapped" again and Joey took me up to see her on the fourth floor, just like he did before. She looked very well after the "tapping" was done and that's the good news. The bad news is that Dr. Edward told me that the result of my latest blood test showed that the drugs, the old and new ones aren't working as well as he had hoped. I don't feel any worse but I guess I will soon. I don't know for sure. Anyway, he said that I shouldn't lose hope because there are other things that he will try, some of them haven't been proven or tested yet. He said he would try whatever he could to help me.

I started to feel scared and depressed again and Mom saw that in my face and voice. She is so wonderful. She sat on the bed, put her arms around me, gently caressed my shoulders and told me in a very soft and soothing way, that we should not worry. We should just take it one day at a time, she said. I thought about it and realized that what Mom said and what Joey always tells me, is right. When I told Joey what the doctor told us, he said that Mama B always told him never to worry about tomorrow, when you have today to get through first. You have to prepare for tomorrow but don't sacrifice today for tomorrow. Live and try to enjoy today first, before you worry about tomorrow. He said Mama B always tells him these things. Thinking about all these things that Mom, Daddy, Joey and Mama B have said made me feel much less scared and depressed. I thank God for that. Now I'm getting tired and have to say good night dear diary.

Friday, June 27th, 1947

Dear diary, I'm very sorry I've not been able to write sooner, but I had to go into the hospital twice and I had a lot of regular and make up school work to do. Although the one new drug I take is making me feel a little stronger and less tired, I still very tired at times. Speaking of drugs, even though that other new drug I tried a while ago didn't help fight my Leukemia, Dr. Edward told me last week in the hospital, that he thinks I'm in remission again. That is I mean, the Leukemia is in remission. I was hoping that was happening, because overall, I've been feeling a lot stronger than I usually do. Of course he couldn't say how long it would last in fact he said he was pleasantly surprised that it happened again. Well if he's pleasantly surprised you can imagine how I feel.

And now for some more good news. Today was the last day of school and I was promoted with my class. That alone made me feel great and the news from the doctor made me feel on top of the world. Well not exactly, but I do feel very good about everything. Wouldn't you feel good too, with all that good news and also knowing that Joey is your "fella". I'm feeling so good in fact, that when Joey suggested that we all, my family and his, go on a picnic to Prospect Park this coming Sunday, I happily said yes. Now I can't wait. Mom and Daddy are looking forward to it too. Heshy asked if he could bring Sarah, and of course everyone said it was okay. I mean, she is almost a part of the family now, just like Joey, but not quite like Joey. Nobody is like my Joey. Mom spoke to Mama B and they decided that they will both share in the making of the sandwiches and other goodies. I bet Joey will not only be helping Mama B, but he'll bring some stuff from Finklestien's Bakery too. I'm also sure that Mary will be doing her part too, because, of course Benny will be coming too.

It's a good thing that Benny's coming, because he has a car and that means that we all can ride there in comfort. Speaking of Mary and Benny, how nice is this. Recently they came over here to visit with me. While they were here, Mary noticed the three ring binder that Heshy had given me, to keep all the lovely notes and poems that Joey has written to me. They both said that it was very nice. Well, right after we had our dinner tonight, Mary and Benny showed up at our house and gave me a graduation present. It was a new three ring binder that they themselves hand decorated with roses on a vine going all around the edges of the front cover. In the center was beautifully hand inscribed with the words. "Love letters for Esther, straight from the heart". When I looked at it, I immediately thought of a song of a couple of years ago, that was sung by Dick Haymes. It was called "Love letters". I loved the song and the way that Dick Haymes sang it. When I opened up the binder, I saw on the inside of the cover, all the lyrics to the song, beautifully hand printed. What a thoughtful and lovely thing to do. Mary explained that it was Benny's idea, and he did all of the printing and artistic work. When I asked her what she did, she told me that she did the most important part, she bought the binder. I don't know it must run in the family, I guess.

Well, I had a very nice day today and I can't wait to go on that picnic on Sunday. Joey and I were taking about going to the beach with all of our friends next week, if the weather's good and I'm feeling okay. We shall see. Anyway, it was such a nice evening tonight, that after Mary and Benny left, Heshy, Sarah, Joey and I decided to go for a little walk to the park and around the neighborhood a little bit. Not too far you know, because I still get tired and sometimes it comes over me suddenly. After a while we walked back to the park and sat down on a bench. Heshy and Joey went over to the candy store to get us some ice cream cones while Sarah and I just sat and talked. It was so nice, just Sarah and I talking. She is such a lovely person and I do love her for being so nice and thoughtful to me. I think she and Heshy will be together forever, just like Joey says he and I will be. I know what Joey says about us is true, because he would never tell me a lie. Now I have to say good night dear diary.

Friday, July 18th, 1947

Dear diary, hello again. It's been a while, but I know you understand why I haven't been able to write sooner. Where do I start, let me see, oh yeah, the Sunday we all went to Prospect Park. I think it was June 29th. Anyway, as I remember it, it was a very nice warm, sunny and beautiful day. We were loaded down with all kinds of goodies to eat, and I was right about Joey going to Finklestein's Bakery. It looked like he bought out the bakery. I even told him, while we were in the car on the way to the park, that I hoped he left something in the store for someone else to buy. He already had his arm around me at the time, but he held me tighter as he told me, in a playful way, that he bought out the whole bakery and it's all for me. When I said that I would get very fat if I ate it all, he said that's good, because then instead of driving me home in the car, he would roll me home. I had to laugh along with everyone else in the car. He never stops making something funny out of anything that's said, and I love it.

After Mr. B parked the car in the Prospect Park parking lot, he started to unload the goodies from the trunk of the car. To my surprise, he pulled out a folding wheelchair that he said was for Mama B if she got too tired to walk. Do you see what I mean when I say that they always seem to think of everything. I had been wondering what she was going to do if she got tired. Joey said that it was lightweight, and that he was going to take turns with Mr. B and Benny in carrying it around. Before going to the picnic grounds, we all went to the lake area which was not too far from the zoo. Heshy, Sarah, Joey and I decided to rent a rowboat and go out on the lake for an hour or less, depending on how

I felt. Heshy and Joey helped me very carefully, onto the boat. Sarah just helped herself on and I wished I could've done the same thing.

Anyway, we spent a very nice hour on the lake, watching the little fishes swimming all around us, and the birds flying overhead. This time I didn't stick my fingers in the water and Joey teased me by saying that I was afraid I was going to get my fingers bitten by the "Itty bitty fishies". I told him to shush, and called him "sweat feet". Heshy and Sarah wanted to know what that was all about, so I told them to ask Joey. Joey of course wouldn't tell them, and just said that it was nothing. We all laughed, but I'm sure that Heshy and Sarah didn't know what they were laughing about. The hour went by too fast, as usual, and then we met up with the rest of our families near the zoo.

We continued on to the picnic area where we had a great time eating the wonderful foods made for us by Mom and Mama B. By the time we finished eating the desserts that Joey bought, we were all too full to walk around right away, so we just sat and talked for a while. That was very enjoyable too. There doesn't seem to be a line between Joey's family and my family. To me, it feels like one big happy family and I love it. Of course I'm including Sarah in our big family too. I think anyone would be able to tell by the different conversations that our families have with one another, that we are all that close. I mean, they can, and do talk about anything and everything with comfort and ease, if you know what I mean. Anyway we all had a great day that Sunday.

On the Fourth of July I was still feeling pretty good and not too weak, so I decided to go to the beach with the gang. When I say the gang, I mean the gang. I mean, everyone was there, all my friends family and even the Bernsteins and their kids and Arlene and her kids. Mary and Benny were there too, but Mama B and Mr. B were not. Well not at first anyway. After we were there for about an hour or so they showed up. It seems that Mama B didn't want to ride on the subway and Mr. B had to work early in the morning. As soon as he got home he drove her to the beach in his cab. Mom and Daddy and Joey and I came with Mary and Benny in Benny's car. I thought that was very nice of Mary and Benny to do that.

I loved watching all the Green and Bernstein kids, playing in the sand down by the water. Joey again rented a big beach umbrella for me to sit under. I did manage to go for a short walk along the water's edge with Joey and it was heavenly. Of course Joey made sure I wore my big floppy hat and a towel over my shoulders. I always love to walk on the wet sand and have the water lick my feet, while Joey has his arm wrapped around me. When I told him how romantic it was to be walking that way, he said that romance only had a little bit to do with it. He said he was holding me so tight mostly to keep me from falling in case I got very tired suddenly. When I looked a little shocked by that remark, he laughed and told me he was only kidding. Of course I knew all along he was kidding. Yeah right! Sure I did.

After a while I was starting to feel tired and so was Mama B. At least that's what she said, but I don't know for sure, because I know how much she loves the beach. I really think that Mama B said she was tired too, because she wanted Mr. B to drive us home. Anyway, Mom and Daddy decided to come home with me and Joey and Mama B and Mr. B. It was a very lovely ride back home. Mr. B being a cab driver knows all the different streets, not only in Brooklyn but in most of the other parts of the city too. He took us along Ocean Parkway, which is beautifully lined with trees, very expensive looking tall apartment buildings and one family homes. I don't know how he did it, but before I knew it, we were on Linden Blvd. and close to home. Mama B put her hand on Mr. B's shoulder and said, "My Giuseppe can drive me anywhere." Mom looked at Daddy and said, "All my Gustav can do is drive me crazy." Daddy looked surprised and asked Mom what she meant by that, while we all laughed.

It was nice to hear Mama B laugh. She's a big inspiration to me, for the way she goes on living each day, in spite of all the bad things that have happened to her in her lifetime. Except for that one time last year, when she questioned why there had to be wars and young boys killed, I don't think I ever heard her complain. I think that's where I get some of my strength from, besides my family and Joey of course. I think I'm beginning to see what Joey meant when he said that he's learned a lot from older people, by just listening to them. I know that I've learned a lot from Mom and Daddy, but now I know I can learn from listening to other older people too.

Monday, July 21st, I have to go back into the hospital, and I don't know how long I'll have to stay. I know I have to be tested as always, but I might be given some new experimental drugs, I'm not sure yet. If I'm given the new drugs, then I'll have to be watched and tested, and then I'll have to be there a little longer. If that does happen, I hope it works and helps me in some way. I also hope that if the new drug does help me, it has no side effects. I've been so lucky so far with no side effects, except for that one time when I had that awful, bad dream. We shall see. Now I'm getting tired again so I'll say good night dear diary until the next time I write.

Tuesday, September 2nd, 1947

Dear diary, I know I have to get you all caught up on what's been happening with me, since I last wrote. The truth of the matter is that not a whole lot has been happening to me. I went to the hospital in late July, like I told you I would be doing. My blood tests came back the same as the last time. The Leukemia is still in me, but it has not gotten any worse, so that was good, I guess. Dr. Edward did ask me to try a new drug and after talking it over with Mom and Daddy, Joey and Heshy weren't there at that moment, I agreed to try it. The bad news is that it didn't work the way he hoped it would, but the good news is that it didn't make me feel sick either. I think it was a whole week that I was in there that time.

I haven't been to the beach since the Fourth of July, because on the days when I felt good and wanted to go, the weather was bad. When the weather was nice, I felt bad. It really didn't make much of a difference though, because on those rainy days, I did go to the movies with Joey and some of the gang. When I felt too tired and weak to go to the beach, Joey stayed with me and as usual, he was wonderful company. On most of those times he actually made me feel better. We would talk, or play cards, or listen to the radio, or watch TV, or whatever. It was wonderful. Sometimes, when I felt strong enough, we would go to the park and sit in the sun for a short while. Of course, you know he made me lunch every day that we were home and Mom was working. Mom has a new name for Joey now. She calls him, "Mr. Dependable". That's why, she says, she doesn't worry about me needing anything when she's at work, because she knows that Joey's with me. Isn't that nice to hear? That's why I feel so lucky sometimes.

This past Saturday Mom, Daddy and Heshy were all working. Joey had worked very late Friday night at his cousin's pizza parlor, and I know he didn't get home until about 1 o'clock in the morning. I know he didn't get too much sleep, because he got up earlier than he would normally, just to be with me. Even though we enjoyed our day together, as we always do, I started to feel a little depressed at one point in the afternoon. It was shortly after we had our lunch and I remember telling Joey that if I don't get better and survive this disease, I will miss growing old with him. The thought of that brought tears to my eyes. Joey quickly embraced me and softly kissed my tears away. He has a gentle touch that gives me such warmth. He kissed me on my nose, cheeks and then my lips. He then looked me in the eyes and told me that he didn't want us to ever grow old together. Before I could say a word, he added that the love we share for each other, will keep us young forever. Our bodies may grow old, but out hearts, souls and spirits will always be as young as we are right now, he said. I held him so close to me and started to cry again, but this time they were tears of pure joy. I never cried and had goose bumps at the same time before. It was weird, but I was no longer depressed or worried about our future at least for a while anyway. You never know when that sinking feeling is going to hit you, when you're sick like I am, if you know what I mean.

Well tomorrow is back to school and I'm looking forward to starting my junior year. I thank God that as of this moment, I feel strong enough and up to it, but who knows about the day or week after. I didn't grow any taller, or gain or lose any weight, so I can still wear most of my clothes from last year, and that's good. I did manage to go shopping with Mom for a few things a couple of weeks ago, right before my monthly hospital stay. Mom also went to Daddy's factory last week and picked out a couple of things for me. Everything I got was very nice and Joey liked them a lot too. Of course you know that means so much to me. Heshy was good enough to pick up all the school supplies I'll be needing, with his discount at Schlossberg's, so that was one less thing for me to worry about. That's about it for now, dear diary. Good night.

Thursday, October 9th, 1947

Dear diary, well the first month of my junior year in high school went well. Of course I had to miss my usual four days while in the hospital, a few weeks ago. Nothing has changed too much with my condition. In fact it has gotten a little bit worse, according to Dr. Edward. I don't feel any worse, not yet anyway. Dr. Edward said that it hasn't worsened enough to get too worried about, so I'm glad about that. On the other hand, I didn't get any better and at first that kind of depressed me, but after the doctor left, Mom told me again to just take it one day at a time. Then I thought about what Mama B said, about living today first, before worrying too much about tomorrow. That seemed to make me feel much better, not great mind you, but better. When I told Joey what the doctor had told me, he said that as long as I still feel pretty good, I shouldn't worry about it. He told me to let us both enjoy each other's company, for as long as we can and not worry or think about those days when I night not be feeling good. That made a lot of sense to me, at the time anyway.

I still have my moments when I get very scared, about what's going to happen to me. It almost always happens to me at night, when I'm alone and trying to go to sleep. On most of those nights I cry myself to sleep. The next morning when I see Mom, Daddy, Heshy and a little later Joey, I feel much better. Mom seemed to know, I didn't know exactly how, that I go through these periods of being scared and crying myself to sleep. When no one was around except the two of us one day, she told me that she knew what I was going through, and it made her very sad. She said she felt helpless to do anything about it. When I asked her how she knew, she told me that she heard me sobbing at night, seen the redness of my eyes in the morning and even felt the dampness of my pillowcase when she went to make my bed, after I left to go to school. I told Mom she should've been a detective or something. She laughed a little, gave me a hug, and told me that anytime I felt like talking about it with her, she would sit down with me, just the two of us and have a nice talk. Then she hugged me tighter, kissed my forehead and told me she loved me very much and will always. I told her how much I loved her and that it would be alright with me, right then and there to talk about my problem.

After I told Mom about all my fears and how depressed I get at night when I'm by myself, she said that if I would like, she'd sit with me in my room until I fell asleep. I thought that was a wonderful idea and told Mom that I would welcome that. Now I don't have that scared feeling as much as I did before. Sometimes I wake up in the middle of the night and feel scared, but that doesn't happen too much. When that does happen, only once in a while thank God, I don't bother Mom I just try to think positive like Dr. Edward once told me to do. It seems to work most of the time. Mom sometimes gently rubs my temples and forehead to relax me and that puts me to sleep.

Last Friday night, Daddy came home after going to the Temple, looking very upset. I was feeling very tired and went to my room to lie down. Joey wasn't here that night because he was working at the pizza parlor. Mom and Daddy must've thought that I fell asleep, because after a while I heard them talking about Joey. I couldn't hear every word, but from what I did hear, I could figure out what they were talking about. Daddy was complaining that some of the elders in the Temple were giving him a hard time, because I had a "goy", a non-Jewish boyfriend. He told Mom that as much as he loved Joey and his family, he was going to have to ask Joey not to come around to see me anymore. He sounded as if he was almost crying when he said that. He then said he would have a talk with him the next day, when he knew Joey would be coming around to see me. I was horrified! I couldn't believe Daddy was saying those words. Then, as I was getting up out of my bed, tears streaming down my face, getting ready to burst into the living room, I heard Mom, crying out loud and asking Daddy why he was talking so crazy.

I came bursting into the room crying and saw that Daddy had tears in his eyes too. He kept saying to himself that he didn't know what to do. On the one hand, he said he loved Joey but on the other hand, he didn't want to be an outcast in the community. I ran into Daddy's arms, crying and asked him to please not send Joey away from me. Daddy hugged me, called me his "Tottala" and said he didn't know what choice he had. He held me tight as he told me that because he cares so much for Joey and his family, he let things go to far with me and Joey. Before I could say anything Daddy kissed my forehead and said that he would have to talk with Joey, no matter what he decides he's going to do. I could tell by the look on Daddy's face that he really didn't want to do anything. Mom was pleading with him to not do something so rash and to not listen to those busybodies, those "yentas" at the Temple. Daddy said, while he wiped away tears from his eyes, "We shall see. We shall see."

Mom came into my room with me and tried to console me, but I couldn't stop crying. When Mom saw that I was inconsolable, she went in a hurry into the living room and started yelling at Daddy. Daddy didn't argue with Mom, he just asked her to please not yell at him, but she did anyway. I don't ever remember Mom and Daddy having any kind of disagreement like this before. After a while I felt guilty about being the cause of them having an argument and I ran into the kitchen, where they now were. Through free flowing tears, I told them how bad I felt for being the cause of them being mad at one another. Mom stopped yelling at Daddy and they both hugged me and Daddy called me his "Tottala" again. Mom told me that I was not the cause of anything but joy and happiness in our house. Daddy strongly agreed with her and told me not to worry. He said that he still has to think about it and talk to Joey the next day.

I settled down after a few minutes and went back into my room to go to sleep. Mom came in with me and assured me with comforting words, as she once more rubbed my temples and head. She even sang an old lullaby in German, just like she used to do when I was a little girl. To my surprise I didn't have trouble falling asleep, but I did wake up in the middle of the night. I don't know what time it was, but I did have trouble getting back to sleep again. I kept thinking about what Daddy said about me and Joey. The worst things kept creeping into my head until finally, I again remembered what Mama B said, about not worrying about tomorrow until you get through today first. I also remembered what one of the nurses at the hospital told me, when I couldn't fall asleep one night. She told me to try to remember other nights that I might've had like that and what happened when I got up the next morning. In the light of day I discovered that none of my fears were founded, and that I worried for nothing. That did the trick and I fell back to sleep again quickly.

Daddy was only going to work until noontime last Saturday, so he could be here when Joey came over. He had to stay at work a little longer to take care of some kind of business problem, so Joey got here first. When Joey came into my room he knew that something was wrong, because he told me, that my Mom looked upset and so did I. After I explained to Joey what the problem was with Daddy, he told me not to worry and that he will try his very best to convince Daddy that we belong together. In any case Joey told me that there's no need for me to worry, because like he's told me so many times before, we'll be together forever. His words as usual made me feel a lot better, but I was still a little worried. After a few minutes I asked Joey to wait in the kitchen for me while I put my bathrobe on. Joey of course had brought some lunch for us. Mom soon joined us at the table and told Joey how sorry she was about the situation. When we finished eating Mom was still apologizing to Joey and sniffling a little. I suddenly got very tired and went back into my room to lie down. Joey sat with me until we heard Daddy come home, then he went out to meet and greet him.

Joey closed the door to my room on the way out, so I wouldn't hear what they were saying. I couldn't stand not knowing what was going on and not hearing anything, so I got out of bed and tiptoed to the door and listened through the keyhole. I couldn't hear every word but again, just like when I heard Mom and Daddy talking the night before, I could make out what they were talking about. Of course the night before I was in bed, but the door was open. Mom, since I've been sick, has asked me to always leave my door open in case I need to call her and also so she could hear me if I was in some kind of distress. Anyway, I heard Joey say things like, Daddy ought to consider that he, Joey, makes me happy and feel good sometimes. I said to myself, sometimes! How about all the time! Then he said that if by some miracle or something, the doctors are wrong, and we want to get married sometime in the future, then he would do whatever it would take to make Daddy happy. Finally, Joey told Daddy that he would abide by whatever Daddy decides, because he didn't want to do anything that would tear our wonderful family apart. I heard nothing for a few minutes, but it seemed like an hour to me. Well not really an hour, but you know what I mean. Then I heard Daddy speak.

"Why couldn't you be a Jewish boy", Daddy asked Joey. He didn't get an answer. Then Daddy told Joey to forget what he said, about he and I not seeing each other again. He said he has been under a lot of strain lately, at work and me being sick. Then on top of all that, some of the elders at the Temple had a big meeting and told him to break us up. He said he was going to listen to Mom, and not listen to those meddling old men from the Temple. I heard them coming toward my room, so I quickly jumped into my bed and when Joey, Mom and Heshy came in I must've had a smile from ear to ear, with tears of joy in my eyes too. Mom also had them. After they all hugged and kissed me, Daddy came in, hugged and kissed me too, and reminded me that he told me the night before not to worry. Then he gently pinched me on the cheek and called me his "tottala" again.

The next day Joey came over and I asked him to please walk with me to the park. It was such a nice day and I wanted to sit in the warm, fresh air for a little while. Heshy asked if he could come with us and of course we said yes he could. As we left our house, Heshy suddenly forced his way in between me and Joey. I was very surprised as he put his arms around us, looked at me, then Joey and said that he was so happy and glad that Daddy didn't make us break up. We all stopped walking, and I know it must've looked strange or funny, when we locked ourselves in a three way hug. I can't begin to tell you how warm and wonderful that felt. We didn't stay in the park too long, because I was starting to get a little tired. Joey said that the visit to the park was just like me, short and sweet. I gave him a little pinch in the ribs. He laughed. We both laughed and then kissed each other with our eyes. He always makes me feel so lucky. Yes, I know I always tell you that, but it's true. Now I am getting very tired and I have to get up early for school tomorrow, so I have to say good night dear diary.

Wednesday, November 19th, 1947

Dear diary, this past month or so has gone by fast. I spent the last week of October in the hospital again, so I was not able to get involved in making a costume for Halloween. I know that some people think that I'm getting too big to be dressing up for Halloween, but all of my friends and I just enjoy thinking up different costumes to wear every year. Not being able to do that this year was a little bit of a disappointment for me. Here's the great part of Halloween this year. When Joey realized that I wouldn't be able to participate in this year's contest, he decided that he wouldn't either. I begged him to go on without me but he wouldn't listen. Inside of me I was really very happy to know that he would do that just for me, because I know how much he loves to put his creative mind to work on Halloween. Heshy and Sarah found out about me and Joey not joining in the contest and parade, and they too decided not to do so too. They all really made me feel like a million bucks. When I told Joey that, he told me that I looked like a million bucks to him. I said that he has never seen a million bucks before so he doesn't know what a million bucks looks like. Then he said, with a big laugh, that's what he's trying to tell me, I look like something he's never seen before! I tried to get mad at him for that, but I couldn't and just laughed with him.

Well anyway, while I was in the hospital, Dr. Edward told me that my tests showed that my condition has gotten slightly worse. Again he said it was not that much worse to worry about just yet. Just like the month before, when he said it was a little worse, I don't feel any worse than before. Actually I feel pretty good except for getting tired so easy and so often. I mean, I'm still able to keep up with my school work, thanks to Joey, Heshy and Sarah. By the way, Sarah has been for a short while now, doing her homework with us at night in my house. She blends in with our family a little more each day and I love it. Between Sarah, Barbara, Eileen, Helen and Mary, I feel like I have a whole bunch of loving, caring sisters. In other words, they all make me feel like the luckiest girl in the world. There I go again. I keep saying that so it must be true.

One day while at the hospital, I had a nice talk with Anne Marie, you know the nurse who let me use her old uniform last year for Halloween. I was telling her that for the last four or five years I've dreamed of becoming a nurse, and she said the nicest thing to me. She told me that judging by the way I treat the younger patients in our cancer ward, she thought I will be a great nurse. The thing that I noticed was that she didn't say "would've been" but "will be" a great nurse. If she can think so positive about me, then I'll have to think that way about myself too. In a way, I'll just be following the doctor's orders, right?

Well next week is Thanksgiving and Mom and Daddy invited the usual gang over for dinner, the Balduccis of course and my Aunt Sherry and Uncle Carl and their families, and a few Mom's and Daddy's friends. Sarah will be there too, but she will be coming a little later for dessert. Joey and Heshy think that's the best part of any dinner. It doesn't show on Joey but it's beginning to show a little on Heshy and Joey's always reminding him of that. He keeps telling Heshy that at his age, he is supposed to be getting rid of his "baby fat", not putting more on. Heshy pretended that he was mad, and asked Joey in an angry way, "Who are you calling a moron?" Then they do their usual laughing and slapping each other on the back. I don't think they'll ever grow up, and I hope they never do. Mom and Daddy say the same thing too. Well anyway, I'm going into the hospital on Friday, the day after tomorrow, and Dr. Edward promised me he would try very hard, to make sure I would go home in time for Thanksgiving. I now feel very confident I will be, so that's good. Now I'll have to say good night dear diary.

CHAPTER 17

Thursday, January 1st, 1948

Dear diary, well the entire holiday season of Thanksgiving, Chanukah, Christmas and New Years has passed since I last wrote to you. The holidays were all good as usual, but I did have to spend Christmas week in the hospital. Dr. Edward arranged that for me, so that I wouldn't have to miss any school days, so that was good. However, tests showed that my sickness is still getting a little worse. I don't feel too sick yet, just a little more tired. My arms, where they stick me with needles, seems to get a little more black and blue each time I go to the hospital. I also notice that other parts of my body are getting a little black and blue too. Dr. Edward said that he's going to try a new drug on me, when I go back at the end of this month. I don't know, it's starting to scare me a little. I'm trying not to think about it. I try to just keep in my mind, the lovely words that Joey wrote for me about always keeping hope in my heart. It's very hard at times to do that, but I have to keep on trying.

Well anyway the holidays were all very nice and I did get my usual nice gifts from almost everybody. Mom made her usual nice dinners and last Tuesday, the day after I came home from the hospital, I did manage to go to visit with the Balduccis and see their Christmas tree, with Joey's and Heshy's help of course. Even though I loved being there and felt very comfortable, I didn't stay too long because I was getting tired. I can't write too long tonight because I have to try to go to school tomorrow and I am getting tired now, so good night dear diary.

Friday, January 30th, 1948

Dear diary, the first part of this month was not too good for me. I felt so tired and weak that I missed three or four days of school. I

316

don't remember exactly how many days it was. In fact Joey, Heshy and Sarah had to practically do all of my homework for me. I'm glad now that they did, because when I felt better and went back to school, I wasn't too far behind the rest of my class. The past two weeks I felt pretty good, even last week while I was in the hospital. I'll tell you what made me feel really good. On one of those days when I felt too sick to go to school, Suzy and her sister Sherry came to my house after school with Joey, Heshy and Sarah. They brought me a box full of pastries that they called, "guayava". They bought it at a Caribbean bake shop. They explained to me that "guayava" is a tropical fruit. Well whatever it is and wherever it comes from, it was delicious. Of course you know that Heshy ate at least half the box. I'm only kidding of course, but he did eat a lot of it. Anyway I thought it was so sweet of Suzy and Sherry to take the time to visit me. I mean, they live somewhere on the other side of Pennsylvania Ave., where our high school is. Not only that, but I know they both work after school, in one of the first new supermarkets in our neighborhood. They are just too nice for me to say in words.

While I was in the hospital I was given a new drug. I didn't have any bad side effects, thank God. I don't know for sure if that is what is making me feel better, because I was starting to feel better a day or so before I went into the hospital. It's a funny thing, but when I'm feeling good and it shows on my face and I guess also in the way I talk and move. Then all of the people around me seem to feel better too. I guess it's like I once heard Mom say, that feeling good is sometimes contagious. Even the nurses at the hospital seem to notice that I was feeling better, because they all came into see me, one or two at a time of course. In fact, by the time Mom arrived one morning, Krissy, a lovely mother of a three year old boy, was fixing my hair for me. She brushed it and tied a pretty pink ribbon around my pony tail. Mom had a smile on her face that lit up the room, when she saw what Krissy had done. See what Mom meant when she said that feeling good can be contagious? Do you also see why most of the time I feel like the luckiest girl in the world?

Well it's just a couple of weeks until Valentine's Day, and I have to start making cards now. I don't know how I'll be feeling in a week or so. At least I'll have to try to make them now and in the next few days. I'm going to try very hard, to make a really special one for Joey. I mean, they will all be special for my family, but because Joey writes all those beautiful things for me, I want to try to write something very beautiful for him. I'll have to think very hard to come up with just the right words to describe how much he means to me. You know, I just remembered what Joey said about how he writes. He said that all he has to do is search his heart and the words seem to flow right onto the paper. That's exactly what I'll do. Well now I'm getting tired so I'll have to say good night dear diary.

Saturday, February 14th, 1948 [Valentine's Day]

Dear diary, I was able to make cards for all of my family and of course Joey too, but I started to get tired again late last week. I asked Mom to buy me some cards for the Bernstein and Green kids and of course she did. She also bought heart shaped little chocolate candies. I was going to ask Heshy this morning to bring the cards and candy over to the kids, but before I could, they all showed up at our front door. I mean the whole gang was there, Helen, Arlene and Barbara too. I'm glad I got to see the kids' beautiful faces light up, when they saw their cards and chocolate hearts. You know they all gave me beautiful cards, that expressed their love for me and that warmed my heart so much. The kids all took turns in kissing and hugging me. They were so cute. The five of them chipped in, with a little help from Helen and Arlene I think, and bought me a little stuffed monkey that has a red heart pinned to it's chest. On the red heart was written, "Will you be my Valentine Esther?"

They didn't stay too long and after they left I had to lie down and rest a little bit. Joey had to work at the pizza parlor yesterday. He had to go there right after school. Thank God Mr. B still takes us to school in the morning and takes us home again on most days. Yesterday he not only took us home, he also took Joey to work. Otherwise he would've had to take the subway and a bus. Mr. B also picked him up again at about one o'clock this morning. Joey has to go back there this afternoon at about one o'clock. One of his cousin's regular workers is out sick so he asked Joey to help him out. Joey said that as much as he would like to spend his time with me, he couldn't say no to his cousin, because he has been too good to him and his family. Anyway, Joey did tell me yesterday before he went to work that he would be here about eleven o'clock this morning and spend an hour with me before going back to work. So, that's what I was waiting for when I went to lay down.

Sure enough, at eleven o'clock Joey came walking through the front door. He was carrying a big package that was wrapped with paper covered with little pink hearts, and handed it to me. The package felt soft and fluffy. I thought to myself that it must be another stuffed animal. I very carefully unwrapped the paper and sure enough, I was right. I had unwrapped a very adorable looking Teddy Bear. Joey had pinned a heart shaped Valentine's Day card, that he made himself, to the chest of the Teddy. Inside the card he had written,

> "To my Esther, my Valentine,
> I couldn't "Bear" to live a minute
> In a world without you in it.
> So always be mine,
> Always be my Valentine!"
> I will love you always and forever,
> Your forever fella, Joey.

Is he something else or what? I threw my arms around him and told him how much I loved him. He told me that he loved me very much too, as I handed him the card that I made for him. I had drawn a light pink heart on a white background. Inside the heart I overlapped another heart, a little bit darker shade of pink. One the top of the card I wrote, "Two Valentines shine bright as the Sun. Across the bottom of the card I wrote, "Two hearts beating always as one". Inside the card, I wrote the words that I had searched my heart for.

> "I hope and pray,
> That you will be my Valentine,
> Forever and a day,
> That you will be mine,
> Forever and for all time."

> I love you!
> I will be
> Your Esther, always!

When Joey finished reading it he smiled from ear to ear, gave me a big hug and kiss and told me he loved it and me. He said that what I had written for him was better than anything that he had ever written for me. Of course I knew that he couldn't really mean that. I mean, after all those beautiful things he has said to me, and about me, he had to be kidding. I told him that I guessed a little bit of him was rubbing off on me, because I don't ever remember writing anything like that before. Then I told him that I did what he always said he does whenever he wanted to write or say something. Search your heart. Once I did that it was kind of easy to write what I did. The words just seemed to flow right onto the paper. He seemed to like that a lot. He laughed a very happy, satisfied laugh and said that made him very glad. I'm thrilled to tell you that while all this talking was going on, he never stopped hugging me. It felt so good and I loved it.

The hour of his visit went by so fast it seemed like only a few minutes. So off to work he went again. Before he left he told me that he will come over to see me tomorrow morning, whenever he gets up. He said it would probably be about noon time, so he said I shouldn't have lunch until he gets here, because he will bring something in for us. When I asked what that might be, he said he didn't know yet but he will make it a surprise. Now I can hardly wait until tomorrow. Not just because of the surprise lunch, but to see Joey, my Joey again.

While we were saying our goodbyes, Mom was making lunch for me. Daddy and Heshy were both working so it was just me and Mom enjoying a nice lunch together. After we finished eating, Mom and I just sat around and talked for a while. Mom is so easy to talk with. I know a lot of the girls that I hang out with, and even some of the girls I know from school, always complain that they can't talk to their Moms, or for that matter even their Dads. They say that because their parents are from the "old country" [Europe] and because they spend so much time working, they don't have the time or the understanding to talk with their children. I don't know about that. My parents, and even me and Heshy are from the "old country" too, and my parents also work hard, but they still seem to find or make the time to talk with us. I mean even when they're tired they listen to whatever it is we have to say. Like I've said so many times before, I'm very lucky, I mean we, Heshy and I both, very lucky to have such great parents..

Anyway, while we were talking I told Mom that because the last couple of months Dr. Edward had told me that my condition has gotten a little worse, I didn't think I was going to get better. Mom put her arms around me and gently hugged me. She told me to try not to think about things like that, to just take it one day at a time. I told her that is exactly what I'm trying to do, but sometimes I can't help but think about it. While the thought of what is probably going to happen to me still scares me, it's not as bad as it used to be. I told Mom that all the love, support and comforting words of encouragement that I've gotten from her, Daddy, Heshy and Joey and his family, have really helped me a lot. At that point Mom started to get a little teary eyed and I apologized for doing that to her. I said that I was trying really hard to be strong in my heart, just live my life one day at a time, just like she, Joey and Mama B have been telling me to. We stayed locked in that hug for a nice long time, until I felt very tired and went into my room to lie down. Mom followed me in. After I put my head on my pillow, Mom, as she usually does when I'm going to sleep, gently rubbed my forehead and temples. The next thing I remember is Heshy waking me up and telling me that dinner was on the table.

I really missed having Joey around here tonight. That's two nights in a row. I don't know if I could stand another night like this. Because he liked what I had written to him in my Valentine's card to him, I thought I'd pass the time away tonight by writing something else for him. I thought I'd make a little, "I miss you" card. I spent half the night trying to think what I'd draw on the outside of the card. I started to look through old newspapers and magazines. I finally got a great idea. I saw a small picture of a pair of beautiful, colorful birds perched in a tree. I very carefully cut it out of the magazine and pasted on the front of a piece of white paper that I had folded in half. Over the picture I wrote,

" WE ARE LIKE TWO BIRDS WHO SING
AND TAKE WING
TOGETHER

And under the picture I wrote,

THAT'S WHY I MISS YOU WHEN YOU ARE NOT WITH ME

Inside the card I wrote,

OF ALL THE LOVELY THINGS YOU WROTE,
AND ALL THE BEAUTIFUL WORDS YOU SPOKE,
THE ONES I LOVE THE MOST
ARE WHEN YOU SAID,
YOU LOVE ME!

I love you too and miss you so much,
Always your Esther!

I hope Joey likes the card. I showed it to Mom and she said that she thinks that Joey will love it because it's lovely. Daddy saw it and said that if Joey doesn't like it, he's going to hit him with a stale bagel. Heshy asked Daddy if he would really hit Joey with something that hard. Daddy asked Heshy if he would rather eat the stale bagel instead. We all had to laugh when Heshy asked if there was any cream cheese in the ice box. When Sarah came over a little while later, Heshy showed her the card and she hugged me, and told me it was so beautiful and touching and that made me feel good. Now I'm sure Joey will like it. Now I'm getting tired again so I'll say good night dear diary.

Sunday, February, 15th, 1948

Dear diary, well my "Mr. Dependable" Joey, showed up at noontime, just like he said he would. Of course he had all kinds of bags in his arms and hands. He immediately announced that we had a few choices for lunch. Heshy, he added, didn't have a choice because he knows that Heshy's going to have some of everything. The first thing he put on the table was a big bag of bagels. That was followed by a bag that had the cream cheese and lox. Next he brought out a freshly baked and sliced rye bread, a box of pastries from Finklestein's and a bag of pastrami and corned beef. You know he didn't forget the mustard and pickles. Heshy wanted to know where the pizza was. Joey said that next week if he gets home early enough, he'll bring home a pizza just for him. Heshy said that would be great, but wanted to know how Joey would be able to keep it warm all the way from Queens. Joey said that just for him, he would sit on it all the way home to keep it warm. Do you see what I mean about my Joey?

When Mom and Daddy asked Joey why he spent all of his hard earned money for all this food, enough to feed and army Daddy said, Joey said it didn't cost him much at all. It seems that a few doors down from his cousin's pizza parlor, there is a kosher deli. The man who owns it is very friendly with Joey's cousin, Jimmy. The man, Izzy is his name, asked Jimmy, if he could spare one of his workers to help him out of a tough spot. Izzy had a catering job to prepare for and a couple of his guys didn't show up, so he needed a hand for a couple of hours. Being that it was a little on the slow side at that moment, Jimmy said sure and asked Joey to help out Izzy.

Joey said that Izzy was so grateful and impressed with the way Joey worked he gave him about two pounds each of pastrami and corned beef and the mustard and pickles too. He was only helping Izzy out for about an hour and a half. Jimmy paid him for the whole day too. Here's the strange thing about yesterday. Joey said that around the corner from Jimmy's pizza place is a bagel bakery. They deliver to most of the grocery stores and regular bakeries in Brooklyn and Queens. That includes Finklestiens, the kosher deli and the grocery on our corner too. The driver, who delivers to our neighborhood, always eats pizza for lunch in Jimmy's and has become very friendly with Joey. Yesterday, The driver came in and told Joey that he was robbed on the way to work and didn't have any money, but was very hungry. Joey of course gave him his usual pizza and soda and also a couple of dollars so he wouldn't be broke. The guy was so thankful that he asked Joey exactly where he lived and told him that he was going to bring over some free bagels when he made his regular deliver run in our neighborhood. This morning he dropped off three dozen bagels while Joey was still sleeping. Half of everything Joey got for nothing he gave to us and of course the other half went to his family. The rest of the stuff he had to buy, but what the heck he can't get everything for nothing.

After he spread out all the food on the table, I gave him the card I made for him and he loved it. He said he couldn't get over how great my writing is. He told me he feels the same way that I do when we're not together, but the difference is that most of the time when he's working he's so busy that he doesn't have too much time to think about it. He added that if he had to stand around and not have much to do, thinking about me would drive him crazy. I guess he knows what I'm talking about in that "I miss you card". Anyway we had a very nice lunch and spent a wonderful afternoon enjoying each other's company. The weather's on the cold side, so I didn't want to go out. Joey went out to buy some ice cream and a large bottle of cream soda. When he got back, he made ice cream sodas for all of us. It was delicious! We all enjoyed it. I was getting tired, as was Joey, so he left early. Now I'm getting so tired I'll have to say good night, dear diary.

Friday, March 12th, 1948

Dear diary, it has been an eventful month or so since I last wrote. In addition to missing my usual school days while I was in the hospital, I also missed three days because I was so tired and weak. I feel okay now, but I got a little depressed when I was too sick to go to school. In fact, not only did Joey and Heshy bring me school work to do, but they practically had to do it for me. Thank God I got over that in a few days. I hope I don't have too many days like those again. The funny thing about it is, just when I started to feel better, I had to go into the hospital for my regular monthly visit. On those days when I didn't feel good, sometimes I couldn't fall asleep. I mean I would doze off with Mom rubbing my forehead, but then I would wake up shortly after Mom would leave my room. Then I started to read again, all the beautiful poems and other lovely things that Joey had written for me, and that seemed to relax me and put me to sleep.

You know Joey has written a whole lot more to me than I've told you about. If I wrote to you every thing that he has written, I wouldn't have the time or the pages left to write about anything else. For a long time now, Joey carries with him his writing pad, and at the spur of the moment or whenever something inspires him, he writes it down right away. He said that before he started carrying the pad around with him, he used to think of something nice to say or write about, and then forget what it was. Now he just puts it down on paper right away. He is so wonderful. Anyway, when I had to go to the hospital, I brought the book of Joey's poems and writings with me, in case I had trouble falling asleep.

Every night I was in the hospital, I had to read Joey's words to help me relax and go to sleep. One night while I was reading the book, it must have been about midnight, one of the night nurses, Karen, came in to check my blood pressure. I don't know her too well, but she seems to be very nice and I like her. She's about twenty two or three and she's built like me. Short and sweet, as Joey would say. When I first met her a few months ago, she told me about a guy she met and liked very much. She told me on my last visit to the hospital, that she is still going out with him and she thinks that he is the one she's been waiting for. Anyway, when she saw me reading from my beautifully decorated loose leaf binder, she asked me what I was reading. When I told her what it was, she said that she had heard about some of the poems Joey wrote for me, from the other nurses. She asked if I would mind if she read some of them and of course I said no. Afterward, I wondered if I did the right thing by saying it was okay for her to read my book, because a lot it is very personal. I also wondered if Joey would mind someone else reading his very personal, innermost thoughts.

The more I thought about it the more I realized that Joey wears his thoughts and feelings on his face most of the time. I don't know how many people have told me that they knew that Joey was crazy about me, just by the way he looks at me and treats me. I did ask him the next day and he told me he didn't mind at all. Anyway, not only did Karen like all the things Joey wrote for me, but she told some of the other night nurses about it and they wanted to read it too. Word got around to the daytime nurses, and they started to come to me to ask if they could see the book. Joey is getting to be very famous with the nurses in that hospital, and in a way, I guess so am I. The main thing is that reading his words of love and encouragement are a great comfort to me. That's the only thing that really counts, and I love it. I never get tired of reading the same words over and over again.

Dr. Edward again told me that my condition has gotten a little bit worse, but he's still trying to figure out what drug or combination of drugs might be of a help to me. I still don't feel too bad, except for the tiredness and weakness. I still do have many days when I don't feel too weak or tired and that's good. I'm trying to do what Mom, Mama B and Joey keep telling me and that is to count my blessings and take it one day at a time. Some days I'm better at doing that than on other days, but I'm still trying. The more I read Joey's words to me about us being together forever and never, ever having to say goodbye, the less scared I get. I mean, I still get frightened when I think about what the doctor's been telling me lately, but after awhile of thinking about what Joey has told me for so long, I feel a little better. Anyway, right now I don't feel too bad and that's good, but now I am tired and will have to say good night dear diary.

Saturday, May 8th, 1948

Dear diary today is Heshy's and my seventeenth birthday. When I was in the hospital a couple of weeks ago, Robin and Rosemary, two nurses who also take care of me sometimes, told me that I'm a lucky girl because so many of the other children in our ward, haven't survived as long as I have. So I guess being able to celebrate my seventeenth birthday, and not feeling too sick is a good thing, although Dr. Edward has told me the last three or four times I was in the hospital, that my condition has gotten a little worse. I do feel a little more tired with each passing week or so, and I find more black and blue marks on my body, but other than that I really don't feel too bad. The doctor did say that he was disappointed, that he hasn't found a drug that would help me, but he's still trying, so he urged me to stay positive. I always try to.

Anyway, Mom as usual, was good enough to give Heshy ten dollars as a present from me. Heshy and I both got very nice gifts again this year. Joey went out of his way to try to make my birthday very special. Of course he makes my everyday feel special. All he has to do is smile at me and I feel special. He started to hand me gift wrapped presents, one at a time and it seemed like there was no end to them. The first one was three new Frank Sinatra records. You know I love Frank Sinatra. The next one was as big as me and when I unwrapped it I saw the largest Teddy bear I had ever seen. Then there was a book of poems about the wonders of Nature by different poets, like Frost and others. I really loved that. There was also a funny hat with a picture of a cat on the front of it. He made me try it on in front of everybody and everybody laughed. Joey said I looked beautiful in it. I don't know if I did or not, but I know that he made me feel beautiful. Last but definitely not the least, he gave me one of his now famous, hand made cards. He pasted a picture of the two of us, with our arms around each other, onto the front of a pink sheet of paper that was folded in half. Over the picture he had written,

"BIRTHDAYS COME AND BIRTHDAYS GO"

And beneath the picture he wrote,

"HAPPY BIRTHDAY TO THE MOST BEAUTIFUL GIRL I KNOW"

Inside the card was written the following lovely words,

"TO THE GIRL WHO IS THE MOST CARING,

WHOSE LIFE AND LOVE FOREVER, I WILL BE SHARING,

THERE IS ONLY ONE THING I CAN SAY,

ON THIS VERY SPECIAL DAY,

HAPPY BIRTHDAY!

I LOVE YOU AND I WILL FOREVER!

And he signed it, "Your forever fella, Joey". I love it!

Well anyway, I'm going to have to go into the hospital earlier than usual this month, because I get tired and weak more often and for longer periods of time. I can tell by the looks on the faces of everyone around me, my family, close friends and the nurses and doctors in the hospital that they are all worried about how I'm doing. The funny thing is that I'm not very scared about it myself. I know that it's because of all the love for me that is all around me, but it's especially Joey's love for me that's helping me cope. I mean, for the last two years he's been telling me not to worry because we will be together forever. Since I have been reading almost all of his writings every night, [some nights I fall asleep before I can finish reading it all], I realize that besides constantly telling me how much he loves me, he's constantly telling me that we will be together forever. I believe that message has taken root in my heart and I think that's why I'm not frightened like I used to be. I will do just like Mom and Mama B tell me and take it one day at a time. Now I'm getting tired so I have to say good night dear diary.

Sunday, May 30th, 1948

   Dear diary the past three weeks have not been the greatest for me. Between missing six school days while in the hospital and another five days because I was too weak and tired, I think I feel way behind in my school work. I mean Heshy, Joey and Sarah tried very hard to help me catch up but I don't think I did too well. While I was in the hospital, getting tested some more, I was having some new medications tried on me. The new stuff didn't help and in fact made me feel a little sick for a while, and the tests showed that I'm getting worse. To tell you the truth, now I'm starting to feel a little worse. I think it was on Saturday afternoon when only Mom and Daddy were there, that Dr. Gold came by to see me. He was soon joined by Dr. Edward and after talking to each other, they looked a little worried about me. Mom and Daddy and the doctors excused themselves and left my room. I was feeling too tired to ask them why they were leaving. At one point when Lydia, another nurse came into my room to check my blood pressure, I saw Mom and Daddy talking to the doctors in the hallway outside my door. They all appeared to be very serious and Mom and Daddy even looked a little pale. I knew then that the news was not good.
   Then a funny thing happened. When Mom and Daddy came back into my room, I asked them what was wrong. Before they could answer me, they both started crying and from either side of my bed placed their heads on my stomach and hugged me. They were both talking in a mixture of German, Yiddish and English. Some of what they were saying I understood, but most of it I didn't. Daddy was calling me his "totala" in the midst of whatever else he was saying. Mom was doing just about the same. I did understand, when they both said they loved me in German and of course in English. Here's the funny part, not laughable funny but strangely funny. While Mom and Daddy were crying, or I should say lamenting over me, with their heads on my stomach, I found myself gently caressing their temples and speaking words of comfort to them. All the while, I myself had a few tears in my eyes, but this time it was not for me, but for them. I couldn't take the sight of them being so hurt and distraught.

After a short while, we all seemed to calm down and Mom and Daddy told me what the doctors told them. Dr. Edward said that he didn't know what else he could do for me, and he told them to make me as comfortable as possible. I asked Mom if he said how much more time I have, and she said he didn't know for sure, but that it wouldn't be too long, maybe a few months at the most. That took my breath away and I almost lost control of myself. Through my tears I heard myself tell Mom and Daddy that everything will be okay, that I will try to be as positive as I can and take it one day at a time, just like she has always told me to do. Then I heard myself say, that everything is beautiful because Joey and I will be together always. I told them that Joey has been telling me that for two years, and I believe it with all of my heart. Then I added I also believe we all will be together someday. I asked them to please not to cry and fuss about me because that makes me feel bad.

They were quiet for a moment or two, and then Daddy said they will do whatever it is that will make me happy. As hard as they tried, I could tell they were both fighting back tears. To change the subject, I asked Mom to tell me the story again about the beautiful girl in her small town in Germany, who no boy would ask to go to the graduation party. Daddy asked Mom what story I was talking about. Mom looked at me with a little surprise in her eyes and said to me that Daddy doesn't like that story because he thinks she trying to say that he wasn't good looking when he was a young lad. Daddy said that's exactly what that story is about. Mom had to smile a little at Daddy, and told him that she always thought he was the best looking guy in their town. Now the surprise was all over Daddy's face, as he said she's finally telling the truth about him and how he looked as a young man. Mom told him he was silly and actually laughed a little laugh. Daddy walked over to her and gave Mom a big hug and said that he always knew she felt that way about him. I was glad to see and hear that. I actually had to smile at his reaction. At that point I was wondering how Heshy and Joey would react to what the doctors told Mom and Daddy.

I think the word about me must've gotten around the hospital because one by one the nurses and even some of the other sick kids came into my room to see how I was doing. For the most part they all hugged me and wished me well. While that felt really good to me, I didn't want to be fussed over like that. It made me feel like I was the center of attraction and I really wasn't because there are so many other kids, mostly younger than me and just as sick, if not worse. Actually, I don't know how I could be any sicker than I am now, except of course if I didn't have all the love that I get from all my family, friends and of course Joey. Like I've said before, there are some kids who don't get visitors every day like I do, and that's really sad.

Anyway, speaking of visitors, a day or two after the doctors told me they couldn't do any more for me I got a big surprise visit from a bunch of my schoolmates. I couldn't believe that so many people were allowed to visit at the same time. They weren't supposed to and it wasn't even visiting hours yet, but because Joey comes to visit me every day that I'm in the hospital, he got to know a lot of the people who work there. I'm not sure, but I think he bribed some of them with pizza or a calzone or something, because that's how he was able to sneak them up, all at the same time. Even the nurses on the floor just winked, told us to keep the noise down and looked the other way and that made me feel so special. Because I had visitors to spare, I asked one of the nurses, Gladys, if she could bring some of the kids who don't get too many visitors to come into my room. Three or four of them were brought into my room, which by this time was really crowded but no one seemed to mind. The kids seemed to brighten up with all attention they got from my schoolmates, and seeing that made me feel good too.

I asked Joey what made these classmates of mine want to visit me at this time and he told me that the day before in school he was still very upset about the news of my condition. He said that it must've showed on his face, because some of them asked him what was wrong. When he told them, he said they felt so bad for me that they all wanted to come to the hospital to see me. Especially since he told them that he didn't know for sure when or if I'd be coming back to school. At first he told them that he didn't think I would be allowed to have visitors, because I was feeling so weak. He told them that he would stop at Dr. Gold's office on the way home from school that day and ask him if it would be alright for me to have visitors, other than himself and family members. When Dr. Gold told him that he thought it might be a good idea, that it might brighten my day, Joey told all the kids who wanted to come, that it was okay and he would make all the arrangements. That's how they all got to visit me at the same time. I loved the fact that they all wanted to come. I thought it was very sweet of them. Then I asked Joey how many pizzas and calzones he promised the security guards and nurses. He laughed a little and said he knew that I'd figure it out, but not that fast. I told him I know him better than he thinks and we both laughed as he hugged me.

The funny thing about my visitors is that most of them are the girls that I met since I started high school. I mean, I'm friendly with all of them and like them all a lot, but I still feel closer to the people I've gone to school with since grammar school. For some reason, I don't know exactly why, they all seem to like me. Catherine Murphy was there, all of her friends from her the neighborhood call her Catherine, [don't call me Kate], Murphy. Bridget Quinn and her kid sister Katherine, [you can call me Kate] was there too. Kate is taller than her sister and always tells everyone that Bridget is older but shorter than she is. That's so funny. Bridget is built like me, or as Joey would say, "short and sweet". Johanna Law and Claire, whose last name I'm not sure of, were also there. It was so nice of all of them to take the time to visit me. Especially since some of them I know work part time after school in one of those new supermarkets. Others work after school at Schlossberg's with Heshy. In spite of what the doctors told me, because of people like these around me almost all of the time, I feel like a very lucky girl.

One of girls, I think it was Johanna, asked me how I rated a private room, she wanted to know is I was rich or something. I said I didn't know for sure but I think my Mom knows, so she asked Mom the same question in the same way. Mom was amused at the "rich" part of the question and told her that from the very beginning of my illness, Daddy's bosses have been very kind to us and they made the arrangement for the private room I always get. I can't say it enough, how lucky I am. Now I'm very tired and have to say good night dear diary.

Saturday, June 26th, 1948

Dear diary, I missed a bunch of school days this past month, but I did force myself to go to school on some days when I really didn't feel up to it. On a couple of those days I had to leave school early, because I felt so tired and weak, and of course Joey and Heshy came with me. I don't know, but I think God is looking after me, because on those days when I did go to school feeling tired, Mr. B. always picked us up, me, Heshy, Sarah and Joey of course. When he notices that I look tired he takes the day off and tells Joey to call him at home whenever I have to come home early, he'll be right there, otherwise he'll pick us all up at three o'clock. I guess when you work for yourself you can do that, but I feel bad that he misses making the money I know he needs to pay for the taxi.

Anyway, I found it hard to keep up with some of my classes because of all the time I missed, but as usual Heshy, Joey and Sarah are all trying very hard to help me catch up. When I told my guidance counselor that I was having a little bit of a hard time keeping up with my studies, he told me not to worry, because I was going to be promoted anyway. He said that because I was a very good student and always tries hard, I was going to be promoted and if I needed additional work to do, before I would be able to start my senior year in September, I would be given make up work to do over the summer. After I spoke to him I wondered to myself why I was even worried about it, because the doctors didn't think I would even be here to start my senior year. That thought for a moment scared me, but I quickly put it out of my head and told myself that no matter what happens to me, everything will be alright. I mean, Joey has told me for so long that we will be together forever and I now believe it with all of my heart. Forgive me, dear diary, I know that sometimes I repeat myself, but hey, that's me when I'm feeling good, so now when I'm not feeling too good, I probably do it more often.

Anyway, the more I hear Joey talk, when he's talking serious talk that is, the more impressed and fascinated by him I become. About a week or so ago, I had what the doctors called a "short or mild remission", a short period of time when I might actually feel as if I'm getting better, but I'm really not. It's just a little break from me feeling sick, that's all. So, while I was feeling better I'm still a little tired, but not sick, I asked Joey to sit with me in the park this one Sunday morning. I mean, the weather was sunny and warm and the flowers and trees were in bloom, it was a really nice day. Of course he said yes and Heshy and Sarah joined us. By the way I'm happy to say that it's been about two weeks now and I still feel not only good but even a little less tired than usual. Anyway, while we were sitting on a bench talking and just enjoying being outside on such a lovely day, this girl Renee Kramer who lives somewhere on New Lots Avenue, I think, came walking into the park with a boy I had seen in school, but didn't know. She use to call herself Rene', but now calls herself Renay.

Heshy said that the boy's name is Calvin and he's in his and Joey's gym class. He said that this Calvin, who he said lives somewhere on the other side of Pennsylvania Avenue, has been bragging to all the boys in school, that he and Renay have been making love a lot lately. Before anyone could say anything, Joey looks at Heshy and said that they were having sex, not making love. Heshy, Sarah and I looked a little puzzled by what Joey had just said, and Sarah asked Joey what the difference is between the two. Joey put on his serious face and said that the difference is, you have sex with a body, but you make love to a person. Heshy, Sarah and I looked at each other and wondered what the heck Joey was talking about. Heshy finally asked Joey how he knows all these things or thinks he knows them. Joey replied by saying that he always listens when older people speak about what happened to them in their lives and about life in general. He added that you can learn an awful lot from them by doing that. Sarah then asked Joey if he was sure he's only seventeen years old, because sometimes when he says things like that, he sounds like her parents or grandparents. Heshy nodded in agreement with her while I just sat there and wondered about my "fella". I'm sure if I think about it for a while I'll figure out what he's talking about. I think my "short remission period" is over because I'm starting to feel very tired now so I'll have to say good night dear diary.

Friday, July 16th, 1948

Dear diary, the last trip to the hospital was probably my last visit there. Dr. Edward told me and my family, that there was nothing more he could do for me. My family, while expecting news like that, took it very hard, much more than I did. In fact, it really didn't surprise me and I kind of knew for some time now that I wouldn't be getting any better, that I wouldn't beat this thing. Everyone was a little surprised that the news didn't seem to bother me, like it bothered them. It's funny, but everyone who comes to see me, my family, my friends and especially my Joey, all come to try and comfort me. I know that and I appreciate it, but now I find myself trying to comfort them, especially my family and Joey. I think all the positive things that Mom, Daddy, Joey, Mama B and the rest of my family and very close friends, have been telling me the past few years, has given me the strength to face what I have to, calmly. Joey has also convinced me that we will be together forever, so I'm not at the moment worried about anything that is going to happen to me. I hope I stay this way all the way.

When Mom and I were alone one day, after I came home from the hospital, she sat down with me at the table for lunch and while we were eating, we had a very nice conversation. Well it was nice as long as Mom was able to control her emotions. Mom would start to tell me about all the hopes and plans she always had for me when I was a little girl and that would make her lose it for a few minutes. To tell you the truth, watching her start to cry almost made me lose control of myself, because I don't like to see Mom unhappy and sad. She got very upset when she said she always dreamed of me becoming a bride and a mother someday. That made me get all choked up too, but I quickly pulled myself together and told Mom, that while I'll never know the joyful pain of childbirth, I felt like a mother to Helen and Arlene's kids, because of all the love they gave to me. As far as being a bride, I told her that I think I did better than that, when I found Joey and his wonderful love for me. As she brushed away some tears, she told me I was right about that, and added that there's nobody better than Joey for me in the whole world. We hugged each other as she said that, and I reminded Mom of all things that Joey had written to me about how we will be together forever. I told Mom that the thought of that has given me the spiritual strength to put up with what has happened to me. I quickly added that all the love and support I get from her and the rest of our family has kept me strong too.

You know I could understand when the "yenta", Sylvia Roth was around, how news travel so fast in our school and neighborhood, but she's not around now and the news of my condition must have spread quickly. Since I've come home from the hospital there's been a steady stream of classmates, friends, family and neighbors in to see me and wish me well. Thank God I've felt strong enough to see them, but early in the evening I start to get very tired and go to bed early. I was very surprised by the visit of some of my classmates that I didn't usually hang around with, but was friendly with in school. It's funny, but before I started high school most of my friends were Jewish and in fact, I didn't even know too many people who were not Jewish, but since I started high school I've met and liked a whole bunch of girls and guys who aren't Jewish. I found that they are really no different that me and my Jewish friends.

Well anyway, this girl who was in some of my classes and who I really like a lot, Tara O'Grady is her name, Joey tells everybody that her last name is really "Rah bump de eh", came to my house to see me. I mean she lives way over on the other side of the high school, a very long walk away. I thought that was so nice of her. One of the reasons why we like each other so much is that she was telling me in school one day, in the lunch room, that she wanted to be a physical therapist when she got out of school, and of course you know I always wanted to be a nurse, so we just hit it off. Joey asked her one day exactly what it is that a physical therapist does and she named a bunch of different things including muscle massage, so Joey told her, he hoped she never rubbed anyone the wrong way. We all laughed. I don't hear Joey laughing too much lately and that bothers me.

After all the strength and encouragement he's given me, I hope he saved some for himself, because since I started to get worse, he doesn't seem like the same guy sometimes. I mean, he still writes things to me everyday and does all kinds of things to show me that he still loves me, but I think he's very troubled over what's happening to me. I overheard Mom and Daddy talking about Joey one night, when they thought I was asleep. Mom was telling Daddy, that she had spoken to Mama B on the phone. She said that Mama B told her, that on many nights lately, Joey would be raging at God for not making me better. He would often cry himself to sleep. My poor baby, my poor Joey. I didn't want him to be that way, but there's not too much I can do about it. I mean, I can't tell him I know about that, because then he might get mad at Mama B or something, for telling Mom these things. I don't know what to do, but I'll just keep telling him that everything will be alright, because just like he's been telling me for so long, we will be together forever. I told Joey that when my time comes, I will be waiting for him to join me so that we can continue our walk through eternity. The thought of that lifts my spirits to the sky. I told him that too, and hoped that he felt the same way. That should make him feel better. I hope that it does. I pray to God that it does.

Now I'm starting to get a little more tired each day, and the only thing that Dr. Edward has given me, is some pain medicine to take when I need it to make me comfortable. I'm starting to take those now too. I don't know how much longer I'll be able to write to you dear diary, but I'll try to write for as long as I'm able to. Now, even though it's kind of early, I have to say good night dear diary.

Saturday, July 31st, 1948

Dear diary, please excuse my handwriting because I'm getting very weak, and writing is a big effort for me right now. I don't know how much time I have left, but I'm okay about it. Joey still comes over every day, and besides him and his family, my relatives and a few other very close friends visiting me, Mom and Daddy won't let anyone in to see me. I don't have the strength to see many people anyway. The only thing that bothers me right now is that I noticed that since I've taken a turn for the worse, Heshy seems to be a little cool with Joey. I don't know if I only imagine it, or if it's true, but I hope they are not having any bad feelings for each other because of me. I don't know, I may mention it to Mom and see what she says about it. Anyway, dear diary as you can probably tell from my unsteady hand, this is probably the last time I'll be writing to you. I love you for the way you've listened to my inner most feelings and secrets for over the last four years. I'll miss writing to you. You have been a great companion. So for the last time I'll say good night dear diary. P.S. I still feel like the luckiest girl in the world.

THE END

or

THE BEGINNING

Printed in the United States
205635BV00001B/337-342/P